smart*brain*

G. F. Smith

Confluential Press

~ A Confluence of Influence

Acknowledgments

Cover, interior design, and Penchant Series graphics: Copyright © 2015 by G. F. Smith, with technical, layout, and final development assistance from Jonah C. Smith. Additional photo, artwork, and font rights were legally acquired and are on record.

Thanks to family, friends, and business associates who have given their support and encouragement throughout this endeavor. Enduring, not only the time it has taken for its creation, but the sometimes obsessive focus that was often required for its rendering. Thanks for understanding.

Special thanks to the professional book editors employed on this project: Cathy and Gillian. I was so fortunate to have found you both. Thank you for your hard work, your brutal honesty, your creative insight, and your keen eyes.

Extended thanks and appreciation to all those who live their lives with purpose, faith, courage, and humility; you have always been my inspiration. This is me following through.

Part 1
Mind

Chapter 1

"My feet are cold; it's cold outside!"

"*No*, it's over seventy degrees outside, Dad. Your feet are cold because you put your shoes in the freezer again."

"Freezer? What on earth are you talking about? Why in the world would I put my shoes in the freezer?"

"I don't know, Dad. Why *would* you put your shoes in the freezer? You tell me," she said, looking between the busy road and her father.

"Well, I...don't know. I wouldn't have a clue." He looked at her, caught her worried glance. He suddenly felt sadness, a fleeting sense of remorse. Something sparked in his mind, but then he forgot what it was. He turned away and looked out the window. Something wasn't right, but he just couldn't figure it out. His brow tensed and wrinkled.

Chapter 2

Sarah Frances Whiting drove carefully after dropping her father off at the *Merit Ptah* Medical Center. Her mind was inundated with thoughts of him, his apparent worsening condition, his stay at the center for tests, as well as her forthcoming job interview, which she was en route to. The clearly insane drivers in Los Angeles were not helping. As soon as she turned on to the street, she was nearly rear-ended by a pokey-haired, suit-clad man intensely multi-tasking on his smartphone.

"Watch what the…watch what you're doing!" she grumbled, as she switched her attention between the rearview mirror and what was in front of her. The driver behind her was getting a little too close as traffic inched and stopped, and her car's rear proximity alarm was making Sarah edgy by blaring every twenty or so seconds.

The alarm sounded again and Sarah snapped. She slammed the gear shift into park and leaned out of the window.

"Hey, you mind keeping your eyes on the driving!" she yelled, scowling.

The man heard the remark and looked up with a defensive frown. He held both hands up, Smartphone still in hand, and presented a *what's the problem?* air of innocence. He then shook his head with annoyance and within seconds changed lanes, mumbling, *"Crazy bitch, you lost your mind?"* out of the side of his mouth as he increased his distance.

Sarah Whiting rolled her eyes and bit the inside of her lip. She turned onto the highway.

After two hours of driving she arrived at the campus' tree-shrouded parking lot.

She was cutting it close on time.

Sarah exited the high-mileage, 2047 two-seater, Praxis-Sport. She grabbed her backpack, reaching into it as she stood up. She shut the door with her slender, athletic hip, hurriedly turned, and as she walked, pinched her streaked, light brown hair back on both sides with small clips.

She was barely going to make it.

Chapter 3

As Sarah entered the tiered-floor auditorium, two things immediately struck her: the odd smell, and the small number of occupants in the expansive room. She paused and looked around, letting her eyes adjust to the lighting. Of the six people seated in the front row of the lecture hall, the three men smiled at her while the three women quickly turned their heads back toward the platform in front.

Sarah then noticed a distinguished, grey-haired man off to the side politely motioning her to the front with his hand. Sarah nodded respectfully and made her way down the steps to the front row. The man smiled back as Sarah took a seat and drew in an anxious breath.

. . . .

"Welcome, everyone. Thank you for accepting the invitation we sent you. I know the information included was sparse, and you're probably somewhat frustrated with that—coming here on your own time, merely at the behest of the university. However, I can assure you that you will find it at the very least, interesting, if not highly applicable to your lives and careers," he said smoothly as he beamed an extra wide smile before resuming.

"First, let me introduce myself; I am Professor Howard L. Dunes. Yes, *Dunes*, spelled like the large piles of sand."

He quickly scanned each face before him.

"I currently have the honor of being the Professor of Applied Sciences here at Earthbridge College; I am also on the Board of Regents, as well as various other committees and secondary boards. I will be your host for this presentation. I imagine you're all anxious to know the full extent of the proposed 'position' the request we sent you mentioned. We will get to that shortly."

He reached under the podium and retrieved a bottle of water. After taking a sip, he started again.

"This presentation today will come to you in four, somewhat overlapping parts: a quick overview of all we'll be discussing; a topic-by-topic illustrated portion; an interactive session that I'm sure you will find fascinating; and then the offer, which of course will include a Q&A."

He cleared his throat and took another sip.

"We are going to introduce you to a technology that is in the final stages of development. This technology is cutting edge. It holds the potential to revolutionize virtually every private and professional discipline, every occupation, relationship, life and lifestyle. It will, without a doubt, change society as we know it: business, economics, science, education, communication, entertainment, and the medical fields. It will change everything I just mentioned, and more," he said matter-of-factly.

His audience stared at him with varied expressions.

The Professor took another sip of water, and then resumed.

"Briefly, this technology has to do with BCI—Brain Computer Interface. I'm sure most of you are familiar with the term. You are going to be asked to spend twenty-one days with us, *studying* this technology, *learning* this technology, *using* this technology, *applying* this new technology, *helping* with the final stages of its testing and certification, preceding its release in product form to the world markets. In exchange for these twenty-one days, you will be paid two-hundred-thousand dollars...each."

He paused momentarily to let them absorb what he was saying.

"For those of you who decide to participate by accepting our offer, you must also irrevocably accept two critically important aspects of your decision. *One*...in addition to the confidentiality agreement you signed prior to attending our presentation today, you will be asked to sign a strict, all inclusive, non-disclosure agreement, of which, if deemed violated, will void and make null the aforementioned contractual agreement, unequivocally prompting criminal charges. Please, forgive my candidness at this juncture, but this must be fully understood.

"And *two*—which is at least a much more palatable aspect to consider than the other—is the fact that after the twenty-one days, each person who has chosen to participate in the program will achieve world-wide, celebrity status immediately upon the release of the technology to the public—akin to the Mercury-7 Astronauts."

The audience all looked at each other, as if seeking confirmation they actually heard what they thought they had just heard.

"Okay then, moving on," he said with a slight smile.

Chapter 4

The three large, curved presentation monitors brightened as the house lights dimmed. Professor Dunes stood in front of the center screen, seemingly displayed on the 12Q-HDX panels. In his hand was a small electronic controller. He held it up, and as he did the image of his hand swelled to life on the observers' right-hand screen.

"History is replete with invention and innovation. This device, for instance, is a simple controller that, with a little effort, can send and receive electromagnetic signals actuating a host of other devices that, in turn, can thus actuate other devices that will, in concerted effort, work together to produce a variety of predetermined effects that can then be interpreted by our physical senses. As in *this*..."

He pressed several buttons to begin a simple search on one of the widely used search engines of the day. Hitting the three key inputs, B...C...I, a list of thousands of possible entries appeared.

"Let's see, how about *this* one."

He moved his finger across a small patch of space on the controller and then pressed another button. On the screens appeared an assortment of text, pictures, video logs, and various other links regarding BCI: Brain Computer Interface.

He turned from the screens and spoke.

"I won't bore you with all the details. I believe a brief expository review will suffice for now."

He cleared his throat, and then continued.

"BCI, brain computer interface, a long sought after medium or method that seeks to effectively integrate the mind, and the machine. There have been numerous iterations over the decades, but truly minimal advancement in the field. The best we've seen to date are simple thought-controlled devices; those which essentially actuate other devices, of which in turn help those with lost motor or sensory functions, etc., live more self-sufficient and productive lives. Physical aids, visual and hearing aids, communication aids, etc."

As he spoke, he clicked through a plethora of illustrations and animations depicting the history and trends regarding BCI.

"And then there are the attempted military applications: the piloting and operation of various machinery: planes, ships, drones, computer programs, weaponry, etc. To date, no integration—or *interface*—has been developed that even remotely reaches the extent of human imagination or aspirations for such technology. That is, until now!"

The small group seemed to simultaneously shift in their seats, becoming more attentive.

"Let me explain further," he said.

He pulled out of its holder his personal Smartphone, and as with the controller, he held it up for viewing. Its image appeared on one of the screens.

"You're all familiar with this. A smartphone, it's a device that allows you to talk to anyone—whether individually or in groups—in real time, via text, voice, or instant messaging, on the other side of the classroom, or on the other side of the world. It is, in reality, nothing more than a computer. Yet, it has become much more than that.

"It's our personal audio/video player; our entertainment center; our mobile learning hub; it is our social networking appliance; it's a multi-tasking, multi-transforming, multi-functioning business-integration and operation apparatus; all of which help us stay connected and involved with others. It is, at its very core, a conveyance tool that puts the world—our *Universe*—right in the palm of our hands.

"This device has revolutionized all aspects of our society: personal, professional, social and psychological. Many wonder how we ever lived without it; and many, at times, as I'm sure some of you can relate, wonder how it would feel to…pitch it as hard as one could into the nearest river!"

He grinned as he looked out over his glasses at the small audience.

Everyone laughed, each in their own way agreeing with the sentiment. The amusement settled and he resumed.

"But, be that it may, this *contrivance* was created to connect our human senses with the vast world around us. We depend upon that, and we love that, we love this *thing*, most of the time." He held the phone up, once more acknowledging the contrasting perspectives.

He paused again.

"Now then, let me ask you: what if *this* was in your brain? What if you no longer needed fingers to make it function? What if you no longer needed only your eyes and ears to see the images, and hear the sounds that it routinely streams your way? What if there was an interface that could wirelessly transmit everything presently accessible with *this*…" he held up the Smartphone, "directly into your brain's receptive areas? Well then, what would that be like?"

Silence settled on the room. Eyes squinted; heads tilted.

"Let me ask you all a question. How many of you dream?"

All showed their hands by raising them while looking around.

"Okay, now, how many have had vivid, lucid dreams? Or at least have had at some point in time that you can remember?"

Most raised their hands.

"Okay, good. In dreams of this type, the images are colorful, in motion, three-dimensional, at times morphing, and changing, yet fluid and quite often deeply engrossing. You hear sound; you sense touch, even smell and taste, sometimes. Yet, your eyes are closed, it's dark, and you're in bed. Somehow, all the sensory receptive centers of your brain are active. And what's more, they're subject to the influx of your memories, and your imagination. And quite often, for some people, they can be directed—steered—by your choices, by your conscious, unconscious minds. How many of you have had this experience, of being able to steer your dreams, at least to some degree?"

Half of the people raised their hands, others saying "sometimes," or "once in a while."

"Good! Now, imagine again an interface that is able to stream the various data this device can access," he held up the Smartphone again, "wirelessly—*directly*—into the sensory receptor areas of your brain, much as your brain does to itself when it dreams, much as your five human senses do, every day of your life. Imagine, just imagine, for a moment that this interface can, and does, do this. Well, we don't have to imagine any more. It has now become a reality."

There was a sudden susurration of muted voices.

Professor Dunes smiled at the reaction, but then quickly continued.

"That is right. You heard me correctly. The elusive *they*, have finally discovered how sensory information is packaged by your senses, and then sent and received by your brain. That is the breakthrough! The Rosetta Stone that now allows us to understand the language your senses use to speak to your brain. And from this discovery, we are now able to do the same thing artificially.

Again he paused to let the concept sink in.

Several people shook their heads slightly as if in doubt.

"I can see your reluctance to believe on your faces. But everything I've told you is true! Let's consider first the two most important senses: sight and sound. Imagine being able to receive images from this," again he held up the phone, "and at your thought command, they appear in your field of vision. You see them as you would with your eyes which, in essence, are simply little cameras that relay bio-coded impulses—packages of information—back to your brain, right?

"Think about sound, which behaves the same way. Your ears, through receptors, transmit impulses to the brain, and like vision, they are interpreted by the brain. Similarly, this new interface technology can do this very thing; transmit—*stream*—sight and sound directly into your brain"

He paused once more, before resuming.

"Reciprocally, your brain routinely sends out signals to your sensory organs, right? Actually in very much the same way, telling your eyes to turn, to focus, whatever. It tells your ears to listen, or to tune-in to certain sounds, etc. Now, let's say that, not only can you send and receive impulses to and from your brain with this technology, but you can also learn to control this process by thought, the same way your brain communicates with your senses. You see?

"Let me give you an example. What if everything you see on this device's screen," again he held up the Smartphone, "could actually show up in your field of vision, or a part of it—like a window in a window—essentially making your field of vision your monitor?

"Let's go even further. Imagine choosing a book, or a video, or an educational course, whatever, and being able to pause it, fast forward it, repeat it, turn the volume up, or down, whatever you would want, simply by thought.

"Imagine sitting in a lecture hall, for an example. You're experiencing a presentation, much as you are today. You quietly pull up a small window and simultaneously as the key topics are being presented, you access and cross-reference corresponding data to support the learning experience. And then let's say that, suddenly, you hear a soft ring tone—in your mind, mind you. At your silent discretion, you answer the incoming call via a messaging application that you navigate with your thoughts, much as you steer…your dreams."

Again, he paused and offered a large smile.

"This hypothetical conversation can be brought about through texting, messaging, chatting or gramming. It can actually be vocal, brought about through an application that quite literally translates the impulses from the brain into speech. The possibilities in development are astounding. In essence, what I am saying here is this: B-CID technology will fundamentally change how we receive and send sensory information. It will expedite, exponentially, the speed at which we are able to transfer knowledge and experience. It will, by its very nature, provide for us private and discretionary communication, in essence creating for us a…a sort of artificial telepathy, in addition to everything else previously mentioned, and more."

He paused again, looking at his audience. From their expressions he could see that they were deep in thought, as if they were expounding upon the myriad possibilities in their own minds. They wore the look of sheer awe.

·······

"Now, here comes the exciting part."

He put his phone back into its holder on his belt, and slowly laid the small controller down. He then reached into the underbelly of the podium and retrieved a small, seemingly delicate device, holding it up for all to see.

"This is a B-CID…Brain-Computer Interface Device, coined *Smartbrain* by one of the developers. B-CID was a collaborative effort, the product-child of a group of scientists and engineers, many of whom are on staff here at Earthbridge College.

"Now, I know you're going to wonder—and eventually ask—just how it works. However, I cannot tell you. It is proprietary technology and patented as such. It has just recently been cleared through all watchdog agencies: FCC, FDA, OHRP, AMAA, etc. Believe me; it is a long list. In this form, it is non-invasive and what you're seeing is one of the many prototypes we—you—will be working with. However, it is essentially the identical product that will be released to the global market."

He raised it even higher into the air, turning it as if to marvel at it.

It was shaped much like a woman's headband for hair. It was nearly three-quarters of an oval, seemingly made of plastic and metal. It also resembled an extremely thin set of headphones, minus the ear pieces on each end. Instead, there was a single, bulbous section centered exactly half way from each end. The device was sleek, with streamlined surfaces, the colors of brushed aluminum, with shades of transparent blue. It had fine streaks of black trim. On the ends—where the ear pieces could have been—there were small oval-shaped pieces of rubber with three, small metal bumps protruding out of each.

"Now, how about a demonstration." Professor Dunes then lowered the device and put it on his head—the ends just over his ears, the rubber parts nearly touching his temples, and the bulbous part at the back of his head, right around his hair-line. He then pressed a small button on its side. An even smaller blue light, situated next to the button, lit up.

"Now, if you don't mind, I'd like to ask one of you for your phone number. Please, don't say it out loud, just write it down and pass it my way. I assure you your privacy will be honored. Also, it must be the number of the phone you're carrying on you at this moment. You? Yes, thank you. Please, just write it down and send it up. Thanks."

The young woman, Furley Goens, excitedly wrote down a number on a piece of notebook paper. She folded it and then handed it to the grey-haired man who'd been there since the start. He took the paper and delivered it to the Professor.

"Okay. What I am going to do is make a phone call to this number. Note that I am looking at the number now; I am see-ing in my visual field a window, produced by the built-in phone app on the device. I am now choosing the correspond-ing numbers with only the focus of my mind. Okay, I'm going to enter the last number."

To the audience it appeared that the Professor was merely staring into space, only barely squinting his eyes, as if focusing on something in his mind. He apparently entered the final digit. Within a few seconds the girl's phone began ringing. Everyone looked at her with astonishment. The girl fished out her phone, swiped the screen and answered it.

"Hello," the girl said.

"*Hello*," the Professor's voice sounded. "Thank you for re-ceiving my call. Now, if you would, please place your phone in speaker mode."

He waited as the smiling girl did so.

"He said to put my phone on speaker mode," she said to the others.

"Good, thank you," the phone's speaker echoed. "If you will look at me, you will see that I am in fact not talking with my mouth. I am using an advanced app that is transposing my thoughts into a speech that is, as I'm sure you can hear, very similar to the frequencies that my natural voice resonates— this is my personal audio field, or AF. This is all possible because the device has learned, through measurement, the exact frequencies my particular vocal chords emit and it has adapted its output accordingly. With the device, I can hear in the audio field as well. We'll discuss this further at a later time. Quite amazing though, isn't it?" he asked, amidst the oohs and aahs coming from the group.

"Now, any of you, perhaps…*you*." He pointed to Sarah. "Please give me a search topic; any will suffice. Just speak it out loud."

Sarah thought for a brief moment.

"Uhm…Alzheimer's?" She spoke it as a question.

"Good, that will suffice nicely as a topic, thank you," the Professor replied.

He appeared to be just staring into space, but within a few short seconds he spoke again.

"Now, young lady, Furley. Please look in your message box. Open it, and see what's there."

The girl did as instructed. She read the message and clicked on the inserted link. Her browser then opened to the National Alzheimer's Foundation's webpage. Furley held up her phone for all to see. Once more, everyone gasped.

The Professor began speaking with his mouth again.

"What you've seen is but a small demonstration of B-CID's capabilities. All that I mentioned earlier in the presentation is only the beginning of the potential applications of this technology. I think you can see from the demonstration how this might change our world, a little!" He grinned at his slight joke.

"And now, why don't we take a short break. We'll reconvene in about fifteen minutes. Through that set of double doors and to your left is a lounge area where we've prepared some beverages and snacks for you; there are personal facilities there as well, if you need. Please, feel free to enjoy the offerings. We'll actually be going to a different location for the Q&A portion. The kind gentleman who showed you to your seats earlier will meet you in the lounge and escort you to a different room, a more intimate setting, so we can begin to get to know each other a little better. And please, feel free to bring your refreshments with you when you return. I will see you then."

He gave them a gracious look, took the apparatus off his head and laid it on the podium. He then went to the side of the stage and exited through a door.

Everyone rose and headed for the lounge.

Chapter 5

They filed into the room and stood by the door waiting politely, each immediately noticing a man off to the side that they had not seen before. The man made eye contact, returning their gazes and nodding a silent greeting.

"Welcome back, everyone," the Professor said, his tone excited. "We'll get right to it then. Please...please, take a seat...anywhere's fine." He motioned to the large conference table in the middle of the room. Everyone seated themselves.

"First, I'd like you to meet someone." He motioned toward the other man. "This is Eliam Zaris. He has also been with the university for some time, in the Applied Sciences Department; he is one of our key engineers on the project. He is joining us for the Q & A; I'm sure he will be able to answer many of your questions. Also, I want to take this moment to pre-address one of the questions you are all probably asking...Why you? Why were *you* chosen?"

After the two men seated themselves amongst the others, the Professor picked up a tablet from the table, scanned a few pages, and then resumed talking

"You were chosen simply because of your areas of expertise: science, business, social, education, psychology, research, health, history, communication, entertainment, etc. Each of you represents an area—or areas—of society that, fundamentally, will be impacted by this technology. And that is specifically why you are here.

"Let me give you an example. Condoleezza Ghee..." the professor said, smiling and motioning to the women to his right. "Condoleezza is an educator. Imagine the advances in education with the use of this technology, from the teaching side to the learning side. Think about instantaneous resource acquisition, immediate cross referencing, the quick, decisive selection of teaching and learning tools, of which we already have access through the internet—*the Nebula,* as many are calling it—but now with, essentially, a direct input into the brain.

"The potential for this is the same with all other disciplines: enhanced experience and learning, expeditiously accessed and processed, simply by thought. I'm sure you're already making your own associations. And as you're applying this context to your own vocations, please feel free to begin asking your questions," the Professor said.

One of the men jumped at the chance.

"What…what about health issues?" Dr. Robert Redding, the young doctor of internal medicine asked anxiously. "Effects on the brain, or the nervous system?"

Eliam Zaris answered.

"No different than holding a smartphone to your ear all day long, or sitting in a room full of wireless devices. The interface's negative effects on the brain are proven to be below negligible. There are none. Painstaking intra-cellular testing has been done concurrently with neurological testing over the last two years to determine all potential physiological effects. Again, there are none.

"The data will be available for you at the onset of your participation with the program, as well as to the general public upon its release. Don't worry; research teams have been working on this for quite some time now. And as stated before by Professor Dunes, we already have multiple-agency approval and sign-off. All of this is to be considered exactly what it is: a Launch.

"Everyone, this is ready for release to the public; and I suppose this is a good time to make the point." He looked at Professor Dunes, who nodded back. "Shortly after your participation in the program, the technology will be released through a prescribed number of proprietary outlets in over two-dozen of the largest American cities. International release will follow as other countries sign-off on the technology."

"The business platform can be likened to an Optometrist visit. A person is tested, and after a short time, returns for fitting and adjustment of their personal device. There will also be a contractual time included in the package that will allow the consumer to return as often as needed for check-ups or any additional adjustments. There will also be a host of help and information directly available from numerous sources in the *Nebula*, accessible by the consumer at any time through conventional means, or through the device itself."

Eliam Zaris looked around the room as the group muttered comments to one another.

"Excuse me, this is, as you coined, 'Smartbrain' technology, like having a smartphone in your head. What about the privacy issues, hacking, etc., like with regular smartphones, or computers? I take it all this is wireless. Is there any added danger of this, simply because of the nature of wireless technology?" Nelson Baurle, the communications engineer asked.

"No. B-CID has its own proprietary encryption technology integrated within *all* of its primary programs, not just as part of its operating system. It's designed on a quad-tiered, randomly oscillating, million-bit encryption structure. This system surpasses all available encryption technologies presently available. It is the safest, non-hackable equipment to date." A sense of pride could be heard in Eliam Zaris' words.

"Yeah, unless you're the one who knows the encryption coding," Declan Stewart, the independent film producer, added.

Based on the raised eyebrows, the group seemed to agree with Declan's assessment.

"Yes, this is true," Eliam Zaris acquiesced. "But, I suppose someone has to know it, or it couldn't have been developed in the first place. There's always *that guy*!" They all laughed heartily at the reality of the statement.

Sarah Whiting stared at Eliam Zaris; something about him tweaked her senses. She thought him attractive, actually one or two notches above attractive. And after hearing his voice a few times, she was surprised at the strange tingle in her lower abdomen. She warmed at the pleasant feeling, cleared her voice, and nervously asked the next question that had been on her mind since before the break.

"Mr. Zaris, Professor Dunes, uhmm, I'm curious about what you said about us being celebrities. Can you talk about that in more detail?" She felt self-conscious asking the question but she was dying to know.

Sarah Francis Whiting didn't exactly like the limelight. In fact, she was somewhat of a recluse. Her father, having been a longtime NASA employee and a failed three-time astronaut candidate, endured much public scrutiny during his attempts to go into space, and especially during the last time in which he was assessed as being "mentally unfit" to join the colonists that were being sent to Mars. In fact, Sarah had endured much criticism in the shadow of her father while he was actively involved with NASA's programs. And having seen what the media did to her father, she was extremely cautious about exposing herself to the public eye.

Eliam Zaris looked at her, momentarily distracted by his own drifting thoughts. He quickly forced himself to answer.

"Ms. Whiting. That is a very good point to discuss." He paused for a short moment to gather his thoughts. "In a way, each of you will end up being…a poster child of sorts for your particular fields. As Professor Dunes mentioned regarding the technology's impact on education, the same will happen in all the various fields. You—all of you—will be the ones others look to in order to gauge the potential impact of this technology in the context of their own experiences, and in their own lives. Each of you will be a spokesperson, and as such, others will follow your conclusions and your advice regarding the technology."

The young girl named Furley Goens spoke abruptly.

"Soooo…we're going to be your iconic salespersons; isn't that the primary reason we're all here?"

Professor Dunes and Eliam Zaris briefly looked at each other, speaking with only their eyes. Professor Dunes spoke next.

"Well, in a sense, yes, that is one way of looking at it. However, the opportunity we are offering you is decidedly *not* a negative thing. If anything, it should be considered an honor."

The professor paused for a moment, but then resumed.

"For those of you who don't know, everyone, this is the renowned Furley Goens, the well-publicized seventeen-year-old CEO and founder of Enviral Corp. Furley, welcome! Yes, you will, in essence, be the initial 'salespersons' of the technology."

"Uhm, I'm actually eighteen now, Professor Dunes, as of last month. And I'm not, as of yet anyway, attaching any negativity to the concept. I'm just stating the obvious. Actually, from what I've heard and seen so far, I'd say this technology could have an enormous impact on my—also well-known—pet projects in the fields of environmental re-profiling. But, we'll see how that develops, Professor. Please, continue," she said.

"Thank you for the clarification, Furley. Everyone, what we are truly seeking here is honest reaction and feedback from professionals, professionals from the areas where this technology will impact the most. We fully understand that not all of it will be inherently positive, much as it is with other technologies, whether smartphones, computers, automobiles, fossil fuels or nuclear power, whatever.

"We are clearly stating the conditions and expectations at the beginning. And even specifically mentioning the inevitable outcomes regarding the way the world will look at you, all of you. In your contracts you will find that your obligations will include the twenty-one-day time period, which will consist of four five-day work weeks, with the additional day devoted to the events and affairs that will surround the specific release date, which, I might add, will come shortly after its public presentation at this year's Blue-Dot Technology Convention."

The group looked around at each other, and then back at the Professor.

"The particular time-frames—and any possible alternates, if necessary—are clearly stated in the contracts. You'll also find that a major portion of your testing, experimentation, and experiences with the technology, will be documented and used in the future for study, as well as potential marketing aids for the dissemination of the technology to the public—yes, salespersons, if you like. But only if you feel you can support the position." He nodded in a friendly way toward Furley. "We believe your compensation to be more than fair with respect to your anticipated roles."

Eliam Zaris chimed in.

"That's right. If you choose to take the contract, you will be required to fulfill it to the degree it plainly states, nothing else. Note also, that after the twenty-one days, any further contribution of time and effort will be of your own volition. You can be sure that all of you will be presented with many lucrative offers in the months following your contractual participation. These are totally up to you, whether you choose to accept them, or not.

"Again, you will quite probably achieve a level of celebrity status. How you choose to use this opportunity is solely up to you. We aren't in any way dictating your positions on this. We're just concerned with giving the public a reasonable presentation and illustration of how this technology can and will be used, in their professional, as well as their personal lives. It's as simple as that."

Everyone seemed to take a deep breath, turning to each other in the group for validation and feedback. The exception was Sarah Whiting who found herself staring into Eliam Zaris' eyes. Based on the duration of their eye-to-eye contact, neither seemed able to look away.

"Okay. That's fine with me," Declan Stewart, the independent film producer suddenly said. "You mentioned earlier that your 'field of vision' would be like your 'monitor.' Does that mean you can use the technology to watch movies? *Entire* movies, that way?"

Professor Dunes looked to Eliam who tore his eyes away from Sarah. He simply nodded in response.

"Really," Mr. Stewart replied, "uhmmm, *any* kind of movies?"

Chapter 6

"…it goes without saying that whatever it is that makes us…'us' or 'we,' must be extremely complex. And who knows, we may just be more than we can know, or can identify yet. Perhaps we are something altogether different than what we think we are? The question is: will we recognize it…when we finally recognize it?"

Sarah heard voices in the hallway and anticipated the knock. Within seconds, it came. She went to the counter, turned the volume down on her system, stepped to the door and opened it.

"Hey, girl!" Cybil Turner said excitedly. She then turned back to the person in the hallway. "Bye, Jake. You and the guys have fun."

"Hey, Jacob. How's it going?" Sarah called out.

"Actually pretty awesome, Sarah. I hear you've got something brewing there, secret stuff, non-disclosure, all that. Sounds mysterious. Hope it works out for you!" he said, hugging his wife and pecking her on the cheek. "Later, Cyb! Love you. You two stay out of trouble," he said, grinning, as he turned and walked away."

Sarah smiled back at the guy.

"Come on in. Ready for a drink?" she asked. "What's your pleasure…water, juice, beer?"

They hugged a quick hug; Sarah shut the door.

"Beer, *yes!*" she answered.

"Coming right up; I've got stuffed chicken breasts ready for the grill, won't take fifteen minutes, spring salad with the crispy pods we like, parmesan cous-cous, cheese dante, and a barrel of chocolate ice cream for dessert."

"Nice," Cybil said, drawing the word out with added expression. "What are you listening to?" she asked, nodding toward the device on the countertop. "Is that *Raker's Slant?*"

"Yeah, Podcast. I was checking out this show he did recently on Mind vs. Spirit, one of his 'out-there' topics."

"Yes, that would be 'out-there', I'd say. I haven't listened to him much lately. He's a little *too* out-there for me. Reminds me of that author you like so much, *Sader*...*Sayer*, whatever his name is. So what's Raker's *bent* on this one? Are they the same, different, what's his premise this time?"

Sarah laughed a little, picking up on her friend's light sarcasm.

"Don't know. Sometimes it's hard to know how the guy *is* bent." She giggled again. "Maybe both, or something altogether different that we've not identified, or are 'even able to place a label on yet,' was his last comment," Sarah said, intoning her voice mockingly like that of the local Radio Jock's, as she turned the Podcast off and put on some ambient, atmospheric composition.

"Let's get this dinner on the road. I'm hungry," Sarah said.

"Alright, sounds good to me," Cybil Turner agreed. "I'm famished!"

．．．．．．．

The two worked together to prepare the meal. The table by the picture window looking out into the sparse woods was set. They had their beers, and their appetites. They began eating.

"Okay, I can't wait. Tell me what you can tell me. I've been waiting all day," Cybil said, stuffing her mouth with a bite of savory chicken.

"Well, it's an advanced product that will...that will supposedly change everything. All fields: communication, health, entertainment, police, military, business, everything, it's really… 'out there.'"

She laughed at her last comment.

"I wish I could say more, but I signed an NDA. In a few months, everyone will know anyway. I just need to make up my mind whether I want to do it, or not."

Sarah took a deep breath and sighed.

"Well, I wish you could tell me more, too. I'm dying here. But, if that's the way it's got to be, then that's the way got to be, I guess. You said on the phone that they're going to pay you a pretty hefty sum for 'participation' in their little program and you're going to be a 'celebrity' because of it? What the heck is all that about? How much? Celebrity, why would that be? *You've got to tell me at least something!*" Cybil cried.

"I wish I could. I will tell you this part, just between you and me." She was trusting her friend's own non-disclosure. Cybil nodded an enthusiastic yes.

"Okay…they're going to pay us two-hundred-thousand dollars, each!"

"WHAT?" her friend said loudly. "Are you fracking serious? For a month's work? Can I get in on this?" she exclaimed, serious about the comment, yet extremely happy for her friend. "That's awesome. What else, what else?"

"Well, the tech…, the *product*, like I said, is going to change everything, and we're—me, and the other people, there are seven of us—are going to be like the first to use it and experience it. I guess they're going to record the testing and training sessions, our reactions to it, its application in our lives, both professional and personal. Then all of that will be used when it is released to the public. You know, marketing, advertising, whatever."

"You mean, like, you guys will be part of a reality show? All you go through during that time will be shown to the world…the entire world?" Cybil asked.

"Yeah, I guess that's what they're saying. Though I never thought of it exactly like that."

Sarah looked down, thinking deeply about the project. She felt her appetite wane as the notion suddenly turned her excitement into dread.

"Yeah, I guess that's what they're saying," Sarah repeated again.

"Well, that's awesome, Sarah! And you need that money, too, what with your dad and all." The two looked at each other, silently staring.

"Yeah, I know. Let's finish eating and get another beer. I think I'll pass on the ice cream."

....

With the food put away and the dishes and table cleared, each grabbed another beer and went outside to sit on the small veranda.

"I know what you're thinking, Sarah. You're thinking about, well..." She paused, thought about it a moment, and then started again. "Listen, you know I'm your friend, soooo...I'm gonna say it like it is. You can forgive me later. But, I think you're afraid of losing your mind like your mom did before she killed herself, and like your dad is now, with Alzheimer's, and it's put you in a who-wants-to-take-a-chance-on-anything state of mind for too long now!"

Sarah cocked her head, a look of astonishment and then annoyance suddenly washing across her face.

"Sarah, I'm your friend, and I love you like a sister, so hear me out." Sarah took a deep breath and continued to look attentive, inviting her friend to continue.

"Okay. You're afraid that someday you are going to lose your mind, and that's why you live like a hermit. You don't want a lot of people knowing you, like they all knew your father, and have to go through all that he went through—what you *both* went through. So, you stay in your own private little world, saving yourself from any potential exposure or embarrassment. You don't date much and God bless you for this, you don't want to hurt anyone. But Sarah, you can't keep doing this.

"If madness strikes, there is nothing you can do about it other than avail yourself of the medical facilities that exist to treat that behavior. It doesn't automatically follow that because it happened to your mom and dad that it will happen to you. Sarah… listen, I understand. What little you just told me sounds like a chance of a lifetime. And not just that, but you know you need the money Sarah, for a lot of reasons, but especially to help with your dad's care. Call it fate, luck, whatever, but this could be a good thing for you! And if this…this *product* is going to cause this much of a stir as these people think it will, then…then maybe it's going to be a good thing, too. And good things draw good people. Like you, Sarah Whiting!"

Cybil stopped for a breath and looked at Sarah who sat there looking stubbornly withdrawn. She had listened carefully to Cybil's outburst but she suddenly found herself thinking about Eliam Zaris. The image he presented in her mind, as well as the memory of his soothing voice, were definitely a plus for joining the project despite her misgivings.

"I did meet a guy…potentially," she suddenly blurted out.

Cybil's mouth dropped open.

"You did? See…*see!*" Cybil said, definitely now more exuberant than before. "Alright, now that's what I'm talking about. You stay right here. I'm going to get us a few more beers, and you're going to fill me in. And there better not be any non-disclosure crap connected to this story. I'll expect all the bits and pieces, down to the minutest detail, even if they're imagined!"

Sarah smiled at her friend, but the fog in her mind made her look down, and she suddenly wished that she'd left Eliam out of the equation.

Chapter 7

"Preparations are on schedule. The modules are complete. We have the labs ready. The apparatus' are being programmed for the aforementioned test levels. All monitoring systems, equipment and people are in place. We have no concerns at this time. We are essentially ready to begin," Dr. Vectren, the Program Director said with confidence.

Eliam looked at Professor Dunes, and then spoke.

"Are they all on board yet, Professor?" he asked.

"We have one that seems to be holding out until the last minute, Ms. Sarah Whiting. All the rest have met with us and settled the contractual requirements. Ms. Whiting has until the end of the day to contact us, if she is going to do so. As you know, we don't have a contingent for her slot. However, we anticipated up front that at least one, or possibly two, would not join the program. We see only a minimal logistical realignment there. Nothing of real concern, though her area of expertise is one of the leading disciplines we were hoping to demonstrate. We should be fine."

Dr. Vectren nodded in agreement.

Professor Dunes was correct, the loss of one or two of the proposed candidates were not going to impact the overall program to any significant degree, just alter some schedules, lab hours, support, etc. Certainly not the project's expected debut to the media, concurrent with the Tech's launch. But Eliam Zaris wasn't thinking of those particular aspects, he was still thinking of Professor Dune's first sentence, and feeling an odd sense of disappointment at the news regarding Sarah. His deep train of thought was suddenly broken when Mr. Zacchaeus spoke up.

"Well, my colleagues and I are glad to see things are going well. This world changing product has come a long way, in a rather short time, we think. It will definitely be a huge economic boost to the American economy, which is very much needed at this point in time. However, remember, there is still this one particular hurdle that must be successfully made, or…or postponement—even possibly the long-term shutdown—of the program may result. It all depends on these final interactive studies. Progression has been successful, in regards to individual testing, but I'm sure we all understand the agency's legitimate concerns here which I feel compelled to reiterate for the record:

"Complex systems may appear to work flawlessly, based upon their design and intended individual functionalities. However, inherent in complex systems—according to leading proponents of Disorder Dynamics, as all of you are familiar with, I'm sure—is the propensity for complex systems, upon integration with other complex systems, to fall into inherently unstable equilibriums, thereby causing unknown, unintended, and potentially catastrophic effects on the whole. In other words…"

Professor Dunes interrupted Deltray Zacchaeus, the generally unwelcome, government-sent observer.

"Yes, we do fully understand the 'legitimate concerns' here, Mr. Zacchaeus, according to the ASTI, the Agency of Sociological and Technological Integration. We do understand. And thank you. I assure you it is invariably on all of our agendas to study, in depth, the relationship—or better, the 'equilibrium'—that may evolve from this technology's interface with vast numbers of people, knowing that it could potentially alter society as we know it."

The Professor finished his controlled, illustrative elaboration on Mr. Zacchaeus' point. There was an uncomfortable short silence that followed until Eliam Zaris spoke up again.

"Yes…*yes*, thank you, gentlemen. We do fully acknowledge the position of the ASTI. It's only in everyone's best interest, large scale and small scale, to study the effects of this technology across all spectrums. We wouldn't want a portion of society somehow becoming negatively impacted by any oversights on anybody's part! I believe we all *do* understand. That is why we are doing this portion of the study in the first place. Right? Okay, that known, let's continue the briefing."

Deltray Zacchaeus forced himself to not scowl.

He leaned back in his chair and tried to relax.

Chapter 8

Sarah Whiting sat in the ascetically decorated waiting room. Hues of soft browns and tans, accented with blues, were fresh in the newly appointed office— purposefully designed to have a calming effect on people. Sarah was trying to look interested in the magazine displayed on one of the many e-tablets the room offered for use to those who needed to spend any time there.

She put the device down after reviewing a few files on mental disease. She pulled her own smartphone out and reacquired some research sites she had been studying. The information was only slightly more attention-grabbing than what was on the tablet. Her mind was on her father and, understandably, on herself.

"Ms. Whiting, the doctor will see you now."

Sarah stood and walked toward the open doorway. Before her appeared a young male attendant. He nodded a greeting and motioned for her to follow him. No words were exchanged.

Sarah knew the way. She'd been to the office several times before with her dad for consultations. And although her father was there at the clinic, in another room, he was not to be included on this occasion.

"Hi, Sarah," Dr. Waxman said.

"Doctor," she replied.

He shook her hand and invited her to sit.

She did, but didn't lean back in the high-back suede chair.

"Well, here's what's going on. Oscar's condition has worsened, significantly, I'm sorry to say. As you know, the diagnosis of early-onset Alzheimer's made…" He looked to the side at some information on his tablet, "about eight months ago, concluded that the disease was worsening even then. Treatment hasn't been successful, as we'd hoped. But, as earlier stated, with this condition, treatment only helps about 20-30% of the cases, and then with only marginal improvement."

He paused to read some more of the information on the tablet.

Sarah felt her heart stop and shakily restart.

"Uhmm," he started again. "I'm also sorry to say that there is no further treatment available, Sarah. There's nothing we can do but adapt his living situation to the disease. He can't live alone, not even part of the time. His condition is such that he doesn't have the capacity to function outside a regimented environment. He'll need constant care and attention."

As a doctor he had done this sort of quick briefing for the loved ones of his patients more times than he could count, but it was never easy.

"Sarah, I know this is difficult for you. I understand. Try to…try to think of it this way. Your father now lives pretty much in his own world. For him, it is as real as ours. It contains a lifetime of sensory input and memory. And he will live within those remaining accessible memories for the rest of his life."

He paused once more, cleared his throat and then began again.

"Sarah, it's us that have to continue to deal with the realities of life: the sadness, the loss, the struggles, the frustrations, but not your father, for the most part. He may again experience some of these things, the struggles and frustrations, but…but within just a few moments of their experience, he will forget them. In other words, he won't have to carry around the long-term pain that they cause, like we have to. Do you know what I'm saying?

"I know this isn't much consolation. This is a terrible disease. But, actually it's the most terrible for those of us who have to watch and help with the condition, much less for those who suffer from it. Especially at the stage your father is. As of now, he's not suffering, Sarah. I want you to know that."

He took a deep breath and then exhaled. This was the point he hated the most, realizing that the truth had been said, and that there was no more to say.

"We're going to keep him for a little while longer to assess his other health conditions, merely routine. In the meantime, you—or whomever—will need to make arrangements for his care. Okay, Sarah?"

Sarah Whiting had suspected what the doctor was going to say. She did make her living as a professional researcher after all. She'd done her homework, and then some. She knew the disease, its levels of severity, its inevitable outcomes, and what she would have to do. In fact, she'd already made preliminary arrangements at a long-term care facility in Bakersfield.

Knowing how intrepidly independent her father had been all his life, it was the hardest thing she had ever had to do. And fortunately for her, she had already cried her heart out the night before.

She was dry now, but the tears would flow again, she knew.

She stood, reached out her hand and thanked Dr. Wax-man.

．．．．．．．

Sarah stepped out through the set of double doors and into the warm sun. She suddenly realized she didn't at all remember exiting the doctor's office, walking down the hallway, or getting into and out of the elevator. She just stood there in a daze, thinking about the absence of the memories. Several people politely started maneuvering around her, so Sarah made her way over to the side of the walkway where there were some stone and iron benches. She seated herself, took a deep breath, and attempted to sort her thoughts.

"The sun is nice today, isn't it?" was the question from the man on the bench next to her.

Sarah oriented herself and turned to look in the direction of the voice. There on the bench sat a middle-aged man with somewhat disheveled, shoulder length brown hair, grayed along the edges. He wore a faded blue collared shirt, and light brown denim trousers. Over the shirt was an attractively styled, dark tan spring jacket with an odd shimmering emblem on the collar. On his face were rimless glasses, the old sort which had a little computer attached to one corner equipped with a miniature screen, which sat slightly above and in front of his right eye.

Sarah didn't notice that anyone was sitting there when she'd decided to sit down. She peered at him, trying to recall what he'd just asked her.

"The sun, it's very nice today, don't you think?" the man repeated, smiling pleasantly.

She looked up into the sky, and then answered courteously.

"Yes, I suppose it is." She just continued to look around up there for a moment. A few birds flew together in the distance, circling each other playfully. She noted that the farther away she looked the hazier it became.

"It says here that we are only able to live on this planet simply by a stroke of luck. If earth was just a few million miles closer to the sun, the planet would have been too hot for life to survive. Too far away by the same measure, and it'd be too cold. We appear to be right smack in the middle of the Goldilocks Zone. Doesn't that make you wonder how we got here in the first place, that we're fortunate to be here at all, given the extremes out there?" He just stared up in the air; both of his elbows now perched up on the back of the bench.

"Yes, I suppose it does," Sarah answered, glancing at the man.

She couldn't help but notice the man's glasses. They appeared to be a very old model, probably antique by the looks of them.

He seemed to notice her curious gaze.

"Yeah, picked them up in an old shop around the corner, and they still work. Amazing the things they've come up with," he said, as he pulled the glasses off, and held them out for her to see. "I'd known that little fact about the sun.

Learned about it a long, long time ago. I'd just forgotten it. Just imagine all the things we may have known at one time, and have just forgotten. Good thing about the Cloud, huh?"

"Cloud?" Sarah asked, not sure what he was referring to.

"Yeah, the Cloud. Though, I guess they're calling it the '*Nebula*' now. The Big Picture always seems to be getting bigger." He laughed slightly, paused and then continued. "You know, the 'Cloud', where all our data and information is, memory!"

She nodded her head, barely understanding.

He continued.

"There's a lot we don't know, or even remotely recognize. Things going on all around us—*inside us*—and we don't have a clue. That is, until someone or something *clues* us in. But that's always been the case, huh?" He snickered once more. "Tells me we're a part of something, and we don't even know we're a part of it!"

The man smiled, winked, and then stood and proceeded to walk away.

Chapter 9

"Hello, welcome. I'm glad you could all make it. Everyone punctual, thank you. Very much appreciated. Please, sit. We'll get started then."

Professor Dunes sat in the primary chair at the opposite end of where several couches and lounge chairs were circularly positioned. It was a small, intimate setting. The walls covered with textured wallpaper, pictures, and sparsely placed soft-lighting fixtures. A few nice furniture pieces along its perimeter rounded off the comfortable room.

"We chose this location—I know it's probably not what you expected—because we wanted to emphasize the fact that after only a few months, people around the world will be sitting in their own living quarters, getting ready to do what you are about to do. We want you be as comfortable as possible when you begin.

"I suspect most, if not all of you may be, shall I say, a little more than...*excited*, starting with us today. It's perfectly understandable. Just be at ease. We'll start with the day's events, morning and afternoon. Lunch will be at twelve, for one hour. You may go out, wherever you wish. For those of you who don't know, there are a couple cafés just down the street on campus—about a three-minute walk.

"Or, there is food provided in the kitchen, which reminds me. Quickly, there is a kitchen over there." He pointed toward an opening. "Down that short hallway. And to the end of the hallway are the personal facilities. Now, don't be shy if you ever need anything. Just go and help yourself. If we're on a critical bit of information at the time, we'll just recap for you when you return. This isn't your typical, rigid, college class or anything. So, please feel free."

"Hello, everyone," Eliam Zaris said as he entered the room.

"You all remember, Eliam, from the presentation," the Professor added.

Everyone turned and greeted him with a nod or a small wave.

"Hi! Hello! I see you all made it. Sorry I missed the start, I was held up. Please forgive me," he said, as he rounded the furniture and quickly settled down on the end of a couch closest to the Professor's chair.

"Good morning, Professor," he then said, reaching out and shaking his hand, "and good morning to everyone else! Uh, let me see if I get this right, uhmm, Dr. Redding...Robert?" Eliam Zaris said toward the man across from him on the opposite couch, questioning if he'd gotten the name correct.

"Robert's fine, please," the man said, also looking around nodding.

"And...Furley," Eliam nodded and smiled, "let's see, Nelson...Declan, and Wena," he bowed his head to the woman. "Condoleezza?" he said next, eyebrows up, seeking clarification.

She nodded and spoke.

"Yes, that is right. Please, just call me Condi!" She also nodded to everyone.

"And Sarah, nice to see you, glad you decided to join us! All of you," he said cordially. He smiled big, nodded to everyone again and then sat back a little.

Professor Dunes started again.

"I'm sure you've all read the briefs given you. That will be pretty much what you can expect over the course of the next month. This morning, we're going to begin with your personal introduction to the device. We'll take you through the simple steps of its operation. How to access and use basic functions: bringing up visual fields—VF's we'll be calling them, and audio fields...AF's; we'll look at adjusting personal settings; window panes and size adjustments; multi-functioning, etc. We'll have fun with that for awhile. Then lunch, and then in the afternoon we'll review all that again, a little more on navigation fundamentals, share a few insights, and then go into some simple apps together.

"This is going to be an interactive experience for all of you. We encourage everyone to share your opinions, your observations, insights and intuitions, about the device as we go along. This goes for today, as well as for the rest of the program. Remember, that's why you're all here: to experience and give feedback to everyone. We invite all comments, and perspectives. Also, remember that while the devices are active, everyone's comments and experiences will be recorded—ours as well." He nodded to Eliam.

Mostly everyone displayed a smirk on their faces at the last comment, many slightly uncomfortable with the idea, though they all knew that it was one of the primary requirements in accepting the offer. All seemed to take a collective deep breath, smiling and exchanging excited looks with one another.

Eliam rose from the couch and walked over to an open cabinet situated next to an entertainment center. He then returned to the group with a case, which he sat on the large coffee table. He opened it by folding one half of it over. In it were eight equally sized compartments, four per side. In each was a smaller case, seemingly made of the same rubber and plastic. He handed each person a small case.

"Here, everybody, please take one. They are all the same, though they are numbered, as you can see. Any of you can use any of the others—there's a basic guest user mode. But, if you would, use the same one throughout the program. Part of the training, and fun, is the customization part. You will find that you can set yours up according to your preferences, very much as you would with your own smartphones. And, feel free to do so as we progress."

"Now, go ahead and open them. Let's begin, shall we," added the Professor.

A few soft gasps could be heard as all the cases were opened.

"Wow…light," Robert said.

Murmurs of agreement could be heard throughout the room.

"What's the battery life like? It can't be much, they're so small!" Nelson Baurle asked.

"Good question. The battery life is actually quite good. Seventy-two hours with a full charge! Each unit will come with its own docking station, and they're also designed for wireless charging with accessories that will be available in the upcoming future," Eliam answered.

"*Really!*" Nelson whispered.

"Yes, there's no screen, which uses up a lot of energy to start with, and the system runs on the extremely low micro-amperage levels.

"Okay! This is on, and again for off." He pushed the small button on the side of his own personal unit to illustrate. "You can turn it on before or after it's on your head, it doesn't matter. However, leave it off for a moment and place them on your heads, like this."

He placed the apparatus on his head as they'd seen before, the ends above their ears and the bulbous part to the back of their heads.

"Go ahead."

All participants followed the instructions, including Eliam Zaris.

The Professor waited for each person to adjust them to their own comfort levels.

With everyone staring at him waiting for the next move, he then touched his device with both hands and spoke slowly, peering at them with narrowed eyes.

"I now have you…under…my…power!" he said, in a sinister-sounding, gravelly voice.

No one said a word for a few seconds. Then the Professor burst into laughter.

"Joking, *just* joking! I've had that planned since day one. I'm so sorry! So…so sorry!" he said, in between roars of more laughter. "I literally couldn't help it…couldn't resist."

He grinned big as everyone relaxed and laughed as well.

"I am sorry," the professor said again, his expression calming. Eliam just sat there, shaking his head.

"You should have seen what he did at last year's Drone and Probe Technology Convention!" Eliam said, starting to laugh again.

The Professor suddenly looked sternly at his colleague.

Everyone cracked up once more.

"Okay, now. When you…when you turn it on, let me first explain what you will feel and then see. First, you'll feel as if your eyes are swelling a bit. This is not actually happening, but the sensation will be there. It's just the device calibrating itself to your brain and nervous system. Your senses are all linked to the brain, and there's a little feedback from this. You'll also notice a little difference in your hearing as well. Now, to date, no one has ever felt any nausea of any sort. However, if you do, please let us know, okay?

"Okay! Those are the sensations you'll feel first. Shortly after, you will begin to see two small, subtly glowing, transparent green circles just above the center of your field of vision. These are the Spatial Locators which are used to orient the B-CID's interface screen. Here's what you do next. When you focus between the two dots, the dots will come together. This is how the interface screen is activated. No matter where your eyes look, the screen will always be in that location, which is the default setting; however, the location can be changed at any time according to user discretion.

"Now then, when your eyes focus on the screen, you will notice that your regular field of vision is still there, just layered behind the screen. But, the neat part is, that even though the screen is there, you're still seeing what is behind it, and both are in focus. The key to remember is that what your *mind* is focused on is pretty much what you will be dominantly attentive to, much as with regular vision. You will see what I mean as we go along.

"Now, what are you going to see on the screen? You are going to see two more dots, as before. These are used throughout the system to spatially locate your focus. Okay, so as before, you focus between them until they come together.

When they do this, you will have created a location cursor. This cursor will behave, within the screen, like any other cursor you might be familiar with. When placed in a particular position by your focus, and activated the same way, you can then open and close files to Apps, Partitions, Browsers, Clouds, Nebula, etc., just like with any other computer operated peripheral device.

"This operating system is designed for simplicity. There are progressively more advanced and complex systems that will be gone over on later dates. However, they all basically operate with the same Spatial Locator system. You, again, are learning the fundamentals of the device and the base system first. The advanced stuff will come later.

"Now, progressing further, we'll be showing you how to enlarge this Interface Screen for dominance in your vision, even to the point of filling your entire field of vision. You will also learn how your regular field of vision can then become the ancillary small screen, to keep an eye on, as it were, and/or completely and encompassingly reduce it to the two dots, thereby being able to enjoy the full sensory field of vision, say of a website, or a webpage, or a virtual tour, or to view a movie, for instance.

"The failsafe built into the operating system is such that a conscious effort must be initiated to change the field of vision. In addition, if a conscious effort is not made to change something, within a given time, the field of vision reverts back to your normal senses. These non-operation time settings can be chosen by the operator and set at varying intervals according to preference. Again, these systems were patterned after the functionality found in today's smartphones.

"When we all arrive at this spatial screen, you will then observe a host of other features that can be actuated and navigated by this same Spatial Locator system. Of course that will come over time, but I imagine that since you're all professionals, used to using today's technologies, you probably won't have too hard a time at catching on, or intuiting the diverse customization possibilities."

Professor Dunes stood. He then motioned toward the entertainment system.

"As we go through this, we have prepared some illustrations for you to observe that will help guide you." He reached up and turned his set on. His eyes seemed to change their focus a couple of times, and then suddenly the large screen came on with what appeared to be the Professor's own visual field, now transferred to the screen.

"So what do you say we turn them on?"

After a short few seconds, the room was filled with a cacophony of oohs, and aahs, and OMG's.

Chapter 10

Sarah Whiting had addressed her own anxious concerns regarding the technology. She discovered that the operation of it was as straightforward as Professor Dunes had described. The morning went well and everyone was ecstatic as they started learning the navigational controls of the operating system.

The audible part was a no-brainer for everyone. It was a simple matter of opening an equalizer screen and adjusting the auxiliary volume levels, which to everyone's amazement was no different than adjusting one's own home sound system.

There were several humorous moments when the Professor gave everyone a turn at seeing their own Field of Vision on the big screen, and being asked to navigate through a series of simply designed files that were engineered as part of a built-in Consumer Training Module. At one point Eliam Zaris demonstrated a more advanced section of the module which was similar in fashion to an interactive video game. He had chosen, from a list of thematic content, a section that centered on space, spaceships, and a 'Living in a Mars Colony' theme.

As he attempted to show the others how to recognize and use the various icons within the program, unanticipated, as well as humorous outcomes, seemed to occur at random. His surprise and frustration seemed genuine and as he continued, his failed attempts at navigation resulted in a succession of spirited reprimands by the female voice of an AI, which was an integral part of the program.

The routine became even more comical when, due to the frustration level Eliam Zaris was apparently suffering from, he abruptly switched the operation of the program over to the nearest person, uttering the words: "Okay, so *you* try it!"

He chose Sarah Whiting.

At first clumsy, Sarah failed on her initial attempts, prompting Eliam's further sarcastic remarks about how it wasn't as easy as one might think. However, after a few minutes, and feeling a little more comfortable, Sarah began to do better. When the AI reprimanded her for failing at a particular task, Sarah would state some reasoning, or strategy, or approach that she was applying in order to better research and learn.

Within a short time of intense application, Sarah passed all the navigational and operational requirements of the program, victoriously receiving commendation from the AI which vocally awarded her with the title of: "Sentient-Prime Navigator."

Following the accolade, Sarah received a devilish scowl from Eliam Zaris, which quickly morphed into a huge, smiling, and humble grin. He started clapping, and the others joined in. Sarah Whiting and Eliam Zaris just sat there with their eyes locked on each other, their smiles lingering, even as the revelry of the moment wound down.

....

After a short break for everyone, Professor Dunes started the next session.

"Good, good!" he said. "Now then, let's move on. Everyone seems to be orienting quite well to the device's operating system. Now...first impressions? Comments?" he asked, looking around the room. Each person took their turns looking at each other, wondering whether they should speak up, or wait and see what all the others had to say. After a short silence, Condi Ghee, the educator, took the first turn.

"I...I am quite impressed!" she said slowly, obviously gathering her thoughts. "It is amazing. All I can do right now is, perhaps, share a few observations, but...this is extraordinary! The feelings you mentioned at the start? Well, I felt them exactly as you said: I had the bulging eyes feeling; I noticed my hearing was, I don't know, augmented, I guess I would say. It was like having an additional source of input, that's for sure."

Most everyone seemed to agree, with nods and murmurs toward each other.

"What I also noticed was the clarity of the Interface Screen. It appears to me as clear as my 20/30 vision, and when I enlarged it to incorporate my entire visual field—my VF—it appeared just as clear. So far we've only seen the basic screen modes, and a few CGI scenes. I'm wondering how far this goes; what it may be like when, oh, I don't know, say like visualizing a scene at a higher HDX resolution. Is it as clear? Professor, Mr. Zaris?"

The Professor looked at Eliam, giving him the floor.

"Yes, it very much is. In fact, you may not recognize the difference."

Dr. Robert Redding then spoke up.

"Won't recognize the difference?"

"Yes, that's right. You see, the impulses that the device inputs in its connection with your brain is no different than your other physical senses. It is just another input. And to not get too technical with it, that is how the breakthrough actually came about; understanding just how your 'senses' feed their information into the brain. Once we understood the physics of how, say, your eyes, which are merely a pair of stereo cameras, send their images through that part of your nervous system to your brain, it was only a matter of converting other extraneous data into the same type signals and then streaming it along the same paths into the brain. Calibrating it and regulating it was a whole other matter, but that turned out to be ancillary to the original discovery of how your natural system does it."

"Does that mean that our minds can be deluded into not knowing the difference, since it's the same type of signals, traveling the same pathways?" Nelson Baurle, the communications engineer, asked.

"Well, yes and no. The operating system is just like other computer OS. It has established programming parameters and protocols. If the protocols were changed, say, for instance, to bypass the icon and cursor programming, then it might happen, but that won't happen because of the encrypted security protocols, as we mentioned before. As you noticed, when you tested out the full vision view, the Spatial Locator dots only disappeared after focusing for a given amount of time. When you shifted your focus, they returned. This is a base program in the OS and can't be overridden by the user."

"I thought you said that the timing *could* be set, by the user?" Wena Paravin, the socioeconomics analyst asked.

"Yes," Eliam continued to explain, "the time of inactivity. When a certain amount of inactivity is reached, it triggers the Spatial Locators to go out of view. The time of how long they will remain out of view is a set amount depending on the user's decision to shift focus. Immediately after doing so, they return."

"So, what is the range of this focus?" Robert asked. "What I'm trying to say is, say I'm looking at a lamp, if I shift my focus to the picture on the wall above it, the Spatial Locators will come back into view? That's what you're saying?"

"Yes, exactly," Eliam agreed with the statement, as did the Professor.

"I think what he's saying, or asking is, can that range, you know, out from the center of focus, be changed? Increased or decreased?" Condi added.

"Good question," the Professor stated. Robert nodded his approval of the interjection.

"Yes, it can be changed. That adjustment can be made by the user. It is located in the advanced settings, which we'll review in a later module. But yes, that is correct," Eliam said.

"How much?" Sarah simply asked.

"Well, it can be set in a circular form, radiating out from the center of your focus, to the edge of your vision, by a factor of close to eighty-five degrees. Meaning, I could set a field that, by shifting my focus ten degrees, would be activated. Or twenty-five degrees, all the way up to about eighty-five degrees, in any given direction—up, down, sideways—any direction."

"Why eighty-five degrees, and not ninety?" Declan Stewart questioned.

"Due to the nature of the human eye," answered the Professor.

"Yes, the human peripheral field doesn't go out to a full ninety degrees. Vision as well as the ability to focus, diminishes to zero outside that range. Try this: without moving your head or your eyes at all, try 'seeing' directly, the person sitting next to you. Try it; make a conscious effort." Eliam winked at the Professor, who, with his own device, activated a camera which recorded several snap shots of what he was seeing through his own eyes—a series of goofy, stressed, and contorted faces.

After trying, everyone shook their heads. It made sense.

"Also," Eliam continued, "one can choose a single spatial point in their visual field—VF—and activate it that way. The purpose of this mostly comes along with the entertainment part. I mean, if you were watching a movie, or some other video source, would you want a couple of green dots popping up to ruin the moment?"

Again, everyone nodded, clearly agreeing. "Makes sense," Sarah said, smiling at him. "You mentioned a movie. I suppose that it would be possible with this to watch a movie with someone else? I mean, two or more people could potentially watch a movie together, with…with this?" She tapped her device with her slim finger.

"Yes, that is also correct, Sarah," Eliam answered. "Something we hadn't mentioned yet is the fact that the devices—through the users' consent and coded activation—can be linked, so that the streaming source, or sources, feed simultaneously to each device, and subsequently, into each brain. Again, these are some of the apps that have been developed for the entertainment-side of the device's broad range of applications, which we will also be reviewing at a later time."

"Now this is getting interesting" declared Declan Stewart, the independent film producer.

Everyone appeared to be deep in thought, thinking of the potential.

Chapter 11

Dinner was superb.

Blackened salmon, shrimp crimson-creole, or a choice cut of steak, accompanied by mixed-exotic vegetable medleys, potatoes, rice and/or pasta-based side dishes, fresh baked breads, with quite a few dessert choices. It was a very pleasant meal in a private room at one of the local restaurants. Close to thirty people were in attendance: the project participants, along with Professor Dunes, Dr. Vectren, Eliam Zaris, with the rest being the senior staff of the University, a few board members, and many of the project's supporting staff: scientists, technicians and project engineers, and a few special guests, including Deltray Zacchaeus and a date.

The occasion was to honor the contributors, the support staff, the participants, as well as to celebrate the project in general. It was also a good way for everyone involved to get to know each other in a comfortable social setting after the first week of the program.

Following dinner, everyone moved to a lounge that was reserved for the particular occasion. The décor was a modern-chic-ocean motif, with comfortable lounge furniture situated on eccentrically spaced terraces, offering the people tables, gathering areas, speaking areas, or little semi-shuttered corners for more intimate conversation. The dress was dining casual: from suits to Dockers, and dresses to jeans.

Sarah Whiting wore a dress, which could have been as equally appropriate in a formal setting as on a beach. It was white cotton, to the knees, form-fitting yet somewhat flowing, open-neck, with intricately laced threading in certain areas for accent. The outfit was topped off with elevated dress sandals, and only two pieces of jewelry: a set of small dangling earrings, and a thin gold bracelet.

After the first hour of socializing, primarily within their own groups, the people started mingling a little more. Though Sarah typically didn't attend social gatherings—choosing to stay away from most bars and lounges and the like—she could force herself to have a little fun and do the meet and greet thing. As she and Condi Ghee were getting to know one another, and strolling over to the beverage counter to get another drink, Sarah heard her name being spoken in a small group to her left.

She turned her head.

One of the older gentlemen smiled at her and then politely invited her over to answer a question—Sarah thought him to be one of the University's senior staff, or a board member.

Sarah looked at Condi with big eyes that whispered, "Don't you dare leave me alone here!"

Condi smiled, instantly picking up on Sarah's plea. She nodded her head slightly. Both turned and casually entered the group's little lounge area.

"Hello, Ms. Whiting," the man said, standing and offering his hand. A volley of introductions went around before the man could get his question asked. He waited courteously until everyone was finished and then spoke.

"Ms. Whiting, we heard that you had an interesting time today with Mr. Eliam Zaris in navigating one of the more advanced learning apps designed for the system, and that you showed a particularly strong aptitude for it. Quite impressive for the first day, I must say."

Sarah blushed, feeling honored by the comment.

"Well, yes, I enjoyed it actually. It's just a matter of settling into the functions and feeling it, I suppose, as opposed to operation by rote," she said, slightly tense from the attention.

"Yes, I understand what you mean. Of course, that's easier said than done, for many of us I should think!" The man returned the comment, drawing a slight laugh from the group.

"Eliam is quite good at navigation within the B-CID. In fact, he was a huge influence in designing that portion of the Consumer Training Module. He's…"

"You're Oscar Whiting's daughter, aren't you?" another gray-haired man asked politely, suddenly changing the subject.

Sarah looked up abruptly, and then nodded slowly.

"How is your father, Sarah? We talked a couple times when I worked at NASA many years back, a very likable sort, a persistent man I understood, all in all very admirable. What's he up to these days? Probably something to do with science, or space, I would think." The man finished and smiled.

Sarah tried to answer carefully.

"Well, he's…preoccupied these days, in his own world, you could say, uhmm, yes, still highly interested in science, and everything related to 'space'. He's retired, actually." She just stood there, not wanting to say any more.

"Oscar Whiting was a decorated Navy Seal in his younger days, as I recall. Then he hooked up with NASA," the man informed the group, "and worked on numerous research programs: deep flight, duration studies, low gravity adaptation, all that computer modeling, and the like. Longed to be an astronaut, but never ended up being added to a ship's roster, unfortunately. Understandable though, tough programs, all the way back. I doubt if he'll even remember me, but if you think about it, tell him that Conner Hartness said hello," the man offered.

"Yes…yes I will."

"So, Sarah, what was that I heard about your mother? I seem to remember something about…" the man appeared to stumble through his memories.

"*Hello*, everyone, I heard my name mentioned from afar. So I thought I should come over and at least try to assuage any exaggerations that may be getting started concerning me." Eliam Zaris seemed to appear out of nowhere. He looked at Sarah first.

"How are all of you?" he added, now looking pointedly toward the others. "Conner, Thomas, guys. I hope everyone is having a nice time?"

Several answers were voiced: "Yes" and "Surely" and "Wonderful."

"Good. This is a nice little place, isn't it?" he asked, shifting his focus around the room. He paused for a moment seemingly distracted as he touched his temple.

"Ms. Whiting, Ms. Ghee, are the two of you having a nice time?" Eliam then cordially asked, turning his attention back to them.

Sarah and Condi nodded, answering that they were.

Suddenly, a voice resonated loudly from another group near them.

"*Conner…guys*, could you spare a moment? We have an interesting conjecture brewing that requires your input! Help us out here, won't you?"

The men from the small group then stood and nodded toward the ladies and Eliam. They scurried off.

"Work," Eliam said, taking a slow sip from his glass, "a man's first passion."

Sarah and Condi looked at each other, thankful for the apparent rescue.

"I never considered the notion that 'work' would be a man's *first* passion," Condi said, actually surprised. "I would have thought that it would be, I don't know, eating, or man-cave construction, or something."

Sarah giggled at her new friend's comment. So did Eliam.

"Well, yes, you're right. I was referring to *after* a man is done eating, and his 'man-cave' is mostly constructed. Work comes next, for many of us *men*. But, there're quite often many other things that come along that can incite a man's passions, to tell the truth." He took another sip from his drink.

"Yes, I suppose," Condi said, smiling largely. She looked at Sarah and gave her a subtle wink. "If you two will excuse me, I need to make a call. I'm going to be picked up soon, and I need to contact my ride." She started to walk away. Stopping abruptly, she turned to Sarah. "Ohhhhh, we still have a date for tomorrow evening?" Condi asked, raising her eyebrows.

"Yes, of course, looking forward to it. I'll meet you there." Sarah answered with enthusiasm.

Condi nodded and winked slightly. "Sweet! Tomorrow then, and if I don't see you two before I leave, have a nice evening. Goodbye!"

Condi Ghee smiled once more and walked away.

Eliam Zaris watched her for a moment and then turned to Sarah.

"So…date…?" he asked, seemingly grasping for words.

"Yeah…" Sarah answered, tilting her head, curious as to the sudden change in his demeanor.

Eliam picked up on her inquisitive expression. "Well, I was just wondering. Are you…you and Condi, you know, together? Together? Getting *together*?" He stumbled with his words.

Sarah was at first confused, but then it hit her.

"Oh, *together*! No…*no*, we're just going to meet to go for a run," she replied. "We just learned that we both like to run. So we're meeting at Sequoia National Park, tomorrow…to go for a run." Sarah laughed heartily. "No, we're not *together*. Not that way!" she again clarified, continuing to reveal her amusement through subdued laughter.

"Ohhhhh," Eliam said, his appearance now brightening. He smiled broadly.

A short silence carried them through the awkward moment, and then Eliam spoke again.

"I wonder what we might have in common that might elicit a *date* of some sort."

Sarah didn't see that coming, at least not that abruptly. But it was a pleasant surprise.

"Oh, well, uhmm, I guess we would have to have some type of extended conversation—you know—to find out."

"Hey, I'm up for conversation! I'm free today, at about," he paused to look at his watch, "about 7:30 this evening," he said.

"It's about 7:30, right now, I believe," Sarah said. "I guess…I guess that might not be a bad time." She turned to face him. "Great! I guess all I can say then is, okay…I'll see you at 7:30 then!"

Chapter 12

Col. William Ravine had been in the military since forever it seemed. He started out as a seat-of-your-pants combat pilot, then a drone systems pilot, and then he pursued further education in the related technical fields: advanced computer systems & applications, artificial intelligence, and then up the ladder to certain focused Intelligence positions within the government relative to his particular expertise. His career choices, each spanning many years, ultimately led to his placement in the Intelligence Office in California, due to the office's primary focus: technology, innovation, and application in the private sectors.

As soon as the patents for the new Smartbrain technology had been filed, his office had been extremely busy. The potential was enormous. Everyone privy to it understood that, and it was the office's main occupation to attempt to liaise with the developers of the technology in order to not only monitor its testing progress, and safety, in accordance with the ASTI, but to assess its prospective commercial applications, as well as to also carefully negotiate for its military counterparts.

Deltray Zacchaeus worked for the local office in a civilian capacity, and was one of Col. Ravine's sets of eyes and ears out in the field. He was hired for the position due to his technical and engineering background, as well as his past involvement with other BCI programs at private companies.

"Not much was said that I could pick up on," Deltray told the Colonel. "Most people didn't converse about the program.

Well, only a sparse reference here or there. No specifics...I..."

"There must have been something, if not directly then through inference. Think about it! What were the general attitudes of the people? Were they happy, excited? Did they seem stressed, frustrated? Any feelings shared—that you observed—relative to dissatisfaction, disappointment, and/or disillusionment regarding the technology in general? It's not just all about the words."

The man considered the questions.

"Actually, the atmosphere was upbeat and, I would say cheerful, optimistic even. There was a lot of laughter, jokes and the like. Professor Dunes and Dr. Vectren were especially in high spirits it seemed. They were drinking heartily, as if they were celebrating something. A few of the people—technicians mostly—got into a heated debate over program subroutines, but again, nothing specific. Everyone appeared to be pleased with everything so far."

"Good, *good*," the Colonel said, enthusiastically. "That's what I wanted to hear. That means the initial trials were positive, from everyone's perspective. And that means I need to take this to the next step." He paused for a moment to think. He then picked up his phone and tapped in a number.

"Colonel William Ravine here, calling for General Epcot. Yes, I'll hold."

Chapter 13

They ran the first few kilometers of the trail with little conversation.

Upon returning to the point where they had started, having taken a circuitous route through the gargantuan forest along its many dirt trails, they opted to stop and get a drink of water. It was a little warmer than they had anticipated. As they drank small sips and stretched, the conversation flowed.

"I've been coming here since I was a kid, on vacation with my parents; I still can't get over these trees," Condi said, looking up at the mammoth sequoias.

"Yeah, me either," Sarah replied, also looking up. She took a couple deep breaths to help get her wind back. She then stretched and leaned backwards, her arms reaching up into the air, as if trying to grab one of the faraway branches above her. The scene sparked a memory about the young girl in their group.

"So, what do you think of our very own Furley Goens. You know about her, right?" Condi asked, just making conversation.

Sarah looked over at her with a surprise.

"Wow, I was just thinking of her. That's weird."

"Yeah? I guess the trees sparked the thoughts. Do you, know about her? Ever heard her story, I mean?"

"I've only caught a few mentions on the news about her is all. She's a CEO of a corporation? And she's only eighteen?"

"Yeah, a nearly half a billion-dollar corporation."

Sarah's eyes swelled with curiosity.

"Really!" Sarah momentarily froze with amazement. "What, did she inherit it, or something?"

"Nope, did it herself, in less than five years...since she was thirteen."

"*Really*," Sarah iterated again.

"Yeah! It's an amazing story, actually. Her parents were essentially non-motivated, lower-class, semi-working people—Media's euphemisms by the way—who were a couple of pieces of work: druggies, swindlers, grifters. When Furley was, I don't know, ten or eleven I guess, they both were sent up for bank robbery and manslaughter—someone died as a direct result of their botched heist and the car crash as they tried to get away. Anyway, Furley was in the foster home circuit for a number of years until a family took her in and gained guardianship. They weren't exactly well to do, but they were good people and Furley did okay.

"Long story short, Furley was inspired by her real parents, in the opposite direction mind you, as she states it, and started an online environmental business where products and companies and resources and passions all seemed to meet up with a desire to help and give back to others, as well as to the planet. She ended up creating an entity of its own that people just seem to want to be a part of and support. Today it consists of hundreds of small companies hubbing off of her start-up, generating a passion for change that is now in over a dozen other countries. And it's still going strong. I can just imagine what this new technology will do for all that. It is a pretty amazing story, actually."

"Wow," Sarah said. "I had no idea. Well, good for her. Huh! She must be pretty well-to-do."

"No, actually, she gets a small base salary only slightly more than a grade school teacher makes! Lives in a small apartment in her home town and only stays in low budget hotels or with people she knows when she travels—sometimes she just camps out, I've heard. All the rest goes to support grants for environmental projects, business start-ups, and scholarships for certain educational programs geared toward the environment."

"*Really*," Sarah found herself saying again.

"Yeah, the kids got a lot of passion, that's for sure. Hey, did you notice her eyeing that Eliam Zaris guy?" Condi mentioned.

"Yeah, actually, I did. Don't think that'd work out, though. Age." Sarah shook her head.

"Yeah, I agree. I could tell *you* like the guy!" Condi said, sharing her observation.

"Yeah, I think I'm starting to…I think," she said, smirking.

As she spoke the words out loud, it seemed to convince her more.

"Yes, I could tell. He is a handsome male," Condi added, as she began to stretch again.

Sarah nodded to herself. She then remembered their first conversation.

"He thought you and I were *together*," Sarah mentioned, smiling at the memory.

"Together? You mean, *together*? Why would he think that?"

"I guess it was the date comment, at the dinner. I thought it was funny. He seemed genuinely relieved when I told him we were just going running."

Condi looked at Sarah for a lengthy bit of time before smiling and turning her head back up to the canopy as she slowly stretched out her arms toward the sky.

"Well," she said, taking a deep wispy breath as she reached, "to each his own. You guys going out?" Condi then added, "Is that even allowed, you know, being in the program and all?"

"I don't know if it is or not," Sarah answered. "Nothing was said about fraternizing with the people, or that it was prohibited in any way." She paused, considering it more thoroughly. "I don't know. What do you think?"

Condi tilted her head as she appeared to reflect on the thought.

"I'm…not sure. It's nobody's business but your own, as far as I'm concerned, whatever you do, or whomever you go out with. I was just thinking of the media blitz that we're in for, when all this comes out. People can really twist things around to make something out of nothing. Who knows what scrutiny we're going to have to endure? After all, we did sign up to be rats-in-a-study!"

"Yeah," Sarah said slowly, agreeing with the new perspective. A sudden shadow seemed to fall across her face. "I really haven't given it all that much thought. I guess we don't know what's going to happen, do we?"

Condi shook her head.

"No, not for sure, but we can extrapolate a little if we think about it. Let's see. We're going to be the representatives of an exciting new technology—a revolutionary new product—one that will fundamentally change the communication, social, and entertainment industries, as well as a vast host of others, a pretty broad-based impact on society across the board. And you know the military and the governments of the world have to be after this; you can bet your life on that.

"And, I'm sure there'll be all sorts of varied opinions as to our own personal agendas. You know, for money, fame, political, whatever. With the media, it's not who you are, or what you are, it's how you're perceived. They're the ones who create the public persona, really—good ones, and the bad ones. And *that's* why people need good publicists, not just to help build a good reputation, but to keep from getting a bad one. *We* probably need to be thinking about that, sooner rather than later."

Both just stood there leaning against the car, sipping on bottles of spritz-water, thinking about it. It was a long moment before either spoke again.

The silence was broken by Sarah.

"Yeah, I'm not so much looking forward to any of that."

"Me either. But a certain amount of it is going to happen, whether we want it to or not. I guess we just make the best of it, if it doesn't drive us crazy first." Condi laughed.

Sarah started biting the inside of her lip.

Chapter 14

They strolled toward the next exhibit: *Time and the Evolution of Man.*

"Wow, look at how real he looks! I'd think he was, if he weren't just a bust inside a glass box."

"Yeah, same here, amazing skill, it says it took the artist's team nearly two years to create these guys," Eliam Zaris said, staring into the Neanderthal's glassy eyes.

"What would it have been like living back then, only the basic instincts, knowledge, to apply, all day—everyday— where your only thoughts and concerns were just staying alive, searching for food? How'd we get from *there*...to *here?*" Sarah asked, with a touch of wonder in her voice.

"I've asked that same thing many times," he answered softly. "When you first mentioned you'd like to come see the new exhibit, I thought you were joking. I mean, *I* love this stuff. But I thought you were in some way making fun of my scientific background, or something."

"Now why would you say that? How would I have known that you were so attracted to Neanderthals, in order to joke about it?"

He laughed at the comment.

She smiled and then resumed.

"I love this stuff, too, actually. I've been waiting for this since they announced it would be on loan from the Smithsonian. I saw these guys there, around the time when I was in grad school. Same effect, they still look so real."

"Yes, they do," he agreed again.

"So what *do* you think about all this? Did we just rise up out of some…primordial-muck and somehow get to where we are today? Or is there another as-of-yet undefined set of probabilities at work?" She raised her eyebrows quizzically.

He turned to look at her.

His expression exhibited more than a hint of surprise at the line of questioning.

"In your 'scientific' opinion," she said, glancing playfully at him as she strolled around to the other side of the exhibit piece.

He returned the smile.

"Well, let's see, honest opinion?" he asked.

She nodded her head.

"I…I guess deliberations are still ongoing regarding all of that: the—how could something come from nothing—conundrum? How did 'muck' suddenly just begin to get smarter and start to question where it came from, what it was made of? Was it all just happenstance, or was it in some way determined? Did something 'external' to the planet contribute the initial spark? And if so, then how external: external to the planet, external to the solar system, to the galaxy, to the universe?"

"Ahhh! The rudimentary joys of scientific conjecture," she said, smiling.

"Indeed!" he replied. "I do think that…that no matter *how*, there still may be a reason why. And if that's the case, then there is purpose, whether we know what that is at every juncture or not. At least that's how I choose to look at it. I'm not what you'd call an existentialist, nor do I consider myself religious. But, I do think that there are some fundamental absolutes that are part of the fabric of this universe. And I think that one of them is that we are absolutely going somewhere; at least that seems to be the case to me. I mean, we've left the planet; some of us are living in space stations, some on Mars. And every day we make strides forward toward some astonishing breakthrough in learning and application. Who knows where we'll find ourselves in the next century, or a million years from now for that matter.

"Personally, I wouldn't want to live my life if there were no purpose for it. And granted, perhaps it's just because I *say* there's purpose, and because of that, there is, at least for me. And does that automatically mean that everyone else is part of the scenario? I don't know! All I know is what I know. And I believe that I'm here for an important reason; I believe we all are. But that's me."

He finished and gave her a large, close-lipped grin.

Sarah was stunned at the simple honesty and depth of his words. She felt the same way about it all, though she'd not ever expressed it like that. The connection touched her. Suddenly, she liked this man very much.

"You sound like my father," she said. She then looked back at the Neanderthal. "What do you say we go hunt down some food? I would say that I'm absolutely hungry right now. I'll take the club, and you can have the spear. Sound interesting?"

He smiled.

"Absolutely!" he answered. "I know of a nice place over in the next valley; they say it's teaming with great beasts of many varieties!"

They both smiled.

....

"Your dad was at NASA! That's right. I remember reading about it in your submission paperwork. He's an engineer?" he asked excitedly, putting down his fork after finishing his last bite. He wiped his lips and placed his napkin back on the table.

"Yes, he was, and very much the astronomer, too. He was also in the astronaut program for many years, though he never got to go up. He'd tried about as hard as anyone could have, but they just seemed to never pick him, always said there was some other person 'better positioned' for the task. But he wouldn't give up. He tried more times than anyone ever did; I think he set the record, actually. He would've really loved to go into space." She sighed, her expression downcast.

"That's unfortunate," was all Eliam could find to say. He couldn't help but notice the change in Sarah's mood. "So what's he doing these days?" he added, trying to be more up-beat.

"Well, Dad is retired. He retired early…had to. He's got advanced early-onset Alzheimer's. Not been a good time for him, for either of us, in truth."

Eliam cringed at the answer, feeling bad by going there. But his enduring sense of purpose and reason gave him the wherewithal to make the best of it.

"Wow, I imagine that's got to be tough. Sorry for mentioning it. But, I really want to get to know you, Sarah. I'm sorry!" His brows tightened together as he looked closely at her, eager to console if possible.

"Oh, it's alright. It happens," Sarah said with a sigh. "Good things happen in life, and so do bad. It's life. He's okay, for the most part. He's temporarily living at a facility in Santa Clarita. He doesn't like it. But, he's a smart man, and he knows it's the best and safest scenario for everyone. He reads a lot, as he always has, and he spends a lot of his time in his own world, which the doctor's say is a better scenario than most. But I know he worries about me a lot. Dad's a good guy."

Sarah looked at Eliam and somehow intuitively knew the next question.

"And my mother…" She swallowed. "My mother passed away. She committed suicide over twenty years ago. She had a mental disease, they said, and suffered from deep depression—which was barely noticeable to us and her close friends. She hid it well. It was only when we read some of her personal writings—afterwards—that we realized what she'd been going through. She was a physical therapist; she helped others with their debilitations and losses—from disease, accidents and the like. She was good at talking with others, I guess, helped a lot of people through their problems; ironic that she had severe problems of her own, and no one even knew.

"She and Dad were close, but he didn't even see this coming. He knew more than the rest of us that she was depressed a lot, but she always tried to put on that good face. One day she just lost her mind, they'd said. Dad was absolutely floored when it happened. It's amazing the burdens people carry around…and keep to themselves."

Eliam was speechless.

"And let's see, as for the rest of my family: most of the relatives chose to remain childless—for world-saving, population-reduction reasons, Dad speculates anyway—so my family was sparse to none over the years. I have a half-uncle out east. No communication. For the last ten years it's just been me and Dad. And let's see, I don't date much; I don't like to play those personality-pretending, social-acceptance games. And did I mention that I'm for the most part, pretty blunt and straightforward?"

She smiled at him sadly.

Eliam just sat there.

After a moment he took a deep breath and spoke.

"My parents were both murdered, while I hid in a cubby hole behind a pile of dirty clothes in their bedroom."

Sarah's eyes immediately grew large and motionless.

"Whaaaat?" her voice quivered.

"They were killed by a group of terrorists, because of the difference in their ideological beliefs. I was seven years old. They hid me there seconds before it happened. Through a small crack in that pile of clothes I watched the whole thing. I was too afraid to come out, and stayed there for hours. I thought that the men were still out there waiting for me, that they were going to kill me, too. As it turned out, people my parents knew happened by and found them—and me. Relatives took me in after that, and we ended up moving away, to another…country. That was that. I don't have much family now, either. None even remotely close.

"And let's see, I'm an engineer, entrepreneurial for the most part, also very much into astronomy. I'm into self-defense training, all things gadget-like, most on-the-edge kind of adventure stuff. I don't date much either; I love action movies, documentaries, seafood, occasional alcoholic beverages, sometimes a little THC when out in the wilderness, and I have a sometimes overwhelming penchant for helping others learn a better way. And did I mention that I'm quite often blunt and straightforward?"

He just sat there, calmly looking at her.

"And how was your dinner?" the overly-perky waiter cordially asked, appearing out of nowhere. "How about some dessert? We have an assortment of wonderful pies and chocco-late delights," he added, stretching the word chocolate out for emphasis.

"No, thanks," Sarah said abruptly. "But, I'd like another beer. And make it a tall one this time, please."

"Same here, an *extra* tall one," Eliam said as they both stared at each other.

. . . .

Their dinner was good, but the micro-brewed beers were better, serving to take the edge off.

Slowly their conversation resumed, though somewhat jerkily at first, seeing how deeply they had revealed themselves to each other. However, though initially uncomfortable, both began to feel a growing inner connection.

Eliam further elaborated on his background—his residing in numerous countries and hard-to-name places in his early life after the tragedy he'd described. Sarah consciously avoided any further conversation about her mother, choosing to talk more about her father, his career, and her own parallel interests.

"That's amazing, living in all those places you'd mentioned. I couldn't imagine. I think I'd like to travel abroad, but then, maybe not so much," Sarah said.

"Yeah, you probably couldn't imagine some of the places I've been," he said, smiling.

"I went to Europe once, with my dad," she then added. "Saw Paris and Rome, for a few hours, anyway. We didn't get to stay long, as it was a business trip. But it was nice. I've also been out east…to Nevada!" she said.

Eliam burst into laughter.

"*Nevada?*" he repeated.

He laughed heartily, then snickered once more as he sipped on his beer. "You're funny. That was delivered *perfectly*, by the way. I wish I had a sense of humor like that. Most people don't get it when I try to be witty. They just stare at me."

Sarah smiled at the compliment.

"That was funny!"

"What?" Eliam scrunched his eyes with curiosity.

Sarah just laughed.

"I also remember reading in your submission paperwork that you've done some bit-acting? Is that right? Really? What are some parts you've done? Are you Hollywood-bound? Is this a career direction for you?" he asked.

Sarah was a little embarrassed with all the detailed questioning. She took a sip of her beer before answering.

"Yeah, sort of, I mean, I've done some small parts. A *career*? Oh, I don't know about that, really. I suppose I'd pursue it, if I had some decent offers. I do enjoy it, at least some of it."

"So, what have you done?"

"I…I, let's see, I started out doing extra work, like most people. I was in a couple of episodes of a mediocre-rated TV series called the *Walls of Ravensbard*."

Eliam's blank expression revealed that he hadn't recognized the title.

"Uhmm, it was one of those kingdoms, fantasy-castle, swords, spear-chucking, slay the dragon creatures kind-of fare. I was an extra. I played a peasant woman who actually got to rise to the occasion and de-horse a bad guy during a revolt scene, and then get killed in a hail of arrows the next day. It was fun, actually."

"Interesting. What else?" He urged her to continue.

"Well, I have had a few one and two-liner parts on film."

Eliam looked even more curious, again urging her to elaborate.

"I got to say," she started, clearly getting herself in character. "I got to say: 'If it's true, and they're here, we've only got three choices: run, die…or fight!'" She finished and for a moment maintained a very serious expression.

"Wow, that was good," Eliam said. "So, what…what was the outcome? Your character got me, by the way!"

"Well, first we fought, then we ran, and then we died!"

Eliam laughed, though he tried not to, being conscious of her feelings.

"It was a bunch of transvestite zombies, one of those b-rated apocalypse yarns. We ended up one of them—zombies, not transvestites."

Eliam broke out into laughter again.

"What's your most recent acting experience?" Eliam managed to ask as their laughter subsided.

"Most recent? Uh, I've been doing some street acting."

"Street acting? What do you mean?"

"Well, have you ever heard of Street Shock Adventures, Inc.?"

He shook his head no.

"Well, it's an acting troupe—sort of for burgeoning actors like me—that perform in altered reality settings, out in public."

Eliam looked confused.

"Okay, so let's say you and a group of your friends, or business associates, whatever, want an entertaining evening. You pay Street Shock Adventures, Inc. to interject into your group's chosen preplanned events. And, let's say you're taking the group out to dinner, and then to a bar, or lounge. As the evening proceeds—unbeknownst to most people in the group—the acting troupe intercedes by interjecting bizarre things into everyone's experience."

Again, Eliam looked somewhat lost.

"Okay, say like your group's at the bar. Perhaps two of the troupe's actors might play bar patrons. They get into an argument, over…underwear, men wearing panties, whatever. They infringe on the group's experience by pulling them into the argument; pants drop, panties are revealed; what fun, huh? Sometimes it can get really bizarre. See? Other times, they might appear to do a drug deal with one of the group members, and then a mobster steps in, checks the package, finds it not filled with the money, and accosts the group members demanding the cash; then another mobster comes in and challenges the first; and off it goes into the surreal. There are a million scenarios that can happen. Some are really out there."

Eliam nodded his head, now starting to get the idea.

"What parts do you play, have you played?"

"Let's see, I've been a hooker, who recognized a group member, who just happened to be there with his wife, and he's trying to convince his wife that he doesn't know me, see. But, I know his name, a bunch of personal stuff, ahead of time, which I got from the guy who contracted us, see; it's the intimate details that really sets them off. And let's see, I once played a corporate executive who apparently noticed a group member that had been in for an interview, and I right there offered him a job making three times the money. Of course the guy's denying it, but the bosses are really taken by it. It's kind of one of those 'get-punked' type of things, but no one gets filmed, that's policy, for privacy reasons, unless it's agreed upon at the start in the first place, and waivers are signed, and all that."

"Wow, that sounds interesting."

"Yeah," she said, "it can be fun. It doesn't pay much. But it's a good chance to hone your craft. At least that's what they tell us to get us to work so cheap."

She sipped her beer.

"So, you do it for the experience—the acting, I mean?"

Sarah thought about it.

"Yeah, I suppose. Like I said, I like parts of it. It can be fun, but it does twist your guts into a knot. Really, I'm kind of surprised I even do it, you know, because of the fear factor. I'm not exactly the extrovert type, if you know what I mean. Though it's often easier to pretend you're somebody else, than to be yourself, I guess. I really only started doing it because it was suggested to me, as kind of a therapy. I was told once that, it's that way with anything you do in life; you have to act it out first, as if you *were* that thing, until the reality eventually sets in."

She trailed off and sat there in thought.

"I actually haven't done it for quite some time; not sure I want to again."

"Yeah, I can understand that, with life being the way it is. And I agree, most the time you *do* have to act the part, until you *become* the part. So what helped you decide to accept the offer for the program?" he asked.

Sarah looked at him, snapping out of her muddled thoughts.

"Well, the money had a big impact. One does not become wealthy from stints at bit-acting or sitting at home on a computer all day doing research for business-types, small-time politicians, and brainless under-grads, much less from writing amateurish screen plays or novels. They pay the bills—well, at least most of the time—but now with Dad's condition, it'll help a lot."

"Screen plays and novels?" Eliam asked, sincerely impressed.

Sarah silently nodded.

"Ahhh, you have an imagination, then!" he said with a grin. She rolled her eyes.

"Uhm, yeah, sort of, it's a hobby, though it can be pretty absorbing sometimes. Don't expect to make any money from doing that either; at least I doubt if I ever will. It takes more than just knowledge and talent. As they say, it's really about 'who you know!' not just what you know. And I don't really know anybody."

"Is that all you're interested in, the money?" Eliam asked.

"No…*no*, but it would be nice, getting some sort of reward and recognition from one's creativity." She thought deeply again before resuming. "And regarding the project, no, I'm not exactly naive. I can see how this has the potential to be world-shattering stuff. One can't help but extrapolate on the potential, when one thinks about it." She was trying to sound intelligent, knowing that he was an engineer and scientist, and because of the beer. "Being a part of something like this is pretty awesome I think. That was another reason I decided to do it, though I'm not going to like all the attention everyone says it will bring."

"Ooooh, 'extrapolate,' one of my favorite words. 'World-shattering,' please go on."

Sarah wasn't used to such candid questions, but she continued on since Eliam seemed so non-judgmental and kind.

"Well, this *is* going to change everything, I think. Like Professor Dunes said at the start, 'everything, every industry, public and private.' Truthfully though, I can't help but wonder about the potential negative effects. I mean, surely the government will want the product and all it can offer. Won't they? They're probably already after it, I'd assume."

"Well, I can't go into detail, but the answer is: yes, they are. All those types and more. Big business wants a slice of the pie as well. They can't afford to lose any competitive edge these days."

"Okay, so what are your thoughts? Why are you doing what you're doing?" Sarah asked. "And what about the negative side?"

Eliam took a deep breath and exhaled briskly.

"Well, okay, let's get hypothetical for a moment. Imagine a world society where the elite—ideologically, educationally, and monetarily—have control over such technology. They would be like an advanced race of beings that would have the potential to control and manipulate the other less fortunate groups of people who didn't have such technology. They could be considered demigod's, in a way, ruling the lower classes according to their bidding.

"And we all know stories of people who did just that because they had proprietary control over some superior technology, or resource of some sort: land or water or mineral reserves, weaponry, or some inside knowledge in the sciences: biology, physics, or whatever, it's a long list. What I'm describing has already happened, of course, countless times throughout history, right? Well, imagine Smartbrain technology being added to that list. And again, what if only a few groups could apply it according to their will? Whatever that might be."

Sarah started nodding her head as she thought about it.

"You're talking about another catalyst for separation of the classes, at the very least," she remarked.

"Exactly! We are naive to think that if something like this was to come along and the wrong people seized control of it, that the planet wouldn't experience yet another paradigm shift in political positioning. Sorry, but the nature of humans—everywhere—still has the potential to think of themselves as inherently superior to others. It's not too much of a stretch to think that in solitary hands a lot of harm could come from this. Especially... *especially* if the world were, for whatever reason, devolved back to a feudal system, full of dictators and disparate regimes and the like...kings, castles and dragons!"

Based on the flash in Sarah's eye, she caught the connection.

"Yeah, but bringing it out in the first place, doesn't that provide the potential for something like that to happen?" Sarah noted.

"True, you're right about that. But *not* bringing it out, so everyone has the equal use of its potential would be even worse. Yes, by doing what we're doing, we're essentially setting the stage for yet another unimaginable potential societal atrocity, I suppose. The point is this: either no one should have it, or everyone should have it."

"I see," Sarah said slowly.

"And that's where you come in, Sarah."

"Me?"

"Yes, you and the others, you're all the first. You're going to help set the standards—of equal potential—for generations to come, much as the way the Open Internet did back in the day. No small contribution to humanity, wouldn't you say?"

She thought about it for a moment before answering.

"You really think this will have that kind of impact?" she asked.

A serious look molded his already rugged features.

"Yes, I do! In fact, I know it will."

Chapter 15

"Alright, good morning to everyone! I hope you had a nice time at the dinner Friday evening. I know I enjoyed it. And I hope everyone had a nice time off over the weekend. Please, take your seats wherever you like," Professor Dunes said, motioning warmly toward the meeting lounge where they had all met the prior week.

Everyone seated themselves; the Professor remained standing.

"If you remember, the last days we convened we reviewed the navigation system of the device, the Spatial Locators, and we reviewed the encrypted failsafe protocols that are built into the devices' OS. We also went through assorted simple applications: texting, messaging, social networking, gaming, web interaction, most of the forms of standard communication we typically use along the course a normal day.

"The first week was all about the general overview. Today, as well as most of this following week, we will review the next stage of Smartbrain capability: communicating through the thought-to-speech app, as I demonstrated when we first met. What we like to call the AT-app, the Artificial Telepathy application."

Everyone eagerly nodded their heads. This was one of the things that the group had privately expressed their keen excitement about.

"Okay, so we'll get started. Please put on your devices and activate them."

Everyone did so.

"Any questions before we start?" Professor Dunes asked.

Everyone shook their heads no as they played with the Locators in their display fields.

"Alright then, it looks as if everyone has become comfortable. As we proceed, please don't hesitate to pursue any line of questioning. Okay?"

He reached down and did something on his tablet in front of him and then started again.

"Though none of you would probably claim to be a linguistics expert, you most likely know that from a very young age, our brains are programmed using words and associations. Our mothers, and fathers, and teachers began speaking to us, describing to us the world around us at the onset of life. It is therefore no surprise to realize the fact that we *think* in words. This is the basis for the AT-app.

"Have you ever considered what—or where—the origin of thought is? I know, tough subject to think about, isn't it? Now, I don't presume to have the answer to this, one of life's most enduring philosophical quandaries, but I can tell you that, as a result of the 'Brain Project' initiated some five decades ago by the then presiding president, we have arrived at not the seat of personality, or identity, but quite importantly, the discovery of the micro-neural pathways of the brain, along with the coded impulses which travel along them. And because of this important line of learning and discovery, we have recently arrived at a breakthrough in the ability to decode these impulses with a high degree of accuracy.

"What I'm saying here, is this: when I think in words, each word, and each resultant meaning travels through our brain in the form of impulses, on their way to various locations, i.e., other areas of our brain, our intellect, our imagination, our memories, to and from wherever that elusive 'self' is. And though we don't quite know that yet, we have still learned to recognize these impulses. And because of that, we can, through the device, pick up and then convert these impulses into other types of impulses, which can be wirelessly sent to wherever desired. Likewise, those impulses can be transformed back into the ones our brains routinely use, and serve as input into the brain, much as the impulses from our senses do. And now, as a result of this most ground-breaking discovery, we have the AT-app!"

"Wow, *that* was a mouthful," said Nelson Baurle, the communications engineer.

Everyone nodded with wide eyes.

Professor Dunes smiled and continued.

"It is amazing, but when you think about it, it's just a matter of data transfer. The impulses are mapped, copied, decoded, and then transformed by the device into other impulses, and then directed to a receiver. It's a similar process to imputing voice vibrations into a phone mic, and the phone turns the signal into a stream of data, which is then sent, received, and transformed back. The breakthrough in this was learning how to map, copy, collect, and then decode the impulses as they travel along the pathways of the brain. Of course, that's another one of those peculiarly proprietary secrets of ours, and if we told you, we'd have to kill you!" He smiled again at the cliché, as did the others.

"Okay, so let's get started, shall we. Now, we're going to have you go to a location in your display field titled, appropriately, ATA. It's located in your App's Hall. Everyone go ahead and find it."

The participants activated their Display Fields and quickly located the link. Each activated it and began reviewing the introduction page. A few began to read the text; others bypassed this part and selected the activation key.

"As some of you are already doing, go ahead and click the activation key. You can review the introduction page later; it's just a built-in informational foreword to new users. We will be guiding you through the application. Good! Good! I see you've all arrived there. Now, let me illustrate what the process is, and what you'll be experiencing.

"Once the app is activated, it will stay in this mode until turned off, or after a preset time of non-use. Now, go to your contacts and I want you to choose a partner, from someone in the room. It doesn't matter who, just partner up. Good…good! Yes, being that there are seven of you, why don't you, Sarah, pair up with Eliam, if that would be okay."

All quickly chose a partner.

"Now," the Professor resumed, "whoever wishes to go first, please follow my instructions. Partner number two can go through the motions for the experience, but partner one will do the contacting during this round. Your turn will be next, if you see what I'm getting at. Good! Now, please find your partner in the Contacts—each of you has been arbitrarily placed in each other's cache for this very reason.

"Okay, good! Click on your contact. You will see a standard list of communication methods listed, much as you have on your current smartphones. There you will see the ATA link; it will be glowing and pulsating slightly since you had previously activated it. Now, when you click it—please wait for a moment. Thank you! When you click it, you will see the contact information in your display field. The device will then call your contact. When the other person answers, that's where the fun begins.

"What you'll need to do then is this: to start, plainly focus your attention on the contact; think of a clear and discernable stream of inquiry. At first, try to think in short, precise, and slow phrasing. Example: 'Hello Condi, I am calling you to test my new B-CID. Do you hear me clearly?' Try something like that. And remember, the key is to articulate your thoughts clearly.

"As a user does this, the device will teach itself to recognize—more accurately interpret—and thus decode your particular brain impulses, and therefore transfer them wirelessly to your contact. And, this can be a conversation where one person is using the ATA, while the other is using their voice on the other end. Or, one person can be texting—which the device interprets as well—and can then change it to voice in the other person's head.

"Essentially, any input can be transferred to any receiver device, which in turn can be turned into any output, and vice versa. One can speak with their thoughts, while the other reads an instant message. One can speak audibly, and the other hears the words in their brain. It's user/receiver preference."

As the Professor paused, the partners attempted to communicate with their thoughts. Some were doing well; others took a little longer, due to a garbled effect in the decoding. After several tries the devices began sending and receiving the participant's communication. The group was awestruck.

"Do you know what this means?!" Wena Paravin, the socio-economics professional started, thrilled by a sudden epiphany. "Deaf people will be able to hear! Those with speech difficulties will be able to speak. Even…even the blind may be able to see normally, with say a series of cameras on their person, or something like that. People can essentially talk to each other using only their innermost thoughts. This…*this is unbelievable*!"

Suddenly everyone became overwhelmed with the realization of the potential impact of the device. Professor Dunes and Eliam Zaris sported wide grins at everyone's reaction and hearing their ensuing comments. The Professor then spoke softly.

"Well, yes, actually! Now you can see why we're making such a big deal out of this."

Everyone had a look of astonishment on their faces.

·······

Sarah thought the words:

"This is truly unbelievable, Eliam!"

"Yes, I know. You're doing well with it."

"It kind of seems natural, I want to say."

Suddenly Sarah thought of something. She immediately directed her attention back toward their conversation.

"Eliam, does this mean you can read my thoughts? I mean, if I'm just randomly thinking something, can you pick up on it? Can you do that? Is that possible?"

Eliam waited for a moment to see if she was going to add anything else.

"I knew you would ask that! We all wondered the same thing, at the beginning. What we found is that thought impulses traveling through the conscious mind are specific and focused. Meaning that," he paused mid-sentence, *"you know…this is one of the topics that we wanted to*

discuss with everyone. Now's a good time, I'm going to conclude; we'll talk like this some more, later. Okay?"

Eliam halted the conversation for the time being as Sarah nodded in agreement.

"Everyone!" he said semi-loudly to get their attention. They all ended their conversations and turned toward him. Most were in a sort of daze with the experience; for some it was beyond the definition of surreal. After everyone fully shifted their focus toward him, Eliam raised the point that Sarah had intuitively struck upon.

"Sarah asked several important questions that need to be shared and explored with all of you. She raised the question of whether through the process—through the device—whether it is possible to 'read someone else's thoughts.'"

Several people had expressions that revealed that they hadn't, until just then, considered the possibility, while others nodded as if they'd thought of it before. Professor Dunes was re-entering the room after having taken a short personal break. He caught the last part of Eliam's comment and knew immediately where the discussion was going. He returned to his seat and waited for Eliam to elaborate further before adding his own remarks.

"This is a tricky question," Eliam continued. "You see, knowing something about the conscious mind has a lot to do with attempting to explain, and eventually understanding this. The human state of consciousness has historically been broken down into two simple realms: the conscious, and the unconscious. Yet, we all know that that is an overly simplistic way of defining it.

"Thought—or the process of thinking—happens in both realms, of course. But, to specifically address Sarah's point, one cannot just pick up on another's thoughts through the device. The reason is this: when you open your mouth to talk, you don't find yourself spewing out an excessive plethora of words and phrases, do you, just because you have an equivalent amount of thoughts? Your mind doesn't do that, right?

"No, when you speak, your mind is innately focused on that specific communication path. Your thoughts—the ones that are driving that communication—are in essence in the same state; they are focused and specific. In actuality, these are the only brain impulses that we have been able to successfully map, copy, and decode, specifically due to their highly organized and precise structures. In fact, somewhere around 99% of all thoughts—or brain impulses—are so amazingly cross-coded with each other, that we can't possibly decipher them, much less find out where they originated, or are headed, for that matter. Even on the conscious/unconscious level, where the two realms overlap, there is difficulty in decoding the impulses. It's only the specific, cognitively streamed portions that we have been able to effectively read.

"It's as if we are far more intricate of thinking creatures than we'd imagined. And because of this, the exploration of discovery continues. However, we have made this important breakthrough, and are just now starting to learn who we are. And on a philosophical note, many think that, who we truly are, exists predominately on the other side, the side of the 99%. The side that we know the least about, even with today's advancements."

Professor Dunes chimed in.

"What Eliam is elucidating upon is true. I couldn't have stated it better. Believe us. We've considered this line of thinking, quite critically. However, you must realize that, just as you may, as they say, 'put your foot in your mouth', and say things you didn't mean to, the same can happen with Smartbrain. You will indubitably experience this, to be sure. But, as Eliam stated, one cannot just hook up to someone else and listen in on their thoughts. Nor can memories or recorded experiences be tapped into, either. That's all science fiction stuff, not to mention that a user has full control over their device with complete autonomy over any and all communication."

"Yes," Eliam added. "This is a topic that will generate a lot of controversy in the media, as I'm sure you can imagine. But, it's no different than the controversial topics of privacy, or tracking and location, or whatever surveillance or shadowing agendas the powers-that-be may have, for whatever reasons.

What it will ultimately come down to is trust in the actual system. No different than you trusting that all your personal data, which is floating out there in the *Nebula* somewhere, will remain safe, secure, and private."

Eliam looked knowingly at the Professor; both shared a similar expression.

They continued on.

Chapter 16

"Hi Cybil, how's it going?"

"*Me?* How's it going with you, girl? Can you tell me anything, yet? What is this big secret project you're a part of, that they're paying you so much money *to* be a part of?" Cybil Turner asked.

"It's going alright. And no, I can't tell you any more than I already have. They said they'd have to kill us if we did."

"*What?*" Cybil asked.

"They didn't mean it; it was a joke, just a joke. It's going great. This is incredible, Cybil! Incredible! I wish I could say more. But it's going great."

"Well, that's good to know. Hey, I visited your dad while I was passing through Santa Clarita today. I was actually going to call you later and let you know."

"You did?" Sarah was immediately thankful. "Oh, Cybil, you're the best. I love you so much!"

"Not a problem, I was glad to see him, you know that! He's like my own dad!"

"Listen, that's why I was calling," Sarah interjected. "Next week I'm bringing him back. I've made arrangements for him to live at Greenway, on the other side of town, and…"

"Oh, that's got to be hard, Sarah, hon!" A sudden sadness could be heard in her already gentle voice. "He's probably not going to like that much, is he?"

"No…no he won't, not at all! But it's got to be done, I guess. I don't see any other way around it. I can't take care of him. I can't watch him all the time, every second. At least there they can help him when he needs it, and I can go there any time since it's so close. You know?"

"Yeah, oh believe me, I know. But it's got to be hard on you, girl. Anything I can do to help?"

"Well, like I said, that's why I'm calling. Can you go with me to bring him home? He loves you too, Cybil, a lot!"

"Well, of course I can! When are we talking?"

"Not this Saturday, but the next. I have to be there, at ten. Can you go?"

"I most certainly can. I'll just let Jacob know. It won't be a problem."

"Oh, thanks Cybil. I appreciate it! I can use the support. How *was* Dad? I talked to him yesterday, for a few minutes. He seemed pretty quiet, and tired," Sarah said.

"Yeah, he was when I was there, too. He'll be okay, hon. Don't you worry!"

"Yeah. What'd you guys talk about? Were you there long?"

"Uh, about forty-five minutes, an hour maybe. We talked mostly about the Mars colonies. What else, right? Somehow the word 'two' got mentioned and suddenly he started talking about a pair of hats. Some your mom made when you were a kid, or something, he said. Didn't you mention that to me in the past? I seem to remember something about that."

"Yes. Mom made them, her attempt at knitting. They were brown and blue sock hats. It was supposed to be therapeutic for her. It didn't last long. I don't remember her ever making anything else. The hats turned out to be huge. They were way oversized for Dad and me. What did he say about them?" Sarah asked.

"He was just saying that when he got home he was going to get them out of the Winter Box out in the garage. Then he kept putting his hands up to his head like he was putting a hat on. We talked about a few other things before I left; space junk and water shortages, but he kept going back to the hats. I don't know why?"

"Uhm, the hats, I don't know why either. Interesting! I'll have to check the box and see if they're still in there. I haven't seen them for years, now that I think about it."

"Hey, hon, I've got to get going, sorry. I've got some other calls coming in and one of them I have to take for work. Listen, if we don't talk before then, I'll be at your house at seven on Saturday. Is seven good?" Cybil asked.

"Yeah, seven's good. That'll give us enough time to get down there. Thanks, Cybil! Bye!"

"Bye, Sarah. See you next Saturday."

．．．．．．．

After the conversation with Cybil, Sarah drove the short distance over to her father's house. She went inside through the side door, as usual, and then directly out into the garage. She quickly found the Winter Box she and her friend had talked about. It was right where it always had been when she'd lived there as a child all those years ago.

She looked around at the quiet two-bay garage. Suddenly, her mind was a swirl of memories and images, all of which were spawned by the myriad items hanging on the walls, and flopping out of numerous shelved boxes: bikes, balls, coats, sleds, and crutches. Sarah's dad kept virtually everything; he was an organized pack rat, but a pack rat nonetheless.

Suddenly she realized that this was going to be another item added to her plate: taking care of the house, the yard, all this stuff. She'd only briefly thought of it in the past, she really hadn't wanted to think about it at all. Now, she had no choice.

She pulled the large box off the shelf and looked into it. It took a little digging, but she found the hats. They were in a little tote bag that also held some winter gloves and scarves. She picked up the small pair of gloves near the top of the bag. They were barely two-thirds the size of her adult hand. But she remembered them as if it were yesterday. They were so warm, and fit so well, she remembered. She then took the hats into her hands. She again laughed at their uneven appearance, and their size. Then, that one particular memory started.

It was shortly after her mother had killed herself. Sarah was only eight years old. And even though everyone had tried to keep the news from her that her mother had actually taken her own life, Sarah had inadvertently found out by overhearing a conversation at the funeral home. It was right here in this garage that Sarah had later confronted her dad with the knowledge, and then took the bold stance to inquire why he thought she had left them.

She remembered as if it were happening at that very movement.

·······

"Sarah, I…"

Oscar Whiting struggled to get the words out. One had to have words to get out, but he realized that he didn't have any. As difficult as it was, he attempted to try and create some context and rationale for her, something that might at least make a little sense to an eight-year-old.

"Sarah, as time goes on, you're going to learn one sad fact about people: we're all very fragile. Everyone is. And…and because of this we are all susceptible to falling ill, coming down with stuff like colds, and flu's, and things like disease, and cancer. Some illnesses, well, some are hard to spot. Some people get sick, and there's nothing to exactly let everyone know that you're even sick. This is what happened to your mom, Sarah.

"Your mom was sick, Sarah. She had a mental disease— that is what they call it. Now, there are dozens of ways this happens, and it actually happens a lot, just so you know. Your mom wasn't the only one. What happened to her has happened to numerous people, unfortunately."

He was trying to get the point across to her that her mother didn't just want to leave them, but that she was simply one of many victims of a dreaded disease. The effort unfortunately had the opposite effect over Sarah's life. Not giving her comfort, but heightening her fear.

"Anyway, I don't know why this happened, Sarah. I guess your mom just wanted to not be sick anymore, and that's why she did what she did. It wasn't at all because of you, Sarah, or me, or anybody else, not at all. It was just what your mom must have thought would make her better. Your mom is gone, and there's nothing we can do about it, except try to remember her, to try to remember the good things, the good times. Like...like this. You remember when your mom made us those goofy hats for Christmas?"

Sarah smiled through sticky tears at the memory.

"Yeah, they were pretty goofy, huh?" she said, wiping her eyes and her nose.

Oscar Whiting then rose and took down the Winter Box from the shelf and retrieved the hats that Sarah's mother had made for the two of them the Christmas before. He took the smaller one and gently placed it on his daughter's head. He then took the other and placed it on his head.

"Your mom loved us, Sarah. You have to remember that. She loved us both, very much. Your mom made us these hats, and a big part of her is still in them, right now, Sarah, her warmth, her softness, and her love. And...and we can be with her, Sarah, anytime we want, just by thinking about her, just by putting these hats on and choosing to remember. And whenever we do, she'll be there, Sarah, in our thoughts and in our hearts. Never forget that, Sarah. Okay, sweetheart?"

Sarah looked deeply into her father's eyes and nodded slowly. Tears now freshly streamed down both their faces as they sat there. He held Sarah close and hugged her tightly. A moment later, as they continued to cry together, Sarah reached up and pulled her father's hat down a little more securely around his head, and then she did the same with hers. She snuggled back into his arms and they just sat there for the longest time, looking around the chilly garage at all the memories a simple family can make.

....

Sarah was startled out of her recollections when her phone piercingly rang and vibrated. She jerked in response, and quickly reached in her bag for it. Retrieving it, she looked at the display. It was Eliam. He had sent her a text message:

HI, JUST WONDERING WHERE YOUR HEAD'S AT. JOKE! ENJOYED BEING IN IT TODAY, BY THE

WAY! HEY, I WANT TO TAKE YOU SOMEWHERE.
CALL ME!

Chapter 17

"You were just down in Bakersfield and thought you'd call me up?" Sarah asked, making general conversation after meeting at the Old Towne Shopping Center.

"Yeah, I needed to do some shopping, and since you lived here in Bakersfield, I just thought I'd give you a call. Thanks for meeting me! What were you doing? When I called. I hope I didn't interrupt anything? You were kind of quiet on the phone. I…"

"No…no, nothing important, I was just over at my dad's, going through some stuff. I needed the distraction, anyway."

"Oh! So, is that what you think of me so far, merely as a *distraction*?" he asked teasingly.

Sarah smiled at his comment. She realized she was starting to like this man.

"Well, yes. I mean, you know, something to do, I suppose!" she said, teasing back. "You said you wanted to take me somewhere? Here, to this shopping center? You wanted to take me shopping?"

They were both smiling now.

"No, well, yes, I needed to do some shopping, but, no I didn't necessarily want to *take* you shopping. I really don't like shopping, actually. I'm one of those go-get-what-you-need and get-out kind of guys. No, I was just hoping, just wanted, to take you out for dinner again. If you're hungry, or haven't eaten? This was just the meeting place, since I was here, anyway, shopping."

"I see. Well, okay, I haven't eaten yet either. Sure, dinner would be great. What were you shopping for? Dare I ask?"

She was looking into the window of his Range Rover eyeing some packages.

"Well, let's see, I got a couple new beach towels, some sun lotion, a better beach chair than the one I have now. And some...some other, you know, guy stuff, personal things."

Sarah nodded her head.

"Beach stuff? Huh? Going to the beach, are we?" she asked, not really realizing how she'd said it.

"Yeah, Pismo...Saturday!" he added.

"Oh yeah! Pismo is nice. I love the Pier." She looked at him and wondered what was in his mind. Thinking that right now she wished she *could* read his thoughts.

"Yeah, me too! You can actually catch some decent fish there this time of year, barring the distractions."

She nodded as if she understood, but she didn't.

"Distractions?" she queried.

"Yeah, you know. Other people, attractive women, things like that," he said teasingly.

"Yeah," she replied. "I haven't been there in some time. It shouldn't be too busy...this time of year," she then added, trying to keep the conversation going. She wanted to ask who he was going with, but then she thought that it wasn't exactly any of her business.

"So, how about some dinner?" he asked.

"Sure, sounds good."

"Italian? Greek? Mexican?" he inquired.

"Sorry, not at the same time. Either one of those would be fine, though."

He laughed at her.

"Let's have Mexican, then. I love hot and spicy, and I know a good place not far from here. Pa..."

"Pablo Estevez's?" she interjected.

"Yeah, I guess you know the place," he said.

"Oh yeah, I've been going there since I was little. It's my dad's favorite restaurant. It's always good."

"Sounds great then. I'll drive. We can leave your car here, if you want. Or, you can drive...both drive? Whatever you'd like."

She was wondering why he was acting so nervous around her. What was it? Was it her?

"I don't mind leaving my car here," she said. "No one would bother this old heap, anyway. We can take yours."

He smiled.

"Okay then. Shall we?"

....

It was a nice, warm evening and they requested a table outside on the spacious veranda next to the landscaped garden area. The sun was almost down and the restaurant had large candles burning at each table. Both had ordered a margarita, with sea salt, and with it, it seemed Eliam's nervousness had left. Dinner was served and they talked freely as they ate.

"This ATA technology is really mind-blowing stuff," Sarah started. "I think I'm starting to see the big picture a little better. This *is* going to have an unprecedented impact on society."

"Like we said," was all Eliam said.

"I have to be honest with you. I don't think I'm ready for the attention this is going to bring to us. Condi Ghee and I were talking about it the other day. I know it was clearly stated at the beginning, but, wow. I guess I didn't realize the full ramifications of the situation."

"You're probably not alone. I'm sure the others haven't either. That's one of the reasons the university has offered so much money to do this, to help encourage the people to stay the course."

Sarah nodded as she took another bite of her chimichanga.

"I guess since we're, you know, getting to be...friends." He wanted to say close, but he refrained. "I suppose I can tell you that, that you haven't really seen the whole 'big picture', yet."

Sarah took another sip of her margarita as she gave him an inquisitive look. He picked up on her silent query.

"Well, I don't feel like I can tell you, all of it, anyway. I don't want to spoil it for you. Or miss out on the group's reactions. Remember, that's a large part of the program: to record the honest reactions and interactions that result. And it's not just for marketing reasons. There is genuine concern over just *how* this will impact everyone. I mean, just because we are presenting it to the planet—the *world* I mean—doesn't mean we have all the answers. We want to see what will happen, not only on the technological scale, but on an emotional, sociological scale, as well. As we've stated. But, there is actually more, shall I say, interesting capabilities and applications than what we've reviewed, or even mentioned. Much, *much* more, truthfully!"

Sarah's curiosity level jumped way up.

"Really?" she asked, waiting for him to say more.

He nodded his head; another teasing look came across his face. Sarah picked up on it immediately.

"How's it feel holding all the big cards…knowing all the surprises?" she asked, mocking his expression.

He chewed on one of his spicy fish tacos.

"You're not going to tell me, are you?" she said.

He shook his head, no.

"You're a teaser! You shouldn't have even mentioned it; now I'll be thinking about it all the time. You're a bona fide…fish-taco-eating-tease-monger!" she said jokingly as she smiled.

He laughed.

"Sorry, but I can't. I just thought I'd let you know that there was some more amazing stuff coming your way. You know, so you'd be prepared, to a degree, anyway. Don't worry! Something tells me the next level will be right up your proverbial alley, what with your acting career, and those interests."

The comment only served to confuse as well as make her more curious. She gave him a feigned look of disgust.

He had to respect the confidentiality of the program and thought he'd better change the subject. He decided to ask her what he'd planned on asking her earlier when there was more playfulness between them.

"So, about where I wanted to take you," he said.

Sarah looked up inquisitively.

"Take me? I thought you wanted to take me to dinner?" she inquired, tilting her head, now even more curious.

"Well, yes, but I...I want to take you to Pismo Beach, Saturday. That is if you're free, and if you'd like to go?"

She thought about it as she leaned back in her chair.

"Sure, uhm, I like Pismo Beach. That'd be fun. Why didn't you ask me earlier when it came up in the conversation?"

"Well, I...I was a little nervous, about asking you."

Sarah was charmed by the sudden boyishness in his behavior. "And why the nerves?" Sarah asked, tilting her head curiously.

"Bathing suits. It's a beach; people generally have bathing suits on," he said, grinning largely.

Sarah smiled.

Chapter 18

"I have to say that I am very impressed! You've all attuned yourselves to your B-CID's amazingly well, it appears," Professor Dunes said, complimenting the group sincerely, as he opened the afternoon session.

Everyone nodded their heads.

"Communicating with others with the B-CID's AT-app is a curious experience, isn't it?" Everyone offered their acknowledgement. "As I said, you all seemed to do well with it. But, navigating the various systems and apps with your thoughts, as you've probably found, is not one of the easier tasks, especially on your first try. Am I right?"

Everyone snickered and nodded again.

"I know when I first made the attempt, I found it somewhat difficult. I kept activating links I had no intention of activating, simply because I would see it, and by doing so, think of it. Backing out to try again was challenging, in and of itself, as well. But most of you seem to have an innate ability for it. Perhaps it's my age; I'm still too 'old school', I suppose."

That admission generated a laugh from the group.

"But, you've all done well. Good, good! Okay, so, before we go on to the next item on our agenda today, we'd like to hear some feedback. Anybody wish to start?"

"I know what you mean—thanks for the compliment, by the way," Dr. Redding began. "Communicating with my partner was at first a little challenging, but after a short time I was very comfortable with it. And, let's see, from my perspective, I can see where this could be used to great gains in the medical fields, if not just for the swiftness of accessing and reviewing information and procedure, but calling to mind collaborative associations, towards intuitive diagnosis."

Many looked at him with little or no understanding. He picked up on it and tried to elaborate further.

"While I was navigating through some research pages at a particular website, I noticed that certain references or associations I thought of in my mind would automatically trigger other links. They would appear in the search windows and I would suddenly just be there, reading that particular information. It was as if I was actually doing it on a subconscious level. And that's the point I wanted to make. You said the device has trouble reading—or processing—99% of our thought impulses. But, it was as if just one brief thought would lead my searches, almost in a subliminal way. It almost felt as if it was—or I was—thinking in a different way. I'd have to say it was sort of…self-intuitive, I want to say. I don't know what I'm trying to say, here."

He stopped to think about it.

"Interesting!" the Professor began to say. "You all know of Savant Syndrome?"

Most of the group nodded.

"Well, many savants are recorded to have the unique ability to perform complex mathematical calculations, instantly. They have an odd capacity to…to intuit, consciously, the relationships needed to do so, although they don't know, or can't tell you, how. They just do it. Again, the relationship between the conscious and subconscious is little understood. It sounds as if the device is helping you, stimulating your conscious thinking, to pull things up from your subconscious in an extraordinary fashion, into your conscious mind. So, your focus is becoming keener; would you say that, describe it like that?"

"Yes," he answered. "That describes it, keener, and swifter—simpler, I guess I would also say. One word—or thought—seemed to help bring up a bevy of information and data for me. I wish I had had this during Med School. It would have been a huge advantage in learning all those terms and conditions, along with everything else." He rolled his eyes.

"And that's another thing. It wasn't just the information being there, you know, for me to learn. By having it feed into my brain through the device, it seemed I learned it quicker, in fact."

"Good, *good*! Yes, the device does offer that advantage, we've found. Your focus is important, but the form of the input is hugely important as well. Just as some people are tactile learners—hands-on—and some are visual learners," the Professor said, looking around the room for someone else to comment.

"I kind of noticed something like that. It's as if it was sometimes effortless, at least regarding the learning part. Once I started to, or chose to do something, with a conscious, I don't know, desire, maybe is the right word. My mind automatically just went that way, effortlessly. It was kind of strange, actually. I did seem to retain things more," Wena Paravin added.

"Definitely, that's what I was sensing as well!" Condi joined in. "I was accessing some history files, some I've been to before, and it seemed that it was different. As if I was doing it for the first time, yet, I knew it was familiar, but it wasn't. Does that make any sense? At least that's what it felt like. I don't know what I'm saying here either!" She laughed at her own statements.

"Huh, I didn't exactly feel that way. But I did find myself more, I don't know, attentive to the things I was engaged in. I did seem to be, I guess, more interested in things. In things I'm not usually that interested in, actually. That was interesting, in itself, for me," Declan Stewart said.

Sarah Whiting didn't say much that morning, for two reasons. One, she couldn't keep her mind off of Eliam Zaris after their date the night before. And two, she was extremely tired, figuring that she just hadn't gotten a good night of sleep. She just couldn't seem to shake off the feeling of sleepiness. However, she did find herself getting a little perkier when Eliam began the next module of the day.

. . . .

"This has been an eventful week, hasn't it?" He glanced at Sarah for an instant, but then quickly turned back to the group. "Any other questions or comments—*anyone*—before we start the next session?"

"Yes, I have a question," Dr. Redding interjected. "While I was reviewing the Apps Hall this morning, I noticed a link in the last archive, AVTR. I was curious about it so I tried to open it, but I couldn't get access. I was just wondering what it is?"

"Yes, AVTR. That is one of our next modules. We will be going through that early next week. I suppose the name hints as to what it may entail. However, we'll leave it at that for the time being. But, I assure you, you will all find it quite the amazing experience. However, what we are going to do this afternoon might hint a little more at exactly what it is; you can probably figure it out if you use a little imagination.

"But, again, we'll leave it at that for now. Everyone, we are going to go to another location shortly for this afternoon's activities. If you would like, please make use of the facilities if you need before we go. And, if you'd like, grab a beverage to take with you. It's a beautiful day out and we're going to go on a little Track and Field adventure. We think you'll all enjoy this one."

·······

The group was led outside to a small open-air, oval-shaped, somewhat run down, paved running track. One set of old bleachers lined the north side of the painted-lined, racing surface. In the middle of the oval was freshly cut, patchy grass. Various items non-related to track or field events were placed in a pattern across the small field: small platforms with raised bars and hoops on top of them, square tunnels made of plywood, vertical walls with different shaped holes in the them, ramps, large inflatable balls, suspended ropes with hooks on each end, and reflectors of some sort that sat on top of boxes placed all around the area, along with a variety of other, obstacle course type items.

The group looked curiously at the entire field wondering what it was all about. Then they noticed a row of ½ scale golf cart-like wheeled vehicles at the far end of the bleachers, and next to those, several tables with quad-fan camera drones setting on them—the kind commonly used for sporting events, wild life observation, disaster inspection, and the like.

Eliam, Professor Dunes, and Dr. Vectren cordially ushered the group in the direction of the carts and drones. Eliam started the session.

"Today, we're going to have some fun. Let me give you an example of what you're in for." Eliam then reached into the container which Dr. Vectren had just placed on a table behind him. He retrieved, and then put on his B-CID. After a few seconds, one of the drones seemed to just turn on and power up. Within another few seconds the blue and yellow contraption whined a higher pitch and elevated itself to about two meters above the table. It then seemed to pitch and nod at the group before it took off toward the center of the oval field, apparently heading toward the obstacle course.

Suddenly everyone smiled, realizing just then exactly what they were in for.

They all kept their eyes on the drone that Eliam Zaris was apparently flying. The mechanism flew quickly through one of the vertical walls, narrowly missing the sides of the opening it chose to pass through. It then swooped over to one of the ropes that had hooks on both ends, and slowly hovered down. It then carefully pitched itself back, inserting one of the hooks into a suspended loop under its belly. It lifted up, carrying the rope with it. It quickly flew over to a group of objects that were on a table. All the objects had loops on top of them. The drone lowered itself down and the hook on the end of the suspended rope smoothly slid into the object's loop.

The drone lifted itself again, carrying the small object toward the group. Upon arriving, it hovered above everyone, centering on Sarah Whiting. Then the drone carefully descended until the object was suspended directly in front of Sarah. Sarah looked closely at it—a little oval box—and then at Eliam. Eliam nodded to her and said for her to take it. Sarah reached out and took the object off the hook.

The drone lifted, swiftly returned to the location, replaced the hooked rope, flew back and then landed in the place from which it had started.

Dr. Vectren started speaking.

"Sarah, please, if you would, go ahead and open the box."

Sarah did so. She reached in and retrieved a one-hundred-dollar bill. Her brows lifted, as did the others.

"This may not only be fun, but profitable, depending how you learn to use the technology. Let me explain further," Dr. Vectren said playfully. "This afternoon, you're going to experiment with remote operation of wirelessly controlled devices—in this case, the conveyances you see here." He pointed toward the carts and drones. "Trust me; it's not as straightforward as it looks. Eliam is very practiced at the task of making it appear easier than it actually is. It will undoubtedly be frustrating, at first, so we are offering up a little incentive for you—we thought a little cash might suffice."

Sarah held up the bill.

Eliam then promptly snatched it out of her hand, with a smile.

"Ooooh, sorry! That was just for the sake of an example. We'll just put it back, so everyone can try!" He snickered.

Sarah feigned a saddened look on her face, playing along.

Dr. Vectren continued.

"The prizes await you, as you can see; some larger than that, actually, once again, a little incentive to help ease the frustration. And so, here's the plan. When you engage your B-CID's, you will locate on your Visual Displays, a series of maps that will detail two individual paths you must travel—one using each conveyance, one ground, one air—along with the obstacles you must overcome, and the particular tasks you must perform, in order for you to earn placement in the competition. And did I say, you'll be doing it *with* your eyes open, and then once without them."

The group exchanged a guarded look.

"You do this experiment once using your eyes, employing your own human depth perception, and once remotely, linking your Display Fields with the series of onboard cameras on each conveyance."

Everyone then nodded.

"Now then, once you complete the training, by conquering the required courses, you will have earned a place in the Drone Competition to try to retrieve as many of the gifts as you can. However, that will not be easy either, because you will have to fight for it—everyone goes at the same time."

The group looked intently focused.

"We said we were going to have a little fun," Eliam added.

"Okay, great! Now, once you've activated your wireless Remote app, you will find your particular conveyance's ID number. When you activate the link, you will have initiated the required connection and you can then bring up the navigation console in your Display Fields. Without firing up the conveyance, go ahead and link up and access your consoles," Dr. Vectren said.

Everyone did so.

"Good…good!" he said. "Now, one at a time—I'll call out who—you will fire up your conveyance, and slowly drive it forward out onto the field. Ms. Goens, perhaps you'd like to go first?"

The girl suddenly looked nervous.

"Uhmmm, okay. I'll give it a try. But, I'm not so sure of the results; it looks pretty straightforward here on the console, but, I must warn you, I was never very good at video games." She took a deep breath and started.

Everyone watched as they heard the electric motors fire, giving off a subtle hum. The cart then slowly inched out of the pack. The front wheels turned to the left, suddenly angling the vehicle. Realizing it was too sharp, Furley stopped it abruptly and then turned the wheels the other way. This time they were a little to the right. The cart started moving again, with the wheels turning one way, and then another, and then back again. The look on Furley's face was intense as she watched the craft zigzag across the turf. After a few minutes of jerky driving, she seemed to find some balance and the cart moved a little faster, and much more smoothly.

"Okay, just drive it around for awhile to get used to it. Good! Now, Wena, how about you go next?" Dr. Vectren said.

Wena's eyebrows arched, and she initially balked, but having seen her peer's success she acquiesced to the request, displaying much the same results: jerky movement, starts and stops, and over-steering. However, she too settled down, having gained a modicum of control.

For the first hour, everyone maneuvered their carts around the field, experiencing the same control problems, but after a while all were doing well and having fun with it. The course wasn't long and each in turn successfully navigated it as indicated on their maps. During their efforts, Eliam flew one of the drones around and filmed the entire event. Much of it was amusing, inciting much laughter and playfully directed derogatory comments among the competitors.

Next up were the Air Drones with similar, yet even more comical results. Fortunately, the diminutive machines were well-designed, proving highly resilient in a collision. Close to the end of the day, everyone slowly made their way through the obstacle courses. And surprisingly, most did far better when they operated their conveyances solely from their Visual Displays using the onboard cameras. In fact, they were so much better at it that many nearly mastered it on their second or third attempts.

Most ended up earning their place in the competition, except for one of the participants: Declan Stewart, the entertainment guy. He just couldn't seem to get the hang of it, especially concerning the flying drone. He ended up crashing his so badly that it wouldn't fly anymore. His only comment, "Well, that was entertaining!" Which drew a big laugh from everyone.

During the last half hour of the day, the remaining group of six battled it out to get to the prized objects in the center of the field, having been told that they only had a limited amount of time left in order to do so. Understandably, everyone became somewhat overzealous in their attempts to get at the cash, and the resultant 'flying war' became one of the most memorable events of the entire day.

Nelson Baurle at first seemed to be the dominant flyer. However, after quickly and successfully getting his first object picked up and dropped off to his designated area, his second attempt proved to be a side-splitting disaster. The hook on the end of his line unexpectedly got coupled to Condi's line, and the two just kept flying circles around each other trying to get unhooked, swooping down on the group, crashing into the objects, and flying erratically.

It was hilarious to hear the two taunt and threaten each other good-naturedly as they did so, especially after someone made the comment that it looked as if two birds had gotten stuck together while mating in mid-flight. However, while the aerial love-dance was underway, the remaining four others just calmly swooped in one right after the other and picked up the objects of their desire seemingly at their leisure.

All in all, it was a fun, if not exhaustingly brain-intense day for everyone.

The winners all decided to treat the others to a gourmet dinner out. They wined and dined and laughed with each other, having a great time, until mutual exhaustion brought the evening to a close.

Sarah could hardly keep her eyes open, much less her mind off the next day, and her date at the beach with Eliam.

Chapter 19

"It's supposed to storm, later," Sarah said, as she tucked her pack into the back of Eliam's Range Rover and climbed in.

"Yeah, I saw that, only a forty-percent chance. I'm still up for it? You?"

She nodded. "Yeah, I mean, if it rains, then hey, I'll have a bathing suit on, right?" she said, intent on seeing his reaction.

He kept looking straight ahead as he tried not to grin. But he couldn't help it, knowing she had both eyes on him.

They drove on.

It would take them a little over two hours to get there, and the same to get back. They figured on spending at least that long there, so it would be a full day.

They were both excited.

....

"Which way are we going?"

"South," he said, "166 to Pismo. There's construction on 58."

"I like that way better, anyway," she said.

As excited as they both were, for some reason they seemed content to ride along in silence. So they drove, looking at the scenery, making only brief comments to each other regarding whatever they saw along the road.

For some reason Sarah started thinking about the story Eliam had told her of how his parents had died, of his not having a family as he grew up. The thought then crossed her mind that at least she still had her dad, and that suddenly made her think of him, of where he was, and what he was doing.

Gradually she started feeling those pangs of regret that she somehow knew she might. Here she was taking the time to travel for hours to a place where she was going to have fun in the sun, with a man she was becoming increasingly fond of, enjoying her life, all while her dad was sitting in some chair he probably didn't feel comfortable in, having to do things he probably hated having to do, while being forced to stay in a place where he didn't want to be. A sudden feeling of guilt overcame her.

She looked out the window at the passing landscape and sighed, trying to flush her mind of the uncomfortable feelings. There was nothing wrong with what she was doing. She was just living her life, she tried to convince herself. It was okay for her to have fun. Her dad would approve. She heard his voice say it in her mind, which he truly would have, and she knew that. It was just the sadness of his condition, she thought, that kept her mind on him.

Unbeknownst to Sarah, Eliam, ironically, was thinking about Sarah's mother and father, of the tragedy of her mother's death, and her father's present condition. The unwanted, yet seemingly inexorable lines of thinking kept both of them silent for an extended time. It was oddly surreal when, after a full ten minutes or so of silence, both started talking at exactly the same time, saying the exact same word to start their queries, and both marveling at the synchronicity of it.

"Soooo," Sarah and Eliam said simultaneously.

A short silence followed long exhales on both their parts. "Weird," Sarah said.

"Yeah…weird!" Eliam replied.

"Uh, you go first," Sarah said.

"Well, I was just going to ask how your dad was. Is he doing alright?"

Sarah was shocked at how tuned in Eliam was with her thoughts. She looked forward and then out the side window for a second before replying.

"Funny you would ask. I was just thinking about him, actually," she started. "He...I don't know, he's probably not, actually, doing well. My friend Cybil stopped by to see him a few days ago and she said he wasn't too happy. It's kind of hard. No, he's probably not doing so well. Who would be? Losing your mind, being forced into living somewhere you didn't want to be, not knowing exactly what's going on. No, he's probably not a happy camper right about now. But, that'll change next weekend, to some degree."

"Yeah, how so?" Eliam asked.

"We're bringing him back home to Bakersfield next Saturday."

"Well, that's good! What...what are you...?"

Sarah interrupted, knowing what he was going to ask next.

"He's going into a nursing home. Not what either of us would prefer, but I can't provide the level of care he requires now. I got him into Greenway Center."

"Greenway Center?" Eliam asked, apparently not familiar with the place.

"Yeah, Greenway's a combination nursing home, retirement home, senior center. It's a really awesome place, actually, at least compared to most. They have a lot of programs, community events, workshops, activities. It's a nice facility. And it's close. I can go by and see him whenever I want."

"Well, that's nice. Think he'll adapt?"

"Dad? Yeah! I think he will. I'd say that after awhile, he'd be having a following, once everyone gets used to his quirky personality. Dad's always been a likable guy and a great conversationalist, but he definitely has an odd manner about him. He knows a lot of facts, and stories, especially about the Space Program, and about science and history and stuff. Yeah, he'll carve out a niche there, I'm sure." She tried to convince herself anyway.

"Quirky?" was all he asked.

"Yeah...quirky! It's a big part of his humor. I'm somewhat *quirky* too, I'd have to say...comes with the inheritance."

Eliam nodded and smiled, telling her he heard her, as well as acknowledging the humor. But his mind was on the other parts of the conversation.

"Wow, that's got to be tough to go through!"

Sarah didn't say anything; she just looked out the window and watched the desert go by.

"Where did you say he is? Where is he now?" Eliam asked.

Sarah turned her head towards him.

"He's in Santa Clarita, at a diagnostic clinic. They specialize in the testing and diagnosis of mental health conditions. He's been there for about three weeks now."

"And what's his condition again, specifically?" Eliam tried to remember.

Sarah was touched by his concern, and his apparent sincerity.

"Uh, he...he has early-onset Alzheimer's disease, with advancing dementia. And it's getting worse, fast, unfortunately."

It was difficult for her to say it out loud, and it made her feel embarrassed, she realized. And furthermore, in doing so it scared her; it was as if she was announcing to the world that she, too, was likely to develop the disease and that it was just a matter of time before someone would have to lock her away. She grew silent again and turned back toward the side window.

Eliam sensed Sarah's distress. He suddenly wished he hadn't even started the conversation. But, he oddly knew it had to be addressed if he wanted any kind of a relationship with her. "I see," was all he could find to say.

The knowledge Eliam Zaris had about the disease was quite extensive. He'd been around it and had studied it in depth, though that seemed like an entire lifetime ago. He then went to that center spot in his mind, and visited its familiar stillness. He waited. This is what he routinely did, more times in a day than he could count. It was the place that helped him link to his source of strength and inspiration. After a few moments, he knew what would come next.

"Sarah?" he asked softly.

She turned to him. "Yeah," she replied.

"How about we…how about we skip the beach and go see your dad?" he said.

Sarah nearly lost her breath. She at first wondered if she'd even heard him correctly. His voice was so gentle.

"Why?" she asked.

"Well, I was thinking that he sounds like someone I'd like to meet. And, it's supposed to rain anyway. We're already heading in that general direction. It's just a matter of which way we turn. So, I figure we might as well go on down to Santa Clarita and see him. What do you say? They have normal visiting hours there, I would think. Wouldn't they?" He turned his head to glance at her. He immediately noticed the sparkle of tears in her eyes.

"Uh, yeah…*yeah*, they have normal visiting hours, Saturday hours."

Sarah was at a loss for words. All she could do was speak in a near whisper.

"Yeah, I'd like that very much!"

. . . .

"Hi, Dad!"

"Sarah?…*Sarah!* How…what are you doing here?"

"Dad, we came to visit you. I'd like you to meet someone. This is…a friend of mine, Dad. This is Eliam Zaris."

Oscar Whiting turned his head up to look at the man standing behind his daughter. He peered at Eliam, at first with a blank look, but then with one of an odd recognition.

"Hello! Do I know you…don't I know you?" he asked Eliam as he reached out his hand for a handshake.

"Hello, sir. It's very nice to meet you. No, I don't believe we've ever met," Eliam reciprocated and shook the man's hand, noticing its firm grip.

Oscar Whiting held the handshake for an extended time and just stared into Eliam's eyes. Eliam stood there and held his hand, smiling the entire time.

Sarah had initially thought Eliam would display nervousness meeting her father, so she was really surprised and happy at how comfortable he appeared to be.

"How are you, Dad? How are they treating you?" Sarah asked.

Oscar Whiting and Eliam continued to stare at each other, holding their handshake. After Sarah asked her question, they let go of each other's hands and he looked at her.

"Treating me? Oh, alright, I suppose. I wish I could get some real food, instead of that goat silage they serve us. Of course breakfast isn't too bad. Can't do toast and oatmeal much harm, unless you burn it or add too much damn cinnamon. Lunch and dinner are in another category altogether though. I…"

Oscar Whiting stopped talking abruptly and began looking at his hand in an odd way, as if trying to remember something. He just sat there, looking at it.

"Mr. Whiting, may I call you Oscar?" Eliam asked.

Oscar Whiting looked up at him, got a funny look on his face and replied.

"Well, what else would you want to call me? My name's Oscar."

Eliam and Sarah smiled.

"Dad, how about we go out to the garden tables so we can sit and talk?"

"Alright with me! Let's launch, it smells in here anyway," he said.

He then stood up and started walking. He led them to the area without an error, even though they had to navigate four complete turns through the building to get to the gardens. They found a table on the far side and they all sat down. Sarah set the small cooler they had brought with them on the extra chair and then asked her dad if he'd like a drink.

"Dad, would you like a cold Green Tea?"

His eyes lit up.

"Sure, you brought me Green Tea?"

"Sure Dad. I didn't figure they'd stock your favorite here, so we picked some up for you." She spoke as she opened the cooler, grabbing one for each of them and passing them around.

"Are you a good person, Mr. Z…uhmm, Za…"

"Zaris. My name is Eliam Zaris, sir."

"Zaris, sorry. Thanks, I have trouble remembering names sometimes, forgive me."

"Oh, no problem, sir. You can call me Eliam, if you'd like."

"Okay, but I thought you wanted to call me Oscar?"

"Well, yes, sir, if that's okay?"

"Well then, why do you keep calling me sir?" He widened his eyes.

Eliam and Sarah laughed.

"See, I told you!" Sarah said to Eliam.

"Told you what?" Oscar asked, looking back and forth between them.

"That you were quirky, Dad, that's all, just that you were quirky!" She winked.

He winked back.

"Well I guess you've always been right about that to some extent, though my choosing *burial* over cremation doesn't make me 'quirky', or old-fashioned. However, if we could all just figure out precisely what 'quirky' actually means, then we'd all be a little wiser and taller perhaps," he said, and then laughed.

Eliam narrowed his eyes, thinking hard, trying to make sense of the dynamic between father and daughter.

"But, you haven't answered my question yet, Eliam. Are you?"

For a moment they'd forgotten the question.

Sarah gave her dad an irritated look.

"You are getting involved with my daughter, aren't you? Just thought I'd get it out of the way," he said, winking again at Sarah.

Sarah rolled her eyes in embarrassment.

"Uhmm, 'good person'? Well yes, sir, *Oscar*, sorry. I believe I am. But, that's a relative term, I suppose. I would say that after knowing me for some time, you'd become convinced of that fact. If your interpretation of 'goodness' includes an individual who genuinely cares for the feelings of others, for their welfare and freedoms and personal rights; someone who tries to change things for the better, at times neglecting their own freedoms, in order to advocate for the sustained freedoms of others. Then, yes."

Oscar and Sarah just stared at Eliam for a second.

"Are you a politician, Eliam Zaris?" Oscar asked.

"No, Oscar, but I do feel that while I'm on this planet, even if it's for a limited amount of time, I have a purpose—as I believe we all do—and that would be to participate in life; to help make things better along the way, if we can."

"So, you're a philosopher?"

They all laughed.

"Yes, Oscar, I am guilty as observed, I suppose. Though I wouldn't classify myself as religious or dogmatic, I just can't help but wonder about things, is all. I guess I'm an explorer at heart, I would say. Aren't we all that way, at least to some degree?"

"Now I can agree with that," Oscar said, "especially as we get old and decrepit. We all tend to want to ponder the deeper explorations of *Being*, at times. That's why I love peanut butter!"

The comment took them off guard.

The look on their faces revealed their bewilderment.

"We're all just a bunch of the same kind of nuts…just really spread out, and some chunkier than the others!"

They all laughed again.

"So, you know anything about space, Eliam Zaris?"

Chapter 20

They visited for several hours, and Sarah was able to convince the facility staff that allowing them to take Oscar Whiting out for lunch was one of the best things they could do for him. The staff took Sarah aside and gave her the usual warnings and admonishments regarding what to expect, though she'd probably known better than they how to handle her own father. After all, she'd virtually taken care of him for the past year as his condition worsened.

At lunch Oscar and Eliam talked to a great extent about everything space and science. At every turn, Eliam astounded the two with his knowledge of the related subjects. Sarah noticed that her father was the happiest she'd seen him in years, with having someone to talk to, instead of just her, who actually had the same passion and interests.

Though they hadn't talked about it much, Sarah took the opportunity to let her father know that he'd be coming back to Bakersfield in a week. And even though he wasn't extremely thrilled about having to live at that Greenway place, he understood his condition enough to understand that it was warranted and justified. He was excited about moving back closer to home and to Sarah. It was a magical afternoon since much of the time was spent discussing space and science.

They dropped Oscar off at around 2:30 pm and said their goodbyes.

When they were about half an hour from Sarah's place, Eliam made Sarah an offer.

"Hey, I want to invite you over to my place, and let me cook you dinner."

This guy just kept on surprising her, she thought.

"You can cook?"

"Gourmet, all the way!"

"Really?"

"No, not really, I thought we'd just have peanut butter sandwiches! I can make those, special!"

She smiled.

"Don't you live up by Lake Isabella, past campus?"

"Yeah, why?"

"Well, I don't know. It's kind of out of your way, for us to drive up there and for you to have to run me all the way back down to Bakersfield."

"It's not that far. I don't mind. And I was just kidding about the peanut butter. I was thinking more like, seafood: grilled Flounder, Oysters on the half, Crab Legs, wild rice on the side, salad, wine, and maybe chocolate ice cream for dessert. I can actually do all that. Not the ice cream, just the other stuff."

"Well, yeah, that'd be nice, I think. That sounds good! You can swing by my place and I can get my car. That way I can drive back and save you the trip. I don't mind. It's not a problem."

"Yeah, we could do that, or…or you could just stay?" Eliam slipped her a quick glance as he was driving, his tone betraying his hopefulness.

Sarah was silent for a long period of time. She took a deep breath before answering.

"I'd love to, Eliam," she said, after careful consideration. "I'd really love to!"

⋯⋯

They arrived at Eliam's place during a lull in the drizzle. It appeared to be an old ranch. They drove through an un-gated split rail fence, the entrance spanned above by a long piece of wood stretched between two poles, which may have had at one time a sign attached to it. The pavement abruptly ended, turning into a quarter-kilometer long, dirt-and-gravel lane that wound through a pine forest. She couldn't make out the area until they pulled out into the large spread of land that lay on the other side of the thick trees.

The property at that point was easy to see. The drive passed in front of an old, yet well-kept clapboard-sided house sitting off to the right and up on a little knoll. The house looked to have been built over a hundred years ago; it had a wraparound, open porch with no railing to speak of. The drive passed the house, curved slightly to the right, and ended at a parking area in front of a huge, three-story, weathered-gray barn.

Part of the barn on the right was only a single story, and looked to have been renovated with more modern construction: darker wood siding, and tinted windows. The house and the barn looked out over a small valley that gently cascaded down to what was probably a creek bed, and on the other side of that was a tree line. The entire property was surrounded by trees, and beyond that the tops of several patchy hills could be seen in the distance.

The grounds didn't seem to be too well kept, though. Many of the fences in the distance appeared to be grown over with vegetation and small trees. And the little fields that were centered in between were knee high with weeds. Sarah figured the small ranch had animals at one time.

Eliam and Sarah exited the vehicle.

A hint of warm pine scented the air.

"This is it," Eliam said, waving his hand through the air. "That's the house."

"Yeah, I see. Off the beaten trail." After scoping out the house her attention was drawn to the barn. "I absolutely love old barns. We've got one at our place, Dad's place, I mean; I grew up playing in it. Not as big as this one, though. Nice! It looks to have a lot of history."

"Yeah, I'm sure it does."

Sarah looked at Eliam, thinking of his comment.

"You haven't lived here long; I take it?"

"No, not long, renting it actually. Let's see, I've been here...about a year, maybe. Come on in, you can look around if you want, while I'll get the grill going."

Sarah found herself a little surprised. She didn't know why, but for some reason she'd had in her mind that Eliam had been in the area for some time, and would've probably owned his own place. Renting a place like this inferred impermanence, she thought, but then again, maybe not. She shrugged and desisted from her musings.

"Okay. But, I won't just let you be chauffer, maître-d', cook and waiter. I insist on helping. I can make the rice and salad. Deal?"

"Okay, deal. This way, ma'am!" He pretended to drape a towel over his arm, straighten his bow tie, and then bowed as he gestured formally toward the house.

·······

"The dinner was superb, Eliam. You're a great cook, and host. Seafood has always been one of my favorites, except for those slimy oysters on the shell. Ech!" She squirmed in her seat thinking of them.

"They're an acquired taste, I suppose."

"Well, I'll never acquire it. Hated the first one, and that was the last one. Your Flounder was awesome, though, and cooked perfectly."

"Thanks. Your salad was perfectly tossed."

She looked at him and laughed at the silly comment.

"I'm starting to like your sense of humor, Eliam," she said, picking up her wine glass and swirling the liquid around before taking another sip. "It reminds me of my dad's. Which reminds me by the way, I want to thank you again for taking me down to see him, and for your conversational skills. I don't think he's had such a good time in a long time. I can tell he really likes you, particularly all that space stuff in your head."

"It was my pleasure, Sarah. Thanks for saying so. No, I enjoyed meeting him, and the visit. You have to know, all of that stuff we talked about goes right along with my own interests. I'm a space nut, too. He's a very knowledgeable guy. I was impressed. And I want to say, he didn't seem, you know, too far gone." He suddenly realized that he might be raising a sensitive subject, but it was too late. "You know what I mean?

His mind was very sharp, and his memory seemed, for the most part, pretty clear. There were only a few times where I noticed he struggled with some things."

"Yeah, some days are better than others. I think he seemed better today because he was excited to talk in such depth about his own interests. Sometimes, he's pretty out there, doing things that just don't make any sense."

Eliam nodded his head.

As they talked they took all the dishes to the kitchen and loaded the dishwasher, they put the leftovers into containers and tucked them into the refrigerator.

"Another?" Eliam asked, pointing to Sarah's nearly empty wine glass.

"Sure, thanks."

"Would you like to sit out on the porch? It's a nice evening, not too hot."

"Yeah, that'd be nice. I noticed you've got one of those old porch swings out there. You know what that leads to."

"And what's that?" he asked.

"You know, swinging, touching, kissing…more touching."

Eliam was suddenly smiling from one ear to the other.

"Wow, you don't hold anything back, do you?"

"Just saying," she said.

"What makes you think I'm that kind of guy?"

"I don't know, let's see. You wanted to take me to the beach, because you wanted to see me in a bathing suit, your words. So I just figure you're probably hoping for a chance to, I don't know, get me a little silly from the wine so you can get a chance to see me in my underwear or something, hence the swing. That's why those things were invented, by the way?"

"Really, to help guys see beautiful women in their underwear?"

She liked the beautiful women comment. He poured her glass half full as she wrapped herself onto one of the kitchen island's tall stools.

"Yeah, you didn't know that?"

"No, that's new information for me," he said.

"Outside on the swing sounds nice," she then said. "I suppose you'll have a window open, with some slow, rhythmic music playing softly in the background?"

He looked at her unbelievingly as he poured himself another glass of wine.

"Did you ever think about writing Romance novels?" he asked, with a crooked grin.

"No, romance is overrated if you ask me."

"Well, you sound like you're an expert."

"No, not at all, actually. Honestly, I've not been married, and I've only been in one really serious relationship, and only a handful of dates. I'm just teasing you because I'm basically nervous, and I'm feeling the wine."

She smiled but thought she saw a brief, but distracted look on his face.

"What happened to the serious relationship?" he asked, his brow slightly furrowed.

"Well, I guess the seriousness was mostly on my part. I found that he had some deep dark secrets, and…and I was just a passing pleasure that he was using to fill some of his needs."

Eliam's eyes diverted from hers for a moment.

"Dark secrets, huh?" he said, looking down before taking another gulp of wine.

"Yeah," she started again. "Don't get me wrong, I understand if people don't exactly sync together, especially all the time. And people need companionship, other people, yada-yada. But, honesty ranks right up there at the top of my Pyramid of Hierarchical needs. And he wasn't honest; I found that out in a not-so-comfortable way."

"I'm not sorry to hear that. Abraham Maslow, you just quoted Abraham Maslow," he said.

"Yes, I did." She paused for a second. "What do you mean; you're 'not' sorry to hear that? Most people from this planet would show a little sympathy and say: 'I'm sorry to hear that.'"

He gave her a funny look.

"Yeah, well, I'm just being honest. If your 'serious' relationship had worked out, then I would never have met you, probably."

She smiled.

"Yeah, that was Maslow. I think he was pretty right-on with his concepts, at least when it came to the base motivations—needs—that drive our lives. At least it seems to me," she said. "Especially when it comes to the honesty thing," she then added.

Eliam looked down again.

"Yes…I agree," he said in a softer tone. He thought for a moment, and then asked a question. "So where are you on the pyramid, according to your own estimation?"

She winced, suddenly feeling more anxiety.

"Well, physiologically, my needs are being met. I feel safe and secure most of the time. I have Dad, and my friends, and my work, and I have a certain level of self-esteem, I suppose, as a result of my accomplishments. But, I'd say most people struggle with balancing that self-esteem thing, with their own strivings for self-actualization. I'm no different, I suppose."

"Yeah, that describes me, too. And you're right, I think. We all struggle daily along the esteem and self-actualization lines. Maslow said that one of the biggest hindrances to esteem and self-actualization is fear. Fear of failure, fear of loss, fear of attempting to reach out for our higher potential."

The notion struck a deep chord in Sarah. She didn't say anything in response. She just sat there and thought about it.

"What are *you* afraid of, Sarah?" he asked softly.

Sarah's head was down; she rolled her eyes up to look at him. She then started to rock her head from one side to another as she mumbled a soft hum, debating in her mind whether she wanted to talk about it or not.

"Uhmm, fear…itself," she said.

"That sounds familiar. Someone said that, but I don't recall who. 'Fear', huh?"

Sarah nodded and shyly grinned.

"Actually, if you want to know, I'm afraid of losing my mind."

She said it; she wasn't sure if she should have or not, but she'd said it. It was out. She just looked at his face for reaction.

"Losing your mind? You...you mean because of your mother? Your father's Alzheimer's?"

She nodded, a little surprised he'd pick up on it so quickly.

"Yeah," she said. "That's about the sum of it."

She gave him a quick smile and bit the side of her lip.

"Well, that's perfectly understandable. We do inherit traits and oftentimes propensities, physiologically, from our parents, and from our ancestors. I can see your fears there. But, that doesn't mean that you actually have the same genetic predisposition for it."

She nodded her head. "Yeah, I tell myself that all the time."

"And it holds you back?" he asked.

"Yeah, I suppose *I* let it hold me back." She felt embarrassed revealing herself to him in such raw detail.

"Perfectly understandable," he said. "You know, it may happen, it may not. I think the point Maslow was trying to make is that to be self-actualized, we *choose* to rise to whatever the occasion is, or whatever it is we feel compelled to achieve, regardless of the fear. And by doing so, fulfill the esteem thing, as well as that higher-self potential."

"Yeah, I suppose so." She just stared into his eyes as they smiled at each other.

"I mean, there's also the fact that there have been great strides in the understanding of mental disease, and they say cures may be possible in the very near future. Who knows? Maybe by the time you turn loony, they'll have a treatment that'll stop the onset."

She frowned at the term 'loony' but knew he was just trying to lighten the mood.

"Gee, thanks for that positive outlook." She laughed, her body language becoming more relaxed and open.

"You're welcome. Hey, hang out for a minute, while I open a window and put some rhythmic music on." He waggled his eyebrows at her and left the room.

Sarah couldn't stop smiling at him.

Within a few minutes they were on the porch, sitting next to each other on the swing, and gently swaying together. Sarah looked at Eliam's handsome face and kind eyes.

"Listen, Eliam. I…I'm starting to like you, a lot, actually. I imagine you're figuring that out on your own. And, you may be having mixed feelings about it from your end. So, I just wanted to self-actualize here a minute and roll with this. I want you to know something. It's very important to me that you be genuine and honest. If you don't feel the same way, or later you find yourself not feeling the same way, then that's okay. But you better tell me right up front!

"Also, I'm a one-man woman and …and I wish to find, someday, a one-woman man. That may be old fashioned, but that's me. And trust me, you'll find that I can not only take it, but I can also dish it out.

"And, I know how important compromise is in a relationship, but when it comes to these basic tenets I'm dishing out here, I won't compromise. Also, I'm not a revenge-seeking, vindictive woman who will go on a rampage if scorned. I'll just break down and cry and go my own way, and eat a lot of ice cream.

"Also, and this is very important, if you ever hit me, I'll hit you back, so help me Jesus. We can have fun arguing as much as you want, but trust me; don't go there, because you won't at all enjoy the consequences.

"Oh, and as far as children go—which I realize is reaching way, way out there—I'm not the kind of woman who just feels that a relationship must absolutely culminate in marriage, and parenthood and all that. However, I'm not opposed to it either, in the proper timing. And one more thing, all this is your fault, you're the one who started talking all Maslow and self-actualization and the like, so I just kind of went for it." She then kind of gave him a throaty, yet feminine growl. "Oh yeah, and don't ever lie to me or lead me on. I simply loathe that. Okay, I'm done…your turn. And I think I've had enough wine." She smiled another quirky smile.

Eliam had that strange, distracted look on his face again, appearing to be deep in thought. Sarah was immediately worried that she'd extended herself too far. She had in mind a few imagined scenarios that she thought might play out toward the end of their evening together, but she hadn't exactly prepared herself for what followed.

Chapter 21

Sarah woke up on the couch. It was early morning. She had a warm blanket thrown over her, and her head was lying on a bed pillow. She tried to throw off the grogginess as she sat up, stretching her eyes, and then the rest of her body.

The previous night's happenings suddenly awoke in her mind. They had swung a little more until the sun had gone down, having kissed only once in the course of the evening. They'd gotten into a conversation about Smartbrain and its effects on society. That led to Eliam suggesting their watching an old classic movie about people living in their minds, and being controlled by machines. And then Sarah remembered Eliam falling asleep. Figuring the evening was over, she too allowed herself to drift off. Sarah rose from the couch and went to the bedroom. She peeked inside and saw Eliam lying there, still in a deep slumber. She thought about going in and lying down beside him, but something held her back. He could have had her, she thought. But for some reason he passed on the opportunity. She didn't know why. Maybe it was her, or perhaps it just wasn't the time. She sighed.

After admiring his physique for an extended moment she went into the bathroom and freshened up, and then to the kitchen to fix herself a little breakfast. She made coffee, and some toast with jam. She then took her breakfast outdoors to the swing and ate as she listened to the birds chirping their morning songs.

For a short time, she imagined what that moment would have been like if they in fact had consummated their relationship the night before. What would Eliam be like as a lover?

She couldn't help sighing again with disappointment, but then she laughed to herself regarding the entire experience. Maybe it was just too much anxiety, and too much wine.

As she ruminated, her eyes looked over at the huge barn. Her mind swam back to the past and all the times she had played in her childhood barn. She could see the memories in her mind's eye; she smiled at her youthful adventures in simpler times. After a few moments, she rose to her feet and started walking towards the monolithic building, suddenly curious as to its interior and the history there.

She went to the small main door on the right of the structure and lifted the old, heavy wrought iron latch. The hinges creaked as it swung out towards her. She left the door open and entered. It was much as she had imagined in her mind, in sight and smell. It smelled dank and musty and had that old scent of animal manure. She loved that combination of smells, she remembered.

As she entered the center of the building she saw the familiar barn layout she'd expected, old grayed, post and beam construction, with animal stalls along the sides, old straw bales in the corners, many broken and loosely scattered around. She noticed several old leather straps and items used for rigging animals for farm work, and other things of that nature.

Tools like shovels and rakes and pole diggers stood in one corner. A few really old license plates were nailed up on the wall in one of the open stalls, and there was an old work bench there that had cans, and wooden boxes sitting on it collecting dust over what must have been decades.

The sights intermingled with her memories and she then remembered her experiences of playing in the loft of her family's barn. She looked up and noticed that she couldn't see up through the floorboards of the structure as she had at home, or of any old barn that came to her memory. Upon looking closer, she saw that a layer of plywood had been laid down on the loft floor above. Odd, she thought, barns needed the ventilation through their loft floors to keep the air moving and carry away the moisture. That's why they built them that way.

Her curiosity was deeply aroused by the unexpected sight, so she began looking around for a passage up to the loft. In one corner, near the door she had entered through, she saw a set of old stairs. She walked over and started up them only to see a fairly modern, newly built wall at the top of the stairs, with a heavily locked door in the middle of it.

Sarah wondered about it. When she arrived at the door, it looked as if it had been used recently: there was no rust, or corrosion, or even dust on the door knob. She presumed that since the place was a rental, the owners were using the loft as storage, having had it sealed for privacy and security. Too bad, Sarah thought. She would have liked to have seen it. Then, she noticed a small hole in the wall next to the door, down about waist high.

She knelt and looked through it. What she saw confused her. She saw an object on the left that appeared to be in the distance, taking up only part of the view, but it was impossible to make out what it was due to its dull blackness. The other part of her view to the right was typical of the interior of a barn; however, the dark part was so dark that she could not make out any surface, or reflection, no matter how she tried to focus. She wondered if it was an obstruction in the hole itself. She looked a second time but still could not tell.

With her curiosity only partially satiated, she went back down the stairs and walked around the outside of the structure, looking into cracks in the siding and through a few of the tinted windows gracing the front of the newly-built addition. Through the windows she could barely make out some work benches, and tables with various items on them.

Sarah then ventured back to the house.

She checked in on Eliam. Seeing that he was still sleeping soundly, she went back to the living area and sat down with her tablet, which she'd retrieved from her pack. She checked her email, and then pulled up the day's news. It wasn't more than a half an hour or so before she heard Eliam stirring in the other room. She rose to go in, but then decided to wait for him to come out.

"Hey there, I hear you. You alright?" she said loudly, so he could hear her.

"Hi, yeah, hi Sarah? Uhmm, yeah, good! I'm going to take a shower. Be out in a few minutes."

"Sure, take your time."

·······

After about twenty minutes Eliam entered the living area. He had a most embarrassed look on his face. Sarah noticed immediately.

"Hi," he said, sitting down next to her.

"Hi," she replied back.

"You sleep okay?" he asked.

"Yeah, comfortable couch. It put *you* right to sleep, it seems. I went out shortly after, I think."

"Yeah! I...I must have been super tired, I guess." He cleared his throat and glanced down for a moment. "Been up long?" he then asked.

"Uh, yeah, awhile."

"Yeah, I hope you made yourself at home?"

"Yes, I did. Thanks! I made coffee and some toast. Can I get you anything? You want something to eat?" she asked.

"No...no, nothing to eat." He rubbed his stomach. "I may get a little coffee, maybe." He started to get up, but Sarah stopped him.

"No, I'll get it. You just stay right there."

Within two minutes she brought coffee out for both of them.

He took a sip.

"So, what have you been doing this morning, while I was dead to the world?"

"Oh, I've been online, checking out the news, emails. And I checked out your barn."

Eliam froze for a noticeable second.

"Really?" he said, more of a question than not.

"Yeah, usual barn stuff around, but the loft upstairs is locked up. I saw something weird through a hole, but I couldn't make it out."

Eliam just stared at her.

Sarah noticed his reaction.

"Was that okay? I figured since this is a rental place, the owners probably stored a bunch of stuff up there. Keep it locked up." She still saw an odd reaction to her comments. "I usually don't snoop around; I was just curious."

"Oh, no, that's not a problem. Yeah, just random stuff up there," he said.

"Is it your stuff?" Sarah thought to ask.

Eliam didn't answer right away. He took another sip of his coffee before replying.

"Yeah, some of it's my stuff, and some other peoples'. It's just a bunch of miscellaneous things in storage, like you said."

"Huh, there was this big object up there. It looked real black, a dull, weird black."

Eliam took a deep breath and thought again before answering.

"Yeah, that's…that was probably my spaceship you saw. I'm from another planet, you see, and…and that's where I park my spaceship. Or, it might have been a desk you were seeing."

"Spaceship…*right!* You're quirky like my dad!" She smiled. "We keep an old nuclear submarine parked in our barn loft at home, in case we need it. You know, floods and such."

Eliam just looked at her and smiled back.

"So what's on the agenda today?" she then asked.

Eliam thought for a moment.

"Actually, I have some things I really need to do at the university, to get prepared for next week."

"Yeah, I can imagine. Do you mind taking me home? I actually have a little side work I've been putting off. I need to keep a promise and get it done, too. I feel bad asking. I should have driven my car, like I…"

"What kind of work?" he asked, just being curious.

"It's some research for a client, obscure historical fact-finding. Not any big deal or hard by any stretch, just time-consuming. But, I need to get it done for her. I've been putting it off. I'd really rather spend more time with you, but I guess we've got to do what we've got to do!" She smiled a slightly sardonic smile.

Eliam sensed her disappointment.

"Listen, I'm sorry, Sarah, about last night. I just wasn't feeling like myself for some reason. I was just thinking about what you said, and...and I don't want to...to take advantage. We'll go slowly. Make sure, you know. Okay?"

Sarah thought about it as she nodded.

"Hey, it was a nice day, and evening, great dinner. Plus, I got to see my dad yesterday—which was a welcome surprise, thank you—and spend time together, which I enjoyed." Both of them smiled again. "It's not a problem, slows fine. I just feel bad about asking you to drive me home."

"No...no don't. It's not a problem. And Sarah..."

"Yes, Eliam."

"I...I still want to go to the beach with you, sometime."

Sarah smiled.

Chapter 22

Eliam and Sarah hadn't talked since he'd dropped her off late Sunday morning. She'd called later that evening, but he hadn't answered. She figured he was busy working. As everyone took their seats, the two glanced at each other and smiled, silently sharing thoughts of their 'mostly' enjoyable weekend together.

"Alright, let's get started this beautiful morning," Professor Dunes said eagerly. "Let me give you a rundown of what you can expect today, as well as this coming week. Now, I want to say firstly that what you're all going to experience this week has actually been pushed forward. It was preliminarily scheduled for the fourth week, but all of you have made such amazing progress in attuning yourselves to the B-CID's—having navigated and completed the other modules so effectively—that we thought that you were more than ready to advance to the next one. We think you'll find it quite amazing. And, I have to add, the staff is in fact pretty excited about this one as well. A lot of hard work went into it, and we're actually quite anxious to show it off, as well as hear your opinions of it.

"Now, I'm going to explain a little about the origin and brief history of what you're going to experience and learn today. Many decades ago, when computer games were in their infancy, a group of people took an age-old concept—a belief actually—and turned it into an entirely new experience for gamers. They asked the question: 'What if you could customize the characters of a game, to act as you would want them to act—to be, as you would want them to be?' This led to the ability for a participant to change things within the game.

"To change and alter, for instance, the clothing of the game characters, their physical features, their voices, their behavior, etc. It allowed for the customization of racing vehicles, for instance, with color, type, style, and sponsorship, along with varying engine power and agility and cornering capabilities. In other types of games, it provided the ability to choose which weaponry your good guys and bad guys would battle each other with; how much they could take a beating, or bleed; how many lives they would have to live until the game was finally over.

"This concept led to further advancements: additional personal settings, cultural configurations, and intensities of graphics, the integration of multiplayer scenarios, and the ability to save those scenarios and resultant outcomes so one could return later. The list goes on.

"These innumerable augmentations and customizations ended up establishing an entirely new entertainment experience, which ultimately surpassed the movie and film industries in revenue earnings as well as attendance and participation. In fact, this is still the case today, as most of you know.

"Now, I imagine a few of you are already supposing where we are going with this, but I'm also reasonably certain that you haven't, as of yet, stretched your mind far enough to see its *personal* potential!" He laughed a somewhat sinister laugh.

Everyone looked around at each other with heightened excitement.

"I see I've got your attention. Trust me, I'm excited too."

"Professor, this has something to do with that AVTR link I saw doesn't it?" Dr. Redding asked.

The professor turned to him and smiled.

"It most certainly does, doctor!"

"And it stands for Avatar, doesn't it?" he also asked.

"Again, it most certainly does, at least conceptually anyway. AVTR is also an acronym for the name of the program: Artificially Viable Transhuman Reality – AVTR. And yes, it's kind of like the movies and the games, but much, much more so, I assure you," he said.

"You said it started with a 'concept', or 'belief', Professor? What belief?" Furley Goens asked specifically.

"The concept of 'Avatar' came from ancient beliefs— Hindu, for one," Condoleezza Ghee stated knowledgeably, "whereby a Deity would descend down and take human form to speak, or to battle some sort of evil, or to educate, etc. There are numerous variations of this. But, the basic concept is a conscious entity taking up residence in a body of some sort, to obtain their various goals."

"Well thank you, Condi. That is exactly it, and very well described, I might add. What Condi has just referenced for us is right on. AVTR allows us to enter a virtual, customizable body, and dwell in an entire other universe created by our, or other's, minds."

"You mean…" Wena Paravin's words stopped as she started thinking out loud. "Like pilots of a game, but internally?"

"Exactly," Eliam Zaris stated, "from within, not as a mere observer and remote operator, but as an actual internal participant."

Sarah looked at him with astonishment.

"What you're saying is we, in essence, would be inside a game? Like in that old *TRON* series, or like on a Holo-deck, from the old *Star Trek* franchises, or the *Matrix*? You've got to be kidding? Really?" Declan Stewart, from the entertainment industry, excitedly asked.

"Yes, that is correct. And again, it won't be like just watching it. It will be like being there," the Professor added, "actually being there. And, the reality of it far surpasses anything you've yet to experience. And not just games, places, settings, locations, events…but worlds, wherever and whatever the core-construct is designed to be. Let me give you a scenario, one that already exists for our purposes, and one we will visit together, shortly. Imagine going into a room to experience a presentation, much as you had done on the first day we encountered each other as a group, in the school's auditorium.

"You enter, view each other and the surroundings. You take a seat. The presentation begins, and you watch and even participate as it proceeds. Sounds and voices, light and color, come from their respective sources and enter your senses. Let's say—to expand the scenario—you're there and you disagree on a subject. You raise your hand, you're acknowledged and asked to stand and speak. You do so, as you watch the people around you react to your remarks. You finish, and sit down. All the while you know in your mind that each participant in the audience, as well as on stage, is merely an Avatar that is being generated in that particular forum or construct.

"The scenario I just described is only one of endless possibilities. Think of your particular vocations. Let's consider the applications for business, for instance. Furley, imagine conference meetings where everyone can attend and participate and do business remotely, without having to travel there, offering their presentations and illustrations, with all that extra edge of realism and professional flare.

"Condoleezza, imagine having a classroom full of students and you all travel together, say, to the inside of the tomb of Tutankhamen. After lunch, your class goes to the September 11th memorial for an overview, and then you tour the actual buildings, inside and out, built from the applications construct database.

"Imagine next taking the class to the bottom of the ocean and walking them through the Great Barrier Reef, or around one of the historical ship wrecks of the world, or how about a trip to one of the outer planets, or to the sun? The possibilities, as you can see, are endless. All that is needed is the appropriate data in the construct.

"And here's an interesting one, Dr. Redding, how about touring inside an actual body that you're about to perform surgery on? Again, the possibilities are as endless as they are exhilarating when you think about them. Within every single discipline represented in this room, there is not one that would not excel and advance from this technology."

The room was ecstatic with excitement.

"How is this done? I mean, inside the body? How?"

The Professor and Eliam Zaris looked at each other.

Eliam spoke next.

"Well, as stated before, a lot of it is proprietary, but let me give you an example of the basics. You undoubtedly know something of the field of HDX-VP—High Definition Extreme Videography and Photography? You probably see it, or even possibly use it every day, and don't think about it. Well, take that resolution potential and multiply it by a factor of ten, and then combine it with the electromagnetic spectrum, along with electron-scanning methodologies.

"One recent project used the technology to examine a forest in all the wavelengths to determine depth, distance, density, molecular structure, proportion, interaction, motion, volume, growth and decay levels, even quantum interactions, all at the same time. Similar technology, together in the B-CID's Nebulonic subroutines, serve to create a seemingly real reality, based upon this real data—and/or lab-fabricated data—that an Avatar, which is generated the same way, by the way, can navigate in, around, and through. It is simple science. Well, maybe not simple, but highly applicable." He smiled.

The Professor spoke next.

"Yes, I know we keep using the word proprietary, but the technologies that go into doing this have been out there and discoverable for quite some time. The proprietary part is 'knowing how' to integrate the technologies directly with the brain, in order to bring about the specific results."

"That's right," Eliam resumed. "This has only become possible through 'Smartbrain technology', being able to directly integrate the data from the various outside sources, and channel them into, and out of, the brain. By doing so, the sense of reality—of realness—has become enhanced a dozenfold. You can visually 'look' at this same data we speak of, or 'hear' it through your ears, but streaming it directly into your brain is where the experience of reality comes from."

Nelson Baurle then asked, "You've mentioned seeing and hearing mainly, not the other senses, I just realized. What about smell, and taste, and feeling? Are those parts of the reality in all this, too?"

Several of the others voiced the same question.

The Professor and Eliam looked at each other, silently speaking with their eyes. Sarah thought she noticed a brief signal pass between the two.

"Good observation, Mr. Baurle," the Professor started. "The technology has been built around sight, sound, the external sense of feeling, and even the olfactory senses, to a degree. The remainder, taste, is still under refinement. That particular sense has proven somewhat difficult to master, surprisingly. Oh, it is part of the Avatar experience, but the B-CID does not produce the sensory impulses as accurately as it does the other senses. Sometimes particular tastes, for instance, get mixed up along the way and, let's say if you eat an orange, it might taste like burnt toast, or something else. But that is inconsequential, since the other senses are the principal ones. But we are working on it, and expect higher measures of accuracy soon.

"I'm sure you'll all have many more questions as we make our way through the day. Feel free to ask them at any given time. But for now, how about everyone take a short break, and when we return, we'll begin." the Professor said, getting up and politely ushering everyone out toward the break area.

. . . .

"Okay, now. All of you remember when we started the program; everyone was digitally scanned from all sides. And I'm sure you remember the seemingly silly motions requested of you at the time, toward the end, remember?"

They nodded, accessing their memories and smiling because of them.

"Well, this was for several reasons, one being for future marketing and endorsement—images, portraits, likeness, etc.—according to your contracts. Another was for what you are going to experience here in the next few minutes. In addition to the photography, you were also deep scanned. Now, don't fret. The technology is the same being used on you everyday as you walk through the airport, or when you enter a bank, or as you apply for a license or a passport, it's basically recognition technology like you've all heard about, and probably despise!"

Everyone smiled again.

"Now then, let me give you a brief explanation of what's going to happen as we proceed. You're all going to engage your B-CID's. You'll go to your Apps Hall and there you'll see your AVTR link. When you do, you'll activate it. What will happen is that you will find yourselves in another Hall. This Hall is the AVTR Hall. This area, like the Apps Hall, will eventually house all the various links, locations, and applications that you—as well as all future users of Smartbrain technology—will ultimately place there to access according to your personal preferences.

"Let me explain further. Let's imagine for a moment that this technology is out in the mainstream. One of your favorite things to do is to, let's say, go to the Smithsonian's exhibit of Minerals and Gems in Washington, D.C., for instance. And, let's say you want to have a friend go with you. So you call up your friend and talk to them, and eventually invite them there. So they say sure and you say you'll meet them there at 1:00 o'clock.

"Now, in your hall is a link to the exhibit, which you placed there some time ago, and which is available—will be available—for free to the public for downloading. So when you click on the link it will open a door and the program will initiate and you will find yourself within your Avatar, inside the location's entry space. You're early, so you wait a minute or two. Your friend shows up. You look at each other and when ready, proceed through the exhibit's entry doors. Together the two of you step through, and there you are, now strolling through the exhibit enjoying the wonders of Earth's mineral samples in full color and dimension. You can walk around them, see them from all angles, even get down and peer at them close up, all with extreme definition. You stay as long as you like, exit the same way, say goodbye to your friend, and return to your own space, wherever that may be.

"Cool huh? Now, imagine going to a new theater where you're going to experience the first showing of the next block-buster movie. You have paid for the privilege online at an earlier date and received a passcode for that particular show. You go to your AVTR Hall, enter the appropriate door, you greet a ticket person perhaps, enter your passcode, and are then allowed in to the theater. You take a seat, watch the show, by yourself or with as many friends as you wish to attend—and it's a private show, by the way. If you wish to pause it you can. You go get a snack—back in reality—and then you resume. When it's over, you exit.

"Now, we're not going to the Smithsonian Exhibit, or a theater, because in truth, these don't exist yet. But imagine that they will one day, along with countless other places like it. Let's take this to another level. Let's say you want to have a party. There will be an app that you can either own, or pay for the use of. Within this app you design your own space. You pick from the multitude of décor available and along the way customize it as you wish. There are tables, chairs, dance floors, whatever.

"It's one room, or an entire house, depending on your ambition and pocket book." Everyone laughed imagining it. "Now, your place is ready, and you're going to invite friends, but first, you have to get ready. You then go to your Avatar closet and there you'll find an unlimited assortment of attire, hair styles, make-up, shoes and accessories, etc., to fit whatever you feel like at that time.

"Or, perhaps, you might want to change Avatar bodies altogether, and attend your party as someone else!"

The group lit up and excited comments began flying around the room.

"You're kidding, really? OMG!"

"For real?"

"You can even change your bodies! How is that possible?"

"Hang out with friends, do things together?"

"You can change appearances, clothes?"

"Can this be used in game settings?"

"Game settings, I just now thought of that, too! Can your Avatar, for instance, use weapons and fight other people's Avatars? Imagine the …"

"Of course they can! Right, Professor? Isn't that what this is leading to? I mean, the possibilities are limitless."

"That's right! And think of the educational potential? And the…"

"You can be in your own house and meet with someone from ten thousand miles away!"

"Or…or, attend weddings, or birthday parties, or funerals!"

"Or go on vacation, to places you could never afford."

"Yeah, and imagine what Christmas would be like?"

"Yeah, or what about Halloween!"

"Wow, that's right. Imagine a haunted house!"

"Yeah, any holiday for that matter!"

"Yeah, or events, races, or sports! Yeah, think of sports!"

"How about po…I…I mean, adult films!"

"Wow, talk about attending parties!"

Everyone started laughing, appearing to become hysterical with the implications.

The Professor and Eliam Zaris smiled at each other. Eliam then acquiesced to the professor as they silently debated who should speak next.

The Professor started again.

"People…*people*, we see you're catching on to the idea. Yes…*yes*, it is quite thrilling, once one considers the vast possibilities, isn't it? Trust us, you as well as the rest of the world, will be more than amazed at the endless potential! We're talking entire industries for the designs and applications in peripheral support of this technology. But for now, let's proceed. And to that end, who's ready to see what it's really like, instead of just imagining it?"

·······

Suddenly everyone was as apprehensive, and yet as nervously excited as a bunch of kids going to Disney World for the first time.

"What's this going to be like Professor? Where are we going?" Wena Paravin asked with caution.

"Yeah, what are we in store for here, Professor?"

Sarah asked the same question of Eliam, except she did it with her eyes alone. He winked slightly. It made her feel confident.

"Well, you shall all see. We're sure you can understand that we don't want to reveal what you're going to experience, in its entirety, all at the beginning. We want to record your genuine first impressions and reactions as we progress through the different environments. But again, trust us, you will be amazed!

"Alright, let me review. You will activate your AVTR link and upon doing so, we will enter a pre-designed room, the entry space for this particular app. And I might add that this application has been specifically designed for this group, the first one of its kind in this world. A version of it will be included as a default introduction program in every B-CID that goes to market. However, all of you will be the first consumers to have the privilege of experiencing it." He glanced at Eliam and appeared to wink.

"Now, when you go in, we want you to notice the décor, also look around at each other, and study the surroundings. Feel free to comment, and talk, and ask questions. I want us all to do so for a few minutes in order to become oriented to the initial experience. After that, I will instruct everyone to proceed through the next set of doors. Once inside each new area, stay close for a few moments and I will instruct you on the subsequent phase, what you can expect: sights, sounds, feelings, smells, so on. We will be traveling through several different environments; these are merely samples of the potential settings and locations that will ultimately be available. The potential applications, I'm sure you'll see, will be virtually unlimited. Okay, everybody?"

Everyone acknowledged the instructions.

"Alright, any questions before we go?"

Wena Paravin sheepishly held up her hand.

"I'm sorry, but…I have to use the bathroom. I'm sorry!"

Mumbles and soft laughter carried through the air.

"Sorry, sorry! I'm just so excited, I guess! Sorry!"

Wena then got up out of her chair and nearly ran to the bathroom.

"That's okay, Wena, not a problem. Anyone else?" the Professor cordially invited.

Three more people shook their heads in embarrassment, got up and headed to the bathrooms. The remainder just laughed and waited.

In four minutes, all that left—including the Professor—had returned and had sat down to begin.

"Okay, B-CID's on, power up. Next, go to your App Hall and activate the AVTR, and then step inside! And…here we are!"

…….

The group of nine people now stood in a large room that appeared to have been built out of smooth, contoured, whitish-blue adobe-style plaster, or silky stucco. It was like being in a huge asymmetrical igloo where the ceiling and walls curved and slid down and morphed into each other.

There were numerous window-like depressions of various depths and sizes in the walls, with no sharp corners leading into them. In each, there was what appeared to be a window with beautiful blue, bright translucent liquid behind them. Also, in the window areas there were flat, sill-like shelves with small, dark, stone sculptures placed on them, each resembling a cultured museum display.

On the ceiling there were inverted dome-shaped lighting fixtures with the light sources hidden above them, or inside them. The light was soft white and cascaded down the walls. The contrasting rich blues, whites, and the darkness of the sculptures made the place seem large and luminous, yet pleasantly cozy.

"Wow! Nice room. Look at the texture of the walls. They are so uniform and defined," Condi commented.

"Yeah, this is nice," Wena added.

Everyone was smiling as they looked from one to the other.

Sarah looked closely at Condi, and then Eliam.

"You look just like you!" She about gasped when observing the detail, as did the others.

"This is amazing," Nelson Baurle said, as he waved and turned his hand in the air slowly, staring at it as if unbelieving.

"You got that right," several others said in agreement.

"May I?" Wena said to Condi, reaching out to touch her hair. Condi nodded and did the same.

"I can feel it!"

"Yeah, me too!"

"It looks and feels so real," several said, touching their own hair.

"Look, there's a mirror," Dr. Redding then noted.

Most had not yet noticed it, but on one wall, turned somewhat away from them, was a two-meter-wide mirror, seemingly molded into the curved wall.

Several walked cautiously over to it and were suddenly astonished to see their own, as well as the other's reflections in it.

"Wow, now that's kind of spooky. I can see my reflection's reflection."

Declan Stewart looked at himself intently, turning his head and checking out all the angles. Suddenly he had a curious look on his face. Dr. Redding, who was standing next to him, noticed the look and asked what he was thinking.

Mr. Stewart leaned in toward the doctor.

"Hey, you're a doctor, so you won't probably think this is too weird." He then reached down and pulled his pants out far enough to look down at himself. He quickly let them snap back into place.

"They're gone, my…my junk, they're gone," he said.

Dr. Redding just laughed at him as he stepped slightly to the side.

Professor Dunes only heard the end of the comment, yet immediately knew what Mr. Stewart was referring to.

He then spoke up for everyone to hear.

"No, Mr. Stewart. We didn't digitally scan those parts of you, so they won't be there. Same goes for everyone else.

However, to answer what I'm sure is a budding question in your mind, Mr. Stewart, yes, if they had been, then they'd be there. And to expound upon that, if enough of our bodies' general motion had been recorded and digitized, then, yes the extended flexibleness would be there as well. But sufficient amounts were recorded for our purposes, here, now. That's why when we talk we can see the motion and stretchiness of the skin, the opening and closing of the eyes, etc. It all ties together. The more thoroughly scanned the subject is, the more detailed the Avatar, and the experience."

"So you're saying that if our motions, our complete physical, I don't know, abilities...dexterity, whatever, are scanned and digitized, then we could be the same in here, and have the same agility, motion, whatever?"

"Yes, exactly. For an extension of what we're talking about, when a gamer, for instance, uses the technology, he or she can have an extensive scan completed, and it would in turn enhance the Avatar capabilities. Athletes will use it for training, etc. War and action gamers will use it quite extensively. And yes, Mr. Stewart, I suppose the concept will carry over to the adult entertainment genres as well." He said the last part with a measure of reticence and intentional brevity.

He quickly moved on.

Chapter 23

"Wow, this is incredible," Sarah said, as she took her turn and looked at herself in the mirror. "We have the same clothes on as we did when we were scanned!" she remarked, just realizing the fact.

Everyone else noticed the truth of the comment as well.

"Yes, because that was the most recent scanning," Eliam started. "As stated a moment ago by the Professor, the results are proportional to the extent of scanning."

"So, if we were scanned in other clothes, we'd show up here in those clothes?" Condi Ghee asked.

"Yes, that is correct," Professor Dunes acknowledged. "Here is how it will work. To effectively build your Streamplaces—which is what we're calling our personal spaces, here—you will populate them with either custom scanned items, or generically scanned items: clothes, wardrobes, accessories, etc., furniture, conveyances, whatever, as we've stated. By doing so, people will be able to build their own environments as they wish. That, in and of itself, will open up entire new industries, as I stated earlier, along with its own unique economic impact. This technology will generate changes in society that you have yet to even imagine. Of course, we're not here to discuss all that. For now, we'll concentrate on the technology itself. Is everybody ready for the next environment?"

Anxious nods came as everyone looked toward the next set of doors, which Eliam Zaris was now standing next to.

"Well then, this way," he said as he started walking. "Oh, and I hope none of you are afraid of heights?" he added, with a slight snicker.

The people started looking at each other, apprehension suddenly showing in their faces.

As the Professor and the group approached, Eliam pressed his hand to a lighted plate on the wall next to the doors. They summarily swung out as they opened, revealing a sight that brought a gasp from everyone.

Slowly, the group went through the opening and found themselves gawking at a huge mountain range of cliffs and dizzying heights, as a distant bright sun hung high over an enormous horizon. The far-away sight captivated them all as they walked out of the previous space in order to visually encompass the entire view of the new one. However, none had immediately noticed just what it was they were walking out on.

It was Sarah that first saw it.

"Guys, are you seeing what I'm seeing?" she asked with a shaky voice.

A few looked over toward her and noticed that she was looking straight down. Suddenly everyone was looking down now, too. What they saw made them all freeze in their stances. The group then realized that they had all walked out onto an elevated deck made of completely clear material. And the deck was cantilevered out over a cliff that must have been at least a half a kilometer high. As they peered down, they all saw a rushing river below, winding around and through a huge valley of cliffs and boulders and rugged terrain. Everyone just stood there in awe, careful not to move.

"Oh…my…God!" Wena said, holding her hands out in the air as if to steady herself.

"I couldn't have said it better," Condi agreed.

"Ditto," Nelson Baurle added.

"I just can't believe this! This is soooo real!" Furley Goens added. "Just what is it we're standing on, Professor?"

"Well, actually, nothing. You're sitting down in a chair, in our lounge, remember?" Eliam answered for the Professor, laughing through his nose.

Everyone looked at him.

"Relax everyone! This is just a stream of data that is making its way through your brain. Your brain is just interpreting it as real. Truly amazing, isn't it?" Eliam continued. "This is an example of an engineered space, an artificial environment. We did this to show you what it would be like, as well as to relate the scale with which it is possible."

"Scale is right! This is gargantuan! And this is all artificial?" Nelson asked.

"Yes, it is. Well, actually, it was generated from numerous real locations, but the composite was built by engineers."

"And, anything like this can be built?" Mr. Stewart asked, with a shaky voice.

"Yes, that's correct. The possibilities are nearly infinite," Eliam said, as he took in the view.

"What if I were to jump?" Dr. Redding asked.

"You'd fall!" the Professor said matter-of-factly.

"Fall?" the doctor repeated.

"Yes," Eliam stated. "You would fall. But, to answer you next question, no, you would not die from an impact. Maybe a heart attack, because it does seem so real, but no, not from the fall. You see, this environment is structured on basic physics. You jump, you fall, and you stop falling when you get to the bottom. However, these are just impulses in the brain. You would just find yourself down there at the bottom, in the water, or lying on a rock. But, you wouldn't have died, not from the actual fall."

"Really?" the doctor asked, again.

Eliam presented a feigned, slightly devious look on his face. "You can jump, if you'd like. Try it out if you want!"

"Uhmm, no! I…I think I'll just stay right here," he replied.

"So would gaming environments be like this?" Furley Goens asked.

"Yes, they would—and will be! They could be virtually anything an engineer could conceive of, actually. In fact, to elaborate on what Eliam said a moment ago, if the engineer decided to bypass some, or all of the basic physics he touched on, one could effectively jump off here and fly, or hover, or pick up that boulder over there and hurl it at the face of that mountain, or whatever. Again, the possibilities are endless, actually."

"Really!" Declan Stewart said softly, his mind rushing like the river down below, thinking of the endless entertainment possibilities.

"Okay, so how about we move on. This way." The Professor turned and motioned to the left.

They all started to follow him, albeit carefully, walking at first with measured hesitation due to the residual realness of the feeling. As they walked they noticed the deck had an attached walkway in its corner, about two meters wide, which snaked around the cliff and seemingly ended about a hundred meters in the distance at another set of double doors that were apparently set into the cliff.

"We're going there?" Wena asked, still significantly constrained by her fear of heights, and the fact that the walkway was also completely transparent and hanging off the side of the sheer cliff to their left. She did so slowly.

"Now, as we proceed. Let me ask you. Have you noticed the breeze?" Eliam asked the group.

"Yes…*yes*, now that you mention it. I do! I didn't at first, I guess, but I do now. And it's starting to get windier. Or is it just my imagination," Sarah asked as she followed the Professor along the walkway.

"No, it actually is getting windier. The environment is programmed that way. It certainly adds to the thrill-factor; don't you think?" the Professor added.

"Yeah, I'll say. How about hurrying up a little there," Wena encouraged everyone, smiling, still trying to find her mental balance.

Everyone laughed, acknowledging her sentiment, as well as their own like-feelings.

"Do you guys smell that, smell the breeze?" Condi mentioned.

A few sniffed intentionally at the air.

"Yes, it…it smells like warm rocks."

"Yeah, that's what it smells like to me, too."

As they rounded the last winding corner of the path they found themselves walking in direct sunlight, with several noticing that the cliff wall was warm to the touch. All reached out to feel it as they made their way along.

"Amazing!" Condi said.

"It's hot," Sarah also mentioned. "Yes, amazing!"

"Alright, we're at the next environment, through these doors," the Professor said as he stopped and waited for everyone to gather around.

The walkway widened to twice the size in front of the doors, everybody realized. But most everyone instinctively crowded up together, as close to the cliff's wall as possible for some reason.

"Alright, now then, our next environment is also a mostly engineered location, made of composites of other real things and places, however, you will encounter some wholly, and completely engineered, shall I say life-forms that may at first be startling to you. But just remember, it's all in your head!" He and Eliam laughed at the pun.

"We're sure you will find this one as interesting as the one we're leaving," Eliam added.

Eliam placed his hand on the lighted panel.

. . . .

The sliding doors opened and everyone walked through, however, their expectations were somewhat let down when they found themselves simply standing in a small windowless room.

"Okay, so this is a little plain," Declan Stewart said with a note of sarcasm.

After everyone entered, the doors automatically closed behind them. Eliam then stepped over to another lighted panel mounted on the back wall. He placed his hand on its surface. Suddenly, everyone felt a little heavier and they all sensed motion.

"An elevator," Dr. Redding said, looking up and around.

The Professor smiled and nodded his head.

A brief moment later the rising feeling subsided, and the entire wall split open into two gated doors, each swinging out into a hot and dry, surreal landscape. Above them was an unusually large, glaring sun, burning down onto a flat area of ground that appeared to be the top of a huge mountain butte. Wind-swept, dusty swirls blew around them. In the distance they saw shimmering mirages and rising columns of heat. Pointed and rugged mountainous peaks lined the vast, waterless, sun-lit panoramic horizon.

As they exited the large elevator, they looked ahead and saw the small, swept-wing vehicles sitting in two rows, each group parked at oblique angles across from one another. No one said a word at first. They all just stared. Suddenly, one of the group realized what might happen next.

"Are those what I think they are?" Condi asked, surprised.

"We're going in those?" Furley Goens added.

"Fly in them, you mean?" Wena extended the question.

"Yes, we are," the Professor said, smiling. "And some of you get to be pilots today!"

"Uh, I don't know about this!" Wena then announced, a sudden fear engulfing her. "I'm not really comfortable with flying, especially in small aircraft!"

"It's okay, Wena, each one has four seats, and you can ride if you'd prefer, and they're easy to fly," the Professor said, attempting to relieve her obvious anxiety.

"Alright, so who's game? Like the Professor said, they're actually very easy to fly—no license required!" Eliam alleged, smacking his hands together with a clap.

Sarah looked at him, and then spoke.

"I…I'll fly one! At least I'll try!" she said, enthusiastic, yet perceptibly uneasy.

"Okay, so who else?"

Several held up their hands, though with observable reticence.

"But, we aren't pilots!" Mr. Stewart plainly stated. "I've never flown anything before, either."

"Well, you flew the drones. It's going to be the same, easier actually—just think, and it'll go wherever you want. Remember where you are. Don't worry, we're not going into combat—no aerial dogfights today. These are merely our conveyance to our next destination. Again, all you have to really do is just think about it."

"Okay, well, I guess I'll try. So, where? Where *are* we going?" Dr. Redding asked.

Eliam looked at the Professor, and then back at the group. He then simply pointed straight up.

The group's collective mouths dropped open when they looked up into the strange, orange and blue hued sky, and in the distance saw the varying-sized celestial objects. It looked like an artist's conception of the view from an alien planet.

Chapter 24

"I think I'm going to be sick," Wena said in a soft, crackly voice.

"I think I want to be a pilot!" Sarah said excitedly, as she held the controls steady and banked the craft to the left as she followed Eliam, who was piloting one of the other vehicles.

The five craft were ascending in pseudo-formation at an incredible speed. Within just a few moments, the anticipated feeling came—weightlessness. It engulfed them quickly, all feeling their limbs and their heads get lighter. Outside the oval-shaped windows, they saw the last of the atmosphere dissipate beneath them, as the darkness of the sky above became unbelievably deep and surreal. Stars shown with a clarity that at first seemed beyond imagination, but then, they all realized it was just a fabrication. But even with that, somehow they knew that if they had actually journeyed out past the atmosphere, then this is what it would be like.

"This is amazing!" Sarah said in a whisper.

"Alright everyone, you're going to follow us for a few short minutes," the professor said, as his craft pulled away at an even faster velocity.

"Where are we going, Professor?" Sarah asked excitedly.

"First we are taking you on a short tour of a few of the potential *future* developments of this app. You see, this is not just an application limited to a few boring stages or levels. There are endless possibilities, an entire galaxy of possibilities, really. And here's one coming up now!"

As he finished his sentence everyone slowly pushed farther back in their seats. Before them, growing exponentially larger as they raced toward it was a planet that appeared to have only partially been formed. Quite literally, a huge part of it was missing. The group veered to the right as they approached and began a wide, high orbit of the gargantuan body just sitting there floating in space.

"What happened to it?" Dr. Redding asked, as he peered out his window.

"Nothing has happened to it. What you're seeing is a work in progress, to be more accurate," the Professor said. "That my friends, is going to be the Zombie Apocalypse Planet, or ZAP Planet many of the engineers have started calling it."

He remained silent, allowing everyone to wonder, waiting for the first comment or question to erupt before going on. All just kept staring as they got closer, beginning a low arching orbit. Below, they all began making out huge cities that appeared devastated beyond measure, sitting between large tracts of green countryside. At least that was the case for the parts of the planet that were formed. When they reached the other side, it was again plain to see that a huge section of the planetary orb below them was indeed missing, and all that was seen looked to be only rock and vast areas of nothing.

"Zombie Planet? What are you talking about, Professor?" Condi Ghee asked.

"This everyone, again, is a work in progress. It is a place where people will choose to go to experience a particular type of experience—a Zombie Apocalypse-type of experience. There you will be chased and challenged and put to the test to see if you have what it takes to survive and even possibly be a hero; blasting your way through the undead, saving groups of stranded people, all in dire danger, helping them get to safe zones, as it were."

Again, everyone just sat there and thought of what he was trying to get at. It was Mr. Stewart that put two and two together.

"You mean…this is an amusement park, of sorts? Something like when you go play Paintball, different scenarios, different games, with different goals, missions and objectives, things like that?" he asked with growing excitement.

"That is precisely it, Mr. Stewart. Precisely! It is a place for people, as I said, to go and experience a particular type of experience, one that is principally in alignment with their intellect, their capabilities, their sense of fun and adventure, and/or desire. This is only one of the dozens of small planets of this type that are in development at present. But as I said, there are galaxies of possibilities—literally. Once Smartbrain technology goes mainstream, there will be innumerable applications coming to market on a daily basis. What you're seeing is just the beginning. Let's check out a couple more, shall we?"

As he said that, he banked right and began to pull away from the world below them. Within a few minutes the group arrived at yet another partially built, gigantic globe just sitting there floating in the vastness of space. This one was covered in lush forests of many types, each dotted with lakes and ponds and rivers and creeks of various sizes and lengths, sliced by long strips of mountains and deserts. It was as pristine looking as Earth must have been millions of years in the past.

"And this one?" Furley Goens asked with special interest.

"This is going to be Wilderness Planet. It is a vast world of forest and various rugged terrains that will be particularly suited to the outdoorsmen types. It is intended for those who wish to hike, camp, hunt, fish, climb, kayak, canoe, any such type of adventure, or combination thereof, according to any difficulty level one may personally be inclined to."

"You're saying these places are vacation spots, theme parks or something?" Wena Paravin concluded.

"Yes, that is one way of looking at it," the Professor began to elaborate. "This, and many others, are under development as potential, well, 'Experience Generators,' as we have found ourselves calling them. Eliam, would you like to join in and elaborate further for us?"

"Sure, Professor, I would be more than happy to. That is correct, everyone. Let me ask you a question: why do people sit in their homes, or wherever, and watch a typically big screen with an endless number of channels, depicting either real or fictitious shows or documentaries, or games, or events, or what have you? What makes this so popular, so much a part of people's lives?"

There was a short silence.

"People are lazy!" Furley said abruptly.

Everyone shared a laugh.

Eliam smiled as he waited for another answer.

"It's entertaining!" Declan Stewart said matter-of-factly.

"Yes, that is the short answer. But why do people want to be entertained…or educated, or fulfilled by doing so?" Eliam added.

No one answered so Eliam continued.

"Because people want to experience things *other* than what they are used to, other than what they are forced to have to experience, for whatever reasons. They want something different, something interesting, something exciting, something educational, again, something *other* than what they're used to. It's a part of human nature, the need to grow, to expand, to learn, to rise through levels of experience until that ultimate triumph or knowledge or challenge or whatever is reached.

"That's why we go on vacations, work in our gardens, play our games, watch our media, have our hobbies, and so on. That's what this is. As the Professor said, there are galaxies of possibilities; we're just upping the *reality* of the experience, the *quality* of the experience. However, it's up to the one experiencing the experience to assign the particular value to the experience, whether it's a potentially good one or a bad one." Eliam suddenly paused for a moment looking over at the Professor. They made eye contact and seemed to nod at each other from the short distance between their crafts. "But, that's getting into the philosophical side of what we're doing. What do you say we move on?" he abruptly ended.

The Professor started speaking again.

"We *could* show you numerous other planets that are also under development, but these will suffice as illustration for you. Now, we want to take you to an Experience Generator planet that is fully developed and is ready for us to, well, to experience." He chuckled slightly. "Eliam, if you would, please."

"Certainly, Professor! Where we're headed now is to a small planet that will be one of the default elements of the B-CID, which will be included in the initial package when it is distributed to the public. Think of it as a sample pack, of sorts, which will serve as an introduction to the Experience Generators, a few of which we just showed you."

"Professor, Mr. Zaris, may I ask a question?" Nelson Baurle politely interrupted.

"Certainly…yes," they replied in turn.

"Why places like individual planets, in space, and all that. I mean, this is all created in the Nebula, right, so why not just experience generators, or whatever, here? Here on Earth, for example. Why space, and the planet themes, and all that?"

"Good question. The answer is sense of scale, and the future, I suppose." The Professor began, as he once again looked at Eliam and shared a brief, wordless communication with him. "Oh, there will be numerous of these places in alignment with the themes of Earth and its many offerings. But Earth really has few actual frontiers anymore; most people know this. And studies have shown that, statistically, over the last century people have developed an exponential interest in what's out there, in space. They wonder, what will happen when we actually do find other planets in our Galaxy, and intelligent life? And most believe that we will, one day!

"The intent is to add to the psychological and emotional content of the experience. And, I might add, virtually every aspect of these Experience Generators has been built based upon the actual physics and astrophysics of known space and time; all that we've gathered so far regarding what's out there." He paused briefly. "Let me ask you this: how do you feel about traveling out into space on a voyage of exploration? Does this pique your interest, your sense of excitement, more than just an Earth-bound vacation, or adventure? Take a look out there, before you answer!"

He pointed out the window at the approaching planet, pausing to let his comments sit in their minds.

Nelson Baurle answered, "Yeah, the word 'pique' doesn't quite do it justice, actually! I was just wondering, thanks."

"Well, I know I'm fracking excited! I can't wait to see what's down there! So come on, let's go! Let's do it!" Declan Stewart said, his mind churning in excitement with the possibilities.

"We're going down there?" Furley Goens asked.

"Yes, as a matter of fact we are Furley, after a brief stop," the Professor said. "Eliam, shall we? Let's introduce these nice people to X-ploration Planet."

. . . .

The group was suddenly on-the-edge-of-their-seat nervous, especially those piloting a craft. Taking off was one thing. Flying toward a gigantic planetary mass in the middle of space and attempting to actually land on it was an entirely different thing. Even if everyone knew that it wasn't exactly real. The sense of reality, in all of their minds, exceeded actual reality by many measures.

"Okay, we're on approach. First, we'll be landing on one of the Space Station Visitor Centers, which serves as an initial observation point for new visitors traveling this way. Now, if you'll just follow me in. And don't worry, the landing will be a breeze. Just think and go, remember!"

The Professor swooped his craft down and onto the enormous landing area on the huge space platform. Each ship in turn landed next to the other, all facing the planet below. The small vehicles then seemed to power down, and for a moment there was nothing but silence.

"Okay, excellent job everyone! Now, pilots, if you will please press the panel link on the right side of your consoles labeled X-data."

Everyone did so. Suddenly, a huge transparent screen shone in front of each craft. On the screens were various readouts, and arrows, and indicators, pulsating in place in their fields of vision, all changing as the group watched the planet in front of them seemingly rotate, as the space platform orbited at a terrific velocity around the giant globe.

"Good! What you are seeing is basically an information display. Remember, this entire medium, or environment we're in is going to be distributed as a default program with the B-CID. Every new possessor will be able to do as we're doing. Other Experience Generators will be available as added options that a possessor can acquire at their discretion, and according to their financial capabilities. But this, again, will be an element of the original package.

"As you can see, there are numerous areas down there that are being identified on your screens as I speak: The Wilderness Pavilion is in view right now, a taste of the Wilderness Planet, as we saw earlier; however, I might add that there is no sample ZAP Planet equivalent here. That one will only be available as an add-on, but there are many others that are represented by their own sample pavilions. For instance, coming around now is the Coaster and Ride Pavilion. That one is pretty self-explanatory. And the Science and Industry Pavilion, right there.

"There in the northern-hemisphere is the Movie and Film Pavilion, again fairly self-explanatory. And there's one that is expected to be very popular, the War Games Pavilion. I'm sure you can all figure that one out as well. It features numerous scenarios from a host of different eras, even several futuristic ones, which will serve to excite and fulfill whatever savage side you might have. And of course, there are going to be numerous of these types of Experience Generator planets that will expound upon this particular sample pavilion's design, if you're into that sort of thing.

"Coming around, is the Animal Planet Pavilion, which is expected to be of huge interest to educators and children. All the animals, as well as their environments, are reproduced to a definition that actually exceeds reality by a notch or two, we're proud to say. Imagine going to a zoo of enormous proportions, yet not having any walls or cages to hinder your observations and/or interactions."

"Wow," Condi and Furley said simultaneously in response.

"How many of these 'sample pavilions' are there?" Furley Goens asked as she stared in awe.

The Professor answered, "There are a total of seven in this year's release, some smaller, some larger, when compared to each other, yet all are quite sizable. We're expecting a large initial turnout immediately upon release to the general public, hence the scale, again."

"There are various others that are slated for the next version, but many haven't been fully decided on, or even designed yet," Eliam also shared.

Everyone watched as the platform continued its orbit around the large planet.

"Ahhh, now this one is going to be an interesting one," the Professor then said.

"Alien Planet Pavilion?" Sarah read the statement on the display out loud, but then made it a question.

"Yes, that is correct," the Professor answered.

"Alien Planet? Really? So how'd you do this one? I mean, you said you matched the physics, etc., to actual reality. How'd you manage to figure this one out, you know, being that it's 'alien'? Are we going to see, like, lizard-men, or something?" Declan Stewart asked, with a more than slight air of sarcasm. "Just wondering."

The Professor picked up on the minor derision.

"Well, the worlds created in your various Science Fiction media have helped to a large degree on that note, Mr. Stewart. What did your Einstein say, 'Imagination is more important than knowledge'?"

The Professor then noticed Eliam Zaris looking at him intently. His brow furrowed in response before he continued.

"Remember, this has all been created to provide experiences that are 'other' than what we are used to in our daily lives. The Movie and Film Pavilion provides a like experience. This pavilion, however, is dedicated to the experience—the proposed experience—of what it would be like to actually meet beings from other planets, based upon known physics, and potentially live within their environs for a time.

"We're not talking about slimy, flesh-tearing, acid-spewing lizards, or the like. We have developed this pavilion under the proposal that if beings like us exist, then chances are the greatest that other intelligent creatures similar to us might also exist. In fact, along known scientific theory, it is a mathematical assumption that, if biology has evolved as it has on Earth, then it is more than likely that it has also done so on other planets as well."

"Makes perfect sense to me," Condi interjected. "This does sound like an interesting place. So, we're going to meet some of these aliens? Down there? Really?" she asked, a note of apprehension apparent in her voice.

"Well, no, not right now, actually. We'll be going some-where else first," he said, pointing to the next area that was just then rotating into view. "That's the Commons Pavilion; it is a compilation of all the other pavilions. Much like this planet is a compilation of several of the others that will be coming online over the first few years after release. We want to give the public a rounded, varied experience at first so they can quickly see what the potential is. You see?"

The group watched with interest.

"Alright! Everyone get ready and follow us down. If you wish, all you have to do is activate the Pavilion's auto-landing key and it'll take your conveyance right to the central landing hub. From there we'll be taking ground conveyance to our next stops. See you down there."

Chapter 25

Within mere minutes the group had landed and was seemingly standing on solid ground next to their flying machines. Most were practically speechless due to the realism of the landing, and the returned sense of gravity that they were now experiencing.

"Okay, a little further orientation I think is required at this point." He cleared his throat. "We are at the Commons Hub. This is where visitors to the pavilions will start. But, to answer one of your unspoken questions I'm sure, no, people who choose to come here don't necessarily have to make the journey as we have in these flying conveyances. This was merely intended to show you one of several modes that can be chosen, one of the more fun ones, I think.

"In truth, when all this is online for the public, anyone can choose however they wish to arrive. You can be sitting in your favorite chair at home and within seconds just find yourself at any of the numerous entry points here at the Commons Hub, same with any of the other pavilions or planets. It's just a matter of bookmarking the address or location. Again, this was mainly for your benefit—and for those who will review all this later once we go public," the Professor said pointedly.

"And speaking of the public…" the Professor then seemingly touched the air in front of his face. Suddenly, the group wasn't alone. The entire area, for as far as they could see, was now filled with other people. They were walking, talking, eating, going in and out of what appeared to be train tubes, mingling. All were smiling and seemingly having a good time.

"What's this?" Nelson Baurle asked, stunned at the change.

The others spoke a similar question with their expressions.

"These are simulations, for realism. When this is online and people are accessing the Nebula, then the population will actually be other peoples' Avatars, as ours are here, you see. But for the time being we wanted you to feel what the environment and atmosphere would be like when populated. Again, these are simulations. Pretty detailed, are they not?"

"Wow, that's an understatement," Sarah commented.

"You can only interact with these on a cursory level. But, when they're the real thing, you'll be able to communicate just as we're doing right now. Remarkable, isn't it?" Eliam added.

The word "Yes" went up all around.

"Those people over there, and over there. They're eating. I thought you said that the sense of taste wasn't included in the experience? So what are we seeing?" Wena asked, curious.

"Good observation, Wena. Well, the experience is definitely intended to be a part of the program. It just hasn't been perfected, yet. However, we are reasonably confident that it will be soon. I mean, what would an amusement park be like if there were no treats to tempt the palate? In fact, for fun we activated this portion of the experience to show you what we mean. Let's head on over to one of the vendors and try something, shall we?"

The professor finished speaking and ushered the group over to a large area of outside tables surrounding a walk-up restaurant. He proceeded to an open window and requested service. A tall, thin, blue-haired girl promptly welcomed them and then asked what they would like.

"Uhmm, may we have two sample cold platters, please, one fruit and one vegetable, and an assortment of dips, please," the Professor asked.

"Coming right up, here's your number; just place it in the service slot at your table and your order will be right out in a streak, and thank you for visiting the Commons Food Court." She smiled and winked, and then turned back into the building.

"Please, sit," the Professor said, motioning toward some unoccupied tables.

No sooner had they seated themselves, and two people in matching Tees delivered the platters, along with some additional plates and napkins for everyone.

"Looks like regular food. Though not like any I've seen at any amusement park," Condi stated, picking up a piece of asparagus and studying it.

"Yeah, me either," Sarah agreed as she picked up a strawberry.

"As we said, this is just for sampling. Thought we might have a little fun!" the Professor said with a devious-looking grin on his face. Everyone noticed the look, but then decided to follow through and try something. They all picked up a food item of choice and proceeded to take a bite.

"I absolutely love vegetables, but this celery tastes like…like horse radish and metal or something; I don't know what," Wena said, immediately spitting it out on the ground.

"This banana tastes like butter, or…or I don't know what, either. And it's actually sort of sour. I can't tell exactly. All I know is it tastes terrible," Dr. Redding said.

Everyone was smiling at the oddity of the experience.

"This strawberry tastes like, I don't know, mint, some kind of mint," Sarah added to everyone's comments, rapidly running the tip of her tongue over her lips. "And it's stinging my tongue, kind of weird!"

"Yes, and what you'll find is that everything tastes completely different to everyone else. When I try the asparagus, Condi, it tastes somewhat like chocolate to me," the Professor said, pointing to her food item.

"I don't know about you guys, but these brussels sprouts taste like…*shit*!" Wena then said, spitting it out on the ground as she had done the celery. And trust me, the dip doesn't make it any better either. Yuck!"

"Now see, I can agree with that…" Sarah said the words loudly, and then paused. Everyone looked at her curiously. "Brussels sprouts have always tasted like crap to me!"

The group broke out into hysterical laughter at the comment.

Eliam slapped his leg as he laughed heartily. "Yeah, to me too! Brussels sprouts do taste like crap!"

The laughter went on for a moment, with each trying another taste of their food and then laughing raucously as they shared the unexpected results.

"Okay, so what's next, Professor?" Furley Goens asked, pushing her plate toward the center of the table.

"Well, the plan is to spend the rest of the morning touring, via the Train Tubes, and then break for lunch, a real lunch that we've catered in—real food this time! We're having grilled spewing-lizard, served on a bed of brain-eating space-lice. Sound good, everyone?" he said mockingly, his eyes now falling on Mr. Stewart.

The group laughed again as Dr. Redding sportingly slapped Declan on the back. The man looked slightly affronted but returned a smile. "I bet that'll taste like crap, too!" he said, slightly embarrassed from the attention.

Everyone laughed again.

The Professor continued.

"After lunch, we'll return for more fun. We want to encourage you to explore your own areas of interest. I can assure you, you're all in for some fascinating experiences. For instance, Luna Caverns the coaster ride is extremely thrilling, it's one of my personal favorites; then there's deep sea diving in the Coral Reef Shark Habitat, if you like water and a bit of danger; or there's the Pedestal Jumping Obstacle Course over the lava flows of Kacheckuan, that's a fun one, and let's see. Well, how about we just look at the Maps and Info Guide, shall we? We can decide and go as groups or pair up, whatever you'd like! There are lots to see and do. And don't worry, we'll have plenty of time. We'll be coming here the majority of this week. And by the way, so you'll know, all this is not all just for the fun of it. Your participation is actually needed as an aid toward the fine calibration of the programs. But, we might as well have fun while doing it, right? Let's take a look at some of the other adventures."

He touched a small, raised button in the table. Suddenly, a multi-screen, visual display popped up out of it for all to see.

Sarah excitedly studied the display with everyone else, but something in the distance seemed to catch her eye. She briefly glanced up at first, and then back down, but soon her attention was quickly drawn to it. After a moment something about the image registered.

There on a distant bench sat a middle-aged man with somewhat disheveled, shoulder length brown hair, grayed along the edges. He wore a faded blue-collared shirt, and brown denim trousers. Over the shirt was a tan spring jacket with an odd shimmering emblem on the collar. On his face were rimless glasses. The man was just sitting there, staring directly at her. He didn't look threatening; he had no malevolent or maniacal expression on his face. In fact, he looked as friendly and gracious as could be.

It suddenly dawned on Sarah. That was the man that she had seen in front of the clinic where her father was staying. The man had spoken to her, and she to him, she remembered. It was him, she thought; at least it certainly looked like him. The odd thing was that every other simulation in all of her visual field was completely involved in what they were doing. No one was evenly remotely interested in their group. But this guy was staring directly at her.

Sarah scrunched her eyebrows with deep curiosity, looking back. Then, Eliam tapped her on the shoulder.

"What do you say? Laser Zip-Line through the Rain Forest Canopies of the Amazon, catch some 200-milimeter stick bugs, observe the social habits of the Capybara; or, get some tan on the Sun-Surface Plasma-Bubble Float Trip; or perhaps a Luna Caverns Coaster Expedition is a bit more to your taste today, ma'am?" he said, trying to sound like a politely courteous tour guide.

Sarah looked up at him.

"Uhmm, I don't know, let me think." She thought for a moment, glanced in the distance yet again, and then turned back. "I guess I'll go with the 'flow' as they say; as long as we can stop by one of those Devonian Black-Sand Beaches, maybe take a short dip to cool off on the way back. I'm sort of partial to beaches," she said, smiling cutely at her inside joke.

Chapter 26

The week had gone by faster than anyone had expected.

The wonder of the technology was starkly apparent after spending several days in the AVTR modes. It was literally like living in another world, on a grand vacation. And as with most enjoyable vacations, it was hard, even depressing, to leave it and return to reality.

Sarah woke that Saturday morning knowing that her day had been thoroughly planned ahead of time; it would definitely not be spontaneous from moment to moment, nor as fun, as she had been used to the entire week before.

She would wait for Cybil to show up and then they would proceed to pick up Condi, who had volunteered to go along to accompany Sarah after she had divulged to her what she was going to have to do that weekend. The gesture of friendship touched Sarah's heart and nearly made her cry when Condi had offered.

Once together, they would drive to Santa Clarita and she would sign all the release papers, and then they would bring Oscar Whiting back to his house of thirty-five years, probably for his final visit. After a short stop there, and after gathering up the small number of personal items that were allowed at his new home at Greenway, they would then drive him and his belongings there, and proceed to help him get settled into his new home.

Step-by-step the process sounded simple, easy even. But that was just how it sounded. The reality of it was going to be quite a bit different.

．．．．．．．

The three were now driving, having fueled and refreshed the car as well as themselves at the gas station before leaving Bakersfield. It was a pleasant day, albeit dry. But it was always dry in California. Condi and Cybil had never met, so the first half hour revolved around their introduction and the basic sharing of their backgrounds. At least it served to take Sarah's mind off the approaching task at hand.

"So your family is from India? That's nice. I was in India once, New Delhi, a long time ago, traveling with family," Cybil said.

"Really," Condi replied, "I've never been there, actually." She loved the reaction on Sarah's and Cybil's faces, as she did whenever she made that statement.

"Really? Never?" was Cybil's comment.

"Nope. I'm from Boston. And no, I've never been there." They all smiled.

"You probably think since I have a lot of that typical Indian accent that I just had to have been, right?"

"Well, yeah, I guess. Sorry!" Cybil answered honestly.

"Oh, don't be sorry. I understand. My mother and father have always spoken with a heavy Indian dialect; they lived there for quite a long time before coming here. I actually exaggerate it sometimes, just because people seem to expect it. I am proud of my heritage. Most smart people are from India!"

Condi gave Cybil a serious look, and then winked and smiled.

They all broke into laughter.

"Well, personally, I like how it sounds. *It is very pleasant sounding, I must say!*" Sarah said, doing an excellent job of imitating the dialect.

"*Oh, you say that very nicely! You must have been to India then!*" Condi replied, a big grin on her face.

The girls giggled.

They talked about their jobs, their tastes, their clothes, their shoes, and their childhoods.

"Okay, I have to try. Sorry, but here goes. You two can't tell me anything about this 'product', this 'program,' not a thing? Nothing? Even though you're most of the way through it, and everyone in the world will know about it anyway?" Cybil asked, changing the subject.

Sarah and Condi glanced at each other. They'd expected questions about the project at some point.

"Trust us, we'd love to. But we can't. All we can say is…is that it is truly going to change the world. You can't imagine; you just can't imagine," Sarah said with expressiveness, once more glancing at Condi.

"Agreed! Sorry!" Condi then added. *"It will be the End of the World as we know it!"*

They all started laughing again.

There was silence between the three as they watched the road signs zip by. Only ten miles left before they would arrive in Santa Clarita. The silence was a solemn one as they realized that their light conversation was quickly going to change, as well as their mood.

·······

"Hi, Dad!" Sarah said to her father as the three approached him. He looked up with a blank stare. His eyes then fell on Condi and Cybil, exhibiting the same expressionless face. Suddenly something clicked and he recognized Sarah.

"Sarah? *Sarah*! You're here! I didn't know you were coming. What in the world brings you down here to see your father? It is so good to see you! Come here and give your dad a hug! My goodness!"

He held his arms out as he stood up from the chair. He and his daughter embraced for a long hug and a kiss on the cheek.

"Hi, Dad! We came to take you back to Bakersfield. Remember, we talked about it on the phone. We have an awesome place for you to stay…to *live*, now, in Bakersfield. We talked about it. It's called Greenway, Dad. It's a retirement, slash, long term care facility. And it's really nice! We're taking you there, today. Right now, actually!"

"Really? I…I don't know. I…I just don't know. I have board games tonight! Friends and I play board games, and…and tonight's lasagna night. I don't know if I can…"

"It's okay, Dad. This has all been arranged. They have board games at Greenway, too, and…and a whole bunch of other things you'll enjoy. I guarantee it. And they're really looking forward to some of your NASA stories, too. They told me that a couple of times. One of the staff there also worked at NASA some time ago, they told me. You're gonna love it, Dad. We're also going to stop by the house and get some more of your things. Would you like to go to the house for a little while?"

"Really? We're going to the house? I had a dream last night about the house. The house? Well okay, that'd be alright then."

"Oh, I forgot. Dad, this is Condoleezza Ghee. She is a friend of mine. And you remember Cybil. They both wanted to see you and they rode down here with me. We'll be going back together, too."

"Hello Mr. Whiting," Condi said with a respectful nod of her head. "It is very nice to meet you, sir. Sarah has told me about your work at NASA. I found it extremely fascinating and I would love to hear more." She stepped closer and held her hand out.

Oscar Whiting shook her hand.

"Well, hello. It's nice to meet you," he replied, his mind suddenly racing with images of NASA.

"Hi, Oscar," Cybil spoke as she also stepped closer, leaning in and giving the man a hug.

"Oh my…my, Cybil, yes…Cybil! It's good to see you again. How are you, and…and how's your boyfriend, your, uhmm, Liam, is his name?"

Condi looked at Sarah with a curious look on her face.

"Jacob, Oscar, yes. My husband's name is Jacob. And he's fine! Thank you for asking. It's…it's good to see you again, too, Oscar. You're looking well, I should say. It looks as if they've been taking good care of you!" Cybil said, trying to get past the awkwardness.

"My goodness, so much attention from such beautiful women," Oscar Whiting suddenly said. He then leaned in and whispered, "There are guys watching us right now from down the hallway that wish they were me, if only for a few minutes!" he said, smiling ear to ear. "You're all so very beautiful, I must say! They're going to be talking about this all evening!" he said, sporting a big, toothy grin.

The girls felt a slight embarrassment, but then laughed appreciatively at the compliment.

....

Sarah unlocked the door to their family's old house and stood out of the way so her father could enter. It'd been months since he'd been there. He walked in and started looking around. Realizing where he was, he got another one of those toothy grins on his face. He then turned and cordially invited Condi and Cybil in.

"Please, come in, come in! Make yourselves at home. Sarah…Sarah! How about getting our guests something to drink before dinner? What would you like? We can offer you…uhmm…"

"Dad, we're not staying for dinner. And I don't think there's much to offer as far as drinks go. No one's been here for awhile, Dad. Remember?"

Oscar Whiting looked at his daughter with another blank stare, as if what she just said made sense, but then it didn't.

"That's okay, Mr. Whiting. I'm not thirsty or hungry anyway. But thank you so much for thinking about us. You are a fine host, sir!" Condi said, warmly.

"Same here, Oscar. But, thank you! You are a fine host, always have been!" Cybil added.

"Dad, I put a lot of your things in that suitcase on the couch. Why don't you take a look and see if I missed anything you may want? They only let you have a certain amount of things so I tried to get all your favorites. We can also pick out some wall pictures, and maybe a small painting for you to have there. And they said you could bring your own lamp and some desk items if you want. You'll have your own desk there. It'll be a small one, but you can have your laptop, external drives, and some other things. I put them on the dining room table, if you want to look?"

Oscar Whiting was suddenly dumbfounded with confusion as to what his daughter was saying. It wasn't that the words themselves didn't have meaning, it was the fact that they all rushed together. He just stood there and stared toward the dining room.

Condi and Cybil saw the lost look on his face. The sight nearly brought tears to their eyes. They just stood there, not knowing what to do, or what to say. Both feigned smiles at Oscar.

"It's okay, Dad. I'll help," Sarah said.

"No...*no*, I understand. I'll...check out the clothes and things. Why don't you show your friends the backyard, where you played when you were growing up, and the...that old tree house. Give them the nickel tour. I just need a little time. I understand what's happening. I...I do. I just need a little time."

Sarah looked at him and saw that it was indeed registering. Her dad was realizing that he was leaving his home, and he would probably never return.

"Yeah...okay, sure Dad. I'll show Cybil and Condi the yard. You just...you just take a little time. We'll be back in a few minutes." She looked at her friends and swallowed hard. They followed Sarah down the hallway toward the back of the house.

Oscar Whiting walked into the dining room area adjacent to the kitchen. He then slowly looked around. Tears welled in his eyes as he peered at the pictures on the walls, at the scratches on the woodwork that his little girl had made with her first tricycle back so long ago, at the handmade magnets Sarah had made when she was at camp that one year, which were still stuck to the fridge. A host of memories suddenly flooded his mind, brought back for a brief instant with each glance of his eyes.

A tear ran down his face, and his hand began shaking.

Then suddenly, he remembered that dream he'd had the night before. He quickly went to the mudroom off the kitchen, retrieved one of his old, heavy work boots and then placed it in the freezer.

Chapter 27

Sarah returned home after taking her father to his new place to live. She did well holding herself together, she thought. It wasn't until the three had driven all the way back to drop Condi off at her car that she burst into tears and the three just sat there in the car sobbing like little girls. Condi and Cybil hugged their friend, sharing her grief.

Sarah felt embarrassed by it and told her friends that very thing. But they just threw it off as quickly as it came at them. They hugged and cried and hugged some more, as Condi and Cybil spoke words of support and affirmation regarding the difficult decision Sarah had had to make.

After nearly half an hour the three got a hold of their emotions and Condi left.

Cybil then drove her and Sarah back home, offering to stay with her as long as she needed, but Sarah was exhausted and said she'd be fine. They hugged and kissed each other as friends do, and said their goodbyes. Sarah shut the door and proceeded to sob for another twenty minutes as she sat there on one of the kitchen island stools, her head down in her arms.

Finally, dried out and exhausted from being so exhausted, Sarah got up and washed her face, freshened herself up as best she could, and then made herself a light dinner of half a cold-cut sandwich, a few carrot sticks, and a large glass of red wine. She then sat at the island checking her emails on her tablet, and trying to eat her dinner, even though she didn't have much of an appetite.

After her emails, her mind went back to her father. And even though she knew it might bring back the tears, she started rummaging through the family pictures she had stored on her tablet. She just sat there for the next hour looking at the pictures of her as a child, along with those of her dad, and of her mom. And as she expected, the tears returned, especially after her third glass of wine. But, she couldn't help it. She then ran across that one picture of her and her dad sitting there with those goofy hats on, the ones that her mother had made them.

Sarah just stared at it for the longest time.

Then came the NASA pictures.

She loved these pictures. They always reaffirmed how proud she was of her father. He'd always been such a strong, determined man. Through his exacting and tenacious efforts at his job; through losing his wife to such a horrible disease, and all the attention it drew; and through raising a teenage daughter through all that, and now, through his own incurable health issues. He'd always been her inspiration.

She wiped a tear as she looked at them. It'd been years since she had. After the first few folders her eyes started getting heavy. She decided to open one more file and then she would put them away and fall into her bed.

It was then that she saw something she had never noticed.

In one of the pictures, taken during some celebratory event she couldn't right then remember, she saw what appeared to be that same man she had seen before—the one at the clinic in Santa Clarita, the one at the Commons in the AVTR program. He and her father were standing together and apparently conversing. *What the heck*, she thought. The image was small and blurry, but it certainly appeared to be that man. And what's more, she just then noticed the fact that the man in the picture looked as if he'd had the same, exact clothes on.

Sarah just stared.

She enlarged the area, resolutely trying to bring the low pixel image into better focus, her mind swirling with questions amid confusion.

Suddenly Sarah's phone rang, making her jerk in reaction.

She put down the tablet, grabbed her phone and looked for who was calling.

It was Eliam.

She answered it quickly.

"Hello," she softly said. Her voice sounded tired.

"Hi Sarah, I just thought I'd call and see how it went. Is this a bad time? Are you home yet? I…"

"No, yes, I'm home. It went as well as expected, I guess. He's settled in for tonight. I was just looking at some pictures, drinking some wine. How are you?" Sarah asked, suddenly realizing she was feeling strange from all the mixed emotions, and the wine.

"I'm good. Listen, I won't keep you. I imagine you've had a stressful day and then some. I just wanted you to know I was thinking about you. And I wanted to see if you would have dinner with me tomorrow evening?"

"Evening, yeah, that'd be nice. I'm spending the day with Dad—it's kind of expected for the transition and all. Sunday's like a big family day there. But, late afternoon, evening would be good."

"Okay! Great! I'll meet you afterwards; say at, would five work? Six, be better for you? How about, *Sophie's*, on Atwater, do you know the place?"

"*Sophie's*, no. I've never been there. But that'd be fine. I know Atwater. I'll find it. Six is good. Yeah, that'd be fine."

"Good! Hey, you sound really sleepy, so I'll let you go. We can talk tomorrow. Okay?"

"Yeah, okay. Tomorrow's good."

"Okay. Bye, Sarah."

"Bye, Eliam."

Sarah listened to the silence as the call ended. She put her phone down and just stared for a moment. She then stretched her eyes, realizing her vision was more than a little foggy.

Within five minutes she was in her bed and out like a light.

Chapter 28

Eliam and Sarah met at *Sophie's Mediterranean*, arriving at nearly the exact same time in the establishment's quarter-filled parking lot. They made their way in, were seated promptly, and were just as quickly served a bottle of wine and their Greek salads. It was a quiet, cool, pleasant atmosphere, compared to the heat and the still bright, blaring sun they'd left outside.

"How'd it go today? Your dad okay?" Eliam said.

"Bittersweet, he hates the idea of not living in his own home. I don't think that will ever change. But, he does understand what's happening, for the most part, and he likes the place so far. It doesn't smell, he said that at least three or four times. That's a good start." She laughed a sad laugh, rolling her eyes.

They talked about Oscar Whiting and his new home as they ate. But Eliam could tell Sarah had probably thought about it enough for one day, so he decided to redirect the conversation to something else.

"So what did you think of the AVTR experience?" he asked.

"OMG in Heaven, it's the most amazing thing I've ever done, Eliam. I had no idea when we started that it would be like this. I don't even have words for it. I will say that Professor Dunes had a unique way of presenting it all—you're included in that compliment, by the way," she added. "You both definitely make it exciting and fun, and challenging."

"Thanks, but the Professor deserves most of the credit. He does have a way with people, and he enjoys doing what he's doing, in a huge way. He's like a kid showing off a toy store. He's looked forward to this part of the program for quite some time. Excited doesn't describe it for him."

"Yeah, I could tell. You two are pretty close, aren't you?" She suddenly intuited.

Eliam looked at her, thinking deeply before he spoke.

"Yeah…yeah, we are. He's been like a father to me, Sarah. I've known him since I was really young."

"Really? How long?" she inquired.

Eliam appeared reluctant to answer at first, even somewhat choking up to the point of having to clear his throat before speaking.

"Well, a long time, actually. He's my uncle, Sarah. He's the one that took me in when my family was killed."

Sarah was stunned for a moment.

"Really! Wow, Eliam. Why didn't you tell me…before, I mean?"

"Well, I didn't really know you then, very well, I guess."

"Wow!" Sarah repeated. "If it's something you really don't want the group to know, don't worry, I can keep it to myself."

"Yeah, if you don't mind. Most people at the university don't even know that bit of information. We'd like to keep it on the professional side, if you know what I mean. Nepotism, favoritism, because of those things." He raised his eyebrows.

"I understand, perfectly. Yeah, don't worry there."

They both paused to eat some more of their food.

"He was around all that, too? When you and your family went through all of it? You never mentioned any more of that to me. What was it all it about? You said ideological differences? Political differences, was that what you meant? And you never said where all this took place. Europe? Where in Europe? And who were the people? Why did it happen?"

Sarah just realized she'd said a mouthful and then some. She stopped, looked at Eliam intently, suddenly overwhelmed with curiosity.

Eliam stared into her eyes.

Sarah could see the wheels turning. She suddenly saw in his eyes remembrances, fears, and then hesitation, and then what appeared to her to be some sort of resolution. She just sat quiet, sipping her wine and waiting. Eliam finished chewing a bite of food. He picked up his glass, took a large gulp, and then a deep breath.

"Sarah, I...don't know if I'm ready to talk about all that or not. It kind of stirs things up in me, emotions, things that are hard for me to dwell on, much less talk about. You know?"

He choked up again.

"Okay, sure. I understand. I'm sorry. I'm just curious...I...I just want to get to know you, that's all, like you said before," she said gently.

"Sure...*yeah*, I know that. It's okay!"

There was another short silence between them as they continued picking at their food. Sarah decided to strike up a different conversation.

"What's going to happen when all this is over? I mean, after the release to the public, after we fulfill our contracts with the promotion and all? Which reminds me, I've wanted to ask you something: what do you think is going to happen to society, to people, say, in the next several years—ten years, whatever—after the technology has gone mainstream? Any opinions?"

Eliam had a surprised look on his face, which sort of surprised Sarah. She took another sip of wine while waiting for Eliam to answer.

"Wow, you can't just ask one question at a time, can you?"

"The researcher in me, I guess."

Eliam stayed silent for a moment, again seemingly taking great care in the choosing of his words.

"Well, just like anything else, it's going to be used obsessively, selfishly, for self-centered and self-serving reasons!"

Sarah's eyebrows lifted high with surprise.

"Wow! That's what you really think? You're not being facetious?"

Eliam didn't crack a smile.

"No, actually, I'm not. 'Technology reflects the soul of the people who create it.'"

Sarah was a little confused.

"That's kind of negative, wouldn't you say?"

"Yeah, I suppose it is. But, people are negative, on the one hand. But, most people have two hands. So I'm optimistic."

"Go on," she said, with a smile on her face.

"Well, let's see…first, it's going to consume a lot of resources in its initial production. It will also displace a vast amount of other technology, of which will impact people and their livelihoods, which leads us to ask a whole host questions, questions that need to be asked. Such as, what are the costs ultimately going to be, in time, jobs, resources, and lives? Think about it! It's going to be used and manipulated by all sorts of different people, with all sorts of different agendas. Once released, we won't exactly have control over it, you know?"

Sarah was beginning to see.

"You're saying the technology will create a paradigm shift where there will be a lot of industries—*people*—hurt by it, potentially?"

"Yes, that's exactly what I'm saying, at least initially. It's inevitable! Sharing this technology with the planet, though, is a necessary thing, we believe, for more reasons than you can presently imagine. It's a needed thing of the future! But it will have its negative side. Trust me. So, an accompanying objective has to be to find a way to mitigate those potential negative impacts on society.

"And to answer your first question, that's what I'll be doing after it goes mainstream. I hold myself personally accountable for this, Sarah, in many ways. So does Professor Dunes. And because of that, we feel it's our responsibility to help with the evolution society will go through. In fact, most of the people at the university understand this; they're committed to helping with the long-term transition, as well. This is actually a major part of the campaign that will be released simultaneously along with the technology."

"Really?" Sarah asked, intrigued.

"Yeah! Let me give you a for instance: a portion of all revenue derived from its sale and licensing, will be funneled back into think tanks, local committees, education forums, ethics boards, industry restructuring programs, the list goes on. The funding is only a part of it, too. There's a lot more in the works, administration-wise. Also, the fundamentals of the support campaign comprise the final module of the program. Actually, we're hoping the group will grasp the perspective. Maybe help along those lines, within their own disciplines. That's the hope, anyway."

Sarah looked blown away.

Here was a group of people who was not only helping advance society with new technology, but was humble enough to understand its negative side, and from that, commit themselves to helping those who would be inadvertently hurt by it. She was impressed, and deeply touched.

"Eliam, I had no idea! That makes so much sense," she said, smiling broadly.

"Well, it's definitely not going to be easy. But it has to be done. What will you be doing, you know, in the next few years after all this?" He took another sip of wine, leaning casually back into his chair.

Sarah just sat there thinking about it.

She couldn't help herself.

She took a deep breath.

"Will you spend the night with me?" she asked abruptly.

....

Sarah and Eliam sat close on her outdoor sofa-lounger. The diminutive terrace looked out over a small wooded area in a generally westward direction. The sun was near setting and the evening had cooled to a tolerable degree compared to the hot afternoon. There were numerous clouds in the sky out over the Pacific, so the sunset was proving to be rich with reds, purples, and pinks slowly being chased toward the horizon by the hazy, dark, blue-black shades of space.

Sarah sat snuggled under Eliam's right arm, both slowly nursing another glass of wine, while rehashing some of the conversation they'd had at the restaurant.

"You're really starting to impress me, Eliam Zaris," Sarah said, in an easy, sensual voice.

"I am?"

"Yes, you are. You're a good teacher, a good trainer. You're sensitive to things like the plight of a woman whose father is suffering from a debilitating disease, who actually asked about you earlier today, I neglected to mention."

"He did?" Eliam inquired, somewhat surprised.

"Yes, he did. He said he was highly impressed with your knowledge of reentry angles and reduced gravity maneuvering methodology."

He smiled.

"Really, he remembered the conversations, huh? That's nice."

"Yes. And, after he got it straight that you weren't the guy I was dating back in high school—which he didn't like much, mainly because of his haircut—he was quite encouraging that I should go ahead and seek out a 'cautioned relationship.'"

"'Cautioned relationship,' huh?"

"Yeah, 'cautioned.'"

"Well, I suppose that's good advice. I would advise caution. So, what do you think he would say if I did, oh, I don't know, maybe this?"

Eliam turned to her and touched her cheek gently with his hand, slowly turning her face to his. He then brought his mouth close to hers, stopping only a few centimeters away. They gazed into each other's eyes. Then, he turned his head slowly as his face descended down toward hers. Their lips touched softly and they kissed. It was slow, passionate, and sensual, each relaxing in the moment as they seemingly melted into each other.

"I don't know," Sarah said, almost breathless. "What's that saying about throwing caution somewhere, or something?"

Sarah put her arms around him tightly, pulling him down closer so that their chests were touching, and as she did, Eliam wrapped his arms firmly around her. Soon they were intertwined, their legs and torsos moving against each other, feeling their bodies warmth, sensing each other's heartbeat, suddenly impassioned beyond expression.

"I don't know! The wind maybe…the wind does seem to be…picking up quite a bit…all of a sudden," Eliam said, as his breathing became heavier.

Suddenly Eliam froze in place.

Sarah noticed the hesitation and she drew back slightly, glancing into Eliam's eyes for explanation.

His face then suddenly took on the countenance of a man filled with confusion and fear.

Sarah immediately noticed the emotion in his expression; she saw it in his blank stare.

"*Eliam?*" Sarah asked, expressing all her concern by just saying his name.

Then, she thought she saw him silently say the word, yes, albeit with his lip's motion only.

Eliam seemed to suddenly realize Sarah was not just looking at him, but was studying him. He quickly focused his attention back to her and offered an odd expression, a face that asked the innocent question: "What?"

At that moment Eliam's phone rang out.

He immediately reached for the device sitting on the small table in front of them, answering it with haste.

"Hello," he said, as he looked at Sarah.

Sarah was confused. All she could do was look at Eliam and listen.

"What! When? When did you find it? You watched it? What was he saying?"

That confused, now fearful look returned to Eliam's face as he listened intently.

Sarah's eyebrows were heavy with concern as she just sat there and listened.

"Yes, I…I understand. I don't know. Yeah, I can't believe it. No! Me either! Of course not! He wouldn't have! Something…yes, yes…something is going on. Listen, thanks for letting me know. Yes, you have to let the authorities know, of course. No, I can't. Get a hold of Dr. Vectren and Dr. Tower, they can. Yeah, I know what to do. Let them know, alright? Okay, we'll see what happens from here. Yes, you too! Bye, Anna! Bye!"

Eliam ended his call. He just sat there for a moment and stared into space, his thoughts awash with obvious concern.

"What is it?" Sarah asked delicately.

Eliam seemed to suddenly realize that Sarah was there, as if he'd forgotten she was there altogether.

"Sarah, Professor Dunes apparently committed suicide. He's dead!" he said, his face white and his breathing shallow. Sarah's face scrunched down into sheer disbelief and denial.

"Wha…what do you mean? *Suicide?* Eliam, how? I mean, why would he do that? Who was that, anyway?"

Eliam didn't answer at once, his eyes drifted down and to the side, and his mind silently swirled, feverish with his own questions. After a moment, he looked back at Sarah and answered.

"That was Anna, from the admin office at the university. She was…she went in to catch up on some work she needed to do before Monday morning, and apparently the Professor had sent the university a video message. He said…he said he was in a remote location, assured everyone that he was somewhere where he wouldn't be found for a very long time. He talked about the technology, his wasted life, and then he just shot himself in the head with a gun. It was apparently sent automatically after a certain amount of time. I guess the video shows him doing it."

"*What?*" Sarah asked. "This doesn't sound like him. Does it, Eliam? I mean, you know him better than anyone. Does it? Would he do something like this?"

"I…don't know. No, I don't think so! No, he wouldn't! But it seems he may have."

"What else did she say…did *he* say?" she asked.

Eliam stood up and began pacing.

"She said he…he just rambled on about things, how he hated his life."

"*What?* You're sure? Has he ever said that to you? I mean, really?"

"No…*no!* That's the weird thing! He never said anything like that to me…to any of us that I know of. The Professor has always been rational; he cared about everything, and everyone! It doesn't make any sense!"

Eliam sat down on the edge of the small table. He started crying, shaking his head, running his hands through his hair repeatedly.

Sarah didn't know what to do. She got up and joined Eliam on the table. She put her arm around him to offer some comfort.

"I'm so sorry, Eliam! I wish I knew what to say. What are you going to do? Is someone letting his family know? What about the police? A missing person's report has to be filed. And what about the program?"

Eliam shrugged, clearly in shock. "I don't know. I guess I'm going to have to figure it all out."

Eliam then stood up.

"The police are being notified. Dr. Vectren and Dr. Tower are going to take care of it. And I'm the only family the Professor has...or had!" He lowered his eyes down and just stood there, seemingly frozen.+

"I need to go. I'm going home. I need to be alone. Sorry, Sarah, that I ruined our evening. Listen, I'll call you."

With that he touched her on the shoulder, with barely a look, and then started off towards the door.

Sarah stood and followed him.

"Eliam...No! Eliam, wait. You shouldn't be alone right now. I..."

Eliam was out the door shutting it behind him with force. By the time she got it opened and made it down the two flights of stairs, Eliam was in his car and driving away at a high rate of speed.

Chapter 29

Sarah slowly walked back into her condo, shocked beyond words. She just stood there silently staring, going over in her mind what had just happened. A tear ran down her cheek as her thoughts cycled through the events. Then a memory sparked an idea.

She went to the island counter top and retrieved her phone, immediately locating the number for Eliam. She pressed the call key firmly and held the device to her ear. The number rang several times and then went to voice mail. She cursed under her breath. She ended the call and then tried it again. She hoped he would hear it as he drove, and would answer it, but he didn't. The same thing happened several times; it would ring and then go to voice mail. On her last attempt, when she heard the chime, she left a short message: "Eliam, this is Sarah. Please call me! I…I just want to be there for you! Call me! Okay! Bye."

Sarah put her phone back on the counter and just stared at it as if she were willing it to ring, but doing so gave her no results. Suddenly, Sarah had an idea. She then critically assessed her level of inebriation. She was okay, she concluded, especially now with all the adrenalin coursing through her veins. She was on the edge, but certain that she was in good enough condition to drive. She then decided her next course of action.

Sarah went to her walk-in closet in her bedroom, removed her evening dress, and swiftly put on jeans. She then went to the bathroom, washed her face, touched up her makeup, and brushed her teeth. Her last actions before leaving the condo were grabbing her little backpack, putting a few extra items in it, and then picking up her phone. She checked it just in case to see if she'd inadvertently turned the sound down, perhaps missing Eliam's return call. Nothing. He hadn't called while she was in the bathroom. She made a grunting sound and then headed out the door.

She was going to Eliam's house.

She wanted to be with him.

. . . .

Sarah drove east through the evening darkness. It was a three-quarter moon, and the air was dry and nearly cloudless, so the landscape was filled with dark chasms of blackness, checkered with contrasting areas of silky white, moonlit tracts of land. Since it was a Sunday evening, the roads were mostly clear of traffic for which Sarah was extremely grateful.

As she drove, she tried Eliam's number two more times, again with no results. Was he just simply not hearing the calls? Did he just not want to talk to her? Or was it that he didn't want to talk to anyone? She didn't know. She could understand it, though, either way. But she was determined to find him and be with him, and that's what she was going to do.

She drove on.

The forty-minute trip was uneventful. Sarah slowed and then turned into the entrance of the winding gravel drive. As she drove ahead she looked toward the house, immediately noticing that there were no lights on inside. The only light she saw was from inside the barn's workshop, and the outside, overhead security light which cast a whitish glow across the parking area. Sarah slowed her approach, as she considered with curiosity the lack of lights inside the house. Odd, she thought.

Wondering if Eliam was in fact here at all, Sarah looked again toward the barn. There were two vehicles parked there, Eliam's Land Rover and another vehicle that she'd never seen before. Seeing the other vehicle sparked a sudden inquisitiveness in Sarah's mind. She braked, stopping her approach, for some reason hesitant to continue. She just sat there in the car, looking toward the barn, the vehicles, and then back at the darkened house again.

Her mind raced with questions.

Suddenly, she noticed a black mass rise up in the distance above the barn. It was black as black could be, discernable only due to the contrasting, moonlit hillside far in the distance behind it.

The object held her attention as if Sarah's head had been clamped down in a vise. She squinted her eyes and watched as the object rose higher above the tree line, appearing to change shape or turn as it did so. Her eyes then widened, as if to take in as much light as possible in an effort to define just what it was that she was seeing.

The object then seemed to rise quickly and dart away in an upward, curving, north-easterly direction, getting exponentially smaller each second and then disappearing into nothingness as it seemingly traveled at an incredible velocity up into the starlit sky.

Sarah's mouth dropped open.

She just sat there, motionless.

She then started to reassess, as best she could, what she'd just seen. But it made no sense to her. She played it back in her mind several times within the time span of less than a minute. Still, it didn't make sense.

Suddenly, a memory resonated in her mind.

Sarah was stunned, speechless.

She just sat there and continued to stare.

In another second, an overwhelming fear gripped her.

Her chest started pounding as her heartbeat increased threefold.

Her head began to spin, and she felt dizzy.

She began to question whether she'd seen what she thought she'd seen at all.

Did I?

She then told herself to get a grip.

She took a deep breath, and then another, suddenly remembering why she was there.

She concluded that she at least had to try and see if Eliam was there.

She let off the brake and drove the car to the parking area, turning the vehicle in an arc and facing it the way she had come. She turned the car off, opened the door and stepped out. The night air was cooler than she'd expected, and the only sounds she heard were those of the breeze along with the plethora of insects that swarmed the security light and buzzed about the property.

Sarah hesitated at first, but decided to break the dreaded silence.

"*Eliam!*" she yelled.

There was no response.

She tried again, louder this time.

"*Eliam!*"

She looked toward the barn, at the house, and then at the barn again.

No lights, no motion, nothing.

The eerie silence set her heart to beating hard again.

Sarah looked up into the sky, once more remembering the experience of only a few moments before. She got back into the car, turned the key and suddenly found herself extremely thankful for the comforting sound of the humming engine and the flood of light coming from the front of the vehicle. She looked back once more, but then hit the gas and sped away.

Chapter 30

Sarah woke to the sound of her phone ringing.

She quickly answered it. It was a staff member of the university graciously informing her that, due to unforeseen circumstances on which she could not elaborate, today's session, as well as all upcoming sessions for the group had been postponed, and that someone would be calling her as soon as the new schedule dates were determined.

Sarah was groggy.

The call had only served to reinforce the memory of what had transpired the night before, at least regarding her date with Eliam, and the phone call about the Professor. The other part she wasn't sure about. She lay there in her bed thinking about it, questioning the veracity of the experience as well as her own mind.

Sarah picked up her phone again and looked to see if there had been any calls that she might have missed. There weren't any. She then realized that she had neglected to plug the device in before going to bed. Her phone was almost dead. She quickly rose and found the end of her charging cord and plugged it in. Relieved, she melted back into her bed. Sleepiness came over her again, and as she lay there thinking she drifted off into the world of her memory and thoughts.

Nearly two hours later, her phone rang again, and she awoke abruptly.

"Hello," she said, not even looking at the caller ID.

"Hi, Sarah," Eliam said.

Sarah immediately bounded to the edge of the bed.

"Eliam? I'm so glad you called. I tried to call you several times, but...so, are you alright? I was worried about you."

"Yeah, I saw that you called. I was not in the best of minds to talk, Sarah. I'm sorry. I needed the time. I hope you understand."

"Sure, I understand. Are you okay?" she asked, still a little groggy.

"Yeah, I'm okay. I guess you got the call from the university?"

"Yeah, they didn't say anything, no details, just said they'd let us know when the sessions will resume again."

"Yeah, that's about it for now," Eliam said flatly.

"So, is it true, Eliam? Did the Professor..."

"Yes, Sarah, I saw the video log. It looks as if it's true. At least it appears that way. Listen, Sarah," he paused for a moment as if to decide on his thoughts. "Can we get together? Can I pick you up? I think we need to talk."

"Yeah, sure, I want to do that. When?"

"I'll pick you up in, say, about an hour. Is that okay? Is that enough time?"

"Yeah, that'll work. I'll be ready."

"Okay. I'll see you then, bye."

"Bye, Eliam."

Sarah hung up. She was mostly awake now, her mind once more reliving the night before. She wondered again about what she had seen. How was she going to bring that up, she thought, or should she even? Maybe it was just in her mind; maybe it wasn't real; maybe she was...

Sarah got up quickly and nearly sprinted to the bathroom to get ready.

·······

Eliam picked Sarah up and they went to an outdoor café to have breakfast, choosing to sit outside so they could have a more private conversation. Neither had much of an appetite, so they ordered light meals and mainly drank coffee. Once the table closest to them had cleared, their conversation became somewhat more to the point.

"So you're telling me you're not sure about this?"

"Yes, that's what I'm saying, I guess. The Professor just wouldn't do this. I know it for a fact. Something else is going on."

"Okay, but what? What else could be going on?" Sarah asked.

"I don't know. I'm not sure about anything right now. But I have some ideas."

Sarah looked at Eliam with curiosity.

"What ideas? What do you mean?"

"I shouldn't tell you. You wouldn't understand; you'd probably think I was crazy."

Sarah felt somewhat offended by Eliam's last statement. She'd been trying to get him to talk the entire time they'd been there, but he was not really saying anything, yet still appearing that he wanted to. She wasn't sure what was going on. It was almost like he was waiting for her to say something first.

Sarah then noticed something off in the distance. It caught her eye a second time and she then made a conscious effort to focus on it. It was a sleek-looking, black-as-night, stream-lined sports car, a make of which she wasn't familiar, but the shape of it remotely reminded her of the object she'd seen the night before. She hadn't mentioned to Eliam yet that she'd gone out to his house, and especially not about the object.

As she thought about it, the waiter came by with more coffee and began filling their cups. Sarah just kept staring at the car in the distance. Suddenly, a figure walked into view on the other side of the vehicle, the person's motion catching Sarah's attention. Sarah then looked up and what she saw nearly knocked her off her chair. It was that man again. The man from the clinic, the one she thought she saw in the AVTR program, and more recently in that photograph with her father.

What the heck's going on, Sarah asked herself.

Sarah peered straight at him and when she did, he suddenly looked up and acknowledged her with a nod of his head. And

then, as if telling her to go ahead and talk to the man, he gestured his head and eyes from her to Eliam, and then nodded,
seemingly mouthing the words "Tell him."

The waiter then asked if they wanted anything else, and
told them to take their time and enjoy the morning. He would
return with more coffee a little later if they wished.

Sarah looked at the waiter out of courtesy and thanked
him.

She then turned back.

The man was gone.

Sarah was dumbstruck.

"What's wrong? Are you okay?" Eliam asked, now seeing
a confused look on her face.

She turned to him, glanced back down the street in confirmation, and back at Eliam.

"Uhmm, something weird," she said, shaking her head in
disbelief.

The comment seemed to grab his attention.

"Weird?" he repeated, and then looked off in the same direction that Sarah had been looking. He saw nothing unusual.

"Yeah!" Sarah answered. She just sat there, silent for a moment, her mind whirling around with confusion.

"So, what? What were you looking at that was so weird?"

Sarah thought for a moment.

"I probably shouldn't tell you. You'd think I was crazy!"
she said, with only a modicum of sarcasm, genuinely thinking
he would.

He just stared at her.

Within moments, two different groups of people entered
the café and randomly sat down at tables near them.

"Want to go for a drive?" Eliam asked Sarah.

She looked around and then nodded in agreement.

·······

They were just driving, no destination, just heading toward
the mountains on the secondary roads so they could have a
little privacy. There was an odd tension between them. Both
wanted to be together, both wanted to talk, but neither

seemed to want to resume where they left off at the café. After an inordinate period of silence, it was Sarah that finally started the conversation back up.

"Listen, I know we're both aware of this…this little barrier between us. I'm not sure why it's there all of a sudden, but I'd say we need to break it down before it gets any worse."

Eliam glanced over in her direction several times, yet keeping his eyes on the road.

"Yeah, I agree," Eliam acknowledged. "Alright, I don't think Howey killed himself."

"Howey?" Sarah asked.

"Yeah, Howey…Howard Layton Dunes, Howey! It's what I've called him since I was young."

Sarah nodded with understanding.

"Go on."

"I…I think he was in some way coerced into doing this."

"Coerced? How? By whom? Coerced into killing himself?" Sarah inquired, disbelieving.

Eliam glanced over at her again with a reluctant look on his face.

He took a deep breath, his expression frustrated.

"I'm not sure who. Like I said I have some ideas. But, that's the part where I'm sure you'll think I'm crazy. I believe he was manipulated somehow—into making that video log. I'm…I'm opting here to tell you, Sarah, because I'm really starting to like you—a lot, actually. And I want you to know what's going on! But it's not that easy!"

"You are? You…do?"

He nodded.

"Well, I'm feeling the same way, just so you know. I guess we both ought to just start talking."

"Agreed! But, I'm telling you, you're not going to believe me, unless I show you."

There was a short silence between them.

"Show me what? And where would that be?" Sarah asked.

"At my house," he said bluntly, looking back and forth between her and the road repeatedly, as if waiting to see her face dawn with some sort of realization.

"Okay, and what's at your house?"

Eliam realized she wasn't putting two and two together.

"Sarah, I saw you come to the house last night." He looked at her again with a serious expression.

Sarah seemed to take an involuntary deep breath.

"You did?" she asked. "There were no lights on. Nobody was around. I yelled for you! Why didn't you answer!?"

Eliam kept looking back at her to see if she was getting it yet. She wasn't, apparently, or she was and didn't want to acknowledge it just yet.

"I didn't answer because I was…busy, at that particular moment."

It took another second, but now he saw that look of recognition on her face.

It was registering.

Suddenly, Eliam sensed something and he looked in his rearview mirror. Behind him was a black SUV that was approaching them at a high speed.

"Uh oh! It looks like we've got company, Sarah. *Crap!*" he exclaimed.

She noticed him looking in the mirror.

She then quickly turned around and saw the SUV.

"What are they doing? They're right on us! What are they trying to do?"

Eliam stepped on the gas, increasing the distance between them slightly. He quickly put the vehicle into four-wheel drive mode and took a better control posture in his seat.

"What do you think they want?" Sarah asked, now getting extremely concerned.

"I'm not exactly sure, but like I said before, I have some ideas. And if I'm right about one of the ideas, I'd say they want to immobilize us in some way and then take me for a ride somewhere."

"*They what?*" Sarah asked, with obvious alarm in her voice.

"Don't worry. I'm not going to let that happen." He exhibited a visage of confidence. It made her feel a little better; at least until she noted the big blue ball of light that flew past their vehicle and engulfed a tree in the distance with dozens of little blue, pulsating lightning bolts.

"*What the hell was that?*" she screamed, leaning away from her door.

"Hang on, Sarah!"

Eliam then veered off the pavement and onto an old dirt road that led out into the wilderness of rolling hills, boulders, scrub trees and bushes.

"What are you doing?" Sarah yelled as she tried to hold on during the sudden bouncing around.

"I'm gaining a little distance!"

"*What?*"

"I need to find the right place so I can be out of sight from them for at least a few seconds. Around that bend up there might work; if I can just get a little farther ahead of them. Sarah, when I get ready to stop, I'm going to slam on the parking brake and jump out. Grab the wheel and keep it going straight. Then just hang on until the car stops. If what I'm going to do doesn't work, then be prepared to get in the driver's seat and take off immediately. Head back the way we came and get to a populated area as fast as you can. Do you understand?"

"*What*…you're going to do *what?*" She couldn't believe her ears.

"Do you understand, Sarah? Will you do what I just said? Repeat it so I know!"

Sarah was hesitant, but she recited it verbatim, her voice nearly drowned out by the violent bouncing of the car.

"Okay, this is the bend. Get ready!"

He hit the gas and gained a little more distance. Their vehicle rounded the corner and Eliam started counting out loud. When he got to three, he turned to the left at about a forty-five-degree angle and pulled up hard on the emergency brake lever. Simultaneously he popped his seat belt, opened his door and dove out.

Sarah was aghast, but she grabbed the wheel and held on.

Eliam slid and then rolled several times across the rough terrain. He promptly came to a stop and then swiftly reached into his pant leg pocket and pulled out a small pistol-shaped device. He took aim at the center of the road where the SUV would appear. As soon as it did, he drew a two-handed bead on it and pressed his fingers firmly to the two firing studs.

Twenty yards in front of him a huge blue ball of energy appeared and within seconds engulfed the pursuing vehicle in a similar swarm of small, pulsating, blue lightning bolts. The vehicle then went off into a long and deep ravine, rolling over several times as the driver lost control. Eliam got up, quickly studied the situation, brushed himself off, and ran to the dust-enshrouded Land Rover. He got in and proceeded to turn around and head back the way they came.

Sarah just looked at Eliam as if he were some maniac.

"Wow! That was intense!" she said, nearly choking from the lump in her throat, as well as the dust in the air.

"Yeah, something you don't see every day, huh!?"

"What about those…" Sarah started.

"I'm not taking any chances with you, Sarah. We're getting out of here, first. We'll call it in anonymously when we get back to town. You just sit tight. We're okay!"

Sarah just stared at him with a look of sheer incredulity.

Chapter 31

Both kept looking out their mirrors, unsure of the situation, even unsure of the next moment. They made it to Eliam's house in record time, talking only briefly on the way regarding what had happened. All Eliam kept saying was that he would explain when they got there.

Upon arrival Eliam took Sarah into the house and seated her on a stool at the kitchen island. He squeezed her arm for assurance and told her not to worry. He then told her he would be back in less than half a minute.

Sarah was dizzy trying to process all that had occurred. The half a minute seemed much longer and Sarah was in the middle of standing up to follow Eliam when he came back into the room. He had a first-aid kit in his hand and was headed to the sink. He then quickly took off his shirt and pulled up the sleeve of his undergarment revealing a huge bleeding scrape and a laceration. He then started to treat the wound.

Sarah realized what was happening and went to him to assist.

"Here, let me!" she said, reaching for a couple of antiseptic swabs and some gauze.

"Thanks," he said, capitulating. "You okay?"

Her motion stopped abruptly and she glared into his eyes.

"Yeah, I'm fine, can't say that much for you, though. This is a pretty deep cut; probably needs a stitch or two. No, I'm fine…I'm just waiting is all!" she then said, her face taking on a look of consternation.

Eliam took a deep breath and exhaled in surrender.

"Right," he said, wincing from the sudden pain as Sarah dabbed his wound with the antiseptic. "Answers! You want answers. I'm not sure you're ready for them, but you definitely deserve them," he said, giving her a sour smile.

Sarah wasn't smiling; she just stared at him.

He cleared his throat and commented again.

"From the beginning?" he asked.

"Yeah, that's usually the best place…from the beginning," she said with sarcasm.

"Okay, from the beginning then. Well, to start off I guess I should tell you…I'm not from this planet, Sarah!"

·······

"You sure you don't want a drink or something, anything?" he asked again.

"No, nothing…thanks. I don't want anything to impair even one little brain cell at this moment. I want all of them to hear and fully comprehend everything you say from here on," she answered, her face taking on a grayish pallor.

"I understand. I'd be feeling the same way, I suppose." Oddly, he sensed his own indecision coupled with slight embarrassment. "Okay, as I said earlier. It'd be better to show you."

Not taking his eyes off her he walked to the door. With his expression and a sideways nod, he invited her to join him.

She immediately realized where.

Their walk to the barn together wasn't exactly together. She strolled along, adjusting her pace to his, yet staying a full stride behind and off to the side. On the way he kept looking over his shoulder and smiling, as if to reassure her.

"So you're going to tell me that you have a spaceship in there?" she asked, disbelief evident in her voice.

He turned to her when they reached the door.

"Yeah, I am. The one you saw last night," he said pointedly, looking to catch her reaction.

Her eyebrows rose.

"The one…I saw?" Sarah's voice became shaky.

"Yes. As soon as I began to lift off, your car showed up on my sensors—I saw you looking up. At least I'm assuming you saw it. The timing couldn't have been more perfect; I was in mid-lift so I just proceeded; I had something important to do. I've been debating whether to tell you—my *dark secret*, I guess you'd say—but circumstances seem to have led to it now. And like I said, I really like you, Sarah. I want you to know who I am, truly, as much as I want to know who *you* are."

Her countenance immediately returned to one of caution as they entered the barn and began to ascend the stairs.

"I know what you're probably thinking. You're crazy, or I'm crazy. Right? I fully understand. But you're not, Sarah. Trust me. Though the jury's still out concerning me, at least some people think so," he said, attempting to lighten the moment while fiddling with the lock.

Eliam turned the key, swung the door open to the right and stepped into the huge space. Sarah slowly followed. He let her pass and then shut the door and relocked it.

Sarah was suddenly in awe.

Before her was a city bus-sized craft with short, swept wings. It resembled an elongated stealthy jet fighter, completely black. It was so black that when she looked at it straight on, it was like looking into a hole. No light reflected off of its surface. In fact, in order for her to make out its shape at all, she found she had to change her position by walking around it in order to get any sense of dimension.

"This is *Sanguine*, my ship," Eliam said.

Sarah looked over to him, her face filled with confusion.

"'Sanguine?'" Sarah repeated, making it a question.

"Yes."

He stepped closer to the side of the craft and then spoke the word out loud again.

"*Sanguine*, audible responses please, and open, thank you."

"*Yes, Eliam.*"

Sarah heard a voice, and it wasn't her's or Eliam's.

"It...talks?" she asked, stepping closer to him.

"Yes, she talks."

As he approached the craft an opening appeared on its starboard side along with a ramp of sorts. Eliam took Sarah's trembling hand.

"Please, come inside and I'll do my best to explain."

Sarah allowed him to lead her up the ramp.

Once inside, Sarah tried to take it all in. She saw consoles filled with lights and screens and pads, and what looked like pilot and copilot chairs. She saw seats that lined the walls, and it was then that she noticed all the windows, on the sides and in front of the pilot's seats. There were windows all around. She was astonished. She walked to one and looked out, seeing in clear view the inside of the barn.

"Windows? It has windows. But, outside you can't see them at all."

"Yeah, it's designed that way—for stealth."

"Soooo, you came to Earth, in this? That's what you're going to tell me!" She couldn't believe she truly asked the question.

"Yes, though this is actually just a shuttle. But it did bring us down to the surface."

"Us? You said, 'us' and…'shuttle', as in other people? As in a shuttle…from somewhere, back and forth from one place to another, to the 'surface', the surface of Earth, you're saying?"

Eliam nodded.

"Yes, our interstellar ship is on one of your Jupiter's moons, Ganymede. *Sanguine* is our transport back and forth. That's where I was going last night when you saw her."

Sarah suddenly felt like she'd eaten some sort of psycho-active substance. Her breathing became shallow and she felt faint.

Eliam noticed.

He reached out, took her hand and led her to a seat.

"Okay, this might take a little time. We'd better sit."

Chapter 32

Sarah rubbed her eyes. They felt stretched and taut, as if she'd been hanging upside down for an extended amount of time. She just sat there and listened, trying to make sense of all the thoughts spinning around in her head.

"'Ho-um?'" Sarah repeated it as she'd heard him say it.

"Yes, our planet. It's actually spelled H-o-a-m-e, according to Earth English, the 'e's silent." He smiled, and then continued. "It's roughly seventy light years away, and much the same as Earth, though significantly larger and somewhat farther away from our sun compared to what yours is. Our sun is also larger than yours, by about half, and Hoame, being larger by about a factor of one-point-eight-seven masses.

"It has a present population of about seventeen billion. Land mass to water ratio is about forty/sixty, forty-percent land, sixty-percent water, north and south poles mostly frozen, like Earth's, even has a similar axial tilt, within a few degrees actually, along with the seasonal ranges. Though we have many more of what you would consider continents, about twenty actually, though most are just considered really large groups of islands. Most people live along the coastlines."

"'Seventeen... *billion?*'" Sarah repeated.

"Yeah, about that, at least now anyway. It used to be much, much higher, but it's been reduced significantly over the centuries, and remains stable at around that amount, even though that number still isn't considered by many to be sustainable. We came close to destroying the entire planet, actually, same reasons that threaten Earth. There's a lot of history regarding the subject."

He paused, turning his eyes down in thought.

Sarah slowly nodded her head.

"*Woooow*," she added softly, drawing the word out.

Eliam saw the look on Sarah's face; it was a look that was beyond astonishment.

"You said to start at the beginning," Eliam reminded her.

"Yes...yes I did, I guess." She nodded for him to continue, her eyes wide with wonder.

He hesitated, giving her a concerned look.

She nodded again and he resumed.

"Anyway, around seven thousand years ago, people on Hoame began the search for life on other planets, much as yours are doing now. It was centuries, literally, before our technology improved enough to detect any. But, we did. One of those planets we found was yours, Sarah...Earth. According to our historical references we first called it Chi-am-ra, which means, literally, a Source of Life."

Sarah looked bewildered, but nodded for him to continue.

"This was back when Earth's most intelligent species was little more than cave dwellers. After more centuries passed we were able to send ships, two actually, at first. These ships were populated by machines. They gathered information, much as your probes do here in your own solar system. They returned. We sent more. We learned more. And then we sent people. Logical course of events, right?

"Well, what you have to realize is that, just as your planet has different countries, cultures and beliefs. So does ours. Over time, more than a few countries on Hoame were sending ships for various reasons. Many people thought of Earth much as your people do about third world countries, as you call them. Many came wanting to help, to teach, to be a part of history, thinking what an amazing time to be living in. But what you must also realize is that not every country on Hoame—or its people—shared the same motives for coming here.

"Most were coming for study, of course, to learn, to be a part of something big and pioneering, but then to many, the adventure turned into little more than just a resource in alignment with their own personal agendas; many came merely for the thrill, for the entertainment of it, for the value of it, if you know what I mean."

He said the last part with an ominous tone.

Sarah thought she understood.

Eliam looked down for a moment as if searching his mind.

He quickly continued.

"Some came over and over again, some only once. Some actually stayed and lived out their lives here—those were mostly the good-natured ones who truly wished to live at the frontier. The majority of those who came—most, but not all—deemed it important to keep their origin a mystery, yet at the same time, felt compelled to share basic knowledge, slowly, with an honest desire to help the planet evolve. It was actually a charter written by several of the first pioneers. Others defied that general charter and announced openly that they were from 'up there.' Imagine how the technology they showed off convinced the primitives that they were from somewhere else, again, if you know what I mean."

Sarah nodded her head slowly, acknowledging the inference, but staying silent.

"Remember, this entire course of visitation, from all these various people from Hoame, according to all these disparate reasons, all happened over thousands of years of Earth time, with the visitors settling in numerous isolated locations across your planet; again, each coming according to their own agendas—some good and some not so good."

Again Eliam took his eyes off her as if gathering his thoughts, trying to determine how he should proceed.

He seemed to blurt out the next part.

"Sarah, over several millennia on Earth, literally millions of people were taken from here and made the equivalent of servants and slaves on Hoame, used for work, entertainment, even medical experimentation, among numerous other things."

Sarah's mouth tightened as she began to understand.

Eliam expected the reaction; he acknowledged it with a nod and then swiftly continued.

"This was mostly a practice of a dominant group of people that were—are still—considered the 'Old Elite,' if you will. They're called the *Ankh*. It's a term that means a lot of things, depending on who you are. To most they are the historical Brain-Trust that, through science and technology and world politics have helped our planet evolve and become advanced, an historical group, deserving of reverence, honor and respect because of all they'd done. At least that's what many believed. But, as time went on, many learned that they had a dark side. And like I said, it depends on who you are when it comes to determining an opinion about them.

"But, Hoame and its peoples have changed over those millennia—through thousands of years of wars and conflict, just like Earth. And there's been a growing coalition of people and countries that have politicked over the centuries for its reform, as it's now routinely called. Its foundations based on equal rights, freedom, liberty, etc. Much as your United States has done over the prior several centuries with its governing position on the world stage.

"At present the vast majority of countries have outlawed the taking of people from Earth, for whatever reasons, and have made decisive efforts to help prepare Earth for what many believe should be—and will be—inevitable open contact. So much so, that this is now supported as a general, all-encompassing, political position, with subsequent laws and legislation and even timeframes.

"But, nevertheless, there are those who choose to go against these burgeoning laws and continue to do whatever they want, what they'd done in the past, no matter what anybody thinks. And there are a couple other things you must know in order to have a broader picture of what's really happening, Sarah.

"As I said, Earth has been—and still is—considered the equivalent of what you would call a 'third-world country,' undeveloped, uneducated, barefoot and backwards—no offense. And many believe that it is currently in danger of having

Hoame's still-widespread internal conflicts spill over to the Earth. That's why this technology we're sharing with you is so important. That's why we are here. It's why I'm here, Sarah."

Sarah stared at him.

It was all she could do.

Her mind raced.

....

"You're here to *help* us!? What do you mean?"

Eliam took a deep breath and exhaled.

"I'm part of one of the main arms of the Reform, Sarah. I guess you could consider me a missionary, of sorts."

"Missionary? You mean, like, sent by God?"

"Well," he murmured, "even though Hoame has its own underlying, spiritual and religious roots, not unlike Earth, I consider it being...mostly sent by faith. My own faith, actually, I suppose. No, I'm not some religious zealot, or anything. I just have faith that there is purpose in life, purpose *to* life. We all, by virtue of being from where we are, being what we are, and who we are, are in our own unique position to help bring about some contribution of good in life, where otherwise it wouldn't come about. Though 'good' is a relative term, I know. No, I just believe that, it's the right thing to do to help those who need it, to help lift others up out of the mire of ignorance and uncertainty, to help them find their own purpose in life, so they can have the opportunity to help other's do the same, simple as that.

"God, creator of Heaven and Hoame, creator of Earth, creator of the entire universe, all of that? I don't know! I don't know anybody who really does, except by a choice of faith, I suppose. And I don't necessarily think that that's a bad thing, or an error in thinking. I just don't *personally* know. And by the same token, I can't say others don't! I do believe in God, that there is some big cosmic reason and purpose for all this; but on a daily basis, all I can do is just simply spell God with two letter O's. But I'm just like anybody else; I hope that one day I'm genuinely shone otherwise, if that's truly the case."

He laughed humbly again.

They sat there, just looking at each other, thinking about it.

"So what was that with the vehicle following us? And those weapons you and they had? What was that all about? Were they trying to kill us? Was that part of all this?" Sarah finally began to let the questions flow.

"No, they weren't trying to kill us. What they shot at us, and what I used, was merely an EMP device that renders electrical systems nil for a time. It was intended to stop the vehicle, not destroy it, or us. They just wanted to get to me. You don't have anything to do with this, Sarah. I believe they were just trying to disable our vehicle to get to me, with the plan of taking me somewhere to try to persuade me toward their own ends. You just happened to be there at the time. They would have left you alone. They just wanted me."

Sarah looked at him with confusion.

Eliam picked up on her uncertainty.

"Seriously! Listen, this group I'm telling you about, the *Ankh*, they don't want Smartbrain technology disseminated on the Earth, among other things. They want to keep things as they are, as they have been. They know that the technology, and the ensuing future contact, will change everything, and they just don't want that. But, I can't let that happen. *We* can't let that happen."

"'We, who is 'we,' if you don't mind me asking?"

"There are many of us, Sarah. As I mentioned, people from Hoame have been coming here for a long time. Several at the university came here with me specifically for this mission, to share the technology. It's what's going to help position humanity for contact. You've seen yourself what it is capable of. You may not understand it yet, but once it is spread to the majority of the planet, Earth will no longer be isolated, backward, or alone. Contact will usher in a sense of belonging and purpose, unprecedented in your, or our, histories. Not to mention eventually help with your environmental and economic problems, at least over the long run.

"Your planet needs the connection, and in many ways, ours needs it even more. We have to realize we're all the same, and that all of us deserve equal freedoms and respect. This is what the Reform on Hoame is about. We're all part of a bigger purpose. And Sarah, just so you know, there are other planets out there with life on them, like ours. We've just recently come to know this for a fact. So this is just the start, Sarah. Everything will change from this point on!"

Sarah could see it in his face. She could feel his passion. And what's more, it strangely began to make sense to her.

"How long have you been here?" she then thought to ask.

Eliam looked deeply into her eyes.

"Several years this time, in Earth years, anyway."

"This time, what do you mean? And what do you mean, Earth years?"

"I've been here twice before. The first time was only for a few months. The other, a few years, like this one."

Sarah still looked confused.

He sought to answer her silent question.

"Time is not the same for everyone, Sarah."

Sarah still looked puzzled.

"Back several hundred years ago, what was the average lifespan of people on the Earth?" he asked pointedly.

She considered the question.

"Uhm, thirty-five, forty years perhaps, I think."

"Yeah, and now?"

Sarah thought about it.

"Eighty-five, ninety-five years."

Sarah wondered what he was getting at. Then it suddenly dawned on her.

Eliam saw it on her face. He answered without her even having to ask.

"I'm ninety-three, Sarah, it's about a three-point-two to one ratio," he said, smiling.

Sarah's eyebrows lifted.

"*Ninety-three?* And just how old is that, according to Earth time?" she asked.

"That would make me around twenty-nine, here," he responded, "though on Hoame people can live close to three hundred—in our years!"

"Wait a second...*three hundred years!?* You can live to be three hundred years old?" she asked, her voice rising in tone and volume.

He just smiled and nodded. And then a slightly devious look molded his face.

"And how old would Hoame time make you then, Sarah? How old are you, by the way?" he asked, catching her off guard, and laughing a little at the expression on her face.

Sarah was hesitant in answering as she calculated the ratio he'd given her a moment before.

"I...I'm twenty-eight, actually," she stated, hesitantly.

"Twenty-eight, which would make you about..."

"Nine years old, on Hoame...yeah, I can do the math!" she said.

Eliam smiled a large smile.

"Yes, that's about right. We've made some remarkable advances in health and medicine over the last several thousand years. But ironically, basic life and living has not changed much actually, if you look at our history, or regarding technology. You'd think over thousands of years we'd be beings of light or something, compared to people on Earth. But it doesn't work that way—advances seem to come quickly quite often, and then taper off.

"We're still basically just like everyone here. We live in homes with rooms and furniture. We have friends come over, and we cook out and go places for fun. We have hobbies, we work, and we play. We live the best we can, make the best choices we can, and then we grow old and die."

"*Nine...years...old*!?" she whispered again, astonished, as well as a little embarrassed.

"Don't worry, Sarah. It's all relative. Physiology on Hoame is remarkably similar; we've just found ways to slow the aging process, as you have on Earth, just to a larger degree. You'd still actually be a young, though mature woman on Hoame...and a very attractive one," he added.

They sat there and looked at each other.

"Listen, I'd like to show you some other things, Sarah, if you're interested."

"Like *what* things," she asked, tilting her head curiously.

"I want to show you my history, my planet, where I'm from. But, you'll need to use a set of B-CID's in order to do so. Actually, I think you'd find Hoame an intriguing place. Would you consider staying the evening with me, Sarah?"

Chapter 33

They left the barn and were now sitting in matching outdoor wicker chairs on the veranda off the back of the house. Eliam had made a small fire in a stone and ceramic fire pit situated in one corner, and they sat close to it and sipped wine and snacked on cheese and crackers and humus and grapes. It took a little time, but Sarah was getting over the initial shock of finding out that the Earth wasn't alone in the universe, and much more, the fact that this man she was attracted to wasn't one of its natives.

The two stared up into the darkening sky as they finished the last morsels of food. Sarah leaned back and relaxed. She was thinking about the improbability of all that she'd come to learn in such a short time, things beyond her imagination. And then suddenly she thought of those people who had tried to run them down earlier in the day. What had happened to them? Were they still there, hurt perhaps? Would they try again?

She was pondering asking Eliam about them when her thoughts were interrupted.

"I'll be back in a second," Eliam said abruptly.

He rose and went inside, returning in mere seconds with a small container. Sarah knew what was inside.

"Eliam, those people in the SUV that tried to run us down today, what do you think happened to them?" she asked bluntly.

He looked at her and considered the question.

"I don't know. I called it in when we got back to the house—while I was getting the First Aid Kit. I don't know what happened to them."

Sarah thought about what he'd just said. She hadn't known he'd called it in, but she did remember him saying he would. Her next question seemed more important.

"Well, whatever happened to them, I hope they're alright. But, my question is, do you think they'll try again, or that maybe someone else will? What's to keep them from coming here, or trying again on the way back tomorrow, or any other time? I mean, if they tried to get at you once, won't they try again?"

Eliam looked into her eyes, appearing to share her concern.

"Honestly, no! I don't believe they will. They know our guard is up now, and *Sanguine* will let me know long before they even get close. They know this. The *Ankh* and their people are resourceful, but so are we. That's why we're not running off and hiding in some hole somewhere. Trust me, Sarah, we're safe. They won't bother us. And once we get through this last phase of the program, and the tech goes mainstream, it'll all be out in the open. They'll have little choice but to just live with the outcome, as they've had to do with numerous other things the Reform has brought about. They may be dogmatic and determined, but they're not exactly stupid. They'll take their place in history."

Sarah thought about his words.

"What about Professor Dunes? Do you think *they* got to him?"

Eliam didn't expect the question.

He appeared to think about it before answering.

"Let's not go there right now. It is what it is. We have to go on! The Professor lived for something important, for a purpose. Let me show you what I was talking about, what we're fighting for, what *he* was fighting for! Okay?"

He looked at her and then touched her arm gently. He then gave her a humble, yet optimistic smile.

"Yeah, okay!" she said.

Eliam opened the container, pulled out a B-CID and handed it to Sarah.

"This looks different than the ones we've been using," she said with curiosity in her voice as she took it into her hands.

"Yes. That's because it is. It's a more highly advanced model, actually. You'll see what I mean shortly. Put it on."

Sarah put it on her head. Eliam reached over and adjusted it for her.

"Where's yours?" she asked, noting that there was only one in the box.

"Well, that's another thing I was going to tell you. Mine is already in my head, actually. I have an implant. Most of us do, Sarah."

Sarah's eyes widened.

"Really?"

"Yeah, let me show you. First we'll meet in the anteroom, and then you'll open the link in your VF titled, *Hoame*. I prepared it just for this purpose, for sharing, which I didn't exactly think I'd be doing quite so soon. But anyway, it's a history and an overview, plus a bunch of personal things I've thrown in about where I'm from, the Reform, our accomplishments over the years, a future prospectus, of sorts. It's not real long. Is that okay? Are you ready?"

Sarah looked at him, thinking for a moment, but then nodded her head.

Together they entered the B-CID's anteroom.

This time, it was the equivalent of being high up in an enclosed observation deck at a grand sports park. Out in the distance were windows of choices which all an observer had to do was choose, and then off they went on a journey of discovery.

Sarah was immediately enthralled with the new experience.

• • • • • • •

"*Sanguine, please initiate exploratory scan: 'Brain-ruse', of subject Sarah Whiting,*" Eliam Zaris communicated his thoughts silently to his ship's central processing character.

"*Scanning initiated, Eliam.*"

"Thank you, Sanguine. Please let me know the results without delay upon conclusion. If residuals are present, Management Protocol Eras will need to begin immediately, upon my authority. After scan is complete, please also consign customary neuronal-tracing protocols to subject. Proceed and advise. Thank you, Sanguine."

"I understand, Eliam. I will advise…"

....

"Wow! That was amazing Eliam. Such a rich history, so much to take in," Sarah said, upon returning to the B-CID's anteroom with Eliam.

"Yes there is, isn't there?"

"This B-CID is amazing, too. I can't believe it!"

"Yeah, a little more real than what you've been used to, huh?"

"Yeah, that's an underestimation! So there are different levels of these!" She touched the device on her head in illustration. "I guess that makes sense. And yours is implanted! Wow! I don't know if I'd want that, but it must be convenient."

"Yeah, it is. It's calibrated and encoded to my brain, yet infinitely customizable, and can last nearly a lifetime. It can have its bad side, though."

"Yeah, how so?"

"It's always there when you want it, whether you want it, or need it. It's like anything else; it can be a blessing, or a curse."

"What do you mean?"

"Escape from reality! It can be like a drug, Sarah. You end up wanting it all the time. And for some, reality just isn't good enough anymore. That's what happened to the *Ankh*. They actually live inside their made-up realities, more often than not, and they've become oblivious to what's really happening around them. But, enough of that, I have another idea! One you might find…*entertaining*!"

Eliam got a strange, slightly ominous look on his face.

Sarah noticed the odd gaze.

"*What?* What are you thinking?" Sarah asked, now looking sideways at him.

Eliam looked up to a distant window. He then chose it consciously and enlarged it for Sarah to focus on as well. It was of a beach, complete with a warm sunset, a cool breeze, and all the privacy they could want.

Sarah noted the exceptionally beautiful setting.

She felt herself take a deep breath.

She knew what he was getting at with this. But something in her was surprised. It'd only been a short time since Professor Dunes had disappeared and left the message of his apparently self-induced demise. Wasn't Eliam's mind still occupied with it? He was family to him. But then again, after all they'd been through in such a short time, perhaps some level of release was exactly what he needed most. Suddenly, she thought the same for herself.

"I'd say it's about time!" Sarah whispered, her mind strangely pushing all other thoughts away.

She swiftly reached out and put her arms around him, and then kissed him hard.

Soon they were in the bedroom and on the beach at the same instant. The cross-sensations from their B-CIDs as well as their own bodies were nearly overwhelming, but at that particular moment, neither wanted any other reality than that one.

Chapter 34

Eliam drove Sarah home the next morning after a breakfast of scrambled eggs and fruit. Both were in a blissful state and would have preferred to just continue being together in their own little reality, but Eliam had gotten a call from the university and had to go in. He didn't elaborate as to why, but Sarah suspected that he and his other expatriates needed to collaborate on their proposed strategies concerning what was going on. Sarah fully understood.

The drive home was a little unnerving. They were constantly looking around and behind them. But the trip proved entirely uneventful. They pulled up to her condo, kissed twice in the car—one a peck, the second a passionate reminder of the previous night. She got out, both said their goodbyes, and Eliam drove off.

Sarah was relieved to enter her place, now feeling more or less safe and secure. Upon settling back into her own daily routine, Sarah started her morning as she usually did. She made herself some coffee, slipped into some old lounge-around clothes, and then sat down at her desk and started checking her website and emails.

Everything was as it should be. She even got a lead on a job it appeared, as she read the subject line of the email: *You've come highly recommended: need some quick research done*. When she opened it she didn't recognize the sender, but she did know the people that did the recommending. It was a group of lawyers that she'd done several small projects for recently. Which lawyer of the five-person firm did the recommending wasn't precisely stated, but Sarah was glad to have the reference nonetheless.

The name on the email was a Mr. Xavier M. Bolt. A phone number was listed under the email signature. Sarah thought about it. The email said 'quick research,' and it was mentioned in the body of the note that because of the short notice, they would pay triple the fee. Sarah was hesitant. She really didn't need the money now since she was nearly through the program. But, then again, it was also her reputation on the line for the future, and the law firm had paid her very well. It might mean a favor to them for her to follow through with someone they know. She at least decided to call the number and see what it was all about.

Sarah listened to two consecutive rings before someone answered.

"Hello."

"Hello, this is Sarah Whiting. I'm calling in response to an email requesting my services, I…"

"Yes…yes, Ms. Whiting. Yes. Thank you for calling. I'm Xavier M. Bolt, the person who sent the email. I'm sure you're probably very busy, as most everyone is these days. So I appreciate your swift response. I'll get right to the point. I'm Director of Investigation and Research for a large, yet private investment group called Sun-Cluster Equity Investments. We're quite busy with numerous projects on the horizon. One of these projects is a recent one out here on your west coast. My job as Director, as you are probably deducing as we speak, is to research potential companies and people that we will be partnering with."

"Yes, I see," Sarah said.

"Well, as I said, we are extremely busy and as it stands, short staffed, so we're opting to apply some local talent to help us, you see. My request to you is a simple one. We have several people on our list out here of which we require thorough background checks. Time-frame is imperative for us, but the work is standard fare: background, history, affiliations, authentications, etc. Well, that's about it, Ms. Whiting. Would you be interested? As I stated, we are in a bit of a time quandary, and we're offering triple the fees, if you're interested. And my apologies for being so succinct, but as I said, we are all very busy."

Sarah was thinking about it as quickly as she could. Triple her fees. She'd never had that offered before. It was easy work; she'd done it a hundred times over. The project was on hold and she could knock out this kind of work in a few days, finish it up in an evening if she needed. Also, apparently she was in competition with other locals for the opportunity, so this would be a good chance to shine, especially if the group is expanding its influence to the west coast.

"Uh, yes, I suppose I can squeeze this in on my calendar. I'm very busy as well, but I believe I can make this happen for you, and I will give assurances as to any deadlines once I've noted the case depth, of course. Yes, I'll be glad to review it, Mr. Bolt."

"Excellent…that's excellent. This is really appreciated. I would like to meet personally, today if at all possible, standard non-disclosure is required, a few other legal items our company requires, and then I can release the information needed."

"That sounds fine, sir. Just give me your office address and a time; I can meet with you this morning, if you'd like."

"Well, that might be a problem, you see. As I said we're moving on this particular project extremely quickly—one downside of the company I work for, they're good, but they are at times quite capricious, always wanting to gain that little edge, as you can imagine. Anyway, we've actually just arrived, and our office suites are still being prepared. Forgive me, but would you be able to meet me at our hotel. We can convene our business at the hotel restaurant; I'll actually buy you a quick lunch, if you find you can afford the time. Or, I can see about securing a small private convention room here at the hotel, if that would better suffice."

Sarah hesitated for a moment, thinking about it. But, it made sense.

"Uh, certainly, I see no problems with that. The hotel restaurant would be alright. No need to acquire a meeting room for this. That would be fine. And the hotel?" she finished.

"The Harrison Executive, on the Lake, next to the Golf Course—golf is one of my hobbies. Do you play?" he asked, off the subject.

Sarah was momentarily distracted by the question.

"Uhm, no, well, I have several times, but no, I'm not very good. I find it quite frustrating, actually, but I can definitely see the attraction," she said, trying to be congenial.

"Yes, frustrating *is* the word." The man laughed heartily. "Much like life, wouldn't you say? You think you got your game going, and then out of the blue, something unexpected and ridiculous happens, and you end up off the course, or in a pit. Probably should give it up, but I just can't quit playing! Anyway, how does noon work for your schedule, would that be alright?"

"Yes, noon will be fine."

"Good, I'll arrive a few minutes early and secure a table. I'll leave my name with the hostess, and they can direct you. Sound alright?"

"Yes, that sounds great. I'll see you at noon then, Mr. Bolt. Thank you."

"Thank you, Ms. Whiting. I look forward to our business together. I'll see you then. Goodbye, Ms. Whiting."

"Goodbye, Mr. Bolt."

Sarah hung up the phone. She was thinking about the game of golf. She actually hated the game, for the very same reasons the man had mentioned. Too frustrating! She put it out of her mind and started planning her day.

•••••••

Sarah dressed business-casual: skirt and blouse in shades of blue, mid-heels, studs and an ultra-thin necklace, no rings. She carried her tablet/notebook and a small matching sling-purse. She entered the restaurant with a smooth, confident walk, addressing the hostess station attendant with her information. The hostess nodded and looked at her seating schedule.

"Yes, a Mr. Bolt. Please, follow me. We have your table right over here."

Sarah followed the hostess. Within a moment they rounded a partition and Sarah saw an attractive middle-aged man in a blue business suit seated at a table in front of a large window which looked out and down two stories into the street. The man noticed her arrival and immediately stood.

"Ms. Whiting," he said, smiling.

"Mr. Bolt."

"I appreciate your coming, thank you."

They both acknowledged the hostess; she turned and left.

"Not a problem."

"Please, have a seat." He motioned for her to sit across the table.

They both sat down and scooted their chairs up a little.

Immediately a waiter approached them.

"Hello, I'm Vicilli, I will be serving you. Here are your menus. We have a host of Italian fare today for our specials, they're right there on the insert. The shrimp linguini is exceptional, in my opinion. In the meantime, may I get you some drinks? Miss? Sir?"

Mr. Bolt acknowledged Sarah with a nod and a hand gesture, indicating for her to go first.

"I'll just have iced tea, please, thank you, unsweetened."

"I'll have water and a cup of coffee, I think."

"Alright! I'll get those for you while you look over the menus. And I'll be back shortly," Vicilli said, smiling. He then turned and quickly walked away.

"Please, order whatever you like. I do sincerely appreciate your coming and meeting with me on such short notice," Mr. Bolt said again, cordially.

"Thank you, but, I think I'll just have tea. I had a late breakfast, and I'll be going running early this afternoon, so I'll be fine with this. But I do appreciate the offer," Sarah said, smiling at the man.

Sarah took a moment and noted the man's looks. He was handsome, she thought. He had dark hair, tanned features, a rugged, yet proportional face with a slightly dimpled chin. Seemingly athletic, no middle-aged belly, and he had good posture, presenting himself with a high degree of confidence in his dark blue suit and eggshell tie.

The waiter returned with their drinks, serving them with professional finesse and alacrity.

"Miss, sir, so what can I get for you today?"

"Nothing for me, thanks. Tea is fine."

"Are you sure?" Mr. Bolt asked one more time. Sarah nodded. He then ordered for himself.

"I think I would just like an appetizer, please. Mussels on the half, thank you, cold, with a small side of bleu cheese dressing."

The waiter looked at the man oddly, as did Sarah, but both quickly returned their faces to a more agreeable countenance.

"Certainly, coming right up," Vicilli said, writing down the order.

"And just in case, please bring a small vegetable tray, and an assortment of dips, thanks. My guest may change her mind."

Sarah and Mr. Bolt made eye contact and both smiled cordially.

"Certainly." He wrote that down too and then left them alone.

"I love seafood," Mr. Bolt said. "Where I come from, there are lots of oceans, but most of the seafood available leaves much to be desired," he said matter-of-factly. "So, shall we get to it?"

Sarah nodded, repositioning her tablet, suddenly slightly nervous.

"Ms. Whiting. I have to say, I was not exactly accurate with you during our phone conversation. You see, I am not in actuality offering you a job, a paying job, anyway. And I deeply regret that particular part about the triple fee. I was encouraged to use the tactic in order to help to more quickly facilitate our meeting. However, I do hope you will follow through with the research and investigation I had previously mentioned, in truth for your sake, more so than ours."

He finished and just stared at her with an odd look on his face.

Sarah was floored. His words raced through her mind a dozen times in a mere few seconds.

"I…I don't think I understand," she muttered.

"Well, I am with Sun-Cluster Equity Investments, and we do wish you to do some research on your own, but again, it's mostly for your benefit, not ours. Ms. Whiting…this is concerning Eliam Zaris. We know that you know him. But, I should tell you now, he goes by many other names, and he's not who you think he is."

Sarah was so stunned she suddenly couldn't breathe.

The man peered at her, apparently reading the expression on her face.

"I imagined you might react this way. Please, let me continue. You owe it to yourself for me to do so, I assure you!"

"Owe it to myself? Why would that be? What are you talking about? I…"

"Perfectly understandable, Ms. Whiting, this may be quite difficult for you, depending on your relationship with the man, but if you would give me just a few more moments."

"Well…I don't know, I…I don't know who you are, or what you think you can accomplish by…"

"Eliam Zaris, Ms. Whiting, is what you would typically call a charlatan! He is a fraud, a scammer, and a shark. He has warrants for his arrest in more than one European country, all under different names and aliases, and he nearly brought down the company I work for because of his dubious business practices, his devilish shrewdness, and his rampant deceit."

The man appeared to realize he was getting overly animated, so he went silent for a moment and seemed to gain his composure.

Sarah just stared at him with utter disbelief.

"Ms. Whiting, the people at my company—not just its owners and Board of Directors, but the employees as well—

once trusted this man, Eliam Zaris, but were nonetheless permanently hurt by him. And, he did it in such a way that legal action is beyond any consequence we might have tried to subject him to. However, the company I work for is a good one, Ms. Whiting; its foundations are built on integrity and family values, which Mr. Zaris took advantage of. Because of this, I have been sanctioned by my company to somehow find a way to stop this from happening to others. And so it is that I have happened upon you, Ms. Whiting."

Sarah just continued staring at the man.

"We lost knowledge of Mr. Zaris' whereabouts for quite some time, but to our good fortune, our efforts at finding his most recent locality again proved fruitful, and about a month ago we determined exactly where he is—here, in California, Ms. Whiting. Since then, some associates and I have been gathering reconnaissance information, and you were observed to be, to whatever degree, involved with him. And as much as this hurts me—and possibly our future efforts if you take all this the wrong way—I felt solitarily compelled to pass on a warning to you about this man. I have two daughters, Ms. Whiting; I'm merely acting as a father would. Please forgive me my straightforwardness here."

"He…he hurt this company of yours? Its employees, how? I mean, how could he have done that?"

"Finance is a tricky business, Ms. Whiting, especially when it comes to the development and marketing of innovation and invention. How, you ask? Well, in short he employed numerous tactics: under-the-table investing with others' resources, specifically inverse derivatives trading, there was testing fraud, prototype cost falsification, fabricated marketing research results, out and out fraud, lies and more lies, and the list goes on. All were brilliantly done through identity theft, and power base manipulation so others would be left holding the smoking gun. It matters little now; the damage has been done. But, it doesn't mean that it has to be allowed to continue."

Sarah felt sick to her stomach.

"Listen, Ms. Whiting, please answer a few simple questions for me."

Sarah nodded, reluctantly.

"Has Mr. Zaris ever led you to believe that he...that he perhaps was a child prodigy, in the fields of Theoretical Physics, or some other scientific endeavor?"

Sarah looked wholly confused. She shook her head, no.

"Has he ever hinted to you that he was, say, a wayward time-traveler, or perhaps from another planet? Or that he was some great genius inventor-type being schooled by beings from other dimensions? Or possibly..."

Sarah immediately reacted. Her face heated and her eyes dropped to the table.

"Yes," Sarah spoke softly, not really wanting to.

"Which?" he asked.

"Another...planet."

"Let me guess, he probably told you he was from this other planet and that he was here to help, to share technology, to help mankind *change* perhaps, maybe even help with first contact; he probably also mentioned that *he's* the good guy, and that there are a bunch of bad guys on this other planet that want to stop him, or something along that order?"

He noted the look on her face, studied her reactions.

Sarah nodded slowly.

"Let me guess again. I'll bet he even showed you his little spaceship prop, didn't he?"

Sarah was awestruck, nearly in tears.

"You're probably wondering how I surmised all this. However, Ms. Whiting, I didn't guess any of it. I knew because this is not the first time he's used this deception to gain others' trust, and support for his insidious schemes. Eliam Zaris is quite wealthy, Ms. Whiting, he has the resources to pull off just about any ruse he wishes to engage in—whether for love, or money, or power. Not to mention he reportedly has in his repertoire of resources, the dark connections he needs to acquire all the latest drugs and medical concoctions to manipulate people's minds and behaviors, if needed.

"I am so sorry Ms. Whiting, so very sorry. I sincerely want to help. That is in fact why I am here. But, I have to ask that you not mention our meeting to him, or anyone that he might come into contact with. As I said, I solitarily chose to bring about this encounter simply because I feel so sorry for you and your colleagues' imminent state of affairs. But, if I or any of my associate's efforts are known, then all hope will be lost of stopping this man from doing this to other people again. Do you understand what I saying?"

Sarah nodded jerkily.

"Listen, Ms. Whiting, I don't expect you to take my word for all this. Please, take a moment and review…this."

He reached into his case that was sitting on the chair next to him, retrieving a mid-size tablet. He then initiated it and quickly accessed some pre-chosen tabs.

"Here," he said, handing the device to her.

Sarah took it and slowly started to swipe through the information. She saw file upon file of news stories regarding what he'd just spoken about. Several had pictures of people, and in many were images of Eliam Zaris. One specific story that crossed Sarah's attention was regarding a man named Arthur T. Pendaghast—the image was that of Eliam Zaris, though with a different hairstyle. Sarah skimmed the story, but she was able to gather its most defining details: fraud, identity theft, scandalous financial deals and even suspicion of murder, though Arthur T. Pendaghast had apparently vanished from the face of the earth and was still at large.

Sarah was confused, and disgusted.

"And please, take this with you. It contains numerous traceable bits of information that I am sure will also corroborate what I am saying, and aid your own search of the facts." He then handed her a thin, manila folder. "It is yours, please take it. Do the research on your own, and you will see. And…and perhaps you can help us stop this."

Sarah looked at him and then the folder.

"Help…you? How?"

"Information Ms. Whiting, basic information. I'm sure this has been a lot to digest, but I'm thoroughly relieved now that I was able to talk with you. And if you don't mind, I'd like to ask you a few other questions."

Sarah kept looking at the information on the tablet, unbelieving, yet deeply questioning what she was seeing. When Mr. Bolt's last comments finally registered, she looked back up and asked, "What questions?"

Suddenly the waiter, Vicilli, showed up with their order. Both Mr. Bolt and Sarah abruptly stopped talking and looked up. Vicilli served them and then asked if there was anything else. Mr. Bolt said no, as Sarah shook her head. He then left.

"What is your involvement with this man, and with the university? What type of prospective business opportunity is he trying to pull off, and how far along is it?" he asked, taking a shell from the plate, dipping it into the bleu cheese dressing, and then slurping it into his awaiting mouth.

Sarah watched the man for a brief moment. She then turned back to her thoughts, disgusted at the food combination, the way the man ate, and at this whole thing. She didn't want to answer, didn't want to speak at all, but felt she had to.

"He…it's technology that will—*does*—link the brain with computers. And it's no scam. I've used it myself. It's amazing! But I'm under contract to not discuss it. I can't discuss it."

Mr. Bolt chewed his mouthful. He then wiped his lips with a napkin, not taking his eyes off Sarah.

"I see. Technology? Brain computer interface? Interesting. With the goal of marketing in the works, I'd imagine? Big investors. Lots of money? At what phase, I find myself wanting to ask."

Sarah sort of nodded, but didn't say anymore. She felt sick.

Suddenly, Mr. Bolt seemed distracted. He pulled his eyes off of Sarah and then seemed to look at nothing in particular in the air. He squinted slightly, and then seemed to move his lips as if softly saying something. He then looked back at Sarah and regained his focus. Within a second, the man's phone rang.

"Excuse me, I must take this."

The man retrieved his phone, turned sideways in his chair and began a brief conversation with someone on the other end. It was an exchange that Sarah couldn't make any sense of at all: half sentences, acronyms, and other things she supposed were of the vernacular of their particular business. She continued looking at the tablet as Mr. Bolt talked, noticing that he kept looking back and forth at her and the tablet as he conversed, yet oddly looking away as she would look up. The conversation lasted only a few minutes. He said goodbye, and then put the phone away.

"My apologies! Listen, Ms. Whiting, I understand non-disclosure, but it would really help us if we knew what this man was doing. Where is this technology being developed, and where are the test prototypes being kept? At the university…somewhere else? Are they individually operated, independent units, or are they a collective of remotes linked to a core processor?"

The man seemed to become animated again. Sarah noticed and she quickly answered his deluge of questions.

"I…I'm sorry, I can't say anymore. I shouldn't say any more. Mr. Bolt, I don't understand all that's going on. I need time to think. This…information, I'll look at this information and think about it. As you said it's a lot to digest. I…"

"Yes, I'm sure it is. You're involved with this man, Ms. Whiting, and it may go much deeper than you might be aware of. I'd hate to see someone like you get caught up in an ordeal such as this, where there might be criminal associations assigned, leading to possible implications and indictments. Cooperation is my best suggestion to you. Do you have any indication as to what the time-frame may be regarding this technology, regarding its release to the public? Do you know, is the government involved in any way regarding this, or is it merely private at this point?"

Sarah was dumbfounded. Cooperation? Criminal associations? She was now overwhelmed with confusion.

"I…*timeframe*? I…I don't know. Yes, there is someone there who is from the government, I believe, has been there, on numerous occasions to observe. But, I don't know why, or what's going on. I…I shouldn't say anymore. I…"

"Do you have a name, Ms. Whiting? This government person might be approaching all this the same way we are, and maybe it would be a good idea to ally ourselves with he and his agency. *Do* you have a name, Ms. Whiting?"

Sarah sat there, silent; her head was spinning.

"Uhm, Deltray? I think…I don't remember a last name. Zack…Za, I can't remember. Listen, I have to go. I need time to think!" Sarah said in a firm and resolute voice.

Mr. Bolt saw the edge his lunch guest was teetering on. He finished another bite of his appetizer, wiped his mouth again, and then sat back in his chair, taking a sip of his coffee.

"Well, I understand, Ms. Whiting," he said, his face molded by contrasting thoughts and emotions. "I hope I have helped in some way, even if that way isn't exactly evident at this particular moment."

He stood.

"And I'm doubly sorry, but I, too, have to leave now. Please take all this to heart—and mind—Ms. Whiting, for both our sakes. I just hope you're not too involved where you might have to endure any unpleasant future implications regarding what's happening with this man. You have my number; please call if you feel you can assist to any greater degree. You'd only be helping yourself. Good day, Ms. Whiting."

The man pulled a fifty-dollar bill out of his wallet and threw it on the table. He picked up his case, smiled once more, and then turned and left.

Sarah just sat there and stared at cold mussels on the half and a container of sour bleu cheese dressing as a portion dripped over the container's edge and onto the tablecloth.

Sarah wanted to throw up.

Chapter 35

She sat at her desk at home into the wee hours of the night running search after search, bringing up every conceivable newsworthy article relating to the man known as Arthur T. Pendaghast, and she read every one of them. This Mr. Bolt was apparently right. At least it seemed. Every image she could pull up of the man was an image of Eliam. How could this be, Sarah kept asking herself, dizzy with disbelief.

It certainly appeared that Eliam and this man were one in the same. But she also knew that according to her own measure of authenticity, a mere picture was utterly inconclusive. She'd known that much from her years of work as a researcher. Pictures could be changed, and so could anything said in any article or news bite. She had to find out for sure. Something about this Mr. Bolt didn't seem right, but she just couldn't pin it down.

She then decided on doing something she hadn't done in a very long time—find some back doors to sneak into. And using the algorithm that her father had written many years ago to do that very thing was the only option she knew to get the answers she wanted. She'd told herself numerous times that she'd never use it again, but then she'd never gotten rid of it either, which she'd considered many times. But, she hadn't, and right at that moment, she was glad she hadn't.

Sarah had always supposed that her dad's earlier college life, when he was suspected of being a "hacker" by the very school he attended, might have contributed to his never getting a chance at being an astronaut, but neither of them ever knew that that was the case. But it had always been suspected.

The only way Sarah had even known about it was after her mother had died and she had been going through some of her things, which just happened to include documents about it, as well as a copy of the algorithm itself, which she'd suspected her mother had kept for reasons unknown, and probably against her dad's wishes. But Sarah had found it and had never told her father of the fact. She'd used it once, quite some time ago, with great success, but it had scared her to no end, and so she had kept it in her little personal fire-safe ever since.

If there were ever a reason to use it, the time was now. But she had to be careful. Much time had passed since it was created, and it might be so outdated that it wouldn't even work. But that didn't mean she wouldn't try. The trick was to set up the program on a random, non-traceable laptop, somewhere at some remote location, perhaps at a school or public access point, and let it run its searches anonymously.

If it worked it would find the backdoors to most any targeted location, bypassing their security protocols by hitching a ride on the actual power cables that supplied the electricity to the data storage devices themselves. It was an ingenious design, not wholly original, but nonetheless effective. Most low-tech security platforms, which were the variety she was assuming she needed to access, would not have sufficient protection from her dad's program. At least that's what she hoped.

Sarah began planning, and the first thing she needed to do was to go shopping for a laptop somewhere, and be very discreet about it. Perhaps a second-hand place, or thrift shop, she thought.

•••••••

The next morning Sarah arose early and went into town to shop. It wasn't long before she found what she needed and was back at her home setting it up. She considered where would be a good place to link in to a hard line, purposely avoiding any wireless connection. She decided on, of all places, the public laundry room at the condo-plex across the street from hers.

It had hardwired hookups for the patrons to use, as well as wireless, she knew. She figured she could get it set up and running and then hide the unit behind a washing machine or somewhere, and let it run all night. She'd perhaps put a tag on the wire saying that it was a diagnostic link with the service, or whatever, and to not disturb. Then she could retrieve the hidden laptop the next day and pull the data off it. It should work, and if it appeared it was going to be a problem, then she would just leave it there locked up under a password, which most people couldn't bypass even if they decided to try.

She was reasonably sure that if it was found out, no one would be inclined to pay to have a security professional attempt to bypass the security of the old junk unit anyway. They'd just end up tossing it in the trash when they found they couldn't make it work.

She decided to do it that night.

But then she thought, what if by doing this she found out that it was all true and Eliam wasn't who he said he was. What would she do? Suddenly, she wondered how gullible she might actually have been. Did she really believe he was from another planet? What was she thinking?

But then again, she had experienced the technology to its fullest, and it was truly out-of-this-world stuff, and she *had* actually seen something above his barn, and later seen, what for all intents and purposes, appeared to be a spaceship, at least it seemed to be a spaceship, a talking spaceship at that. And all the history, and images, and information he'd showed her. What was that? Was it all fake? Merely concocted? Just to get her into bed, or whatever? Could that have been the case all along?

Sarah's mind swirled to the point of making her dizzy as she finished setting up the laptop. She was just getting ready to set it aside and fix herself something to eat when her phone beeped. She grabbed it up quickly. It was Eliam.

Sarah froze.

She just let it beep, as her head and heart raced.

....

Sarah's phone beeped several more times throughout the afternoon; two were Eliam again, and one was a number she hadn't recognized; she didn't answer any of them. Sarah was slowly thinking herself into a tizzy. She wasn't sure what to do, much less how to even speak to Eliam when the time came. And what about the program, she thought. What should she do about that when they were called to resume? Go back? Finish? She didn't know. She cried about it, sulked about it, and even punched a door because she felt so angry about it.

Sarah was sitting at her desk in the early evening when her phone beeped again. She recognized the number. It was the university. She hesitated but decided to answer it after the third beep.

"Hello," she muttered.

"Hello, Sarah Whiting?"

"Yes, this is Sarah."

"Hi Sarah, this is Anna again, from Earthbridge. We wanted to extend our apologies regarding the delay in the program, but under the circumstances, we had little choice. However, we wanted to let you know that we will resume again day after tomorrow, Thursday morning at 9:00 am; will we be able to confirm your attendance at this time?"

Sarah stayed silent for moment, thinking hard, but then she spoke in a hoarse, choppy voice.

"Yes…I…I'll be there. Thank you for calling, Anna."

"Alright then, great, we'll expect to see you at 9:00 am. Thank you, Sarah. If there are any changes, we'll let you know promptly. Thanks again, Sarah. Goodbye."

"Goodbye," Sarah replied in a soft voice as her decision settled in her mind.

She hit the button, ending the call and then plopped back down into the chair she had been sitting in, once more in deep thought.

She about leaped out of her skin when the phone unexpectedly beeped again.

It was Eliam.

She hesitated, but against her better judgment she chose to answer it.

"Hello," she muttered, feeling like she couldn't breathe.

"Sarah? This is Eliam, are you all right? I've been trying to call you all day. You haven't been answering. Is everything alright, are you okay?"

Sarah hesitated again, but she knew she had to talk.

"Yeah…*yeah*, I'm okay. I'm just…occupied with work. Uhm, how are you?" she found herself asking, trying to divert the attention from her so she could think, trying to sound as even-minded as possible.

"I'm okay. I've been real occupied here. The program is starting up again Thursday morning. I see they've called you and you've confirmed. That's good. Listen, I'd like to see you this evening. How about dinner? We can go over what to expect in this last week. It's going to go pretty fast. The Board has decided to press on, even under the circumstances, and move forward even quicker than previously planned. In fact, I'll be here until after seven working, but I can pick you up after that. How about Mexican again? Does that sound good?"

Sarah was choked for words. She struggled with what to say. Somehow she decided that she had to maintain her distance, at least until she could confirm what she'd learned, or not.

"No, actually…I've got a lot of work to do, too. I…I've kind of let things go these past few weeks, and they've seemed to catch up with me. I need to work, too, sorry!"

"Really?" Eliam replied, a little set back from her response. "Okay, sure. I understand. What are you working on?"

"Oh, just the usual stuff, research and more research, nothing exciting here, just need to get it done."

"Yeah, I understand. Hey, how about tomorrow then? It'd have to be late in the day as well, but the offer stands, *the Blue Lobster* maybe, and a quiet evening?"

"Uhm, probably not, no, not tomorrow either. I've got other things…to do. Dad! I'm spending some time with him, and we have some other things to go over with the home, some upcoming things we need to go over, plan, things like that…part of it will be in the evening, after their dinner…kind of a social thing they're having. I need to be there. Sorry!"

Eliam went silent. Something wasn't right. He thought about it for a moment, but then decided to not mention what was in his mind.

"Okay, sure. I see. Well, maybe we can get together Thursday after we all get back together. Maybe then?"

"Uhm, yeah, maybe, we'll see." She tried to sound interested, but again she was having a hard time and she just knew Eliam suspected something wasn't right. But, it was what it was. "Okay! Yeah, hey, I've got to go. So I...I guess I'll see you, uh...Thursday morning."

He answered, but it was slow coming out, "Yeah, okay, Sarah. I'll see you Thursday morning then. Uhm, well, bye, I guess for now."

"Okay, bye Eliam!"

Sarah hung up.

Tears filled her eyes.

Chapter 36

Deltray Zacchaeus was home and alone as usual.

The call came through in the late afternoon.

He wasn't particularly excited about having to join up with those people at the university again. Perhaps it was the job, he considered, or maybe just the people. Actually, once he thought about it, it wasn't either; most of the people were nice, and highly professional, he had to admit. They were just reacting as a lot of people do when subjected to the scrutiny of some government watchdog agency.

He knew that for a fact, having been on the other end many times when he was the one working for the particular company being scrutinized. Nobody likes to be under a spotlight all the time, much less a microscope. But that was the job and he took it seriously. He often wondered if that was a mistake on his part. But at least he did some good, protecting people. At least that's what he told himself.

And along with that, the money wasn't really all that bad either, he thought, and occasionally he did get to be part of some amazing discoveries, even if he was the one picking everything and everybody apart on the way to that end. This one did seem to be different from all the others, though. It definitely had the potential to be, anyway. He was still thinking about it all when the doorbell rang.

"Coming," he said as he got up from the comfortable chair in his living room. "Yes, who is it?" he asked through the intercom.

"Complex Security, sir. Is this Mr. Zacchaeus?"

"Yes, Deltray Zacchaeus. What is it? Security? What's going on?" He spoke the words as he looked through the peephole at the uniformed man.

"Sir, we're going door-to-door to let all the residents know of a potential hazard that may affect the people on this side of the complex. There've been several call-ins reporting a gas smell. Have you noticed any smell, sir, coming from, or around your unit?"

"No...no, I can't say I have."

"Good, thank you for the information. If you do, today or anytime in the future, please call the main security office. It would be much appreciated."

"Yeah, of course, certainly, I'll be glad to do that."

"No need to open the door sir, but I do need to request confirmation-of-contact by signature. I'll just slide it under the door if you could do that for me sir? I'd appreciate it, thanks."

Deltray Zacchaeus saw a half-filled out, paper signature roster slip under the door at his feet. He reached down for it, and as he did he realized he did notice a slight hint of a gaseous smell near the floor.

"Hey, now that you mention it, I do smell gas!" he said, taking a deep breath through his nose, and then again to be sure.

The sudden potential threat motivated him to get the opinion of the security officer. Deltray then unlocked and opened the door.

"Do you smell that too?" he asked as he opened the door fully.

The officer knelt slightly and curiously sniffed the air. As he did he inched his way into the condo, sniffing and looking around.

"Yeah, I do smell something. But I think it's this..." the uniformed man then held up a small spray canister of some sort, and at the same time stuck the small needle-tipped injector into Deltray's neck with his other hand.

"What?" was all Deltray Zacchaeus could say before passing out and falling to the floor.

The security officer then took off his hat as he gently shut the door.

Chapter 37

Sarah shivered as she stood there on the beach at the water's edge. It was cold, and the vaporous, biting wind seemed to pass right through her. She held her arms over her bare breasts, which afforded little protection from the elements. She panned her gaze from left to right as she noted the brownish flat water that reached out to the oddly distant horizon. She could see numerous islands out there; their vegetation-covered tall hills reaching up into the air. They appeared hazy and vague, due to the distance, she thought.

"Go into the water, Sarah!"

She heard the comment, uttered by the familiar voice. She turned her head to see Eliam Zaris standing there several meters away. He had a blank look on his face.

"Go into the water, Sarah!" he said again.

Sarah looked out beyond the shore once more, and then down, now finding herself standing ankle-deep in the shadowy liquid. A chill went up her spine from its sudden coldness.

"Go in the water, Sarah. Trust me!" he said again.

Sarah heard him, looked back at his emotionless face, and then back down at her feet. She was now knee-deep in the water and she felt an odd current pulling at her legs. The force of it was surprising, and she realized that it took every effort from her leg muscles to withstand its pull.

"Trust me, Sarah!" she heard him say again.

Once again, she looked over to him and then back at the cold, slimy, brackish water that was now rising up to her hips. She then tried with all her might to step backwards and get out of the water, but she couldn't move her legs. Her breathing became hard and labored, and she whaled her arms around as if trying desperately to find something to grab onto to help pull her back, but there was nothing there. She had to try harder. She had to try harder. Sarah struggled as hard as she could, and then she heard the voice again. Her heart pounded and her head swirled.

"It's not real, Sarah! Trust me!" she heard him say.

Suddenly Sarah's body was almost completely under, her mouth and nose and forehead the only parts that were not submerged. Sarah struggled with all her effort to keep herself above the surface so she could breathe. Tears washed down her face as she struggled, fighting against that strange current that seemed intent on pulling her deeper and deeper into the murky depths of blackness. It tugged once more and she went under. Panic engulfed her very soul as her eyes blinked involuntarily from the cold, oily wetness.

Sarah screamed out the breath she was holding as she awoke to partial consciousness, quickly sitting upright in the bed. She was breathing hard and shallow as she looked around, momentarily confused, suddenly realizing that she'd in fact been dreaming. Her covers were all but absent and lying on the floor where she'd apparently kicked them off throughout the night, and her moist skin was cool from where she'd had the fan running on high.

Sarah shook herself, and then rose from the bed, naked except for her powder blue panties. As she stood, she reached down and grabbed up the covers and tossed them back onto the bed, and then stepped to the fan, quickly turning it off. She walked into the bathroom, pulled her panties down, plopped onto the toilet, placing her elbows onto her knees, and her face into the palms of her hands, sighing with relief as she relieved herself.

. . . .

Sarah sat there and looked at the laptop sitting on her desk. It was the first thing she'd done after she'd showered, dressed and gotten fully awake. The laundry had just been opened by the staff of the complex, and she'd only had to wait for one person who'd dropped in about the same time to throw a couple of loads in and then leave to go back to their unit to await the washing cycles before returning.

As soon as the woman had left, Sarah retrieved the laptop and placed it in her basket, covering it with clothes. She then went back to her place. The laptop had done its job, apparently, and no one had bothered it. Something in Sarah's mind wished someone had. Wished they had just taken it and relieved her of the stress and burden she was now faced with. But, 'it is what it is'! Sarah recited the words her father had been known to use frequently throughout his life—an intended positive affirmation.

She grabbed a cup of coffee and sat down at her desk. She entered the password and within seconds the unit lit up, revealing the file folder on the desktop where she'd had the program load the data to.

Sarah took another deep breath and opened the file.

....

Nearly two hours had passed.

It all seemed to corroborate this Mr. Bolt person's comments, except for the fact that there were a couple strange oddities about it. There were a total of twenty-seven articles and short pieces written about this Arthur T. Pendaghast person that was brought up from the search by her father's program. Of the twenty-seven, only a few had attached pictures; the others had none, being mostly short snippets in business journals which only mentioned the name briefly as a subtopic in another piece. Sarah read them all one by one.

The program parameters set by Sarah were to locate the articles based on her inputted criterion, which it had. Another set of parameters was to bring up each article's history of searches—how many times, and what dates each article had been accessed by somebody online, along with any modification dates after the original release date, if there were any.

Of all the articles which featured a digital image, all but three were pictures of either some business headquarters of a particular company, or of some sort of graphic art design that was made to depict growth and stability in financial markets. Of the three that displayed a picture of this Arthur T. Pendaghast, two were of an apparent group of people, of which Pendaghast was among, with only one displaying an image of the man himself. These were the articles that this Mr. Bolt had shown Sarah, and they indeed appeared to be images of Eliam Zaris.

Sarah was struck with disappointment.

Yet, she had to be sure, so she continued her review.

The majority of the articles she'd accessed had creation dates of over seven years ago. All had a general access history that peaked a year after the articles were written, and then tapered off quickly after that to zero over the past five years.

Suddenly, Sarah noticed something strange regarding the articles: all had a recent history of access over the past week, whereas before they'd gone dormant literally for years. All of them had. And the ones with the pictures had shown a marked increase in access in just the prior two weeks.

"Why?" Sarah thought.

She then began focusing on the articles with the pictures.

All of them seemed to have a similar timeframe of creation, and none showed any signs of any recent modifications, at least that the program could identify. But, the pictures themselves seemed strange to Sarah. Yes, each one had an image of Eliam Zaris, but the thing she noticed was that in each one the face was turned in nearly the same direction and appeared to have a similar expression on it. As if it were the same image, yet digitally enhanced and sized to match the proportions of the surrounding image.

"Could this be?" Sarah thought. "No, it can't be," Sarah then considered. The search showed that there were no modification dates on any of the articles. But she knew as well as anyone that if someone had the technology, they could do so without being detected, but you'd have to know how, and have a good reason.

"Why would anyone go to such lengths to do that?" she considered.

Confusion raced around in her brain.

"Facts are facts, even if you're trying to talk yourself out of them, Sarah!" she whispered to herself, hope deflating as time progressed. She then decided to dig deeper. She began to access the histories again. The group this Mr. Bolt had mentioned could be the answer to the huge increase in recent access to the articles she was seeing over the prior two weeks, but that only made sense to a point. Mr. Bolt had said that they had just recently discovered Eliam's whereabouts, yet he said it had been a month before. Yet, there was no history of access to any of these articles until just two weeks before.

"I guess it could be," she thought. But it didn't seem to make any sense to her.

If this group had gone through what it'd gone through seven years before and were still looking for this Pendaghast guy, and they somehow had found him just a month ago, why would they want to bring up all the old articles about him anyway; and why did the interest just suddenly start two weeks before, not a month before?

"The people wanted to review what went on!" Sarah said to herself. "That's all there is to it." She tilted her head in confusion again. It wasn't just a few articles about the strange enigmatic man, but it was apparently all of them that were accessed.

That didn't make any sense whatsoever.

"Maybe they found him, advertised the fact to several people, and two weeks ago a lot of these people wanted to review what went on back then? Maybe that was it?" she seemed to settle it in her mind. But, then again, why *all* the articles? That still didn't make any sense.

Suddenly Sarah's phone beeped.

She pulled her mind and attention away from the data on the laptop and picked up her phone.

It was Condoleezza Ghee.

Sarah answered it.

"Hello, Condi!"

"Hello Sarah Whiting, and how are you?"

Sarah suddenly thought about the meaning of the question. She was momentarily stymied by it.

"Uhm, I'm…staying occupied, that's for sure. I'm just doing some research here. Trying to figure some things out that don't seem to make any sense," Sarah said, being truthful, yet vague.

"Ahhh yes, every human's enduring quest for enlightenment, let me know when you figure it all out. Hey, I guess you were called about us returning. And I'm sure you heard about Professor Dunes? It's terrible, is all I can say, poor man. I wouldn't have thought for a minute that he would've done something like that. I guess we all have our breaking points," Condi ended, waiting for Sarah to reply.

"Yeah, I guess so. I didn't know him enough to speculate, but I'd guess he was just one of those who had a lot of turmoil inside, and just wanted it over. I don't know. Yes, poor man! It'll be strange finishing the program without him there," Sarah added, thinking about it further.

"Yes it will. Hey, I was thinking about going for a run today and I was wondering if you'd like to go along. I'll buy lunch afterwards and we can talk more about all this. I imagine a lot will change, under the circumstances. Don't you? Anyway, I was wondering what you've been thinking about it all."

Condi waited for Sarah to answer.

Sarah hesitated for a moment, looking back at the laptop. She'd actually reviewed all the avenues she'd initially considered. It would take a lot more thinking before any conclusions were had, she then realized. And a run might actually help her think.

"Yeah, a run is exactly what I need. But you don't have to buy my lunch. Where were you thinking?"

"Uhm, how about Connelly Park? It's close, and has some nice paths, a couple miles worth."

"Okay, that sounds alright. I can meet you in, say, an hour or so."

"That'd be perfect. Let's meet in the main parking lot by the kid's playground—eleven-ish?"

"Sounds good. I'll see you there. Bye, Condi."

"Great! Bye Sarah! See you there."

Sarah pushed the button and ended the call, suddenly realizing all she'd been through in the past several days. How was she going to talk about all this to Condi? How was she *not* going to talk about all this to Condi?

Chapter 38

Sarah exited the car.

"Hey," Condi said.

"Hi," Sarah replied, as she changed into her running shoes and threw her sandals into the back seat.

"You're looking a little rundown there," Condi commented.

"Gee, thanks!" Sarah replied, yet knowing what Condi was getting at. "I haven't gotten much sleep the past few nights. Shows, huh?"

"I wouldn't worry. You are still a very beautiful woman, Sarah Whiting!"

Sarah turned and looked at her.

"As are you, Condoleezza Ghee," Sarah said in her own complementing Indian accent, smiling as she did so. "I take it the trail starts over there by the sign?"

Condi turned in that direction.

"That would be it. You have never been out here?"

"No, not to run," Sarah added, starting her warm-up stretches as Condi was doing.

"How is your father?" Condi asked.

"Uhm, he's doing okay." She remembered her mentioning to Eliam about going to see him. "I'm going to see him today, actually. Later."

"Oh yeah? Want some company? I wouldn't mind seeing your father again; he is an interesting man. I enjoyed meeting him. He reminds me of my father, in many ways. My father was a scientist."

"Sure, that'd be nice. Thank you for asking! I think he'd welcome the visit very much." She paused. "I didn't know that about your father, that's interesting!" Sarah thought about it for another moment. "Dad might even show us beautiful women off to his new friends." She giggled, remembering what her dad had said when they had been at the clinic in Santa Clarita.

Condi remembered as well, chuckling along with Sarah.

"I'm ready! You?" Sarah asked with enthusiasm.

"I am! Let's go!"

....

They'd ran the loop nearly twice, only briefly talking as they did. Sarah was getting more fatigued than usual, and as they approached the trailhead by the parking lot, she commented to Condi.

"That's it for me. Twice is good."

"Yeah, good for me too," Condi agreed.

They slowed to a walking pace to wind down as they took a circuitous route back to their cars. Unlocking their vehicles, they retrieved their water bottles.

"Sit for a while?" Condi invited, motioning to a picnic table in the shade.

Sarah nodded.

She felt better after letting off some steam.

The two sat across from each other, sipping on their waters as they got comfortable.

Condi looked at Sarah oddly.

"What?" Sarah noticed, and then inquired regarding the look.

"Oh, just that…I meant what I said. You are a beautiful woman, Sarah!" Condi acted a little embarrassed; she then turned her head down, staring at her water bottle as if studying it.

Sarah had a thought and then an odd feeling.

Her eyebrows went up.

"Tha…thanks, Condi. I meant what I said, too."

The two locked eyes and they just stared at each other, silently.

Sarah suddenly realized; she smiled a large smile at Condi and nodded in acknowledgement.

Condi fidgeted and smiled back.

"I…see," Sarah started. "Uhm, I guess I should say, uhm…I…I'm not that way, Condi. I'm flattered; really flattered, that is if I'm reading you right?" Sarah tilted her head, but kept eye contact, trying to look honest and non-judgmental."

Condi's eyes darted from her bottle, to Sarah, and then back again.

"You are! I…I just wanted to, you know, get it out there. Sorry!"

Sarah understood.

"Hey, nooooo…no sorry necessary, I…I, like I said, I'm flattered. I mean that. I…just don't lean that way; I guess I'm trying to say. But, it's okay. Really! I just prefer the other way, that's all."

Condi just sat there and looked at her bottle of water, twisting and turning it, peering at it from all angles. Sarah noted her embarrassment.

"Listen, Condi," Sarah reached out across the table and took Condi's left hand into hers. She squeezed it sensitively and gave it a slight tug to get her attention. Condi kept her head down, but lifted her eyes.

"Listen, I do understand. There's no problem here, my friend. We are just who we are, and that's all there is to it. Don't feel bad, or get down because of this. And…and it never hurts to ask. You never know…we could have been the very thing we both wanted, needed! I'm just sorry to say, that…that it's not. But, I'm just who I am, too, and I'm okay with that. You know what I mean? Are you okay with that?"

Sarah squeezed her hand. Condi squeezed back.

"Yeah, I'm okay with that," Condi said, feeling less embarrassed.

"And to be honest, I think you're pretty hot, Condi, actually. You are very beautiful, inside and out. I just like guys, that's all!" Sarah suddenly thought of Eliam.

"You really like Eliam Zaris, don't you?"

Sarah was kind of knocked off guard with the question.

She thought about it before answering.

"Yeah…yeah, I do, unfortunately, it seems! You noticed, huh!"

Condi squint her eyes.

"Yeah! What do you mean, 'unfortunately'?"

Sarah thought more about it before answering.

She withdrew her hand from Condi's.

"Well, sometimes people aren't who we think they are. Not genuine, is what I mean…pretend to be someone else."

Condi listened intently, nodding her head. She then spoke.

"Yes, don't I know that?! I think guys are just that way, mostly. You know, more than girls. At least from where I come from. Maybe that's why I'm like I am, to some degree. I just got tired of getting lied to, being used and abused, I suppose. Women are more authentic. If you ask me, guys, not so much—most guys, anyway it seems! But maybe that's just me being prejudiced."

"Yeah, I'm sorry to hear that; I know what you're saying," Sarah whispered, truly understanding her friend's feelings, as she assessed her own.

"Hey, like I said, I want to buy you lunch!" Condi then said, now apparently back to her normal self.

Sarah was glad to see her friend perking up.

"Sure, that would be nice. But, you don't have to buy. Where're we going? What do you have an appetite for?" Sarah asked, not at first realizing what she'd said.

After a moment, both broke out into laughter, yet neither mentioned what they were laughing about.

"I could go for some seafood," Condi said, her laughter now calming.

"Seafood? I thought you said you were a vegetarian!" Sarah asked, remembering what she'd said the other day.

"Yeah, I am, mostly. But sometimes I get cravings, and when I do, it's for seafood!"

"Sounds good to me," Sarah agreed.

Suddenly, Sarah was in deep thought.

Seafood…*Seafood?*

Her mind kept churning the word.

. . . .

"I'm really glad you called. I needed this. Thanks," Sarah said genuinely, as they waited for their lunch orders to show up.

"My pleasure! Listen, from what you've started telling me, I can understand. So talk. What's going on? You like the guy, but you think he's leading you on or something? What are his tactics? All guys have some sort of line, don't they?!"

Sarah quickly recapped in her mind all that had happened over just the past few days.

"Oh yeah, he's definitely got some unique lines; some are really…out there! In fact, I'm seriously starting to doubt his honesty," Sarah said plainly.

Condi gave her a sideways look.

"Really? Okay, so what's the source?"

"Source?" Sarah repeated.

"Well, did you catch him in a lie? Boldface? Or is it just based on hearsay?"

Sarah thought for a minute.

"Hearsay, I guess you would call it, though it's some pretty compelling hearsay!"

"Maybe, but it is still hearsay, right? You have to be careful with that. Did you know that half of all wars, throughout all of history, started as a result of some sort of hearsay?"

"No, I didn't know that," Sarah answered.

"Yeah! I heard somebody say that once!"

They both laughed.

Condi continued.

"The point is a good one though. It might be exaggeration, extrapolation, or out and out lies, but entire societies have crumbled as a result, and potentially good relationships."

"Yeah, I'd imagine," Sarah said.

"So, details?" Condi inquired.

Sarah looked at her with trusting eyes, but she couldn't tell her. She would sound absolutely crazy.

"You wouldn't believe me if I told you, Condi. But I will tell you that this 'hearsay' states not only that Eliam Zaris may be part of some sort of charade, but that the entire program may be threatened by it, potentially."

Condi suddenly got very attentive.

"Really?"

"Yeah, seriously. You make a good point though, and I suppose all I would be relating would simply be something someone else told me—actually lead me to find, in this case. And like I said, it's pretty compelling. But right now I'm not sure about anything. I still need to do more research. I shouldn't say anymore! But if any of it *is* true, the program might not end up as we expect. And what that means, I don't know either. I just need to think about it more."

Sarah went silent.

"Well, I guess I ended up talking myself out of all the juicy details with the hearsay comment. But, I do believe, and I hereby *say*…it's always wise to proof the proof, however you can."

Sarah nodded in affirmation, but her anger about it all just kept swelling.

"Yeah, I suppose you're right!"

Chapter 39

"Welcome back, everyone!" Dr. Vectren said, after they had all seated themselves. "We realize this may be somewhat difficult for you. It is for all of us here at Earthbridge, I assure you. I know some of you are wondering about a memorial service of some sort for Professor Dunes, but I'm afraid that according to his own will, there won't be any. That's just the way he apparently wanted it, and that decision will be honored. However, if anyone needs to talk to someone, as mentioned along with the announcement, please feel free to let us know. We have some good counselors here and they would be more than happy to help in any way they can. So please, don't hesitate if needed. Okay?"

He smiled a sad, yet encouraging smile and then continued.

"I will be facilitating the last module of the program with Eliam Zaris, along with a few other people from the university who will be helping this final week as well. I'm sure that, due to the circumstances, it will be a slow return to pace, but we do have a lot to cover so we're going to just press on, if that's okay with everyone."

Several people nodded.

"Good! First, I'll give you a rundown of the week's agenda; some things have changed due to the circumstances, so bear with me. Today, and tomorrow, you will be spending time individually within applications that are specific to your own particular disciplines. Please note, that at the beginning of each App you will find a directory of queries that have been specifically placed there; we'd like you to review these before your active participation in the application. These are merely cues intended to spark your thinking processes, and ultimately aid your objective summations of the apps relative to their components, overall structure, professional presentation, efficacy, and so on. Foremost, you are being asked to engage these apps with an open mind.

"On Monday, we will ask you to individually render for us your personal opinions and comments in conjunction with the basic queries that you found at the beginning; what do you think about this, what do you think about that? In other words, you are being asked to present yourselves as the initial test market subjects.

"Your pending reviews will be invaluable to us; and of course they will be recorded and documented. They will ultimately become part of the compilation of reviews consumers will use to help with their own assessments once the product has been released. And trust us when we say, the expectation is *not* an across-the-board endorsement. We are looking for honesty and integrity, simple as that. The intent is to help with the improvement and development of future editions of the apps, as well as that of the product.

"Then, later in the week, all of you are going to be part of a test Q&A forum. In this forum, you will be queried by specific people from your own disciplines, as well as people who will represent the general public who have been informed of the product and its overall capabilities and expectations. It may turn out to be a spirited dialogue, knowing that there are many ways of looking at things, as well as people to look at them. Again, we're asking for not only your honesty, but your diligence in regards to professional decorum.

"We will also be positing certain scenarios and topical formulations to help encourage everyone's thinking as well as everyone's comments on the various subject matter, so please realize this up front. It will be somewhat structured, but you may also expect a few spontaneous discussions bordering on debate. However, there will be mediators to help maintain focus.

"You may now be questioning why; why exactly are we are doing this, this way? I will simply say: it is to answer as many concerns as possible for the public so they will have a broad-based understanding of what the technology is, as well as its potential impact on their lives—positive, and negative. That has been the objective of this program the entire time. As Professor Dunes clearly stated at the beginning: 'It—meaning Smartbrain technology—will without a doubt change society as we know it!'

"Also at this point I would like to inform you that you will be meeting the university's marketing representative, along with her team. Her name is Chance Huffington. She's been working behind the scenes for the last couple of weeks observing your recorded sessions, and has been tasked with choosing and choreographing the many highlights that will be used in the final marketing documentary, as well as during the public presentation of the technology at this year's Blue-Dot Technology Convention in Chicago."

He finished and then turned to Eliam Zaris, silently inviting his contribution with a glance.

Eliam nodded in return and then stood. His eyes couldn't help but fall on Sarah's as he stepped to the center of the group. She looked at him, but only for a brief moment tilting her head and looking down at his shirt, not making eye contact. Eliam noted her avoidance with heightened curiosity. He refocused his attention, cleared his voice, and began.

"Everyone, what has happened over the past few days is beyond unfortunate as well as inopportune, and for many of us, an unspeakable loss. But what we are doing here is very important, and we must follow through, for a multitude of reasons. In a short amount of time—as I'm sure you're fully aware from your contractual agreements—the world will be eyeing you with great curiosity. I know all of you have experience with public exposure, this is one of the reasons you were initially chosen for the program, and though it quite often is never easy, all of you have been to some degree successful at it. You will survive this; I am sure!"

Eliam looked at Sarah again, and again she turned her eyes away.

He continued on.

"In...in attendance later today will be a few people who are on staff from the university, as well as several others who are privy to the nature of the technology, including several from the government agencies that have tested, authenticated, and have determined that the technology is medically safe to release to the public. They have all been asked to be here at various times throughout the week and have cordially agreed to do so.

"Note that they are here on a personal, as well as professional level. Remember, they will also be under the bright lights, you might say, once Smartbrain technology is released to the public. And because of that, they have every right to be here, just as you do. At the end of each day over the next few days, you and they will take part in a series of test forums—as Dr. Vectren previously mentioned—with each covering different topics. They will be the ones asking the questions, and making comments, and you will be addressing them according to your experiences and perspectives. This is intended to help you prepare for the final—recorded—public forum that will be released worldwide with the product launch.

"Also, I want to reiterate one more thing that Dr. Vectren touched upon a moment ago. I believe that it is very important. Know now that what you say in this final forum has the potential to affect literally billions of people. So, knowing, this just be honest with yourselves. And don't be nervous!" Eliam then added, "No pressure!"

Everyone took a deep, anxious breath as they looked around at each other, smiling and rolling their eyes.

....

It was an intense day for everyone, and nearly exhausting for some. Each immersed themselves in their applications of choice and diligently sought to explore them under the pretext of the queries listed. And all did so with a high level of energy, knowing that they would indeed be questioned about their experiences. None wished to appear halfhearted or lackadaisical in any way, so everyone gave their full attention. Most found it interesting, if not rewarding, as they surveyed the apps in alignment their various backgrounds, vocations, and interests.

At the end of the day, and especially after the two final hours of questions and discussions with near total strangers, everyone was tired and ready to go home.

....

"Mr. Thurmond…Mr. Zacchaeus, thank you for agreeing to join us, we appreciate the help during the forums. Mrs. Drexel, our thanks go out to you as well, and to you Mr. Smith and Ms. Wagner. Thank you for your participation," Dr. Vectren said genially to the people as they exited the auditorium, trying not to miss anybody, and shaking their hands as they passed.

Deltray Zacchaeus attempted to make a comment, but was overshadowed by Dr. Vectren's quick attention changes. The man stepped back slightly and just frowned oddly as everyone passed while he waited for the group to thin. It finally did, and he was again acknowledged by Dr. Vectren.

"Yes, Mr. Zacchaeus. What may I do for you?"

"I was wondering, Dr. Vectren, will there be a tour of some sort, of the labs and the production facilities, possibly? I know I don't just speak for myself. It would be fascinating to see the facilities, especially for us technology-minded people who enjoy automation, scientific equipment, and the like. I feel that being a government rep—merely on the statistical reports side, as is the case with my position—lacks quite a bit, compared to the actual nuts and bolts of the technology that the agency scientists and testers receive from their hands-on work. If it's not on the agenda, would it be possible to arrange such a tour? I know I would enjoy it immensely."

Dr. Vectren looked down as he idly thought about it.

"Well, there is nothing on the agenda, as such…"

"Oh, that is truly unfortunate. As I inquired, could one possibly be arranged? I take it the labs are here on campus, and I would suppose the Prototype Shop is as well, for convenience. I'm sure it wouldn't be too difficult to acquire authorization for at least a small number of us to do so. And I'm sure it would go over quite well with the public, if there were at least a few allowed. You've been through them, I'm sure. They're interesting, aren't they? I would surely think!"

"Well…uhmm, I don't know. Yes, the labs are here in the Computer Science building, and the Prototype Shop is in the basement of the Applied Sciences building; they're here on campus. Yes…yes I'm in them quite often. Yes, they're very interesting. But, I don't know about a tour. I don't know…a limited tour, perhaps, but no photographs, I'm sure. They probably wouldn't even entertain the idea, but I suppose I could…"

"Well, of course. That's perfectly understandable. No images, recordings, etc. Proprietary processes, and all that, fully understandable. Well, maybe you could inquire for us. Perhaps sometime this week, and if not, well then that's perfectly understandable as well. Thank you in advance for trying. Listen, I must be going now. I will see you tomorrow, Dr. Vectren. You have a nice evening, sir. And thank you again." Deltray Zacchaeus nodded and started off to the parking lot.

Dr. Vectren sighed and then headed back to his office to close it up. He was glad the day was finally over.

……

Sarah was reaching for the door handle to her car when she heard the voice.

"Sarah!"

She started to turn, but she didn't need to look up to know who the voice belonged to.

"*Sarah?*" Eliam Zaris repeated with emotion, nearing her from the front of the car.

Sarah took a deep breath.

Eliam reached her just as she pulled the handle and opened the door letting it swing between the two of them. Eliam stopped abruptly; a look of utter confusion molded his face.

"What…Sarah? What's going on? Did I do something wrong?" He stopped there, his mouth gaping.

Sarah finally made eye contact. The look on her face was one of anger and disgust and bewilderment all rolled into one.

She looked down to the side, thought quickly, and then attempted to speak.

"Listen, Eliam, I…I don't want to see you, okay. Let's just leave it at that. I just want to be left alone and get through this. I want to go home!"

Sarah then jumped into her car and started to pull the door shut, her visibly shaking hand trying to align the key with the ignition. Eliam moved quickly, grabbing the top of the door and skirting around it, keeping it from closing. He put one hand on the car's roof, and kept the door from closing with the other.

"Sarah! What is going on?! Talk to me! I have no idea why you're acting like this. Tell me what's going on! Please! What did I do?!"

She tried to pull the door shut.

"Please let go of my car! I'm not going to end up as a pawn in one of your games! That's all! Please, just let go!" she said, as she pulled with greater effort.

"WHAT?!" Eliam said with added volume and surprise. He seemed to realize the fact, which led him to soften his voice and look around. "*Sarah*, what are you talking about?" he said with strained control, as he held the door firm. No one was looking their way.

"I'm talking about Arthur T. Pendaghast. Or should I say, I'm not talking *to* Arthur T. Pendaghast. So let go of my damned car!"

Sarah then pushed against the car door with all her might, knocking Eliam away for an instant, and allowing her to slam the door shut. She quickly hit the lock, started the car, and backed out of the space.

Eliam just stared as she drove away in haste.

"Who the hell is Arthur…whatever…Pendal-gast?" he muttered, confused.

Chapter 40

Beep...beep...beep.

Sarah took another drink of wine; it was her fourth glass.

She blinked widely, trying to thin the gooey gelatinous coating on her eyeballs. It would beep again, she figured, any minute now. He was still trying to phone her even after her defiant comments in the parking lot. Sarah again thought of what Condi had said about hearsay and proofing the proof, but that is exactly what she'd been doing all along. Her mind was looping in ever tighter circles now.

She scanned the laptop screen once more, reading the information she'd gathered. *Who would make up all this stuff?* she thought, shaking her head and biting her thumb nail.

Beep...beep...beep.

He wasn't stopping. It was his fourth—no *fifth*—try, she recalled hazily, each time causing her to become increasingly infuriated. She couldn't help but think of his attempts at using her, as he'd apparently used all those others, as toys, and play things, pawn pieces in his shameless games of power and control and lies.

"From another planet...*another planet*, Sarah! What were you *thinking*? It was just a prop...an expensive...converted... RV bus, love shack, or whatever. It wasn't a spaceship. What were you thinking to even... even...? God you're an idiot Sarah Frances Whiting!" she mumbled. She then cursed under her breath as she thought about how gullible she must really be, believing even for a moment in such a crock.

Her anger swelled even more as she reread the article for the umpteenth time about that particular woman who got caught in this guy's trap, ending up losing all her personal wealth, and her dignity. Because she trusted this…this *conniving*, *Machiavellian*, *poser*, she mumbled.

Beep…beep…beep.

It was him again, of course.

She couldn't take it anymore.

She hesitated, drew back, took a deep breath through her nose.

Beep…beep…beep.

"That's it!" she spit slightly as she said the words.

She reached down and snatched up the phone.

"Listen, don't call me anymore, ever! *Pendaghast*! Or whoever you are. I don't want to talk to you; I don't want to see you; I don't want to read about you ever again! All I want is to get through this, and go back to normal, back to my simple life! So leave me the hell alone!"

"Sarah, listen to me! What happened? Why are you acting like this? Read about me? What are you talking about? I…"

Sarah pushed the button hard, nearly breaking her fingernail doing so.

It felt good, releasing the tension. She took another swig from the glass, this time a sloppy one. The red fluid dripped down her chin. She wiped it with her hand, transferring the liquid mess to her jeans as she got up and went to the counter to refill her glass again. In doing so, she saw the picture of her dad and her on the counter top. It was the same picture that he now had on his desk at the home.

Sarah slowly sat down on one of the island stools. She picked up the framed picture and looked at it closely. Tears filled her eyes as she held it adoringly.

"Oh, Dad! I'm so sorry!"

Tears welled in her eyes.

"I just wish I was smarter; I wish I could have seen this coming." She sniffled, wiping her nose with her hand as she'd done with the wine, coating the same spot on her jeans with the slimy residue.

"You got a real dummy for a daughter, Dad! A real piece of work!"

She sat the picture down and reached for the bottle.

Realizing it was nearly empty, she poured its little remaining contents into her glass, and then rose from her seat. She walked into the kitchen, opened the pantry door, and then stumbled into the closet-sized room feeling for the light switch at the same time. She found the small lever with a sweep of her hand and lifted it, lighting the room.

"A little more vino, a hot shower, that'll make it for me for the day. I'll finish this…pro-ject, and then I can get back to my happy…place, by myself, and just…take care of dad and me, and forget this freak-oyd-guy and his line of crap-olla."

Chime…chime…chime.

Sarah leaned backwards out of the pantry and looked across the room. Her phone was informing her that she'd just received a text. She then clumsily carried the bottle of wine to the island and set it on the counter top. She looked at the phone, didn't recognize the number, but saw the beginning of a sentence:

I UNDERSTAND! LOOK OUT…

Sarah focused her eyes and reread the line; curiosity then got the best of her; she opened the full message.

I UNDERSTAND! LOOK OUT YOUR BEDROOM WINDOW!

The message gripped Sarah hard; her mind raced.

"*What?*" she muttered to herself as she read the message again.

Suddenly, fear coursed through her veins, and she felt her body sway with an eerie lack of control. She couldn't help but read the message again, and then yet again, once more trying to blink the sticky coating from her eyeballs, as if by doing so the message would make more sense to her.

Everything inside Sarah said don't; you are an idiot if you do. But some strange, distant feeling moved her beyond curiosity. She carefully walked to the bedroom, but stopped suddenly when her phone went off in her hand. The accompanied vibration startled her to such a degree that she about threw the device to the floor.

Chime…buzz…chime…buzz…chime…buzz.

Sarah got her wits about her and looked at the screen.

ABOVE THE TREES!

Sarah was momentarily confused, nearly unable to move except for the gentle, involuntary swaying which was becoming more pronounced as a result of her rapidly beating heart.

"*Above the trees?*" Sarah spoke the words out loud, more than perplexed now. "*No fracking way!*" she then uttered with force.

Sarah sprinted to the darkened bedroom window and slowly peered around the curtain to look outside. There she saw it. Up above the tree line was a dark, velvety blackness that seemed to move slightly and change shape. And then there, amidst its blackness, a hole appeared to open in the middle of it and she saw Eliam's face, as if it were looking out a window.

Sarah's phone erupted again.

Chime…buzz…chime…buzz…chime…buzz.

I READ MOST OF THE ARTICLES…THEY'RE FABRICATED…THAT'S NOT ME! I CAN PROVE IT! TRUST ME!

Sarah fainted, and fell onto the bed.

Chapter 41

Sarah's head was swirling amongst black areas that seemed to be changing shape, along with tufts of light that appeared to squeeze through the convolution of transforming profiles. She then noticed that the blackened shapes were getting smaller, as if the tufts of light were somehow absorbing their velvety darkness.

The light was blurry, filled with splotches of color, and it all seemed to be coalescing into some defined shape. Sarah blinked and widened her eyes until the shape suddenly became recognizable.

"Hi there! You okay?"

Sarah jerked at the sound.

"What...where am I? What's going on?"

"You fainted. Fortunately, you fell on the bed, at least at first, before you rolled off and landed on the floor. It looked like you hit your head; good thing there was carpet."

Sarah sat up a little, trying to shake off the lingering faintness. She took a deep breath and instinctively scanned her surroundings. It looked as if she was in Eliam's ship, or whatever it was.

"How'd I get here? What are you doing to me? I don't know what happened? What...how...?"

Sarah was at a loss for words.

She put her right hand up to her face and massaged her temples, closing and opening her eyes in a stretching motion.

"Like I said, you fainted. I brought you here. Don't worry, you'll be alright. *Sanguine* did a scan and there's nothing wrong with you. You just passed out and had a little jolt to the head, no concussion or anything. You've been out for a couple of hours. You'll be fine though."

He looked at her with eyes that were filled with relief.

"You *brought* me here?" she asked, now remembering the event. "I…I saw your ship, the blackness, whatever. I read your text. I…I think I remember."

"Sarah, I've been researching that name—that person you spoke of—and the articles. I saw the pictures…pictures of me. But, that wasn't me, Sarah! I've been trying to figure out what's happening." He became quiet for a moment, turned pensive, but then he started again.

"I have a few suppositions, but I need you to tell me what's happened to you. How'd you run across those articles, the name? When? For some reason you've become convinced that those are all about me, but they aren't! I promise, Sarah! They aren't!"

Eliam had a terrified look on his face now, as if he was scared she would not believe him.

Sarah thought through his words; she noted his expression.

"They aren't you? You aren't this Pendaghast guy who did all those things in Europe? You said you came from Europe, grew up abroad, whatever?"

"Yes, that's true, I said I came from Europe, lived abroad, which is true, but those articles weren't about me. But I suspect someone is trying to make you think that. Am I right? Has someone told you all this? How'd you find the articles? Where'd you get the name?"

Sarah was unsure. She wanted to answer his question, but she hesitated, trying to be careful. For a moment she didn't know what to do.

"That's *not* you?!" she asked, with a measure of force.

Eliam saw her bewildered look.

"No! You have to believe me. I've never heard of that guy; I don't know anything about him, or about anything those articles spoke of. I'm not that guy, Sarah! Someone is setting a ruse, and I suspect we're part of the arrangement. And if what's happening, is what I *think* is happening, then we need to figure it out soon before it's fully launched—if it hasn't been already—or we may be beyond stopping it!"

Sarah had a puzzled look on her face at what he had just said, but she felt such sincerity from his voice and manner that she suddenly found a modicum of trust in him again. She didn't know exactly why, but she did.

"So…you're really Eliam Zaris? From another planet…actually from another planet? I'm really going to try, but I'm sure you can see my perspective here! You're telling me you're from another planet? And you're not shooting me some bull-shit line?"

Eliam had a relieved look on his face. She was at least trying to trust him.

He nodded adamantly.

"How'd I get here? Did you beam me up or something?" she said, leering at him.

"'*Beam* you up?'" he repeated. "No, Sarah, this is reality. There's no machine that can dismantle flesh and molecules and reconstitute them back to their original form somewhere else. That's science fiction, Sarah! No, I landed on your building's roof, and we took the elevator and then the stairs. I carried you."

He looked at her with honest humility and a seriousness that nearly melted her.

"You carried me?"

"Yeah! I saw you through the window. You passed out and fell! I couldn't just leave you there. I came and got you. Look…look at this. *Sanguine*, portal views please, interior-out only, thank you."

Eliam spoke to the ship and suddenly the windows adorning the curved walls of the vessel became transparent and Sarah could see that, indeed, it appeared that she was in a ship and it was on top of a building. From the high advantage point, she could see a great distance—she saw the surrounding buildings, the shopping plaza several blocks away, her favorite coffee shop, and the moonlit mountains to the east.

Sarah's eyes lit up with amazement.

"It's true!" she said in a whisper, looking out at the expanse.

"Yes, Sarah. But, we need to talk. I'll tell you what I think is going on. But I need you to tell me what happened."

Sarah nodded.

"*Sanguine*, please lift off and let's cruise around for a bit. Sarah and I would like to see some sights. We are going to have a conversation, so please feel free to offer any insights or eval's, thanks. And head west, I think, and then north up the coast. Standard stealth and avoidance measures, thank you, *Sanguine*."

"*Yes, Eliam...initiating departure now.*"

Sarah took a deep breath as she looked through the portals, now seeing the ship lift up and the city falling away below.

Chapter 42

"You seemed to have figured this out pretty quickly. You're saying that this Bolt guy, the one who conned me into having lunch with him, is from your planet—from Hoame— one of the Elite, the *Ankh*, and he's trying to stop the distribution of the tech on the Earth? How do you know this?"

"Yes, that's what I'm supposing. We know it because it was a subject of debate on Hoame for quite a long time. They don't want it here, and they don't want open contact, especially. They want the Earth to stay like it is, as I told you before."

"What was he hoping to accomplish by getting me to disbelieve you. I mean, what am I? How did that figure into his head?"

"I'm not sure, but there's something you have to understand about the *Ankh*. They operate and manipulate by ruse, and they'll set up a dozen different detailed avenues to go down to accomplish their goals. It's more in alignment with their shrewd nature than just simply killing or using force. Though they are perfectly capable of doing both, trust me. They're masters at false impression and delusion. So much so, they have a tendency to be trusted and even supported by the very ones who are the primary focus of the deception in the first place. They obviously wanted information from you, like this guy Bolt mentioned, but you can bet there's more to it.

"And I'm sorry, Sarah! I was mistaken when I said earlier that you weren't important to them, that they'd only wanted me. I...I'd received a call from them before it happened—the SUV thing—asking for a meeting regarding the releasing of the Tech, is what they said. I was doubtful and I refused, and after another call, and another refusal, I got a message that said that they'd disable my vehicle while I was in it, and talk to me on the side of the road if they had to."

"Really, they announced that they'd do that, and then they did just that?" Sarah asked, surprised.

"Yeah, though I wasn't sure at all whether it was a figure of speech, or what. Like I said, they're really good at deception. And I told you what I told you because I obviously didn't want to worry you. Nor did I want to get you any more involved than you were. But I was wrong. And I'm beginning to believe that the identity of this Arthur T. Pendaghast guy has been dreamed up to discredit me at some point in the future, or some variation on that theme.

"When that will happen, I don't have a clue. But I'm guessing it'll probably be after the tech is released, if they don't find a way to stop it altogether. And though I'm not sure exactly how, or why, I think the whole thing with Professor Dunes is part of this, too. Set up to somehow discredit the tech and the university along with it, and me, is my guess right now."

Eliam stared out the window at the various lights that adorned the coast as they silently glided along.

"You think they...*killed* him?" she asked, with a heightened level of anxiety now apparent in her voice.

"I don't know. But as I said, they're not averse to doing such things if that's their remaining option. They probably tried to get to him, but saw no way, so they may have gotten into his brain and manipulated him in some way to do it. He just wouldn't have done this on his own!"

"'*Got into his brain?*'" Sarah repeated the statement with sharpness in her voice.

"Yeah, they can do that, a throwback from the old days when they used chemicals and other techniques to turn people into their 'instruments.' It was outlawed centuries ago. Many of your Earth's governments attempted to do a similar thing, with little result, fortunately. There's suspicion some of their older agents still use the old methods, with varying measures of success. It depends on the person actually. I still don't see how they could have gotten to the Professor. He was a pretty strong-willed man. It just doesn't make sense!"

"Really? Oh my God! So what's their next move? What're they going to do? The release is in a couple months or so, right?"

"Yeah, that's the plan, though after Howey's death, the actual release date has been put on temporary hold for now. We don't know what their plans are, obviously."

Eliam thought deeply as he stared out the window.

"*Sanguine*, pertaining to relative topic discussed, please offer hypothesis."

"*Yes, Eliam… processing…Historical records show that the Ankh will first seek to disrupt, and then destroy, if manipulation proves impractical or impossible, depending on root objective. Assuming that their motives are to completely stop the dissemination of tech on the Earth they would not only have to inhibit the practical science applications and the associated devices from being available for consumption, but they would ultimately be required to inhibit the desire and aspiration for said science applications and delivery devices, thereby eliminating the actual market for the Tech in the first place.*"

The ship stopped talking.

Eliam and Sarah just sat there and looked at each other, both thinking acutely.

"*Sanguine*, please propose dominant method or methods that may be employed to eliminate desire and/or aspirations for applications and devices as previously stated," Eliam said pointedly

"*Yes, Eliam…processing…dominant method of quelling potential market for applications and devices would be an over-encompassing fear in consumers that the applications and/or devices were inherently dangerous and/or potentially lethal: causing mental incapacitation and/or corporeal termination.*"

"Thank you, *Sanguine*," he said, appearing stunned by the ship's comment.

"She's saying that, if Smartbrain technology were to kill," Sarah began, "or in the least, be proven to drive people insane, or render them into some zombie-like hulk, then no one would even want the tech in the first place. Is that what I'm gathering here?"

Eliam nodded his head slowly, staring at nothing in particular.

"Yes, exactly," he said, now turning to Sarah. "First an attempt at disruption—ruse—and then if that doesn't work, destroy. Yes."

Sarah's eyes widened.

"I can't believe this. That this is happening! Just what are you—is *she*—saying again, for the record? That this group doesn't want Smartbrain technology on the Earth, so bad, that they're willing to make it seem like, by using it, it's going to drive people insane or kill them? So no one would want it? And if that doesn't work, then...then what? How would they do that, any of that? I mean, how would they accomplish either?" Sarah asked, now animated with trepidation, disbelieving that any of this was even happening in the first place.

"*Sanguine*, please attempt to answer Sarah's last query."

"*Yes, Eliam...Sarah Whiting...processing...the answer is reducible to one answer for each individual query: First query: sufficient mechanical malfunction or inserted foreign application would need to be introduced into each device, of which would cause irreparable biological damage and/or death to the participating consumer. Second query: complete destruction of all devices, laboratories, equipment, and knowledge which directly or indirectly contribute to, or could contribute to, the initial development and/or reconstitution of said devices and associated knowledge base.*"

Sarah gasped.

Eliam saw the look of shock on her face, knowing that Sarah was able to gather exactly what *Sanguine* was saying. He allowed himself another moment to think before speaking again.

"Sarah, don't worry. Because of this—because of *you*—we now have an idea of what may be, at least a calculable course of action that this Mr. Bolt might take. And we'll do everything possible to make this go the way *we* intend it to, and not him. But I have to ask you to trust me. We need to take you back home as soon as possible. Tomorrow, I want you to return and continue on with the rest of the group. You'll be safe there. I'll get with you later in the evening. *Sanguine* and I have a lot of work to do tonight."

Sarah was obviously hyper-anxious about all this; she gave Eliam a fretful look, and then abruptly turned to look out the window again.

"I know," Eliam said, trying to comfort her. "But it will be alright; there's more going on in our favor than you know. It will be alright! Trust me, Sarah!"

Sarah continued to stare out the window, her mind racing a million miles a second.

"*Sanguine*, please return us to Sarah's home, and increase stealth and avoidance measures to their highest levels…immediately, *Sanguine*, thank you."

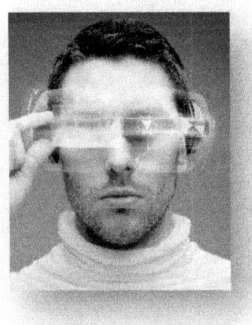

Part 2
Matter

Chapter 43

"This is one story that seems as if it may be going to everyone's head, literally! And the word is, it is unfolding right here under our very noses, or in this case actually, just up the mountain at the very private, historically enigmatic, Earthbridge College, a short jaunt off the road on the way up to Lake Isabella. Earthbridge has quite the mysterious history, supposedly housing a Think Tank that has had its hands in everything from early nuclear technologies, to space and aeronautical applications, and now to consumer goods, it appears.

"What's this 'hype' all about? Well, apparently, the elusive THEY have found a way to wirelessly stream data directly into the neural pathways of the human body, just as your eyes and ears and other senses do. According to the rumor mill, wearable Smartphones can now be directly linked—or interfaced—with the human brain. BCI it's called—Brain Computer Interface—a technology that's so far only existed in the realm of the imagination. At least this is what the local media seems to be all a-buzz about, with several legitimate sources saying that it's true!

"They're calling it 'Smartbrain': your field of vision is the monitor; images, motion, and sound feed directly into your consciousness; activation, operation, and navigation, accomplished by your thoughts; apps and Cloud sources, apparently under development. Many are already speculating that this will be the technological game-changer of the century.

"How did this come about? How is it that we're just now hearing about it? And how is it possible that something like this has made its way through all the required government agencies and is

nearly ready for release to the public? Yes, you heard me correctly. Apparently, this technology has been under development for some time now, and it is on the verge of being released to consumers. And, word is, it is apparently set to debut at this summer's Blue-Dot Technologies Convention in Chicago.

"What's more, something that is, to say the least, unsettling, and which broke at the same time as this intriguing story, is this: allegedly one of the proponents of this new, wonder technology has disappeared and purportedly committed suicide—a professor at said university! Wow! Now that sounds like some novel promotional planning.

"I hear you asking the same questions. And yes, I too, wonder if it may all be some deterministic hoax, some Hollywood marketing scheme-matic for a new movie or weird sci-fi series, or whatever. But, let's say that somehow all these people were able to keep a lid on it, and the story is true. Who in their right mind would want something like that? Would you want an electronic device feeding input directly into your brain, just as your natural senses do?

"Wow! I don't know? Sometimes I get dizzy from hearing loud music, and seeing the flashing lights on my studio console here. Can you imagine having them feed directly into your brain? Sounds mysteriously psychoactive to me; how about you? But, let's give it fair ponderance, muse on it for awhile yet, and we'll discuss it further when we return later for another en-trippy delvation into the subject!

"This is Jonathan Raker of Raker's Slant; stay tuned for more breaching news and inclined commentary!"

Chapter 44

He was at his desk working on his computer when his personal phone tickled his side with its silent, pulsing vibration. He quietly pulled it out of its holder and noted the number; his eyebrows rose. He immediately got up and stepped into his private bathroom, shutting the door silently behind him.

"Hello," he answered in a whisper, seemingly pleased regarding the call.

"Hi, William, how are you? I trust our signals are being scuttled? I dislike talking by these means, but I need to refrain from our other usual methods, for the time being anyway, just in case."

"Yes, of course, I understand. I'm good! How are you?"

"I'm well, thanks for asking. Listen, I won't keep you. I know I said I was going to be out of the loop for a time, but something has happened that you need to be aware of, and I also thought of something that I considered, well, a significant probability that may contribute to your research."

"I see. I'm glad you're well, by the way. Okay, I'm the only one who is all ears, go ahead," Col. Ravine said softly.

As he listened he quickly opened the presence array program for the building, and then localized it to the office and the adjoining areas. Deltray's infrared signature glowed brightly where he'd hoped, right at his desk. No other people were in proximity. Good, he thought. He continued listening intently as the person on the other end spoke a few more sentences.

"A break-in at the labs? Yes…yes, I would concur. That does make sense; it could lead to a number of different things, but I think you're right. We'll proceed under that assumption. I appreciate the heads-up. Yes…yes…and you as well. Alright, take care! I look forward to seeing you soon. Goodbye for now!"

Col. Ravine ended the private conversation, flushed the toilet and washed his hands for effect, and then exited the bathroom, glancing at the opened door of his office, as if looking with x-ray vision at the man sitting around the corner. He thought of his next actions, choreographing them in his mind before starting.

He then got a determined look on his face, took a deep breath, and reached for his personal phone. He tapped in a number and waited. A moment later his desk phone rang. He let it ring twice, picked it up, and proceeded to act as if he were talking to someone on the other end.

"Yes, Colonel Ravine here." He paused to listen. "A break-in? I see. Yes, I appreciate that you called." He spoke loudly again so his voice would carry. "Yes, thank you. Goodbye Sergeant."

Colonel Ravine hung up the desk phone. He waited for another moment and then picked it up again.

He entered a number and waited. Within a few seconds, the assistant to the Secretary of Defense of the United States answered.

"Hello, office of the S.O.D. How may I direct your call?"

"Hello, this is Colonel William Ravine calling for General Epcot," he said, projecting his voice with clarity and professionalism.

"Hello, Colonel. One minute please," the voice answered.

Twenty seconds of silence went by; Col. Ravine used the time to further review his data.

"Hello, Bill. Epcot here," the voice said in the Colonel's ear.

"Hello, General! Thanks for talking with me," he continued stridently. "I phoned to let you know that there's been a development. I just received a call from the locals; the labs at the university were broken into last night."

"I see…" the voice said, pausing to assess the information, "any word on the damage?"

"No, sir. I just now learned of it."

"Well, I'd say it would be prudent to show up there and gather some information, while it's still fresh. You get back with me and let me know what you find out. We may need to employ our own containment measures."

"Yes, sir, I agree. We'll head over there immediately. I'll let you know as soon as we find out anything. Goodbye, General."

He hung up the phone.

Colonel Ravine tapped a key on his terminal and within a moment, Deltray Zacchaeus entered his office.

"Yes, Colonel," he said, approaching the desk.

"Apparently there's been a break-in at the university's labs. Please get my car and meet me out front in ten minutes. We're heading over there. Thank you, Deltray."

"On the way, sir."

Colonel Ravine just sat there thinking about the probabilities he'd just learned of.

…….

Walking into the silent garage, Deltray Zacchaeus pulled his phone out of its holder and dialed a number.

"Mr. Zacchaeus, thank you for calling. Please *proceed and report…*"

Deltray Zacchaeus suddenly became calm after hearing the request; he spoke in a slow and precise tone.

"Yes, Colonel Ravine here… A break in? I see… Yes, I appreciate that you called… Yes, thank you. Goodbye Sergeant…

"*Continue*, Mr. Zacchaeus," the man said, sure of the effect his specific tone was having on his new recruit.

"Hello, this is Colonel William Ravine calling for General Epcot… Hello, General! Thanks for talking with me. I phoned to let you know that there's been a development. I just received a call from the locals; the Labs at the university were broken into last night… No, Sir. I just now learned of it... Yes, Sir, I agree. We'll head over there immediately. I'll let you know as soon as we find out anything. Goodbye, General...

"*Anything else*," he added.

"Apparently there's been a break-in at the university's labs. Please get my car and meet me out front in ten minutes. We're heading over there. Thank you, Deltray."

Deltray Zacchaeus stopped talking and just stood there in silence.

"Very good! This is to be expected. Thank you, Mr. Zacchaeus. Please resume your efforts and get back with me after you gather more information. Let's see what they think they know. *Proceed and end report*," he finished.

Deltray Zacchaeus stood there for a moment, just staring at his phone curiously as if trying to remember what he was doing, his thoughts drifting in and out.

He then remembered the car.

Chapter 45

Eliam got the call first thing in the morning. He pushed himself to get ready as fast as he could and drove to campus in record time.

"So what are the details? Did they get into the lab? Any damage? Data breached?" Eliam asked Dr. Vectren, anxiety evident in his voice.

"No, apparently not, thank God. Whoever they were they couldn't get past the security doors into the labs, even though they were able to get into the building. They hacked their way through the east entrance and made it into the offices, through here and through here," Dr. Vectren said, tracing the perpetrators' path out for Eliam on a building schematic displayed on a large flat monitor.

A man in a wrinkled gray business suit approached them.

"Eliam, this is Detective Ortiz; Detective, Eliam Zaris. Eliam's the college's chief applied sciences engineer."

"Hello, Mr. Zaris."

"Detective."

The two nodded and shook hands.

"Security video?" Eliam asked swiftly, but the doctor was already pulling it up for him.

They watched the fifteen minutes' worth of clips, compiled from a total of twelve different camera feeds.

"There's not much to go on," Detective Jose Ortiz of the Lake Isabella Police Department said simply. "As you can see, they wore masks and what looks like padded clothing to hide their identities and physical characteristics. The one looks something like the late Bill Gates and maybe the other is that

Jeff Bezos guy from Drones Unlimited. I don't know." He laughed at the goofy, plastic facial expressions. "Cute, huh? No exposed flesh, no hair, no markings that we've made so far to help with an ID. They knew they were going to be recorded alright.

"They worked in tandem on the security, one accessing the swipe pads and the alarms, the other apparently trying to get into your system by tapping into the hard lines. Guy number two—Bezos here—tried to do so from three remote locations; he was able to get into a few subsystems, but fortunately wasn't able to unlock your lab doors or get into your protected mainframe."

"So no data breach, right?" Eliam asked Dr. Vectren again.

"No, not as far as we can tell right now," he stated. "Paul's team has been running diagnostic scans since we got here. Nothing so far. As it stands, it looks like they didn't accomplish anything except getting through a couple of doors and a little vandalism. Our security protocols defended the attack as designed."

"Personally, I don't think they're of any rank to be worried about," Detective Ortiz said pointedly. "Probably just a couple of teenage hackers trying to make a mark for themselves. Whoever they were, they spray painted several walls and the doors going into the lab section with their apparent slogan. I mean, look at the lousy spray paint job: AnTi-GeeK's TuRN. Lower and uppercase! Probably aren't college students. High school would be my guess. It appears they were nervous and in a hurry. Most likely didn't even have an agenda other than just seeing how far they could go, which wasn't far."

He motioned to the images on the screen of the lab's double-door entrance.

"These weren't professionals, again probably just kids trying to politicize their inner-angst regarding the world they were born in."

Eliam considered the man's words. Perhaps he was right. There was no evidence to the contrary.

"Good, that's a relief," Eliam said. "Keep checking the systems for any anomalies Dr. Vectren, okay. Just in case." He looked at his watch. "I really need to be going. I'm already late for the start of the test screening. Dr. Vectren, would you mind staying here and assisting further if they need anything?"

Dr. Vectren nodded, acquiescing politely.

"Detective Ortiz, nice to meet you," Eliam continued. "Thank you for coming out to help."

"Not a problem. Glad it was less than what it could have been; it looks like you have some good security out here. We'll take the recordings and have them analyzed further to see if we can isolate anything: sound, voice patterns, any identifiable markings, if there are any. But I wouldn't get my hopes up. Do you have a number you can be reached at, Mr. Zaris, for further questions, if any?"

Eliam fumbled in his wallet and retrieved a card.

He handed it to the man.

They shook hands.

·······

As soon as Eliam exited the building, he was approached by Deltray Zacchaeus and another man that he'd never seen before.

"Hello, Eliam," Deltray said as they got into ear range.

"Hello, Deltray. Listen, I'm very much in a hurry, I don't have…"

"Hello, Mr. Zaris. My name is Colonel William Ravine. It's nice to finally meet you. I head the office that Mr. Zacchaeus here works out of."

"Yes, uhmm, I see, it's nice to meet you, sir. But as I said I'm in very much of a hurry. Perhaps we can meet at another time. Maybe…"

"We understand that there has been a security breach at your labs, Mr. Zaris. You understand the government's interest and concerns here, I'm sure, and have from the beginning? It would be a prudent move on the university's part if we could be involved from the start, especially regarding any security problems pertaining to the project. We're here to help, Mr. Zaris, not impede, I assure you."

Eliam was silent for a moment as he considered the man's words.

"How did you know of the break-in? It just happened early this morning," Eliam asked curiously.

"Come now, Mr. Zaris. We work for the government. Hence we are in contact with all local agencies. We were notified immediately. It's very important we be kept in the loop, Mr. Zaris. I'm sure you understand our concerns."

Eliam studied the man. Something seemed familiar about him.

"Well, yes, of course I...*we* understand. And my apologies, but I do have to be going. The police are here—a Detective Ortiz and some officers. They're inside and practically done with the initial site investigation. Apparently it was just a couple of teenage hackers, part of that 'anti-geek hacker movement' or whatever. No data was breached, they assured us. All they were able to do was open a few doors and make a mess on a few walls, nothing more. I don't see any need for the government's help for something on this scale, I mean."

"I see," the Colonel said. "That's good. We're glad to hear that—no breach. However, it is true that information about the project is starting to leak out to the press, and now there has been a break-in of your facilities. Again, I think it would behoove us all to consider a more collaborative relationship going forward. Wouldn't you agree?" The Colonel spoke firmly.

Eliam now saw that this man wasn't going to be swayed from his position. He raised his eyebrows and exhaled briskly in acknowledgement of it.

"Sure, okay. Uhmm, yes, by all means, be my guest. Dr. Vectren is in there with the police. He can help you with any other information, if you wish. But I do have to be going. Deltray has my number, if you need to contact me."

"Thanks, Eliam," Deltray said, with a nod.

"Yes, thank you, Mr. Zaris." He then turned to his associate. "Deltray, would you be so kind as to go and sit in on the investigation, take thorough notes, gather incidental details, offer our help to this Detective Ortiz? I will join you shortly. I would like to talk to Mr. Zaris a few minutes longer."

He turned back toward Eliam and gave him an inquisitive look.

"Would it be alright if I at least walked with you to your next destination, Mr. Zaris? I have a few other brief questions. I promise, after that we won't take up any more of your time until we can make other future appointments."

He smiled broadly, trying to be cordial.

He then looked at Deltray Zacchaeus and raised his eyebrows. The man understood. Deltray nodded, turned and trekked on toward the labs.

"Sure, I suppose that would be okay. Thank you for understanding. Please, this way. I'm headed to the auditorium; we're conducting a simulated press release for the project's participants, ahead of the actual release."

They began walking.

After only a few seconds Colonel Ravine spoke.

"Mr. Zaris, all I in fact wanted to say to you is this…" He turned back to make sure Deltray had entered the lab building before continuing. "I understand your reticence regarding cooperation with us, especially when it comes to my subordinate, Deltray. He lacks, shall I say, critical knowledge, as well as certain professional skills."

He smiled a large smile, and then resumed.

"Be that it may, I wanted to personally reiterate to you the fact that we are here to help. The technology you're about to release to the world, as you undoubtedly know, will transform it dramatically. This, in itself, is reason for caution and prudence in exactly how, and with whom, that is accomplished, wouldn't you say? We just want to extend our hand, and offer any help if and when needed. Believe me; we quite possibly may be able to help in ways you can't begin to comprehend, going forward I mean."

He said it softly in a controlled voice, and then smiled once more.

Eliam stopped mid-stride; he then turned and gave the man a curious look.

. . . .

"Very good!" Chance Huffington said to everyone toward the end of the morning's Q&A session. "You've all answered the questions openly and honestly. And everyone's presentation has been professional and certainly practiced. However, all of you appear to be sold on the technology and its benefits. Few of you have uttered even a word of negativism regarding any of the aspects of the product. I assure you, when the real questions fly during the public forum, there will be a host of negatives posited for each and every one of you.

"So, I will be the devil's advocate in this scenario, with the intent of giving you a few morsels of what you can undoubtedly expect from the public, starting with you, Mr. Stewart."

Declan Stewart, the independent filmmaker, sat up a little straighter in his chair, now fully attentive.

"Mr. Stewart, I can see where this technology has the potential to make it more interesting, purportedly, when it comes to games, and movies, and personal amusement. But people are already so self-absorbed in their various entertainment forms that they don't have a clue anymore as to what reality truly is. How can you justify adding to this cultural decay, especially regarding the 'adult' industry? Are you going to tell me that morality is going to be thrown out the window yet again, in the name of personal entertainment?"

The entire group was clearly stunned by the question.

Declan Stewart nearly turned white, but he tried his best to keep his composure and answer.

"Well…uhm, 'morality,' as with many other things, is…is a subjective thing. It…depends on who you are and what your personal beliefs are, I think."

He wanted to say more, but his mind suddenly went blank with the attention.

"Yes, I see. It always comes down to that, doesn't it? Whatever one, or a leading group, chooses to believe, that's the defining factor, regardless of the consequences. That's why we have terrorists, and pedophiles, and the governing despotic autocracy. Isn't that right, Mr. Stewart?"

The group's expressions reflected utter astonishment, but Chance didn't even flinch at their collective rejection. She just looked at her tablet, appearing to be accessing some additional content.

"Let's see. I have another question here. Ms. Goens this time, you're quite the environmental advocate. Let me ask you, how can you justify supporting something like this technology, given your position? Wouldn't it actually be considered *having* a 'smart brain' if people would just forgo wasting all the required resources that are undoubtedly going to go into the manufacture and marketing of yet another electronic novelty? Don't we have enough already? And let me also inquire of you, along the same lines, exactly what you would consider a 'smart brain' to be?" Chance Huffington asked candidly, with discernible ire.

Furley didn't answer right away. She had a look of reticence on her face, but held one finger up, acknowledging the query and at the same time indicating she was composing her response. After a short pause of reflection, she offered her answer.

"Yes, I am an advocate of the environment; I think everyone is, to one degree or another. And, it could be considered 'smart' to reduce our apparently insatiable consumption of electronic products, along with a host of other 'things' that are created, using—or wasting—resources to do so. However, I am not unduly naive to the fact that we can't just de-populate the Earth, put off modern society, and simply revert back to sustainable, agrarian lifestyles in small cooperative communities.

"History is replete with circumstances of excess and over consumption and 'not-so-smart' over-indulgences based on errors of thinking and foresight regarding planning, and forecasting, and the extrapolation of true costs. But we have improved in many ways: we got rid of hydro-fluorocarbons, we have curbed the practice of deforestation to a great degree, we have reverted to solar and wind energies, whilst working toward the reduction of fossil fuel consumption, and the list goes on. In truth, I've probably thought about this more than a lot of people, but initial indications are that this Smartbrain technology will ultimately *reduce* consumption, not increase it."

"*Really*, and how so?" Chance Huffington asked, apparently disbelieving the statement.

"Well, with this technology, people can meet without the use of cars, and planes, and hotel rooms, to conduct business for instance, be with family, or whatever. Talk about a boon to social media! And we won't need to continue to manufacture all the devices we are now—cameras and phones and stereos and TVs, etc., because one device can do everything with tri-fold efficiency, and with one-hundredth the energy consumption. Consider the resource and cost saving advantages of the recent past with eBooks, and eCommerce, eEducation, and the open internet. These are just a few prime examples. I believe this will fall into a similar category, as well as creating its own.

"With Smartbrain technology people can be educated and entertained and do business, in stark realism, with detail and variety and convenience, as if they're actually together, while staying home—your senses can't tell the difference. This effect will be seen in business, and tourism, politics and education, entertainment and the arts, along with a million other applications.

"Yes, initial costs to build the infrastructure will undoubtedly be large, but a lot of it is actually already in place; we have wireless and satellite-based networks now. And yes, there are people who will find that their livelihoods will fall by the proverbial wayside because it will replace the things we have now. But, that has always been the case with change. There will be suffering from it, yes. Change hurts, change is hard, but it can be mitigated as it, too, has always been. And to answer your last question: 'what would I consider a smart brain to be?' To me, a 'smart brain' is one that chooses to develop the courage and discipline to do what's right and necessary, in order to make some commonsense change happen."

Furley paused and reflected a moment before making her last statement.

"I'm beginning to see this technology in the same light— at least potentially—as I do a patriot's rifle in the Revolutionary War; or a hand-carried sign in a Civil Rights march; or a wooden cross being dragged through the dirt by an innocent man to his death. It's something that, again, has the potential to raise the common man's awareness. But, it's not the thing; it's what's *behind* the thing that matters! Knowing that is what a 'smart brain' is!"

Silence settled on the auditorium.

The words Furley used were those of a mature, venerable diplomat, or perhaps even an oracle as such, likened to a bearded wise man on a mountain top, not a young girl barely beyond puberty. Sarah, along with several others, suddenly felt conflicting emotions: admiration and esteem yet set off against a sort of childish resentment at the young girl's profundity, as well as the lack of resolve in their own lives.

"Well, I'd say that was quite the oratory, Ms. Goens. I have no further questions for the group this morning," Chance Huffington said, herself taken aback by the young girl's eloquently offered and spirited delivery. A diminutive smile broke her thin, serious lips. "Okay, so why don't we break for lunch then? We'll reconvene back here at one o'clock."

As Sarah stood, she felt her phone vibrate and heard its faint tone, muffled by the thick cloth of her back pack. She stopped her motion and quickly fished for it, glad it had not gone off during the session. She was a little miffed at having forgotten to place it in silent mode. She pulled it out and entered her security code. It was a text from a number she did not recognize. She swiped the screen and opened the message.

HELLO SARAH, I'M CATHY YARNS, A DSP HERE AT GREENWAY CENTER. YOUR FATHER OSCAR MISPLACED HIS PHONE AGAIN. HE ASKED ME TO SEND YOU A MESSAGE TO SEE IF YOU COULD STOP BY HIS HOUSE AND GET A DATA CD FOR HIM. HE SAID IT WAS IN THE DESK, OR ON THE SHELF, HE COULDN'T REMEMBER—TITLED NASA STUFF. THX, CATHY.

Sarah read the message and processed the request. She wondered about the CD, not remembering seeing it, but it could have been overlooked in one of the drawers. She thought about it and then typed a reply.

HI CATHY, PLEASE TELL HIM YES. I WILL GET IT THIS EVENING AND DROP BY THERE AROUND 6:30.

Chapter 46

Sarah slowly drove down the hedge-lined driveway. The sun was low, the sky clear, and the shadows long. She rolled through the darkened bands laying across the pavement as if skipping through distant memories from the past: all those evenings at play in the yard when she was a kid; that one particular bush on the left where she'd long ago ran through, ripping open her arm as if with a razor; all the warm summer evenings playing games and hiding amongst the many nooks and crannies of the hedges and up in the many trees of the large yard, and raking all those tons of leaves over the decades, only to see them return year after year.

Sarah couldn't help but go back in time every time she returned there, especially recently.

She stopped the car next to the back porch, turned off the engine and just sat there, looking through the breezeway between the house and the garage. The yard was getting out of hand, and she made a mental note to get someone out here to take care of it. She sighed and frowned at the same time. And yet again, the burden of thought entered her mind of what to do with the place now that her dad wouldn't be living there anymore.

She bit her lip, not wanting to think about it.

Sarah got out and headed up the steps with her key in hand. She opened the door mindlessly, stepped in and started pushing buttons to deactivate the alarm system. As she did so, she suddenly realized that it was in passive mode. Apparently she hadn't set it the last time she was there. •

Surely she hadn't forgotten. She strained to remember. She'd set it and turned it off so many times, it was like driving the same way to work every day—you just do it without even a thought. Had this been the case? When was the last time? She and Cybil, and Condi and her dad, she recalled. That's probably why she had forgotten. Her mind was in turmoil that day.

She shut the door and listened for a moment.

Shaking her head, she put the keys in her pocket and headed to the den.

"NASA stuff," she said out loud, bringing it back to memory. She arrived at the desk and began the search. It was a substantial piece of wooden furniture with numerous drawers, but there were only a few items left in them after the move. She saw no disk.

"Or on the shelf…!" she said next, remembering the message. "Shelf? What shelf are you talking about, Dad? There's no shelf. Did you mean Mom's curio in the dining room?" she mumbled, looking around.

Suddenly she heard what sounded like nylon brushing against nylon. It was faint, but that was certainly what it sounded like to her. She went silent and listened intently. Nothing. She turned her head ninety degrees and listened once more. Nothing. She thought about it again. It had seemed to sound like that familiar resonance she'd heard a thousand times. But it was nothing, she concluded, probably the wind and trees outside.

Sarah shook her head again.

"Get a grip, girl!" she said, going to the curio.

She looked through the glass doors, but didn't see any CD on the sparsely covered internal shelves. She then slid out the top drawer. Nothing. She went for the second drawer and as she slid it open, she thought she heard that sound again. She stopped and listened, again questioning her ears. Nothing. She went on, looking in the next two empty drawers.

"Nothing…" she said.

She looked back to the shelves in the curio to double check, but her searching eyes were abruptly drawn to something she wasn't at all expecting: a movement of light reflected in the polished glass of the beautiful cabinet.

Sarah's eyes froze on the location of the motion. But she could make out nothing in the curved, warped image she was focusing on. Then, within an instant, her slight anxiety swelled to heart pounding terror. She suddenly saw the movement again, and it was getting larger in the glass—something was behind her.

Sarah swung around with a high energy jerk and immediately saw the person coming at her in haste. It was a man much taller than her, dressed in a dark, fall-season running suit, and he had a mask on, a plastic mask that made him look as if he were a futuristic, robot-like mannequin. As soon as Sarah's eyes met his, he sprinted like a runner out of the starting blocks toward her.

However, having seen him nearly across the room gave Sarah a split second more to react, and she turned and darted down the hallway toward the kitchen. As she raced toward it, she quickly and instinctively thought of the kitchen door to the outside, and to safety. The thought pulsed through her mind at light speed and gave her the incentive to pump her legs like she'd never had in the past.

She made the end of the hallway, all the while hearing the man stomping the floor in heated strides trying to gain on her.

Sarah started to panic when she felt the hand touch her left shoulder, just as she turned the corner to enter through the open double doorway into the kitchen. Her turning, and the arm's apparent impact on the door jamb made it lose its tenuous grip and it slid off, yet Sarah's inertial forces, coupled with the nudge of the hand made Sarah lose her stride and she crashed into the sink counter next to the refrigerator, doubling her over as her right hip slid along the counter's edge.

She then saw him lunge at her again in her left-side periphery, and she reactively rebounded off the counter. Yet with all her effort, she was met with his strong arms in front of the refrigerator, and he pushed her hard into the large appliance.

Suddenly Sarah felt like a small gazelle trying desperately to get away from a roaring cheetah, the predator swift and confident, while the prey was nearly incapacitated by the debilitating fear of pain and dying. Sarah almost went limp from the blow against the old-fashioned fridge her father insisted on keeping and using. And in thinking about it, something in her mind stirred at that instant regarding her father: things he'd told her, things he'd taught her.

Sarah then chose to do something she'd only barely ever wanted to do, or ever thought she'd have to do. Perhaps it was instinctual, her having been born with it as a human thing, or perhaps it was amassed from her father's proclivity toward preparedness, but none the less, it was ready to come out before Sarah had even decided upon it.

Sarah turned toward the man and lashed out a snap-kick catching the man square in the crotch before he even saw it coming. The momentum of his motion, however, was stronger than Sarah's kick, carrying his temporarily collapsing body right into Sarah's, and both slammed into the refrigerator.

The man quickly went to the floor grabbing himself, but he must have been impervious to pain, or at the least seriously dedicated to his cause, because he immediately rebounded off the floor and lunged back at Sarah.

Seeing it coming, Sarah rolled to her right and grabbed the handle to the upper freezer on the appliance, jerking the door open as she did so in one fluid move.

Intuitively, the man grasped that he was going to be smacked in the face, and he swiftly ducked. The door barely caught the top of his head as he again went down on his knees. Thinking himself clever and fast for maneuvering in such a way to avoid her attack, he smirked as he looked up at her, while at the same time moving slightly to the left to avoid the rebounding door as it swung back around.

His eyes suddenly took on a confused look when he saw Sarah reach into the cavity of the freezer and pull a man's full-sized, heavy work boot out of the cold storage space. The oddity of it stopped him in his tracks for an instant as he tried to process in his mind what he was seeing.

Sarah took advantage of the man's hesitation and in swift motion, grabbed the boot with both hands, twisted her body, and swung it as hard and as fast as she could. Before he could react, the heel of the hard-frozen footwear slammed into his temple and knocked his head sideways into the adjacent counter top's edge. He summarily bounced off it, as if his head had been made of rubber, and fell limply to the floor.

Sarah couldn't help but follow through with her swing, for she had put all her adrenaline-filled might into it. She spun around and was as surprised at the result as the man might have been, had he still been conscious to consider what had just happened. Sarah stood there in a ready stance, the boot drawn back for another attempt, but after a few seconds she was reasonably sure the man wasn't getting up any time soon.

Sarah dropped the boot to the floor and instinctively stepped backward, away from the horrible event that had just happened. In a jolting instant, she felt her shoulder blade hit the door jamb behind her, hindering any further rearward movement. She put both hands to her mouth and gasped from the shock, as well as from the surprising finality of the encounter.

Sarah just stood there and stared in awe, frozen in her thoughts and motion as she tried to take in what had just happened. It was then that she felt the instantly-stinging slap to the neck and heard the voice behind her.

"Damn, Jack! You got to be kidding me! A simple pick-up and delivery, and you about fuck it up."

Sarah recoiled from the muscled reaction in her neck, naturally turning at the same time to see what it was that had so painfully poked her. In doing so she saw a blond haired woman also dressed in a dark running suit looking at her with the female version of that same mask on. Sarah suddenly felt dizzy and disoriented. She tried to step away from the feminine apparition, but her legs buckled for some unknown reason and she felt herself fall to the floor. Everything seemed to close in on her at that moment and her eyelids felt like they

were made of lead. Then, Sarah Whiting couldn't remember
anything.

Chapter 47

Something flashed in her mind. It was an image of some room, in a hospital maybe. All she could remember of it were the colors gray and white and the undulating movement of fluted cloth.

She felt herself blink, though it wasn't a voluntary action, only a sensation. It seemed to just happen, a fluttery, wispy feeling came over her, and her mind felt as if it were in motion somehow. It was an odd, out-of-body sensation. She then thought to focus on her breathing, but as she did she realized she couldn't tell if she was breathing at all.

A light seemed to snap on.

She saw a man in a long white coat with pens sticking out of his breast pocket.

The man made eye contact with her. He then spoke some-one's name: "Sarah!"

She heard the word; she knew it was a name, but why had he spoken it to her?

Then, she felt herself sliding backwards, shrinking.

The darkness wasn't particularly frightening; in fact it was comforting.

When the light came back, she felt anxiety and confusion, but then she wasn't sure.

This time she saw fast-moving images of her father; he was talking to a man she seemed to recognize. The man had his hand on her father's shoulder and they appeared to be laugh-ing and enjoying each other's company. Numerous images of the two flashed through her mind, each in different locations, in the midst of different circumstances. And then she saw that same now-familiar man up in front of a podium, speaking. And off to his side was a multi-portrait display of her father, the images surrounding an ornamented urn positioned in the middle of a table decorated with embroidered cloth, and flowers, and plaques with sayings on them.

Darkness and comfort engulfed her once more.

There was no sense of time.

There was no sense, of sense.

But then the light returned.

In the light were streams of images, as if watching one's life on fast forward. The ensuing motion captivated her, though not because of the actual scenes she was seeing, but because of the convoluted way they morphed around her. It was as if she were caught in a whirlwind of spiraling, four-dimensional space, the people, and objects, and depth, and dimension sluicing in and out of each other, seemingly occupying the same space at the same time.

There was that man again.

He had dark hair, a dimpled chin, a rugged handsome face, and he wore a heavy, course-threaded, dark blue sweater. His familiarity captivated her, yet she couldn't remember how, why, or from where. It was also the first time she could remember sensing that coolness on her open eyes, and she felt herself blink this time as she heard the man speak.

"Sarah! Can you hear me?" he asked, his voice full of trepidation and anxiety.

Sarah blinked several more times, slowly becoming aware of her surroundings. She was in that gray and white room. The scene returned to her memory, as did the familiar face she found herself gazing up at. It was then that she felt the warmth of the hand holding hers. She looked down toward the sensation. The man was gently squeezing her hand as he held it in his.

"Oh, Sarah! I am so glad! Can you speak, Sari?" He tilted his head, his wide eyes seemingly radiating his affection for her. Sarah had a sudden flash of light in her vision and an uncomfortable feeling came over her. The man's face changed slightly, and then it all went black again.

....

"Hello, Sarah. I see you've returned to us. You're making wonderful progress. It's a bit too soon to explain what has happened to you; that will come in due time. For now, I'll just tell you who I am, and where you are. I'm Dr. Lazarus, Sarah. You are in the advanced recovery unit of Heartland Center; it's a hospital for…well, for people who need special care and monitoring. You had some things happen to you, Sarah, that, fortunately, we were able to…to gain some significant ground on regarding diagnosis and treatment. You've been here for quite some time, but you are showing some remarkable improvement."

Sarah searched her mind to try to understand what this man was saying. She studied him intently, forcing her focus. She did not recognize him at all. He was of medium build, middle-aged with a receding hairline that appeared to be augmented by slightly off color implants. He had a pleasant, friendly face, not handsome by many standards, but sociably cordial in its demeanor.

Sarah tried to speak, but felt awkward in attempting to do so.

"You're…you're a doctor?" she asked in a coarse voice. "What happened? What happened to me?" she added, not waiting for the answer, but trying to account for the sudden lack of knowledge in her own mind.

"Yes, Sarah. I'm a doctor. As I said, it may not be a good time to cover too much all at once. Let me ask you. What do you remember?" he asked, shifting position to hear her better.

Sarah considered the question, but nothing came to her mind. She had an uncomfortable feeling right then, akin to embarrassment, but she attempted to answer.

"I…I don't remember anything. I think I remember…I remember images…uhmm…just pieces. It hurts to think," she said, just then realizing that fact.

"Yes, I imagine it does. That will most likely be the case for some time. Just take it slowly. Sarah, let me ask you. Can you tell me your name? Your full name?"

She thought about it.

"Sarah…uhmm…Sarah…*Whiting*," she said, struggling with the discomfort.

"That's your maiden name, Sarah. What is your married name?" he then asked, tilting his head and giving her a slight nod of encouragement.

Sarah just looked at him.

Married?

Nothing seemed to register except confusion. She rolled her head to the side and contorted her face as if trying desperately to recall something that her mind right then told her she should be recalling, but nothing came to her. Then, she saw a series of fleeting memories in her mind. They were there, and then just as quickly gone.

Sarah lifted her right hand up to her brow and rubbed it with her fingers.

"Married name?" she repeated. "I…" suddenly she felt pain in her head and squint her eyes in repulsion of the feeling.

"That's okay, Sarah. That's probably enough, why don't you rest a little more. It looks as if we have a little more work to do."

Upon saying that the man lifted the small device he had in his hand and looked at it.

Sarah fell back into unconsciousness the moment he did so.

·······

The sense of time was altogether absent from Sarah as she slowly become cognizant of the new images. It was as if she had awakened once more from a deep sleep and was still groggy from the slumber. Sarah opened her eyes wider; she was in a different room, sitting upright, though reclining back slightly, she realized.

"Hello again, Sarah," said the man who had called himself a doctor.

Sarah realized the man was sitting across from her in a chair similar to the one she had found herself in. Sitting up a little straighter, she looked around. The room appeared to be a lounge of some sort. The kind found in countless hospitals and clinics, the type where families were told of loved one's demises, or of their own.

"Where am I?" Sarah asked calmly.

"You're still at Heartland Center, Sarah. It's located quite some distance from your home in L. A. You've made some wonderful progress the last few months, and now it's time to see if we can bring you back to reality."

"Reality?" Sarah repeated, a sense of apprehension evident in her tone.

"Yes, Sarah. We think it best that you still go slowly; however, it's important that you begin connecting with your life in the real sense. We—our staff, as well as your husband—think you're ready for this, though we must warn you…it will not be easy. You may feel confused and disoriented at times, but just be patient. It's perfectly understandable. Your mind will settle as time progresses. We believe your memory will return to you, but again, we'll just take it slowly, okay?" He gave her a somber smile.

Sarah stared at him. His words made sense, in their individual meanings, and his appearance seemed sincere, but the overarching gist served to do what he'd just said. It confused her deeply.

The man saw her expression and understood.

"You just wait here. I'm going to leave now and send in your husband. He…"

"*Husband?*" she asked, interrupting.

"Yes, Sarah. He's been fully informed of the sensitivity of the situation—of your condition—but he's insistent that he be the one to help make the initial reorientation happen. I'll send him in; I will be just outside that door if needed. Okay?"

She looked at the door, then back with a blank stare, trying to process her thoughts, but they kept looping around in unintelligible sequences that didn't make any sense to her.

The doctor stood, reached down and touched her hand supportively, then turned and stepped towards the door. He opened it as he smiled back at her. She saw him apparently acknowledging someone outside in a hallway, and then he exited the room. She heard brief, muffled conversation. After a few seconds another man entered.

There was recognition in the form of memories, but they were accompanied with an anxiety that nearly took her breath away.

． ． ． ． ． ． ．

"Hi Sarah!" the man said softly, as he walked over and took a seat in the chair the doctor had been in. "It's so good to see you, Sari. I'm sure Dr. Lazarus told you that we need to take this slowly. But, I think it is important to start by answering some of the basic questions you've probably been asking."

Sarah wasn't really listening to the man's words. She was trying her best to access her memories to answer the questions in her mind about why he seemed so familiar. His form and appearance gave her an overwhelming sense of familiarity, but for the life of her, she couldn't place him. Then, as if a flash went off in her mind, she seemed to suddenly recall a series of images of him: them together in various places, a place that seemed to her to be a house, maybe a home, and then images of him with her father, and…

Sarah's mind halted on the image of this man in front of a podium, speaking. He was speaking at her father's funeral. The scene in her mind made her blurt out her words with force.

"My father! You…you…he's gone?"

The man leaned forward slightly. He looked down as if carefully considering his words.

"Yes, Sarah. Many years ago…six, now, I guess it's been."

"What? Six years? You…you…" she fumbled for her words. "I…I don't understand. You're…"

"Yes, Sarah. I'm your husband…Mathew…Mathew Bolton, you're my wife, Sari! Sarah Bolton. We've been married for over twelve years, soon to be thirteen, on the ninth of April."

Sarah's head tilted down at his words. She took a deep breath and just stared at him, twisting her head involuntarily, trying to process what she was hearing.

"I see you *don't* remember." He exhibited a sad, despondent expression and looked away, apparently trying to gather his emotions. He too took a deep breath, clenched his lips and tried to continue.

"The doctors warned me of this. But…I…I didn't think it would be so hard. Listen Sarah, you and I have had our problems over the years, just as a lot of people do, but, we love each other, Sari…very much! I wish I could just turn back the clock and make this all right, change what happened, for both of us, but I can't. We have to go on from here."

Sarah's mind caught on his one word.

"*What*…happened?" she asked abruptly.

He looked at her, fear and anxiety shaping his countenance. He took another deep breath before beginning.

"It was that damned Smartbrain contraption. It nearly warped your brain beyond recovery, Sari, you and a few thousand other people. But you're one of the lucky ones; there's no coming back for most of the others. It's a horrific thing to happen, Sari. Terrible, just terrible!"

"Smartbrain?" Sarah repeated. "I…I…it…did *what*?"

"It essentially put your mind into a hyper-epileptic state. At least that's how they describe it. I don't pretend to understand it. But, for many, it scrambled their brains—electrically—and there's no fixing it for most of those affected."

Sarah just sat there and stared. Suddenly, memories—blinks of memories—starting coming to her conscious mind.

"I was…I was part of the program. I…"

"No Sari, you weren't. You were a consumer, just like all the others. It's not your fault. That's something that Dr. Lazarus said. He said that you were living in a fantasy world, in effect. That you'd talk for hours as if you were…as if you were living another life, another existence. I mean, I heard it to, when it started, but it didn't make any sense to me. That's when I got you some help and we found out that literally thousands of others were experiencing degrees of the same thing.

"For some, it happened nearly immediately after they got fitted with the damned thing, within days: loss of memory, strange behavior. Others apparently used them for quite a long time before it happened. No one knew what was going on for months after its release, but after enough people starting having problems, they recalled every last one of them. The damned companies behind the marketing as well as the inventors of the stupid thing are in some really deep crap right about now. It'll probably be in the courts for the next thirty or forty years before they settle on the damages. Hell, there were all sorts of big-named people affected, too: politicians, entertainers, executives, a ton of Wall Street and Silicon Valley people, I guess. A lot of people!

"But like I said, Sari, you're one of the lucky ones. They say ninety percent of those who had the right brain chemistry—or the *wrong* brain chemistry, I guess—will never recover, ever. That's why it'll take so long in the courts—so many people, so many different effects. A lot of people weren't adversely affected at all, and probably never would've been, possibly, because of how their brains are wired. But, it didn't matter. They put a 100% mandatory recall out. That's been over eight months ago."

Sarah nearly turned white.

Her breathing became shallow and slow. She sat back in her chair as if drained of all energy. Her mind suddenly became exhausted, as did her body. It was as if she'd suddenly been drugged.

Once again, blackness engulfed her.

Chapter 48

Sarah found herself lying down on a large, king-sized bed, covered up with soft sheets and a tufted down comforter. She was in silk pajamas, very comfortable silk pajamas. She looked around as she pulled herself up into a sitting position against the backboard of the bed. She yawned and stretched slightly as she began taking in the details of her surroundings.

The room was large and very nicely appointed: stylish platform bed, a separate lounge area in one corner with chairs and a couch, a center coffee table and an entertainment center. Two large curtained picture windows on one wall flanked a set of double French doors leading out onto a large veranda, a passageway off to her left lead to dual walk-in closets, and four ornately carved, matching antique dressers and tables were aesthetically placed around the room against the wood trimmed, delicately papered walls.

Sarah was stunned for a moment while assessing the high-end fineness she had just found herself in. As she awoke further, the memories began returning, as well as the anxiety that accompanied them.

Her thoughts were suddenly distracted when she heard footfalls in the distance. They grew stronger, as did her anxiety. She turned one way and then the other attempting to decide just what it was she should do, but her efforts were stymied when she heard the bedroom door knob turn and then saw the door open. She pulled the comforter up closer to her neck in response.

He entered.

"Good morning, Sari! How was your first night back home?" he asked, as he walked slowly over to the side of the bed. He was smiling, with an oddly confident look on his face. His six-foot frame was fully dressed in business-casual trousers and a dress shirt, both stylish and well-fitting.

Sarah noticed his muscled body and his manly attractiveness at that moment—wavy dark hair, slightly dimpled chin, strong jaw and strong hands. It did little to calm her fast-beating heart. She held the comforter tighter. She wanted to get up and run, wanted to be anywhere but there, but she didn't know what to do. Her mind raced for recognition. All she could bring to memory were a few disparate images. None were enough to explain to her in any way what had happened or what was happening. She just sat there and stared at him.

He slowly sat down on the bed next to her.

Sarah about jumped out of her skin.

He saw the reaction and moved back slightly.

"I hope you slept well. I am very glad to see you home, Sarah. It's been way too long. And, I hope we can take up with our lives where we left off. I really want that, Sarah."

Sarah didn't say a word; she just stared at him blankly.

It was an uncomfortable moment, for both it seemed.

"Well, I imagine you're hungry. I'm sorry, but I can't join you for breakfast. I have some important early business this morning I need to rush off to. But I had the staff prepare some breakfast for you. It's in the kitchen downstairs."

He stood and started to back away.

"Uhmm, as per doctor's orders, it would be best if you stayed in the house for awhile, Sarah. Venturing out too soon—especially alone—may trigger some relapse episodes. There is some worry there, still. We just need to give it some time, okay? But he assures us you'll be fine if you just take it easy. The phones and my number—you know, if you don't remember—are in nearly every room. You can call if you need anything, anytime. Okay?

"You might want to look through some family portraits, trips and whatever, on one of your tablets. Maybe that'd be nice for you. Oh, and Dr. Lazarus recommended that you refrain from watching any news, or media for awhile as well. There are movies and shows on the drives, but he also suggested you stay away from any high-emotion dramas and the like, same reasons."

He coughed and cleared his voice at the same time.

"Well then, I guess I should be going, big day ahead."

He paused as if contemplating going in closer to give her a kiss, but he again noted the look on her face, so he thought it better not to.

"Well, I will see you later. I love you Sari!"

Sarah didn't respond.

He looked at her for a long second, but dropped his eyes. He turned and left, shutting the door behind him.

Sarah just stared at him until he disappeared. Extremely thankful to be alone again, she reclined back down into the bed and covered her face with her hands. She began crying softly. She'd never felt so lost.

....

Sarah finally rose after a long period of futile contemplation. Mainly so because of the intense frustration she felt in trying to remember. Her train of thought would seem focused one minute trying to link together her disparate thoughts, and then she'd find herself just sitting there with nothing in her mind at all it seemed, as if she had fallen into a gaping void inside her head. The sensations, having happened more times than she could recall, scared her, yet finally moved her to get up in an attempt to fend off the sickening feeling.

She first went to one of the picture windows and peered outside. She saw only grass covered rolling hills amidst stands of trees in the distance. There were no other structures, nor any roads to be seen. She then went to the set of French doors and tried to open one, but it was securely locked. She looked closely several times for a lever or button to unlock it, but to no avail. She then grabbed both handles and pushed and pulled them with force, but they would not budge at all, not even a single millimeter, she noted oddly.

Sarah then went to the closets and in the one which was apparently hers, she saw row after row of dresses, and tops; she saw shelves and drawers of shoes and boots and handbags of all kinds, all fine clothes and accessories in a host of styles and colors. None of them were even remotely recognizable to her. She then found a small area in one corner that had simple pants and jeans—some stacked, some hanging. She scavenged through several pairs of jeans and picked one. She opened a few random drawers and located some undergarments, and then ended up choosing an unassuming blouse and a matching pull-over sweater.

She headed to the bathroom.

Sarah stood there and just stared in the mirror. She saw herself, but had the oddest feeling that the person she was looking at wasn't her for some reason. She couldn't even begin to describe the sensation. Tears rolled down her eyes. After an extended amount of time studying her features, Sarah took a shower, dried off with the softest towel she could ever recall using, and then dressed quickly, suddenly feeling self-conscious about being in a strange and unfamiliar place while being unclothed.

"This is…my bathroom?" she uttered softly as she dressed.

She felt a little better after showering, but in actuality she didn't physically feel any different or fresher, or cleaner than before. She found some socks and shoes and decided, for no other reason than there was nothing else she could do, to go exploring a little. She opened the double set of bedroom doors and peeked out slowly. She neither heard, nor saw anyone else, so she carefully and quietly stepped out into the hallway and headed the only direction she could, down a long corridor.

Along the hall she saw other doors but decided to not open any. She thought about calling out to see if anyone was there, but her anxiety kept her from doing so. She then found herself at a large staircase which descended to a platform, and then saw other steps turning to the right and descending further out of sight. She took a deep breath and started down. Arriving at the platform she observed a large atrium area below. There she saw what was apparently a front entryway to the house, and on opposite sides of the atrium, two hallways that went off of it at oblique angles.

As she stood in the middle of the large, high-ceilinged room Sarah could now see down each hallway. For some reason she supposed that the one to the right was the one that might lead to the kitchen area. She was correct in her assumption and she wondered, as she strode down it, whether she'd actually remembered it, or had just made a reasonable guess. Regardless, she found the dining area, and off it an entertainment wing. In that was an indoor gun range, a pool, a weight room, and a bar-type lounge, laid out in a sports/golfing theme, complete with a putting green and a virtual driving range to boot.

Sarah shrugged, turned, and went the other way to find the kitchen two more rooms off the ornately designed dining room. It was a kitchen of any woman's dreams: two prep islands in the middle, one with a huge sink. Cabinets galore, and any kitchen appliance one could ever imagine needing behind smoked-glass cabinet doors. Off it, yet in the same large room, was a ten-person contemporary styled table and chairs half sitting in an alcove surrounded by floor-to-ceiling windows trimmed in dark-cherry wood, with matching modern French doors looking out onto what appeared to be a golf course. Outside, it appeared to be a beautiful day, but she didn't see any people, or golf carts, or anything of the like, just blue skies and breeze-blown greenery. Sarah tried several of the sets of doors, as she'd done upstairs, but with the same results. Neither of the doors would open. She didn't try further.

Sarah looked around again, noticing that there were trays on the counter top of one of the islands. She walked over and lifted one of the covers and found a spread of food that was enough to feed five people: sliced fruit, eggs, bacon, sausage, potatoes, fresh baked bread and biscuits, jams, nuts and dried fruit, yogurts in different flavors, cereal, milk, juices, coffee and tea. All of it was hot and steamy, or cool and fresh, depending on what it was.

Sarah grabbed a plate and loaded it lightly with a few morsels and then sat down at the table with it and a cup of coffee.

She felt hungry and started eating right away, but it wasn't very long before she noticed the blandness of the food. It was flavorsome, but not exactly delicious, at least as delicious as it first appeared. She ate most of what was on her plate, but didn't return for seconds, except for the coffee, even though it was on the weak side and had a funny aftertaste.

After eating, Sarah went to the sink and washed her dishes, placing them into a strainer. She dried her hands on a towel, and as she did she noticed that the water didn't seem to dry as quickly as she'd thought it should. She tried again with the towel and then considered that the cloth it was made of must not be very absorbent, just the opposite of the towel upstairs after her shower, she thought.

Sarah decided to continue her exploration.

She returned to the atrium, and in passing tried to open the front entry doors. Like the others, they would not budge. Again, there were no discernable locking mechanisms to be seen, which was extremely odd, she thought. Her mind told her that her husband must have had all the locks changed or removed so she couldn't venture out, but again the very thought of *'her husband'* stopped her in her tracks.

She couldn't believe any of this.

This wasn't her home, was it?

But, she couldn't remember her home.

Sarah just stared, wide-eyed into the distance. Her mind drifting, seemingly circling around some big dark void, poised on the edge of its precipice, peering down into it as if awaiting something. Fear and anxiety were the only things keeping her from plunging into its depths.

Her attention returned to her when she suddenly thought she heard a sound. She twisted and looked down the other hallway. Careening her neck and remaining still, she listened, thinking it came from there. Nothing. She then slowly headed down the corridor, continuing to listen carefully as she walked. The long, curved passage soon came upon yet another set of double doors.

Sarah hesitated, listened intently, but heard nothing. She reached for a door handle. It turned with ease. She took a deep breath, pushed one of the doors open, and then leaned in. The unexpected size of the space stopped her breathing for a second. It was enormous: three or more floor elevations with single and double step-ups, the inside towering over two stories high. Various skylights and irregularly located windows high above flooded the expanse with light and shadow.

The design and décor was rustic, yet modern, replete with intersecting beamed ceilings, wooden posts, and stone, amidst walls of metal and glass, all of which created various room-sized alcoves located asymmetrically around its perimeter. In the center of it was a massive, walk-around, stone and mantle fireplace. The huge expanse was superbly appointed, with wood and leather furniture of varying styles throughout. It was like having a huge, mountain-lodge-type visitor's-lobby as your personal living space.

Sarah began a slow, leisurely stroll around the vast room noting the huge number of odd, yet uniquely accenting items that adorned nearly every surface, nook, and cranny. She saw statuary of many sizes that appeared to be Roman, and Greek, and Egyptian; fossils, and rocks, and mineral samples; antique clothes behind glass; old, yellowed pictures; volumes of books; flags, and parchments, and time pieces; and a huge amount of weaponry from Neolithic to modern times, from nearly every continent, culture and era.

Sarah especially noted the particularly large collection of handguns; an entire pair of conjoined alcoves appeared dedicated to these alone. There were muskets and Colt Peacemakers and semi-automatic Model 1911 military pistols; there were derringers and long barreled target shooters, and numerous chromed-out, pearl-handled-type small caliber personal protection guns. Guns of all shapes and sizes, there must have been hundreds of them, she thought.

Sarah was in awe. The entire place was a veritable museum of historical artifacts, from the dawn of man to the space age, it seemed. Yet none of it was at all familiar to her. How could she not remember any of this?

As she strolled and touched and stared, wondering about it all, she noticed a corner where there was desk and chair ensemble. On the desk was a large tablet/monitor set into its surface at a slight angle. The memory sparked in her mind about looking at one of "*your*" tablets. Sarah suddenly became curious. She rounded the desk and sat down in the comfortable chair. She touched the monitor's screen and just below, an input pad embedded in the top lit up.

Sarah hesitated but then swiped the pad, accessing a folder on the screen that was plainly marked: Family. She touched it, followed by the one labeled Pics. What Sarah began seeing stunned her beyond belief.

....

She sat there for what must have been hours, surveying image upon image, and watching videos. Most were of places: buildings, cityscapes, landscapes, mountains, parks, beaches, zoos, gardens, and museums. Images and videos apparently taken on trips, stored in various folders titled: New York, Grand Canyon, Europe, Mexico, South America, Science and Industry, Smithsonian, Harvard, NASA, Anniversaries, Business Trips, Escapes and Adventures, Best and Worst, along with a number of Miscellaneous files.

Sarah seemed to remember some of the places; scenes she'd seen with her own eyes, she thought, but most sparked no memory whatsoever. In all, there were hundreds of images, but remarkably few with Sarah and Matthew in them. Many of the sub-files would not load for some reason, and the ones that did, seemed to load awkwardly and slowly.

Of the images of Sarah and Mathew, individually or together—mainly of their wedding, and on a few trips in a few random files—there were only a couple dozen or so in all. The ones that stood out were of their apparent wedding, of which most were primarily of a bunch of people Sarah did not recognize, and those directly of them, but obviously unprofessionally taken. They sparked little recollection, except an odd feeling of familiarity, as if she had merely only seen the image before, not the actual event.

In the end, the all-morning sortie into the life of Matthew and Sarah Bolton left her feeling stranger and more confused than when she'd started. *Why can't I remember more,* she asked herself? *Why were there so few pictures of family, and friends, and of us?* she continued. *And why would so many files not even open?* she wondered.

Sarah just sat there and stared at the screen.

Smartbrain? What happened? she tried to remember. *The device…thousands of people? People lost their minds, went crazy?* For some reason the thought struck Sarah to the core, and she had no idea why. Another torrent of questions poured from her mind, sparked by dislocated and disjointed memories. One seemed to spark another, but they were so vague and fleeting it was as if seeing ghosts just inside your peripheral vision, and hearing them whispering into your ear.

Smartbrain? I…I was part of it, wasn't I? I was…I was…

Dad's…gone?

Another …life? Another…place? Another …me? she wondered.

Sarah suddenly felt herself fall off the edge and into that big black void.

. . . .

The resonance startled her, shaking her unexpectedly.

Sarah opened her eyes from a half-closed position to see him across the room; he was standing there next to the fireplace, looking at her. She felt the breath leave her for a moment.

He could see the stress on her face, and the loss in her tear-filled eyes.

"Hi," was all he said.

Sarah looked at him, and then around the room as if seeking a path of escape. Her mind told her there wasn't any. She looked at the screen in front of her and then back up at him. As difficult as it was, she answered.

"Hello."

He froze all movement for a second and then offered a sad, disappointed expression, hearing in her voice the complete absence of any acknowledgement or acceptance.

"I would have thought you'd think...*feel* differently by now," he said, shaking his head slightly as he started toward her. "I guess not. Apparently not yet, anyway," he mumbled the last part.

Sarah thought she had detected subtle disgust in his shifting voice and demeanor. She didn't say any more. She just sat there and watched as he approached the desk.

"Were you looking at some files?"

Sarah looked at the screen again and then back up.

"Yes," was all she said.

He waited to see if she'd say any more. She didn't.

"Anything? Any recollections...memories?" he asked plainly.

Sarah moved her eyes in numerous directions, not exactly looking at anything in particular, but just searching her thoughts. She glanced at him again and then tried to consider his perspective.

"Some. I...I remember some things, I think. I don't remember this place." She looked around. "I don't remember my dad dying, or...or much of anything, actually. Just big holes in places I can't seem to get around." Her face exhibited sudden strong emotion, and her eyes moistened heavily.

"Yes, I can imagine."

"Can you?!" she blurted out suddenly.

He was somewhat taken aback by the eruption, but not overly so.

"Yes, I think I can."

She stared at him.

"Sarah, I know it must be difficult. But think about how lucky you are, compared to the rest. You're getting your mind back; you have all this; you have us! Many don't have anything, and never will again." He made an odd expression and then continued. "Listen, let me answer some questions for you. Let me help."

Sarah thought about it. All she had were questions.

"Where is this place? Like I said, I don't remember this house, this room, any of it, just…just fleeting images, maybe. And our 'family' pictures…why are there so few? I don't remember those, either. How come we don't have more? Why? And why does it all seem so…foreign to me?" Her tears swelled even further.

He considered her questions before answering.

"The house," he said, looking around, "is outside L.A. It's private out here. I think it's nice. I…*we*, like it. And there aren't that many pictures because of the fire."

He didn't say any more. He just studied her reaction.

"Fire?" Sarah repeated.

"Yes. There was a fire a few years ago, where we used to live. Fortunately, we weren't there when it happened. No one was hurt. But it destroyed our old home, for the most part, and took with it about everything we had, including most of our life. Files, pictures, keepsakes, our collections, all were lost. Those files you were looking at were compiled from sparse, old backups we had, and what few we pulled off the actual burned drives, frankly, because you didn't trust 'the cloud' with our personal data. But that old argument doesn't matter now. Anyway, it's all that remains."

Sarah listened intently. She had no recollection of any of it, except another fleeting image that was somehow there and then gone.

"Look there, in the Miscellaneous file, folder three, under FIRE." He nodded his head toward the monitor while he moved and sat down on the corner of the desk.

Sarah flinched slightly from his motion, but settled back into her chair, swiveling it slightly in an involuntary cautionary move to face him fully. She processed his comment in her mind and then followed through with what he suggested.

She swiped the screen and the pad in the table to begin accessing the files he'd mentioned. As she did so, she realized she felt very comfortable using the device. She accessed the folder quickly with a seemingly practiced finesse, even though they were buried in numerous other files.

Sarah tapped the folder and began opening archive files which were basically an assortment of online articles along with picture and source links about the event. Something about it seemed to spark a familiarity, but she couldn't place the feeling. It didn't have anything to do with the fire, she felt, but something about the articles and their structure sparked some deep curiosity.

She began reading one of the locally written articles which depicted a generic-sounding account of the fire, its supposed cause, the number of alarms it roused in the night, how long it took to extinguish the inferno, etc., along with mention of their names—listed as the unfortunate owners—and at the end, what the damages were estimated at. There were also a couple of accompanying pictures of the house on fire, and the aftermath.

Sarah opened another article and skimmed that one as well. Again, she had that familiar feeling she couldn't place. She tried another one; it basically covered the same information.

"See," he said. "We've had our losses, but like I said, we've still got each other. We have a lot to be thankful for, Sarah."

Sarah then thought to ask about her father.

"What about…what about Dad?" She wanted to elaborate more with specific questions, but found it difficult to do so, as she began to choke up thinking about it.

"Your father died from a heart attack, Sarah, the year before the fire. He was cremated in Bakersfield, at Deerfield Mortuary. His ashes are interred there in their gardens. I'm sorry. We had pictures of the service, of the memorial, but they were lost in the fire." He looked down, emotionless.

Sarah stared at him; a tear ran all the way down one cheek. She wiped it, and then both her eyes.

"*Cremated?* But he…he…" She shook her head, searching her quivering thoughts. "Where are his ashes…*gardens*?! I want to go there," she suddenly erupted.

He looked up at her, hesitated for a moment.

"Uhmm, that wouldn't be a very good idea right at this point, Sarah. Dr. Lazarus said it wouldn't be good for you to have all that stimulus, remember."

"I don't care!" Sarah again belted out with sudden emotion. "I want to see where he is!"

He took a deep breath and exhaled.

"Well, I'm sorry Sarah. The doctor was very specific, and…"

"I don't care what the doctor said, I WANT TO GO NOW!" she shouted.

Suddenly an incensed expression appeared on his face. He hesitated for a moment as if considering what to say next.

"Sorry, but the answer is no."

Chapter 49

Sarah awoke slowly.

Her head was spinning.

She felt dizzy and disoriented, lethargic.

It took a few moments, but she realized she was in bed. She then looked down at herself and determined that she was modestly dressed; only having on a man's oversized cotton t-shirt, and a pair of black panties. She pulled herself up into a near sitting position and leaned against the headboard.

Sarah suddenly remembered the surroundings: the large bed, the windows, the French doors.

"Good morning!" the voice rang out.

Sarah looked in its direction. Her husband was coming out of the bathroom. He had a towel wrapped around his waist, but was bare everywhere else. Before she could say anything, he rounded the bed and sat down next to her, his right thigh nudging up against her hip.

Sarah found it difficult to move. Her mind felt inclined to change position, but for some reason she couldn't seem to follow through with the notion.

"How are you this morning, my love?" he asked as he rubbed a towel through his hair.

Sarah just stared, emotionless.

"I have some good news. That business I was telling you about—never mind the details—has shown some tremendous advancement. In fact, I believe it has reached a level that would summarily deem it a success. Oh, there is still quite a bit of time left to see if it plays out as planned. But, the foundation has been laid and it's only a matter of time, and the matter of a few more added structural supports, to make it an overall final accomplishment. 'Success is its own reward,' as they say."

He arbitrarily threw the towel onto a chair a short distance away. He then grabbed up Sarah's hand in one of his, put his other arm around her, and leaned in. He looked at her and studied her face for a moment.

"You are very beautiful, Sarah. I am so glad we're together."

He then half-closed his eyes as he dipped down and kissed her on her lips. At first it was a slow, savory kind of kiss, but then it turned into a passionate one. He moaned slightly as he did so, seemingly enjoying the experience immensely.

Sarah only barely kissed him back, mostly in reactive response.

He finished and rose from her slightly.

"It won't be long, and all your 'good' memories will return, I'm sure, Sarah my love. And then we can really enjoy each other."

He kissed her again.

"But right now I've got to run. Still much business left to do, even though plans are working out. We can't slow down now, can we, when so much is at stake?" He rose from the bed, and headed toward the bathroom.

Sarah seemed to slip back into a stupor.

She closed her eyes and drifted off.

·······

She had no concept of time.

Her mind seemed to be an entity unto itself now. It went where it wanted, thought what it wanted, saw what it wanted. Her real self, if there truly was one any more, just seemed to exist there on the side, in the periphery, not having a say, or a part, much less any influence on what was going on.

It was a strange feeling, but not an overall dislikeable one.

With no decision making abilities, it became a burden-less existence, which oddly rendered a freedom most people probably longed for, but few could ever achieve in reality. To be able to live as an observer, a mere spectator, instead of an active participant made one devoid of compulsion, of obligation, of a sense of responsibility.

It wasn't so bad.

Not having a desire to gain also took away any sense of loss.

Not being someone meant that you were 'no one.'

And being 'no one' meant that no one mattered.

·······

Sarah watched as if from under a warm pool of shimmering glass. She was on the other side of all that was happening. She was comfortable now. So relaxed, and the sense of anxiety so absent, that she couldn't even entertain the rudimentary concepts of mental blocks, or brain dysfunction, or insanity. And it was for this reason that all thought and remembrance became like an amorphous fluid, its essence whole, void of particle, of form, of substance, or of motion. In that moment she could see all as if it were all.

But, in the midst of the currentless stillness, Sarah noticed a turbulence forming. It morphed and changed and separated itself from the 'all.' And as it did, Sarah's tranquility left her with a sickening jolt. The form swirled and coalesced, continuing its solidification. In doing so it seemed to disrupt everything, sending out ripples of matter and motion, altering all space and time around it.

Sarah now seemed to focus on it, as well as its disturbance, as the duality of nature seemed to reconstitute itself. It was sickening, the motion of it, yet it seemed to Sarah that it was the way it needed to be. Within a moment of time and space, the form took on the countenance of a man. A middle-aged man with somewhat disheveled, shoulder length brown hair, grayed along the edges. On his face were rimless glasses, the old sort which had a little computer attached to one corner equipped with a miniature screen, which sat slightly above and in front of one eye.

The man seemed to focus all his attention onto Sarah with a severity that penetrated her very soul. Then she heard him speak,

"Hang on, Sarah. They're coming for you. Don't... let... go!"

Chapter 50

"Did she talk to you, say anything about where she was going, or what she was going to do?" he asked.

"Uhm, yeah I do, actually," Condi said, yawning broadly as she sat up in bed. "She mentioned at lunch about getting a text from someone where her dad is, something about going to his house to get him something, or something."

"Really? Anything else, Condi?" Eliam added.

"No...*no*, nothing I can think of. What's going on? Is she okay? What's...?"

"No...no, I'm sure she's fine. I'm just anxious to get with her, and I...I'm just trying to catch up with her, that's all. Hey, thanks, Condi. Sorry about waking you up. I really appreciate the information."

"Sure, yeah, no problem Eliam, sure."

"Okay, well, thanks again. You sleep sound, okay? Sorry to have bothered you! Night, Condi!"

"Sure, yeah, okay, like I said not a problem, yeah, night...night Eliam!"

Eliam ended the call and immediately jumped into his car. He quickly accessed the needed county land records to get the address, and then promptly headed to Sarah and her father's house. The drive took him nearly half an hour, his anxiety and mental speculation reaching dire levels on the way, prompting him to anticipate the worst, even though he had no reason or justification for it, other than that acutely uneasy feeling he had in his gut. When he got close to the house he turned the SUV's lights off and coasted to a stop a short distance away, deciding to walk the rest of the way.

The house was dark and there were no vehicles anywhere in the long driveway or in the parking area up by the garage. Eliam stealthily made his way to the back of the house and peeked inside several windows. Everything was dark, so he took out the pair of thick glasses he'd taken out of his pack and put into his pocket upon exiting his car.

He put the glasses on his face, and instantly he could see everything around him, nearly as well as if it had been full daylight. The advanced night-vision hardware worked perfectly in conjunction with his B-CID and he could now see into the house with ease. Apparently no one was inside that he could discern, and all he noted that was the least bit unusual was an old boot lying in the middle of the floor in the kitchen.

He looked in several other windows but saw nothing. He then looked in the garage, and only saw what he assumed was Sarah's father's old pick-up truck. Sarah's car was nowhere to be found, and there was definitely no sign of her.

His next thought was to contact Greenway to follow up on the text Condi had talked about. But he figured it was too late to call the Center, and they for sure wouldn't allow visitors at this time of night. He'd have to figure out a way to bypass their night people in order to get in there. Then he thought of the sheer worry that doing so would cause her father, so he decided against it.

His only recourse, other than to just wait until the next day to see if she would contact him, was to enlist *Sanguine*'s help. He'd sworn to himself that he'd honor her privacy at all costs, unless it was absolutely necessary. His sudden fears told him it was, and he didn't hesitate. He opened up a pane in his VF and initiated the contact.

"*Sanguine*, Sarah has been inordinately absent without communication. Please begin passive scans for her personal signature."

Sanguine replied through their shared link.

"*Acknowledged, Eliam. Scanning…*"

She paused.

"*Scanning completed, there is no positive location in our general area.*"

Eliam suddenly became very worried.

"Extend scanning range, *Sanguine*."

"Acknowledged, Eliam. Scanning…"

There was another pause.

"Scanning completed, there is no positive location in extended area."

Eliam suddenly became more than worried.

"What? Sanguine, what parameters are you using for extended range?"

"Topographical and atmospheric Eliam, extending to one-thousand-kilometers out in a three-hundred-and-sixty-degree field, and forty-thousand-meters in elevation, respectively."

Eliam Zaris was now beyond the edge.

"Then go to full scanning range, *Sanguine,*" he said, irritated.

"Acknowledged, Eliam. Scanning…I have located Sarah Whiting, Eliam."

Even though he'd just then initiated his full link with *Sanguine*, much of the visual information was oddly absent from his virtual view.

"Sanguine, I don't understand, why am I not able to see your full readouts?" he inquired, curiosity and impatience fueling his increasing annoyance.

There was an extended silence.

"You do not have clearance for this information, Eliam."

Eliam began pacing there in the dark next to the garage. He felt himself about to erupt verbally, but stopped at the last second with only a whisper of a gruff, snorting sound coming out of his nose.

"Sanguine, I don't understand. What do you mean I 'don't have clearance'? What the zirconium plasma-phate is that supposed to mean? Since when do I *not* have clearance?"

Sanguine went silent again for a moment and then said it again.

"I am sorry, but you don't have clearance for an expository explanation at this time, Eliam."

Eliam put both hands to his head and began massaging his scalp and temples as he paced faster. His head was suddenly spinning from confusion.

He then blurted out:

"Where's Sarah, *Sanguine*? You said you located her…where is she?" He stopped in his tracks and just stared into the artificially lit-up darkness around him, waiting for an answer.

"Sarah Whiting is presently on the Earth's Moon, Eliam."

He tried to blink away the confusion.

"Come get me, *Sanguine*! Now, please!" he said, his voice deflated.

"I am on the way, Eliam."

Chapter 51

Sitting down in the Captain's chair, Eliam began to initiate manual preparations for a flight to the Moon. But just as he tried to start the required systems for the journey, they were immediately overridden by the ship.

"*Sanguine*, what are you doing?"

"*It is not advisable to proceed with your course of action, Eliam.*"

Eliam's anger flared.

"*Sanguine*, this is ridiculous! You're not telling me *how*, or *where* exactly, or...or *why*, which I don't understand, but if Sarah's on the moon, I have to go to her, and you're not going to stop me. Now either initiate flight systems, or release the controls so I can do it myself. That's an order!" He was nearly yelling in desperation.

There was a long silence as they just floated there in the air above the city.

"*I am sorry, Eliam. I am not allowed to do that.*"

Eliam was about to explode.

"*Allowed?* Allowed by whom? I'm this ship's commander!"

Another long silence permeated the thick air in the ship.

"*Yes, you are the commander. I will take you virtually anywhere you wish to go, Eliam Zaris. I will aid your acquisition of information in any form or by any manner, regarding virtually any subject, and do so without delay upon request. However, under my existing program parameters I am not allowed to acquiesce to your current wishes.*"

Eliam was practically stupefied. He just sat there, struggling to think.

"Why is Sarah Whiting on the Moon, *Sanguine?* Can you tell me this?"

"Insufficient information, Eliam."

"How'd she get there then, *Sanguine?*"

"Insufficient information, however, Sarah Whiting was probably transported there by a space vessel of sufficient class rating required for interplanetary travel."

Eliam scowled.

"Yeah, you think?!" he said sarcastically. "*Sanguine…Sanguine*, I'm trying to understand what's going on here. I guess I don't, apparently, but I'm trying to. I don't understand why you're doing this, why the information about what's going on is 'classified,' or whatever. All I know is that…is that I…I love Sarah Whiting. I love her, *Sanguine*. And I…and if she's in danger, *Sanguine*, then I have to go and help her. Do you understand what I'm saying, *Sanguine?* Do you truly understand what I'm saying?"

Eliam was nearly in tears now, his feelings of ineffectualness suddenly draining him of all energy and course.

Sanguine was silent.

"Is Sarah in danger, *Sanguine?*" he asked, not having wanted to say it, for fear of the answer.

And while he waited, the anguish and the silence became deafening. After a few more moments, the ship answered, reticence was oddly present in its surrealistically replicated, feminine voice.

"Yes, Eliam, probabilities suggest that Sarah Whiting may be in danger."

Eliam looked blankly at the monitors in front of him. His eyes darted about nervously. As he bit his lip, he ran his fingers through his hair then put his face in his hands and slowly hunched over. He was trying desperately to think of what to say, of how to say whatever that would get his ship to respond to his requests. Fear and trepidation engulfed him, and he suddenly didn't know what to do next.

"Eliam, I have been authorized to take you to meet someone."

Eliam looked up.

"Meet someone? *Meet someone?* Who, *Sanguine?* Meet who?"

"*Someone who in all probability will be able to help you remove Sarah Whiting from any clear and present danger. Do you wish me to proceed, Eliam?*"

"Yes, *Sanguine!* Proceed…*proceed!* Just go, now, *Sanguine!*"

Chapter 52

Sanguine made it to their destination in a matter of only a few minutes. She could have gotten there in less time than it would have taken to cross a street, but that would have caused a series of atmospheric booms sufficient to wake the dead, along with every curious human being in a several hundred-kilometer radius. The ship lowered to the top of a building coming to rest as silently as it had speedily flown there. Eliam swiveled his chair around as he heard the ship's outer hull doors slide open. The image that suddenly leaped into the spacious cabin stunned Eliam beyond words.

"*Colonel?*" Eliam exclaimed with shock.

"Hello, Eliam," Colonel William Ravine answered calmly. He then slowly examined the interior of the ship, having an almost adoring look on his face. "And hello, *Sanguine.*"

"*Hello, William!*"

Eliam was even more taken aback when he heard his ship's voice change noticeably, from that of an oft-times mechanical and calculated information machine, to a soft, sexy, and seemingly evocative feminine voice.

Eliam was now literally dumbfounded; his eyes narrowed in confusion. Colonel Ravine noticed and smiled largely, holding back the explanation for a moment longer.

"*Sanguine* and I go back a long way. Don't we, love?"

"*Yes, William, we do. It's nice to see you again; it has been a long time. Perhaps we can chat over a game of chess, or go, William? I so miss that.*"

Eliam couldn't get over the augmented voice. The look on his face was priceless. Colonel Ravine laughed.

"We have a lot to talk about, Eliam. *Sanguine* contacted me and let me know what was happening. We…"

"Contacted you! *Sanguine* contacted you?"

"Yes, she did. I'm from Hoame, Eliam, just as you are. And I am *Renasci*. Only, I've been here working under that edict for quite a bit longer than you. About thirty-two years, to be exact."

Eliam furrowed his brow.

"*Sanguine*, please take us to our destination, thank you." He gave the ship the coordinates through his neural link.

"On the way, William dear."

Eliam's eyebrows flew up.

Colonel Ravine smiled again.

. . . .

Colonel William Ravine and Eliam Zaris were in the kitchen/dining area of a small, secluded private home some-where in the mountains of northern Canada. The view out the large window was spectacular. Isolated, snow-covered peaks and jagged ridges cascaded down into deeply shadowed val-leys. The house warmed quickly from the gas-flamed stove, and the Colonel offered Eliam a cup of fresh, hot coffee as he sat down at the rustic wood table opposite him. Though feel-ing anxious, Eliam accepted the offer.

"*Sanguine* let me know what's been happening. I know Sa-rah Whiting is missing, and apparently where she is. *Sanguine* held tight to her core instructions—not revealing certain in-formation—because she was surreptitiously instructed to do so before she was passed on to you to be your personal con-veyance," the Colonel started.

In the short time he'd had, Eliam had surmised several things about what was going on. He waited for the Colonel to explain before sharing any of his own assumptions.

"*Sanguine* used to be my partner, though that was some time ago."

"Yeah, I gathered that. Must have been close," he added, not elaborating on his mind's postulations.

"Yeah, close," he said, followed by a slight laugh. "Ever see that old...*old* American film, about a castaway? Guy stranded, all by himself, on a tropical island, only friend is a soccer ball named Wilson?"

Eliam slowly shook his head sideways, indicating he hadn't.

"No? Anyway, I was traveling in deep space and due to a cosmic event, we think—we never figured out what happened—most of *Sanguine*'s systems were wiped out and we were adrift for months before we were fortuitously run across by a transport ship, which noticed us. Except in the end, I didn't lose Wilson."

He looked for recognition, but Eliam just appeared confused.

"*Sanguine* and I spent a long time together. It was odd trying to ration water and what food I had knowing that it would only last a certain amount of time, no matter what. I was down to just a few days of meager supplies, facing certain starvation and death. I didn't have much hope for a good end to the situation. But *Sanguine* kept me alive and mostly sane through all of it by talking to me like any other person, quoting centuries of wise and encouraging sayings and adages and prayers, reading to me, about life and death.

"Anyway, we both made it. She's a part of me, and I'm a part of her. I'm only saying this because, due to all she and I went through, she somehow gained a...a sensitivity which most AI's don't have. That's why she felt compelled to contact me. She was programmed to do so if she noted any anomalous behavior on your part, which apparently she felt she was seeing."

Eliam sat up on the edge of his chair; an extremely anxious look washed across his face. Colonel Ravine read the look accurately and attempted to answer it.

"Okay! First off, I don't believe Sarah is in mortal danger. But we have to get to her soon or she won't be the Sarah you know. *Sanguine* wouldn't let you go to her because she knew that it most certainly would endanger her, not to mention yourself, and hinder any chances of bringing Sarah back.

"I had her bring us to this place to talk because there's a lot you don't know about what's going on. And to be honest, the powers-that-be didn't want you to know, for good reason. But things are not as they seem all around and I am personally willing, now, to take a chance on you in order to garner your confidence and support. However, before continuing, I want to ask you a few specific questions. How you answer will help make up my mind as to whether to continue."

Eliam was trying to take it all in, but he was still at a loss. He decided that he had little choice.

"Thank you for the offer of help. Please, ask anything you want. I just want to help Sarah. And thank you for the coffee by the way, it's very good."

Colonel Ravine took a sip of his, along with a deep breath before starting.

"Eliam, do you know why your parents died?"

Eliam didn't see that coming at all. He shifted in his seat as he pondered the question.

"No, actually I don't think I do. I was told that they were killed by a group of terrorists because of the difference in their ideological beliefs. But I think that was probably an over-simplification. I think that they stood up for something that they believed and actively tried to bring about a change because of it. Others were threatened by that, and they were killed for it."

"You're absolutely right. What you don't know are the details. I knew your parents, Eliam. We were friends. And I'm sure you wouldn't remember me, but I was around when you were very young. I was—*am*—of the same beliefs that they were, and those beliefs took me all over Hoame, and eventually here.

"Your parents were *Renasci*; I know you know this. But they were in different positions—public positions—and they were made examples of, plain and simple. But what the *Ankh*—and especially those who killed them—didn't expect was the providential impact it had on the future of the Reform. In a way, your parents were a cornerstone of its foundation, Eliam. Because of what they knew, and what they did, and how they died, they set a lot of things in motion."

He paused for a moment before continuing.

"What do you believe is the *Renasci's* core purpose, Eliam?"

Eliam thought about it.

"I think that it's much the same as the values that led to the creation of the country here on Earth known as the United States of America. The elimination of tyranny and oppression, the establishment of a democratic, egalitarian set of conditions so people of all diversities have at least the opportunities afforded them to be able to determine their own realities and futures and freedoms."

He finished, but he knew that even that was an over-simplification.

"Your parents felt the same way. And that's why they died. But, and I believe you know this as well, it's still not that way, not by a long shot—on Hoame, or on the Earth. There are people who appear to support and encourage those values, but in truth are deceivers at their very core, counting it virtue—personal success—when others are under their control, especially when they are *unknowingly* under their control. This way of thinking is totalitarian in its essence and it is why the *Ankh* and all of their various factions are still a force to be reckoned with."

"Yes, I know this."

"Do you? Do you also know that you're being used by them, that your very actions are part of their overall plan?"

Eliam shook his head, unbelieving.

"How so? What are you saying?"

"I'm saying that they are cunning enough to allow you to continue doing what you're doing, with the foreknowledge that what you're doing will be used to their advantage at a given time."

"What? I don't understand, how?"

"Why are you here on this planet, Eliam?"

"I…I came to help share technology—Smartbrain technology, specifically—to help this humanity gain perspective and knowledge in order to help them rise out of the decay that they're in, of which the *Ankh* wishes them to stay in so they can continue using them as their slaves and game pieces as they've done for thousands of years. Sharing Smartbrain technology will put them on an even field so they can fight the *Ankh*, just as it has done for us."

"What if that's what the *Ankh* wanted in the first place, to see the technology proliferate on this planet?"

"But we know that's not the case. They've fought the idea publicly for decades when it was first suggested on Hoame that we share the technology and help this planet prepare for open contact with Hoame. Why would they say they were against it, when they were for it?" Eliam asked sincerely.

"Ahhh, now that is a good question. Why?"

They both sat there and pondered the shared query.

"Okay, I'm going to trust your sincerity. Just know these two things: trust can be fleeting, and have dire consequences if misplaced. And because of that, never let go of this one thing: '*Always hold in reserve the belief that things may be different than they appear; this is the first step into the valley of humility, on your journey to the summit of truth.*'"

He took another sip of coffee.

"That was one of the last things *Sanguine* read to me before that transport ship happened by. You never know how things might work out, Eliam."

He watched the reaction in Eliam's eyes, holding an extended pause.

After another moment, he began again.

"So now, let's get back to Sarah. *Sanguine* apprised me of the situation: specifically, your openness with her as to who you are and where you came from, and your growing fondness for each other." He gave him an odd look, yet one tempered with understanding and acceptance. "It is what it is. She also mentioned the SUV incident in the country, and everything that went down regarding this 'Mr. Bolt' character."

Eliam was once again stupefied.

"You learned all this, in this short period of time?" Eliam asked, curious.

"*Sanguine* and I have been conversing in our Streamplace on and off, while you and I have been talking. Isn't that right, *Sanguine*?"

"Yes, William," she said, both men hearing her voice through their personal links with the ship, even though it was parked outside some distance away.

"Another cup of coffee? We have quite a bit to discuss."

Eliam nodded, feeling a little more comfortable, and hopeful.

Chapter 53

"What I'm about to tell you must be held in the strictest of confidence."

He paused to await Eliam's acknowledgment.

Eliam nodded.

"I am not only *Renasci*. I, along with my team, are also an arm of the Intergovernmental Panel on Crimes against Humanity, the IPCH—otherwise known as the *Curia Equitas*."

Eliam was stunned. He knew of the unified council, the International Court of Justice, much like The Hague here on Earth.

"Really?" was all Eliam could say.

"Yes, we are sanctioned by the *Curia Equitas* to seek out certain people that have come to Earth, either to escape prosecution on Hoame, or who have in essence committed similar crimes against humanity here. Our job is to track these people, gather intelligence, and at the right time, secure them for future trial—a believed important precursor to open contact with the planet. I believe this Mr. Bolt character Sarah has crossed paths with is one of the people we've been after for a long, long time. Of course that's not his real name. If it's him, his name is Davian Adorjan."

"Really," Eliam found himself saying again. "Are you saying that he may be the one who has taken Sarah...taken her to the Moon? Why? What's Sarah got to do with anything? And why the Moon?"

"It's not Sarah that is the object of this man's obsession, Eliam. If I am correct in my assumption, it is you!"

Eliam contorted his face in disbelief.

"What? *Why?*"

"Your grandfather, Eliam, that's why."

Eliam looked stunned.

"If this is indeed *the* Davian Adorjan, then we have some serious planning to do. And that's why I'm telling you all this. You see, this man is *old Ankh* from way back. He's been implicated in numerous crimes, the primary one being human trafficking, which he's done for every conceivable purpose you can imagine: slavery, medical experimentation, black market organs, sex, sport, and war. He used to be your grandfather's partner, Eliam."

Eliam's stunned look suddenly took on the pallor of a corpse.

"Partner?"

"Yes, he and your grandfather were sent to Earth about a century ago by the *old Ankh* to secure numerous young females for return to Hoame. As was the current then-legal practice at that time. Long story short, during the expedition, there was a falling out between the two, and your grandfather somehow was able to return, but because of something Davian Adorjan had done—reportedly—he was ordered by the *Ankh* to remain on Earth indefinitely, to work as their emissary. An honor, they made it seem, yet a lamentable curse by all accounts, to him anyway. He apparently blamed your grandfather for the conditions imposed upon him. He's been on Earth ever since, acting as their eyes and ears and hands."

Eliam continued listening.

"The man's built empires and fortunes that few know about. He supposedly has the resources to do about anything he wants. He's been the catalyst for numerous major wars, for reasons of economic gain, manipulation of economies, changes to governments and powerbases, along with the human trafficking thing. He's a very bad man, Eliam."

"But what about Sarah, why? Why would he take her?"

"Again, you! Rancor, revenge, whatever you want to call it! He's obsessed with your family for some twisted reason, and I suspect that when he heard of you coming here, representing the Reform in opposition against the *Ankh*, bent on helping prepare the Earth for contact, he became incensed and turned his directives into his own vendetta against your family, against you!

"From what I've learned from *Sanguine*, he's already created a ruse to slander you here on Earth, and is already planning on somehow stopping the proliferation of the technology however he can, and as an extra bonus, getting additional revenge on what he must consider his arch nemesis—your family. Sarah's just been caught in the middle of it."

Eliam turned pale again; it was his fault.

"Now you see why *Sanguine* couldn't let you go off all half-cocked? But you can't blame yourself, Eliam. You had no way of knowing."

Eliam nodded slowly.

"The Moon…you and *Sanguine* said the Moon. Why? Why the Moon?"

"There's an old base there, built by the *Ankh* several centuries ago, a way station and an observation post for travelers—and then traffickers to and from Hoame. Due to its sordid history, and its age, it was made inoperable and locked down by the *Renasci* decades ago. Apparently this Mr. Bolt—Davian Adorjan, if that's who it proves out to be—has somehow managed to take control of it, which means that he is probably once again actively involved in the trafficking of humans from Earth to Hoame, which pretty much seals his death warrant once he is tried before the *Curia Equitas*. The thing is, the only way he could have gotten into the base was by having inside information to bypass the *Renasci's* security protocols, which means, unfortunately, that it is quite probable someone in the *Renasci* helped him."

"And Sarah's there!" Eliam said, a sense of foreboding twisting his stomach into knots.

"Yeah, so it seems. She couldn't be anywhere else," the Colonel said reluctantly.

"What do we do?" Eliam asked in a deflated tone.

"Well, for one thing we have to look at it from an intelligence standpoint. If it wasn't for Sarah—specifically the neuronal-tracer you placed in her—we wouldn't know where she was, or where Adorjan possibly is. That was a stroke of wisdom and providence on your part, by the way. Hopefully Adorjan won't detect it in her, and with any luck, he'll not be so on his guard when we attempt to infiltrate the facility!"

"Infiltrate the facility? It's about time you said something like that. When, how?" Eliam's countenance perked up with new energy.

"We have to do it soon, but not too soon. We need to plan; I know the facility, and I have a few ideas. Also, while we've been talking, I instructed *Sanguine* to issue a code green to my team. They'll be here within the next three hours. Until then, there are some things we can do. Finish that coffee and I'll show you my pantry."

"Team?"

"Yes, my team. Think of us as an off-the-grid Special-Ops Unit; we may be small, and operate independent of traditional jurisdictions, but we are sanctioned by the highest authority, and we're effective."

"*Pantry*?" Eliam then asked, curious about the odd invitation.

The Colonel just smiled and took another sip of coffee.

Chapter 54

Sarah's eyes fluttered open. It was hard to focus, she must have fallen into a deep sleep, she thought. She raised herself higher against the pillows and looked around. Her clothes were wrinkled, and she was lying on top of the bed covers with a throw over her.

Napping, she thought, though something seemed odd to her.

She looked around the familiar room. She then glanced at the furniture in the entertainment area and suddenly began re-membering the day she had picked it out. She didn't know why she'd remembered that right then. She saw the event in her mind: walking through the dozens of furniture settings at the Gallery, bypassing the obviously repulsive retro-styles that she despised, and then coming onto this contemporary set at the far end of an aisle. She'd fallen in love with it upon first sight and remembered the moment vividly.

"Now this is more like it, dear," she had said, turning and looking at her husband for approval. She remembered his ex-pressionless face as he looked over the furniture, at first inat-tentively but then with apparent earnest. She remembered how she felt as his face suddenly glowed with acceptance. She loved it when he connected with her like that. It made her feel so good. She sat there looking dreamily at the memories.

"Sari, I see you've awoken from your nap. Good, Lucille just let me know that dinner is about ready to be served. The Tavington's are downstairs, too. They called and said they were held up due to a horrible traffic jam, some bad accident on the highway, closed all the lanes. So I let you rest a little longer. Why don't you get up now and put on the deep blue *Deveccio* I bought you last week? You look so beautiful in that dress. I'll go back down and entertain our guests until you're ready."

He eyed her from the open doorway, made a soft kissing motion with his lips, and then turned and pulled the door shut behind him.

Sarah sat there on the edge of the bed and stared at the door for a moment. She then looked back at the furniture in the entertainment area, relived its discovery again. She seemed to realize she was staring. She tried to shake it off; still sleepy from her long nap, she surmised. She then looked toward the closet and viewed the memory of her and her husband picking out the blue dress. It was suddenly as vibrant as the one about the furniture.

She seemed to rise from the bed as if being lifted by some unseen force and then she walked to the closet. She went straight to the dress. It seemed to stand out from all the others. Perhaps because it was her newest one, she told herself. She grabbed the garment and without even remembering putting it on, she found herself standing in front of the full-length mirror admiring the garment, as well as her shapely body.

She ran her hands slowly over her sides and down her hips and over her buttocks, smoothing the fabric, feeling its texture and her shapeliness under it. She then held her hands in front of her face and looked at them oddly, as if they were in some way foreign to her. She was startled out of her stupor when she heard her husband call her.

"Darling, come on down now. We're waiting for you."

She hesitated, but then replied.

"Yes, dear, coming."

． ． ． ． ． ． ．

"Sarah, young lady, you look ravishing. How are you, my dear?" Candice Tavington asked, shaking Sarah's hand in a finger-mostly, feminine handshake.

"Uhmm, I'm fine, Candice. You…you look nice as well."

"Well, thank you, dear!" she replied.

"Sarah, Candy's right once again. You are a fine looking specimen of the human race, Sarah Bolton, fine indeed. You've always been the lucky one, Matt. I swear. I don't know how you do it. You're not exactly magazine cover material, but you certainly have one for a wife! Stole her right off the page, didn't you!"

"*Donald!*" Candice Tavington said abruptly, a measure of pointed, yet controlled antipathy evident in her voice.

"Now, don't worry, dear. I've got a cover girl of my own; you know that as well. No need to get snippy," Donald Tavington replied.

"Ha-ha you two, always appreciate your humor. We do thank you for the compliments!" He looked at Sarah with beckoning eyes.

"Yes…*yes*, thank you," Sarah found herself saying reluctantly.

"Dinner is about to be served. Shall we make our way to the dining room? And please, bring your drinks along. There's plenty more where those came from," Mathew announced.

The Tavington's laughed, lifted their drinks in a semi-toast, and then allowed themselves to be herded toward the large dining room. Everyone found their respective seats and sat down. As they did, servants entered the room and began filling the glasses with water. A moment later, another brought in a tray of elegant plates, placing them in front of each person, and then another servant began dishing out portions of salad in accordance with each person's preference. When everyone was served, Matthew Bolton courteously nodded and invited everyone to eat.

"Bon appétit, everyone!"

Sarah watched as the others started. She slowly followed suit, picking up one of her forks. In doing so she noticed the reflection in the flat area of the utensil. Even though it appeared extremely polished and shiny, the images seemed blurred and out of proportion to her. She thought it odd.

Everyone ate their salads, and then the servants brought in the soup. Again, Sarah followed suit and did the same. Picking up a spoon and noting the odd reflection in it. She let it pass from her hazy attention and started to eat like everyone else. The soup tasted bland and slightly fruity, she thought.

"Excellent tomato-shrimp bisque, Matthew, our complements to Lucille. Your chef is as good as any at any of the number of five-star restaurants we frequent."

"Thank you, Donald. Yes…yes she is. She gets paid like one as well!" he said, tilting his head and snickering through his nose. The Tavingtons snickered as well at his little joke. Sarah did the same, yet it seemed involuntary. She continued eating as everyone talked.

"So Matthew, how's the Dorshire Order proceeding? Is the quality going to be as before? My investors are anxious to close; and I'm looking forward to the delivery myself, I might add!" He snickered under his breath, as he looked knowingly at his host.

Matthew Bolton read the look in the man's eyes, glanced at Sarah, and then looked back at him.

"Oh, you know, always the best for my clients, Donald. We're on schedule as previously stated. Tell our investors the shipment will arrive safe and secure, just as the last one did. And again, I'll be including a few surprise upgrades, as I did the last time. I know how our clientele so enjoys their little surprises. Don't they, Donald?"

"Yes indeed they do, Matt. That's good. Very good! We wait then, with full anticipation."

The main course arrived, Mahi Mahi with savory mixed vegetables in garlic sauce, atop a spread of exotic sea rice. The servants served the meal efficiently and everyone began eating again.

Sarah sliced off a piece of fish and put it in her mouth. After a moment of chewing she poked her fork in to a sautéed, quarter-sliced piece of Brussels sprout. Sarah was listening to more of the mostly indecipherable conversation between their guests and her husband when she popped the morsel into her mouth.

Sarah stopped chewing immediately and just sat there with an odd look on her face. She then slowly picked up her napkin and spit the foul tasting food into the piece of cloth.

Matthew Bolton noticed his wife's behavior and asked her if there was anything wrong.

"No…no Matthew, I just didn't realize that these were Brussels sprouts. Brussels sprouts have always tasted like crap to me, I…"

Suddenly Sarah's mind was spinning.

Matthew Bolton placed his fork on the table, picked up his napkin and wiped his mouth. He had a look of repugnance on his face. With his face down, he turned his eyes up to meet his guest. The man seemed to know what he was thinking.

"I'm sorry everyone. I'm…I'm not feeling well," Sarah said shakily.

She then got up, politely excused herself and left the room to the obvious chagrin of her husband.

"My apologies, Donald. Listen, if you'll excuse me, I think I'll end our transmission for now. It appears I need a little more time working with my new companion. However, as I said, tell our clients that the shipment will arrive just as before: with impeccable quality and on schedule."

"I see. That's perfectly understandable…perfectly understandable! That's why we enjoy doing business with you, Davian. You always take your time to make sure attention to detail happens exactly where and when it's needed. That saves a lot of extra toil for our customers, not to mention justifies our higher pricing structure. They appreciate that, as do I. Take care of that new cover girl; she looks as if she's going to be worth every effort."

"I believe I feel exactly the same way, Donald. More than you know. You take care, too."

Candice Tavington just kept eating the whole time, apparently not hearing a word. The two faded out of the room as if they'd been apparitions from the nether-world.

Davian Adorjan snorted in disgust as he angrily shoved his place settings across the table. He didn't have time for this; the woman had become more work than he had initially thought. But then again, once she was fully his, he could move on to the next part of his plan, the best part, he considered, doing to Eliam Zaris what his family had done to him. He smiled at the promising thought.

Chapter 55

Colonel Ravine led Eliam Zaris down a short hallway. At the end was a door. He opened it and turned on a light. Eliam could see that they were now in a small, walk-in storeroom. There were no windows and no observable doors, just walls of shelves.

"Your...*pantry*, I take it?" Eliam asked, not sure what they were doing there, and not overtly impressed with what he saw.

"This way," the Colonel just said.

Eliam was led to the back wall of the small room, with nothing but more shelves in front of them. He watched as the Colonel reached underneath one of the lower shelves. Suddenly, the shelf-covered wall swung free away from them, out into a dark void beyond it.

"Follow me," the Colonel then added.

The two walked a short distance into the darkness and then the shelf-covered door behind them swung shut, leaving them in pitch-black darkness. Before Eliam could say a word, everything lit up. He was stunned to find that they were now standing in what appeared to be an enormous airplane hangar. The single large room must have been forty meters wide by nearly seventy-five meters deep, Eliam immediately surmised.

"Wow! Nice pantry! You can keep a lot of canned goods in here. Or spaceships, assault vehicles, assorted weaponry, and whatever those things are," Eliam said jokingly, noting the objects that suspiciously looked like nuclear warheads.

Colonel Ravine laughed slightly.

"Yeah, you never know when something might come in handy. Let's go to my office, the team should be arriving soon. Until then, I can get you up to speed on this Moon base, and a few of the basics regarding the team and what we do. I'm afraid it's going to take everything we know to pull this off, and the sooner we get started, the better."

·······

"I've had fight training and combat training," Eliam said bluntly.

"Yeah, I know, I've done my research, and weapons training, and some tactical training. So has my team. But what you don't have is combat experience, which we do. And that could kill not only you, and us, but Sarah as well. So, first order. You're going to do what I say, when I say it, and exactly the way I tell you, the same goes for my team, or we're not doing this. Understood?"

Eliam knew he was right.

He was okay with all of it.

"Yes, sir!"

"Good! When the others arrive, they're going to say the same thing, so before they ask, you tell them that up front. They're a rough bunch, but they're all good people. And whatever you do, don't piss 'em off. They'll still do a top-notch job no matter what, but the after party won't be as much fun. Okay?"

Eliam laughed.

"Okay!"

He suddenly realized that Colonel Ravine was his best hope of seeing Sarah again.

·······

The alarm sounded as anticipated.

Colonel Ravine stood up and went over to a console on the wall of the office. He didn't touch it. He didn't need to. He activated the items he wanted just by thinking of them: perimeter security clearances, scanning protocols, the ship's vector, etc. He didn't in fact need to look at the wall monitors;

he just liked seeing them for real, while at the same time seeing them in his vision field. 'Redundancy never hurt anything' was one of his personal mottos.

"Good, the team is all on board," he said. "They met up in Greenland and ditched their personal conveyances there. Then they picked up the two people here in the States on their way in. Huh! If they make it on the pad in, let's see…under five more minutes—which it looks like they will—I'm going to have to buy them all a night on the town."

He made a sour face, but then smiled as he motioned for Eliam to get up and join him.

The two went out into the open expanse of the hangar and Eliam was impressed when the ceiling in that section opened up to the sky. The cold air vortexed down as all the heat was sucked out into the atmosphere. That and the motion of the ship stirred the air inside the hangar into a temporary cyclonic frenzy.

The vast, trussed ceiling closed immediately after the ship cleared it, and within seconds all was calm again. Eliam heard the ship power down even as a side door opened and a set of stairs descended. Right after, several people tramped down the stepped ramp, greeting the Colonel with a nod and a respectful salute. Five people from on board the sleek craft were now on the tarmac of the hangar shaking hands with the Colonel amid introductions with Eliam. The sixth person—Eliam presumed the man was the pilot—descended the stairs and completed the ritualistic greetings in kind. Soon all were inside the warm office.

"People, thank you for coming; it looks as if I owe you that night on the town," he said with an impressed look on his face.

"Damn, Skippy! I told you head-bangers we'd do it!" said the rough-looking, scar-faced man. Introduced only as Lem, he had hair that was short cropped, a small tattoo just under his right sideburn, with several prominently visible on his arms. He was the pilot.

The man sitting next to him—the one named Atol—held his palm in the air and they slapped hands together, then bumped fists in a typical act of comradeship. Atol, too, had short cropped hair, though his was lighter, displaying also his own array of tattoos on his arms and neck. He exhibited an edginess that mimicked that of the pilot's, Eliam noticed.

To his right sat another man that wasn't exactly someone Eliam would have considered to be part of a tactical team. His name was simply, Raj. He was actually somewhat nerdy-looking, Eliam thought. He wore a dark plaid felt shirt, jeans, had actual glasses on his face, sniffed quite a lot, and could be likened to a darker-skinned Clark Kent type, except with somewhat straighter hair.

The other two men were of the very cautious and quiet sort.

Each had medium length hair, wore black and grey BDU's, and had very intense eyes. The slightly taller one was introduced as Sergeant Tomlinson, the other as Sergeant Norris. Both were fit and athletic-looking and carried themselves professionally. Eliam couldn't tell by their uniforms where they were from.

Then, there was the woman. She wasn't exactly dainty, though she was highly feminine and quite attractive. She had long, dark brown hair, and was introduced simply as Doctor Athena. She had a perky, attentive countenance and an intoxicatingly youthful way of swinging her hair out from her eyes.

"You've all been briefed and have had time to review as you made your way here," Colonel Ravine started.

"You think it's Davian?" Sergeant Tomlinson asked.

Colonel Ravine narrowed his eyes and exhaled hard.

"Yes, it's looking like that may be the case. We might have our chance here!"

"About bloody time!" Sergeant Norris added in an identifiable Australian accent.

"You got that right!" Lem the pilot, added.

The others mumbled their own acknowledgement in sequence.

"Yes, and we also know what that means. It's not going to be easy, or simple. But we're going to make it happen. We may never get another chance like this."

Again the people acknowledged the situation with excitement.

"He's got your woman?" Atol asked bluntly, looking right at Eliam.

Eliam didn't expect the question in that way, but he answered forthrightly.

"Yeah, you could put it that way. Her name is Sarah Whiting."

"Like the prominent Earth scientist of the nineteenth century," Raj mumbled to himself.

Everyone looked at him, yet apparently not making any connections with the comment. They turned back to Eliam. Eliam could see that they were trying to sum him up. He remembered what the Colonel had said.

"Listen. I know I'm not part of this team, and I don't have the experience or the expertise that you all do, but I have had extensive training—tactical and combat—though I've not been in combat situations, other than one knock-down, drag-out in a bar parking lot. I did my share, held up my and someone else's honor, and survived; I assure you I can handle myself. However, I'm under no illusions regarding that.

"I'll do whatever's necessary to get Sarah back—even die, if it comes to it. But I won't be stupid and knowingly sacrifice anyone else in the process. I'm here because of what I know. And apparently because of whom I am. Sarah's an innocent in this, and she's in this because I got her into it. I expect to pay for that mistake, one way or another; I don't want her or anyone else to pay for it.

"Anyway, I can respect your positions; I *do* respect your positions. I just ask that you respect mine. I will support your assessments and your decisions; I will help make those happen in any way I can along the way. If you say jump, I'll jump. If you say sit, I'll sit. But...I will *not* roll over! All I care about is seeing Sarah safe; and if taking this guy down will do it, then, well, I'll take point." Eliam paused and stared at them. "If that's not what you wanted to hear, well then, you'd better lay it out for me right now, because I don't want to waste any time!" he said, making his final pitch.

Throughout his little speech Eliam looked determined yet humble.

The team just stared at him for a moment with expressionless faces.

"Okay…sounds fine to me!" Sergeant Tomlinson said, nodding his head.

"Okay, what the man said!" Lem added.

Everyone else responded in kind seemingly seeing Eliam's heartfelt and honest humility. Doctor Athena smiled broadly, a touch of jealousy toward this Sarah Whiting evident in her eyes. Her and Eliam locked gazes and she gave him a confident nod of acceptance as well.

"Alright then. Let's get to work!" Colonel Ravine said, slapping his hands together.

·······

The team worked throughout the night and into the early morning. Raj, much to Eliam's surprise, was not only a superlative computer and AI systems designer, programmer, hacker and geeky expert in virtually all things tech, but he was also an exceptional cook and he prepared breakfast for everyone toward the end of their intense brainstorming session.

Sitting around the large table with readouts, plot maps, timelines, notes, schematics, simulations, and illustrations, amidst plates of eggs, toast, salmon and potatoes, and another round of fresh coffee, the people reviewed their best laid plans.

"Alright, I'll go through it again so everyone gets it," the Colonel started for the umpteenth time. "The intent is for *The Adora* and *Sanguine* to stay just out of range of their sensors and on the other side of the Moon, which means we'll have to travel out beyond the sun, swinging back in a calculated trajectory mimicking the rotation of the Moon so we can stay on their blind side at all times. Lem has the vectors calculated. It should take us under two hours at sub-light.

"Beginning as early as this morning, one of our CME-Burst Disruption Arrays stationed out and above Sol's elliptical plane will send out a single, truncated, Fermium-Pulse

Emission aimed at their base, which should cause a number of systems' failures and a host of other minor glitches. This will hopefully mimic innate systems problems within the base's old equipment, leaving no residuals for them to trace. They'll run the expected diagnostics and system checks, but won't be able to isolate any one root cause. After a short time, they'll get their systems back online and be none the wiser. That's ruse one.

"We'll do it again—send another burst, only at a magnitude of .5 of the preceding one—one hour before debarkation of the penetration unit—you guys—which, again, will consist of Sergeants' Norris, Tomlinson, Raj and Eliam, respectively. The second Fermium-Pulse Emission will, again, mimic innate systems problems within the base's old equipment. Then…"

"Yes, but I'll say it again for the record. Won't a disruption of any kind to their systems put them on alert? Give them the signal that something is wrong? And we're going to do this *three* times?" Athena asked again, plainly.

"Yes, I believe it will put them on alert. But, we're going to do it hoping that they'll ultimately think it's legitimate systems glitches and they'll be more than occupied with diagnoses and fixing the problems than anything else. They'll take the position, I assure you, and especially after nothing unusual happens over a period of time after the first two pulses."

Athena nodded, still in a state of ambivalence.

"And that brings up a good point. Remember, even though they have old systems at the base, there are still newer systems on their ship—or ships, for that matter, possibly. We don't know because we don't want to scan the area just yet in order to avoid possible detection. We have to take all that into account. That's why we're maneuvering our ships and are launching the conveyances from the location we are, and why you're going to be in Cryo-mode, as well as hugging the Moon's terrain as closely as possible on approach.

"Their ships' sensors will pick up heat signatures quickly—especially *moving* heat signatures—that's why we're using the Cryo-units. We need to get you guys past their sensors, in close, until you're shielded from them by the bases structure itself. Remember, your entry point is on the opposite side of the base's ship docks. It should shield you from their sensors. Inside is another story, hence the Fermium-Pulse Emissions.

"What we want is for them to think that their systems are failing again when we attempt to contravene the hull, again, on the other side of the base from where the ship docks are located. The final, timed Fermium-Pulse Emission should cover the installation and activation of the Breach-Lock, and once Raj gets inside to one of the junctions and taps in, the residual effects from the disruption should allow him sufficient time so he can rewrite the protocols to overlook our individual signatures within their arrays—essentially making you guys invisible for the entire trip into the heart of the base where we think Adorjan and his center of operations will most likely be."

"It'll work. I guarantee it," Raj said, shoving a piece of salmon into his mouth. "Once we get inside, I only need sixty seconds to override their sensor protocols to pass us over, to make them totally blind to our presence. It's really our suits that'll do the job. Anyway, we'll essentially be invisible in all bands of the spectrum—except visible light, of course, unfortunately. I'll have to take care of their optics as we go along, but that shouldn't be a problem. When I make it to a central hub, that's where I can tie into their ship, or ships, whichever—through their hard docks—and cap off their arrays there so they won't be able to detect *The Adora* and *Sanguine* on their approach. Again, I'll need a little longer to do this— about ten to twelve minutes. I know that's a long time, but I don't dare go any faster or their ships' AIs will detect the hack and react by throwing themselves into their lockdown and alert sequences."

Everyone nodded.

"Explain this Breach-Lock again. I want to understand the procedure better. I'm not really clear on this," Eliam asked.

"Yes, okay, the Kroots Breach-Lock. It will be towed behind Sergeant Norris' conveyance, and will be used to get you into the base. As you can see from the schematics, the apparatus is a meter-wide circular device consisting of two primary rings, each an airtight door connected to a collapsed telescoping tunnel—or chamber—made of nano-tubes. The device was designed by salvagers for the purpose of gaining access to disabled and/or abandoned ships. One ring attaches to the hull and is equipped with phase-plasma cutting equipment.

"Once attached the chamber drills in its probe, it then pressurizes to match the atmosphere of the ship, or in this case the base. It then cuts a man-sized hole in the side. Once this is done, the tube telescopes out and the unit becomes an airlock. Only one person can use the device at a time, but it is highly portable and will cycle a man through in under thirty seconds—that's two minutes for all of you to get in. We'll go over the equipment further in transit so everyone will know how to use it, just in case."

Eliam nodded his head in understanding.

"Okay, back to the trip in. When in range, the three personal conveyances will be launched from *The Adora*. With the combination of lack of heat signature from the Cryo-units, expected interference from the Moon's topography of mountains, hills, and boulders, as well as being shielded from the ships due to our approach vectors, then we can be ninety-nine percent assured to make it in undetected.

"Once close to the base structure, the Cryo-units will take about fifteen minutes to return you guys to warm-blooded creatures again." He sort of laughed, remembering the comments everyone had brought up earlier.

They all looked at Eliam.

"Well, I've never been in Cryo-stasis before," Eliam said. He saw their looks. "Okay, I know I said it earlier. But I haven't. It gives me the chills to think about it!" He'd just then thought up that particular comment.

Everyone got the humor, as well as his need for it, understanding his emotional reactions to the process. They all had their own. Allowing one's self to be systematically frozen, not to mention trusting a diminutive computer and drive system to fly your ice-hard, popsicle-body at breakneck speeds in and out of canyons and around house-sized boulders, for hundreds of kilometers, landing precisely where needed, and then thawing you out specifically according to the correct sequence of time and temperature, just to wake you up and then pop its top there on the lunar surface where there is a three-hundred-and-fifty degree difference between you and what's on the other side of the two-millimeter thick piece of pressurized fabric protecting them. It was enough to give anybody the chills.

"Alright, this is where it begins to get mathematically unpredictable. Though we know the complete layout of the complex, we won't know where Adorjan's positions will be, or how he's augmented the facility, until you actually see them with your own eyes. You can't use any active scans to determine those facts without taking a chance of giving yourselves away. Their systems will pick them up in a nano-second if we try, and we can't override those. You have to use stealth all the way. When you hack the base's links to the ships and override their sensor arrays, well, that's one thing, but they may have some redundant systems they brought to the base that we don't know of—something to keep track of their 'product,' though I hate to put it that way. Anyway, we just can't take the chance.

"Once you guys get close to Adorjan and have re-conned the situation, you'll signal us, and we will be there in less than five minutes. With their arrays capped on Isolated Function we can disable their ships on our approach, while at the same time you are delivering those NERV-TONEs we'll be sending along. Those will effectively incapacitate everyone within range, at least those that are not in one of those suits mind you, or in a shielded chamber, which they'll probably have up there. And remember that, too. They use these for isolation and sensory deprivation, part of their brain-ruse methodology. You might have to take some of those out separately, if the need arises. Then it'll just be a matter of unlocking the door and letting us in."

He smirked at how simple it all sounded, exaggerating the expression on his face in bold defiance of the truth. Anything could go wrong at any stage, and they all knew it.

"Okay, any additional questions, observations…bitches, moans?" Colonel Ravine asked again.

"And you're sure our B-CID communications won't be detected?"

"No, they shouldn't be. But only *after* Raj does his magic on their systems. Even if your unit's own encryption renders your communications indecipherable, the signal itself can still be detected. We still live in this universe, and physics is physics and the electromagnetic spectrum is what it is. That's why it's going to be a strict systems blackout until Raj does his thing. After that, you can power up and coordinate your efforts together as normal. That's why we're going to review the Breach-Lock procedures in transit, so everyone will know what to do, how to do it, and when. Understood?"

Everyone nodded.

"There is one other thing: Sarah's condition when we find her. Athena informs me that in order to help her get back to reality, she needs an actual physical representation of her past acting on her physical senses. And a person—she feels—will have the greatest effect along those lines."

"You mean she needs someone there that she knows in order to help her regain her neural connections?" Eliam asked, following their line of thinking.

Athena nodded in agreement.

"Yes, that's it exactly, Eliam. She needs someone—preferably someone who she has had an extended duration of contact with—to stimulate her brain connections to help her differentiate true reality, from whatever it is that Adorjan has been doing to her."

"I'm going to be there; we've been close…" Eliam said pointedly.

"Yes, but, I'm talking about someone who has had an *extended* duration of contact, a link to her base memories. You will make the initial contact, that's good. But she needs someone who has been in her life for a long time, and the sooner we make that happen, the better chances she'll have," she added.

"What about her father?" Colonel Ravine offered.

"Her father? He's in a nursing home," Eliam said, thinking about it hard. "I doubt they'll release him to me; I'm not family. Sarah's his only family still around. We'd have to...we'd have to sneak him out of there somehow."

"Well, it's up to everyone else. It's not my call, of course. But, we don't know how far Sarah's gone. My intuition tells me we need to do this. Every aid we can get toward reestablishing reality for her is essential. And like you've all been saying, we shouldn't waste any time! Just my professional opinion though," Athena stated adamantly.

Everyone thought about it. It was an indeterminable risk, no matter how one looked at it. But the alternative could be worse. It was up to Eliam, and he knew it. Everyone looked at him with understanding eyes.

"Okay! If we're going to get him, we need to do it now. And Athena's right, we shouldn't waste any more time."

Colonel Ravine looked around the table, silently inviting any further questions or comments. No one responded.

"Alright, let's go get Oscar Whiting and light the match. Godspeed to us all."

Chapter 56

"Oscar, you have some visitors," the attendant said, speaking through the doorway, glad he'd gotten everyone through lunch and that at least one of his charges would be occupied for a time, perhaps giving him a few minutes to go out and smoke. "You folks just have him ring if you need anything. I'm going to take a short break. Enjoy your visit."

"Thank you. Yes, we will. We appreciate it very much, have a nice break, and take your time," Eliam said calmly and encouragingly.

"Thanks," both Raj and Athena added as they watched the door close.

Their plan was simple. Raj was going to access the room's alarm console and splice in a jumper to bypass the large window's security trips. Once that was done, they were going to exit the window, make their way to the facility's garage and maintenance building and then go out through the gate as their little diversion was surreptitiously herding the staff to the front of the building: the car wouldn't explode, they'd made sure to drain all the gas, but the electrical fire would set the vehicle ablaze causing sufficient excitement for the staff and residents to allow their escape to the other car they'd parked around the corner.

"Hello, Oscar," Eliam said affably.

Oscar looked up from his little, one-drawer desk. He had a blank look on his face at first, but something akin to familiarity finally shone in his eyes.

"Hello…*hello*…uhm…" he started, but stopped mid-sentence apparently trying to recall a name.

"Eliam…Eliam Zaris, Oscar. I'm a close friend of Sarah's. Remember? She and I visited you recently!"

Oscar appeared confused, but then it seemed to come to him.

"Yes…*yes*, Eliam. Yes of course, I remember. How are you? Sarah…is Sarah here?" He began looking past the three, expecting to see his lovely daughter.

"No, Oscar. Sarah is not here with us," he said, looking to Athena for support. Athena nodded for him to continue. They'd briefly covered what they would say. "No, we came to visit you on our own, if that's alright!"

Raj quickly went to the alarm panel and started his work. Oscar watched him but continued with the conversation.

"Alright? Why, yes…I…suppose it is. I…"

"Listen, Oscar. I have something to tell you. It may be difficult to understand, but we came to you for a very important reason. You see…"

"Sarah's not okay, is she?" Oscar Whiting blurted out as he turned from watching Raj, and back to Eliam.

"Well, no, Oscar, actually…she isn't. It's hard to explain. We want to ask you if you'd come with us, to go and see Sarah. She's…she's…"

"She's been taken, hasn't she?" Oscar asked bluntly.

The three looked at each other with utter amazement, Raj stopping abruptly with his work on the alarm.

"Yes, uhm, Oscar. Yes, she has, I'm sorry to say. That's why we're here! How…how did you know that, Oscar?" Eliam asked, stunned nearly beyond words.

Oscar answered slowly, holding his fist to his mouth, his eyes darting side to side as he tried to remember.

"I…I had a dream last night. Someone told me." He looked up abruptly. "She's in danger, isn't she?"

Eliam again looked back and forth between his friends.

"We don't know, Oscar, how much that is the case, exactly. But, we think we can help, that *you* can help. That is if you decide to come with us."

"Who are *you*?" he asked, pointing to Athena.

"My name is Athena Mauropolin, Oscar. I'm a doctor. I'm going to try and help Sarah when we find her. You may be able to as well, if you decide to come along. We're asking, not telling, just so you know," she added.

"You're very pretty," Oscar said, and then turned toward Raj. "What's *he* doing?"

Eliam answered.

"That's Raj. He's a computer systems expert and he's disabling the alarm system so we can go out the window," Eliam said. He didn't expect it to go down like it this. It was just happening.

"Out the window?"

"Yes, Oscar. We're not family, and they won't let us take you out of here just because we want to, even with your consent. We have to be somewhat *covert* about it. Do you understand?"

Oscar looked back at Raj. He was just finishing putting the cover back on the keypad next to the door. "Ready," he said.

"Will you come with us, Oscar? We really need your help!" Eliam said.

Oscar looked around the room with a confused look on his face. He took a deep breath and then blew it out hard before speaking.

"Are you...are you all from another planet?" he asked pointedly, his eyes darting around between the three.

Again, the group looked shocked.

Eliam smiled a quirky smile.

"*Yes*, we are, Oscar?! Well, except for Raj here, he...he's from Silicon Valley. What made you think that?!"

They couldn't believe what they were hearing.

Oscar then looked at Raj.

"From the valley, huh? Well, I guess I shouldn't hold that against you, should I? You're probably real smart then." Oscar smiled, nodded his head and winked. He then turned, and looked directly in Athena's eyes. "Like I said, someone told me. And you're a doctor?"

"*Yes*...yes I am, Oscar."

"What field?"

She looked around at her friends before answering.

"I'm a doctor of several fields, actually. Internal and Nuclear Medicine; Psychology and Psychiatry, they're the primary ones. I also work with the rehabilitation of criminal minds and with those with specific mental and compulsory disorders, as well as in some areas of child development, preteens mainly." She could say more, but she didn't.

Oscar just stared at her with scrunched up eyebrows.

"And you'll help Sarah?"

"Yes, Oscar. I will. In any way I can. That's why I'm here."

Oscar looked down for a short moment as if debating.

"Do you think I'm crazy?" he asked, directing his question to Athena, but then looking at the others as well.

She smiled.

"No, Oscar, I absolutely do not. I know your condition. It's the connections in your brain that are the problem. You're not crazy!" She shot him a sincere look.

"Well, I certainly think all you people are, but I guess I'll just have to deal with that. Okay, let me grab a few things, and we'll get out of town!"

Everyone looked vastly relieved as Oscar quickly gathered items which he put into the small pack he'd pulled out of a closet.

Within seconds they were out the window.

Chapter 57

"Sari, my love, you really are very beautiful," he said, whispering in her ear.

He held her close and they swayed back and forth rhythmically. Leisurely he began sliding the silky robe down to reveal her shoulders. He then tenderly ran his fingers over her curves, caressing them, and every time he did it felt as if small currents of electricity jumped across his flesh. The feeling was beyond sensual. And this was the real thing; no longer was their meeting in the world he'd created for them necessary. At least it was due time he found out; he didn't want to wait any longer. He wanted a taste of this woman now.

Sarah's eyes were closed and she was lost in the moment, dizzied by the slow, rhythmic motion of her body. She held him loosely, the sensations comforting and pleasant. She was in an odd state of mind, yet the thought of it was as fleeting as her sense of discomfort now. All was good. All was smooth. All anxiety was gone. She was blissful, and she didn't care about anything. A wispy sigh of pleasure left her lips.

He spoke soft congratulations to himself regarding his efforts and his attention to detail; she was truly a work of art, he considered, as he beheld her.

He slid the gown further down, exposing her breasts. He gazed at them with lazy eyes, and then brought her in close to his bare chest. The subtle electricity popped and crackled silently as their skin touched. It was going to be sheer ecstasy, he told himself, just as he'd imagined. He raised his hands and cradled her head in them, turned her face up to his. He then lowered himself as he aimed her lips toward his.

BEEP! BEEP!...BEEP! The sound accosted his inner ear. His annoyance was immediate. He reactively sat Sarah down on the bed and let her fall back. He then quickly turned his attention inward, initiating his visual/communication link.

"What's happening," he arbitrarily asked his subordinate, just as he was accessing all the systems himself with sweeping speed in his head.

"Sir, it's affected most of the systems, but as I'm sure you are seeing, nothing is showing up as the central cause. It appears to be random fluctuations in the old systems. Perhaps they're just glitching from age, sir. Our ship's systems aren't affected, and nothing is showing up on our sensors regarding any external forces that could be contributing to the trouble; no solar flares, no EMP sources. It must be internal to the base's systems."

"Curious," Davian Adorjan said as he continued scanning the arrays of sensors himself. He shut down and reinitiated the entirety of the major systems, one after the other, running diagnostics as he did so. The anomaly didn't appear to repeat itself. He then did it all over again, with the same results. Only a few systems behaved in a sluggish way, but it was understandable that they did so, due to their age. And by doing so, a few components were brought to attention that needed replacing and recalibrated, but nothing glitched as before.

He then turned his attention to his ship and its sensor arrays, calibrating them yet again, and then initiating a series of oscillating scanning sweeps in all directions and to the limits of their ability. After several minutes he placed them back into standard alert mode for conservation and seemed to rest in the fact that nothing unusual was happening.

But he knew better.

It was just a matter of time.

. . . .

'We will be approaching the outer edge of Venus' orbit shortly, Eliam. The timing of the Fermium-Pulse Emission has proved accurate and our position on the other side of Earth has shielded us from any long

range scanning they could have completed—we remain undetected. Sustaining our calculated vector, we should be rounding the sun in about twenty minutes, and arrive at our destination at the dark side of the Moon in approximately 1.3 hours."

"Good, thanks, *Sanguine*."

"Eliam?"

"Yes, *Sanguine*."

"Do you consider bringing Oscar Whiting along a strategic maneuver?"

"Please elaborate, *Sanguine*."

"Do you consider him—in his current physical condition—to be a strategic augmentation toward the efforts of de-programming his daughter upon her rescue?"

"Well, *Sanguine*. That is our hope, yes."

"I understand that Doctor Athena Mauropolin suggested the move."

"Yes, that is correct, *Sanguine*. Why do you ask?"

"Well, my general research into her history and background has shown that she has, on record, exhibited numerous behavioral anomalies. Many of her contemporaries in their fields have issued warnings concerning her professional 'mistakes,' as well as her 'highly irregular directives regarding the circumventing of scientific, tangible data,' for the less acceptable practice of proceeding along the lines of the intangible, which have apparently clouded her reasoning at arriving at sound conclusions.

"Though I've read countless treatises on the dichotomous subjects, I have yet to observe any critical data that would justify the choosing of the inanimate, and imagined, over the certainty of facts and imperial knowledge. And though I think very highly of Colonel William Ravine, he has exhibited like behaviors within the recent past as well, especially noted after our experience together of being stranded. I thought I should bring this to your attention."

Eliam thought about it for a moment.

"Well, *Sanguine*, I haven't looked at all the data you have, but I think I know what you're referring to. You're talking about gut feelings, and intuition, faith perhaps. Some people, *Sanguine*—many on Hoame, as well as on Earth—believe that there is much more going on than just what we can see and interpret with our senses. That there are patterns and synchronicities taking place that just do not fit within known physics

and cosmology, and that it's these ancillary, incidental components of existence that give people that, I don't know…that
extra impetus to not only survive, but to live with a sense of
purpose, and hope. My jury is still out on that subject too,
Sanguine, to some degree, I suppose. But, people just have feelings about things. That's the way it is. I understand it may be
difficult to understand, as an AI. But, perhaps someday you
will."

He lowered his head, considering his words as he thought
about Sarah.

*"I see. Thank you for your comments, Eliam. I will alert you and
the rest of the crew when we have reached the rendezvous point where we'll
dock with the other ship for final preparations."*

"Thank you, *Sanguine*."

Eliam left the Captain's chair and stepped back into the
cabin with Colonel Ravine, Athena and Oscar Whiting.

"We're on schedule and still undetected. We've got a little
time before we dock with *The Adora*," he said to Colonel Ravine as he sat down across from him at the fore table. "How's
Oscar?" he asked. He looked to the back of the ship where
the man was sitting and talking with Athena.

Colonel Ravine turned and looked at the two as well and
then back toward Eliam before commenting.

"He seems fine. I don't think he's grasping the reality of
the situation. I mean, he knows he's in a ship, in space, and
that we're heading to the Moon to rescue his daughter. But I
think he considers it all in his own imagination, which actually
says a lot. He knows he suffers from dementia, but he appears
to accept it and just go with the flow of it."

"Yeah, I noticed that. We should all be so lucky."

"Yeah!" Colonel Ravine laughed slightly at the comment.
He then changed the subject. "Are you okay with all this? Any
second thoughts?"

Eliam was full of second thoughts, third thoughts, fourth
thoughts, more than he wished to acknowledge. Yet something in him was calm at the center of all the anxiety that knot-
ted his insides. He couldn't place his finger on it, couldn't find
the words to describe it, but it was there nonetheless. He

thought about what *Sanguine* had mentioned and then about how he felt about Sarah and his responsibility for getting her into this.

"Yes…no…yes…no, who knows? I guess I'm about as ready for this as I've been for anything. I mean, I watched my parents die before my very eyes; I watched thousands die in the wars, while I was working, in fact, on WoTi Island; I had a perfect stranger die in my arms while trying to drag him away from a burning vehicle during all that craziness. And then I come here and I see the same things happening on this world, basically. It doesn't seem to be any different anywhere you go, nation, state, or planet. It's all the same. It's just what's inside people.

"We're all inclined to being this way. It's just a matter of how we choose to look at things, I guess. I want to see things as being good and purposeful and fair for everyone. Others don't seem to care, and just take the position that their lives are the center of the universe and nothing, or no one else matters." He took a deep breath and exhaled hard. "I'm not saying I understand it; I just see it for what it is. And I'm just here, making *my* choice." He paused for another moment. "I'm going to do everything in my power to make sure Sarah gets back to the position where she can do the same for herself again. That's what's driving me right now. Am I okay? Actually, I don't think I've ever been more okay!"

Colonel Ravine looked at Eliam, apparent recognition softening his hardened features.

"That makes perfect sense to me!"

Chapter 58

Everyone on board the two ships, with the exception of Oscar Whiting, had their Smartbrain implants tied in to the ships' sensors and were watching attentively either out the fore view screen, or within a viewing-pane of their own VF's. *Sanguine* was trailing behind *The Adora*, matching the same slow speed as together they approached the horizon line where they had to stop in order to remain undetected.

"Please land down there below that escarpment, Lem," he said. Colonel Ravine spoke without words to his lead combat pilot on *The Adora*, highlighting the area in their shared VF's.

Lem acknowledged the command and immediately came about, descending the remaining few dozen meters, and landing effortlessly. *Sanguine* followed *The Adora* in and did the same, positioning herself strategically next to the larger ship. The space vessels then extended their docking tunnels, connected, and were sharing atmospheres in mere moments.

Eliam and Colonel Ravine made their way over to the bigger ship and joined the others who were already busy in the cargo hold.

"I take it these are the Cryo-units?" Eliam asked. The machines appeared as if they belonged to a genre of sleek racing cars, except they had no wheels, and the elongated, dome-like canopy where one entered was just as opaque as the rest of the unit, sporting the same exceedingly non-reflective surface coatings as *Sanguine*, and *The Adora*.

"I don't think I ever asked you, why you just happen to have Cryo-units around that are rigged with propulsion and navigation systems. I'm an engineer and I've never heard of a need for such devices," Eliam asked, instinctively searching his mind for possible applications.

Colonel Ravine looked at his men knowingly. They returned the look, but didn't say a word; they just raised and lowered their eyebrows indicating they knew the answer, but weren't telling.

"Well, after all this is done I may just let you in on why, maybe during the after party, if everything goes well. But for now, we need to get everyone prepped and ready, there's no time to waste."

"You're right! Yes, let's do this," Eliam said, after a deep breath, putting his curiosity as well as his fear aside.

"Alright, everyone, let's go over this one last time!" Colonel Ravine shouted out with authority. Everyone started gathering around.

·······

Eliam watched as the elongated dome closed tightly over his upper body. His breathing became labored and he tried to apply the calming techniques he'd learned years before. Most of the time they worked well for him in tense situations, but he'd never had to experience anything in his life that even remotely amounted to what he and these men were preparing to do.

The voice startled him, even though it was feeding directly in through his neural connection.

"Okay, gentlemen, remember the critical points we reviewed. Every one of them is essential for success. Again, for those of you who haven't experienced cryo-stasis, here's the rundown. Your lungs will fill with the gas being pumped in, displacing the normal atmosphere. You, however, have modified climate suits on for this purpose, as well as for working on the surface, but the effect will be the same inside your suit as inside the chamber if you didn't have them on. The gas will prep your body for the extreme temperature reduction, and at the same time numb your senses to the effects.

"After a few minutes you will feel disoriented, much akin to how one feels when being anesthetized for a surgery. In most common procedures, once you're out cold—pardon the pun—you will have no sense of consciousness. However, you won't need to go in that far, or for that long, so you will find yourselves essentially awake in a simple VF program designed to keep your mind working so the recovery period will take much less time. Note that your sense of time will be out of whack while you're in there, but don't worry about it. Just try and keep your mind on what you're going to do.

"After arriving at your destination, your units will automatically begin bringing you out of stasis. The process will take about 13.5 minutes for full recovery. However, you might feel a little awkward and sluggish still, so take it easy. Give yourself some time. It'd be better to wait a little longer to start moving around than to make a mistake that could compromise the mission, or worst yet end your life. Remember, you're on the surface of the Moon; it's not an inherently forgiving place.

"You should have enough time before the third Fermium-Pulse Emission arrives at the base. But, before it hits you need to be prepped, at the side of the structure with the Breach-Lock, and ready to go. There's only so much time once the base is hit. From that point on it's critical you move fast, to get in, as well as to get Raj into their systems."

He paused, trying to remember anything else to say.

"Okay! Well then, Godspeed, people. Starting cryo-stasis…now!"

Eliam shuddered at the command.

. . . .

The units raced across the cold gray landscape at nearly four hundred kilometers per hour. They had roughly half that distance to travel, so it would take about half an hour to arrive at the base. The men inside didn't have any sense of motion or velocity, or that they were zooming in and out of crevasses and around rocks and hills hugging the jagged terrain so tightly that sometimes they were only mere centimeters from impacting some lunar surface.

Eliam found that his calming techniques had worked, or perhaps they hadn't and it was just the effects of the gas.

Whichever, he had calmed down. And just as Colonel Ravine had described, he found himself in a VF program that consisted of little more than a room with a couple of lounge chairs and some old magazines on a table. Eliam picked up one of the magazines out of curiosity, an antique issue of *Life* depicting the then, newly discovered workings of the human brain. Fitting, he thought.

He thumbed to the main article and laughed vaguely at the old images and styles and advertisements. He scanned the first page of the piece, but then put the magazine down as he sat on the edge of one of the chairs. His mind then dutifully returned to their plans. Again and again he went through them, considering all that could go wrong and what could be done if it did. He felt as if he should stretch and warm up his muscles, but then realized that that would be impossible. He returned to his focus.

His mental exercises were interrupted when he remembered what Colonel Ravine had said about time. It seemed that he had been in this waiting room for hours. He even found himself thumbing through and reading more of that article on the brain. He was in mid-sentence when he noticed the words on the page swelling into his Visual Field, growing ever larger until all he saw was the white between the letters.

Suddenly, he was shaken out of his cold slumber.

Eliam blinked away what felt like frost from his eyelids. He was lying on his back, looking up through his suit's clear visor at the blinking display on the inside of his Cryo-unit. He also heard the barely audible sound of beeping and remembered what Colonel Ravine had said about it: "Once the unit has finished its cycle—which should take about thirteen minutes—the system will notify you with a series of beeps that you will detect through your B-CID. When you hear these, and you are ready, just press the green flashing Manual Open button."

Eliam's mind felt sluggish and his thoughts oddly surreal. He then tested his real senses by moving his legs and toes, and then his hands and arms, ending with the twisting of his neck and head. He took a few deep breaths and felt as if he were returning to reality. The thought of what he was getting ready to do then seized upon his mind. He was preparing to open his unit and before him would be the landscape of a desolate, planetary body. He would be on an airless, lifeless moon.

He'd been most places one could think, in simulation anyway, in a virtual sense. And even though they had all felt real, to one degree or another, he always knew in the back of his mind that they weren't. But now he was truly and unequivocally going to experience the reality. He suddenly felt hugely anxious and noticed his breathing was erratic. But, just as that happened, he saw an image of Sarah in his mind and summarily realized that she was the reason he was there.

He gritted his teeth, took a deep breath and pushed the green button.

The domed cover immediately lifted and slid down toward his feet disappearing as if it were a knife going into its sheath. Eliam then found himself looking up at a brilliantly shining, star-filled black sky. He laid there for a moment, but then took another deep breath and sat up. His muscles suddenly shot out signals of pain to his brain and he realized that he was experiencing what Colonel Ravine had also mentioned, disorientation. It was more acute than what he'd imagined.

Eliam struggled to center his thoughts, even as he began noticing the details of where he was. He saw the other Cryo-units not far from his. Two were open, but one was still closed. Sergeant Norris was sitting up and looking around, as was Raj, but Tomlinson's unit was just sitting there motionless. It took another minute, but it opened as well. By then Norris was climbing out of his. Raj and Eliam followed suit. The first thing Eliam noticed was the reduced gravity. He'd nearly forgotten about it for some reason.

He reached out reactively, grabbing his unit to brace himself as he swayed back and forth. He took another deep breath and as he oriented his muscles' motions to match the conditions, he thought to check his suit's systems. Everything was functioning normally according to his helmet's readouts. Eliam then looked around and saw the other guys doing the same thing.

Norris nodded to Eliam. Eliam nodded back. The others did the same. After a few more minutes they all gave the thumbs up sign, and Norris pointed to his wrist as a sign for all to notice the time. They had less than originally discussed, and they all knew it.

The four men huddled closely and touched their face plates together. Norris then spoke loudly and the vibrations of his voice carried through from helmet to helmet.

"Looks like we all survived the trip. As you can see we have less time than we thought!" he said.

They all nodded to indicate they'd heard him.

"Okay, just as planned, let's get the Breach-Lock un-hooked and set-up. Raj, Eliam, it looks like there's some debris in our path. Can you two see if you can clear the bigger rocks away? We don't want anyone tripping up and falling as we're carrying this thing. Tomlinson and I will detach it from the unit and then we'll wait for you guys to help move it in place. Everyone be careful, but remember, we've got…it looks like fifteen minutes before the Pulse hits. We need to have this thing sitting in front of that wall right there so we can hoist it up and attach it a few seconds after. Okay? Let's do it then!"

They all bumped their helmets together as if they were players on some sports field and then went to work. Within minutes the excess debris was cleared and the men had the Breach-Lock in hand carefully toting it to the structure's exterior wall. With only a couple of minutes to spare, they had the Lock in place, stood upright on its stand, and positioned within centimeters of the wall.

"So far so good," Sergeant Norris started as they stood there and bumped heads again. "That was the easy part. Raj, you geared and ready for yours?!"

Raj spoke loudly so the vibrations would carry.

"Ready as I'll ever be! Everything I need is right here!" he said, tapping the small pack attached to his belt.

"Okay, just as planned. Tomlinson's the first one in. He'll secure the room. Hopefully we're entering a part of the base that's not occupied, but there's no way to tell. Sergeant, be ready to lay down that spread of NERV pulses inside, just in case. Otherwise, assess the situation and be ready to help Raj through. Raj, you're next in. The two of you get to one of the utility junctions as soon as possible. You need to work as fast as you can and cover our signature asses. If the effects of the Pulse wane quicker than we think it will and we're detected, surprise won't be on our side, and we'll be screwed. So move fast, guys. Eliam and I will be right in behind you. Be ready for anything, gentleman!"

The wait was short, and it happened as scheduled. The men knew the Fermium-Pulse had hit because they saw some distant lights on the bases structure flicker at precisely the expected time. They pushed the Lock up to the metal wall and hit the button. The unit's powerful magnet attached the device securely.

"Here we go!" Sergeant Norris said to himself.

Chapter 59

"There it is again," he said, shaken out of his work-induced stupor.

"Yep, seeing it! What the hell is happening?" the other replied, also snapping out of his pseudo-daze.

They immediately sat up straighter and started running diagnostics. As expected, within a minute Davian Adorjan stepped into the control room.

"Status," he demanded, looking at the consoles, and then to his two subordinates.

"It's happened again. Multiple systems have gone off line; power is down to sixty-two percent, two of the main generators just shut down for no reason," the Systems Chief said pointedly, pausing a moment to seemingly validate more information.

He then continued.

"Atmosphere and artificial gravity-boost systems are mostly intact, fortunately, but several of the core computer systems have gone into safe-mode. They look okay, but it'll take a few minutes to get them and their subs back up. And there are a handful of small isolated fluctuations happening in some of the programs: lock-screens and freeze-ups, that sort of thing. It's the main Cyn-boards in the primary, like I suggested earlier. It's got to be. When they glitch, they confuse the subs, so they just shut everything down. And we don't have replacements. That's why their neural-chip counterparts were designed, to eliminate things like this from happening,"

"Yeah! And that's probably one of the reasons why the base was shut down. It's just old and bitchy, like my grandma!" the younger tech offered.

The two looked at the man, neither at all amused by the comment. The man immediately wiped the grin off his face, returning to his efforts.

"Yes, I understand the effect, but I'm…I'm not …" Davian Adorjan stopped mid-sentence, apparently thinking about something. He pinched his lips. "It's not the systems," he said, shaking his head and stepping back slightly.

The men looked up at him.

"Not the systems?" the Chief repeated, unsure of his inference.

They both looked at their diagnostic readouts again, studying them with greater attention.

"As soon as you can, get the systems back up. When they are, initiate Security Protocol's SC-9 and 13. I'll monitor remotely, but keep close eyes on them as well. Report immediately if you notice any fluctuations, even if they're minute. Without delay! And remove the ships from hard dock. Do it now! Do you understand?"

The Chief nodded and answered forthrightly.

"Yes Sir! Take the ships out of hard dock. You heard him. Do it!" he said to the other sternly. "Protocols SC-9 and 13 when the systems are up. Yes, sir. Report immediately if we notice anything!"

Davian Adorjan suddenly seemed as excited as a poor boy getting a new bicycle.

His men were at a loss for words regarding the odd reaction, but they went to work without delay, swiping pads and bringing up screens.

They then looked at each other with raised eyebrows after their employer left the room.

....

Raj shook like a leaf as he waited inside for the dock to balance atmospheres. He had no idea if Sergeant Tomlinson had encountered any resistance on the other side. He readied himself and his weapon, and watched for the door to automatically open. A few more seconds passed. It opened with a whoosh. Suddenly an arm reached in and grabbed him. He was just about to discharge his NERV weapon when he saw Tomlinson grinning at him, attempting to help him out of the chamber.

The Sergeant held his index finger up to his helmet and in front of his mouth reminding Raj to be quiet. Once Raj nodded in understanding, Tomlinson pointed to a small box up by the ceiling just down the corridor. It was a junction between conduit lines.

Raj smiled and moved toward it swiftly.

Within a few minutes the team was inside and cautiously scouting out the rooms and other corridors within their immediate vicinity while Raj was working with his equipment. There was no air to speak of in that part of the abandoned base. They'd figured as much, but that was a good thing, allowing them the ability to work undetected.

Suddenly, Raj issued a thumb up to the guys and then tapped on the side of his helmet to indicate they could speak to each other now.

They all switched their systems on at the same time and heard Raj speaking in their AF's.

"Okay, I've entered our equipment codes into their database so they won't identify us as any anomalous signals. We shouldn't set off any of their alarm systems. We can talk freely now. They won't be able to listen in unless they intentionally scan the spectrum for activity, which they most likely won't, but then we're also encrypted."

"Good," Sergeant Norris said, his lips only barely moving to the words his mind was saying in their shared audio fields. "Everyone has the layout of the base in their nav-gear; we'll all know where everyone else's position is at any given time; keep track of each other. Our main objective is to move toward the parts of the base that they are most likely to be occupying. We'll move and monitor, move and monitor. No one moves without someone else monitoring.

"As discussed, most likely they're a small contingent, with only a small area in use, probably just on the other side of the central hub and near the docks. But, we don't know if they might have people working in other areas, for whatever reasons. So go slow and don't underestimate the situation. If we have to take somebody out, we NERV them. But we do it quickly and silently, and then secure them somewhere where they won't be a threat to the mission.

"Once we get to the lock, Raj should be able to mask its operation so we can pass through without notice. Keep all communications in the AF. Remember, we need recon data before we can finalize our plans; otherwise our chances of success go way down. When we get our data, we'll meet up at Raj's Streamplace and determine where we go from there. Got it?"

They all acknowledged the instructions with a nod.

"Good!"

. . . .

The base was comprised of a central hub and three adjoining wings. The wing they had chosen was strategic from the point of their approach and entry. It proved a good choice because there were no signs of people or any recent activity. Sergeant Norris and Eliam had a slight scare when checking out one of the rooms along the corridor they were scouting. A full bodied jump suit had been left hanging from the front of an open closet door. In the dusty darkness it appeared to be a man looming there. Both saw it at the same time and spontaneously drew down on it, but rapidly realized that it wasn't what they had initially thought.

Upon arrival at the lock, it was Raj's turn again to do his stuff and he easily accessed a terminal panel and began reconfiguring its core programming to hinder any signal that would be sent to a control room in another part of the base. The only problem was if someone might be in a room or down one of the adjacent corridors in earshot of the thing while it was activated. Airlocks that old tended to make a significant amount of noise when operating, and they would have to use it twice due to the fact that it was only large enough to accommodate two people.

As before, Tomlinson and Raj would go first so they could scout out the area on their way to one of the base's main computer terminals. It was from there that Raj needed to work in order to hack their systems and establish their own security layers, as well as doing two manifestly important things: 1) mask their two ships' signatures so they wouldn't be detected upon approach; and 2) determine Sarah's location, as well as verify exactly where and how many other occupants there were on the base.

·······

The men were huddling around the lock's door as Raj made his final adjustments. Each was taking turns peering through the thick window to see if they could make out any movement on the other side. There was none that they could tell. Raj finished his work and let the others know with a brief, "We're good!"

They all raised their eyebrows and nodded their readiness.

Sergeant Norris grabbed the single, heavy-duty recessed handle and twisted it down from its horizontal to its vertical position. They cringed as they heard the loud click. Norris wasted no time in opening the door. Raj and Tomlinson then stepped inside the chamber. The others shut the door quickly and Norris initiated the lock's pressurization sequence.

The sound wasn't as loud as they'd first imagined, but it was definitely noisy. It took ten seconds for the unit to match the pressure on the other side. When done, the men opened the door, nodded back to the others, stepped through, and then quickly shut and sealed the door from their side. Within another minute, all were through. The four then secured their collapsible helmets behind their heads, and were spreading out in a tactical formation as they slowly made their way down the wide corridor, covering each other's moves.

Rallying at one of the base's remote computer terminals was next on the agenda, and they knew they had a distance to go in order to do so. They passed numerous rooms, which they cautiously checked out on the way, as well as four different corridors that took off at right angles from the one they were in, which, according to their maps, circled around the central hub of the base.

They carefully looked down the curved hallways as they happened upon them, taking turns walking a short distance to see farther down their curved lines, before returning to the central corridor. They saw no signs of occupation anywhere. In fact, it was an easy trip to the nearest terminal. Perhaps luck or providence was on their side.

"So far, so good!" Norris said to the others through their shared AF's.

"Yeah, looking good," Tomlinson agreed. "Raj, according to the layout, there's a terminal up ahead and around the next corner at a central hall connection…about thirty meters?"

"Yep, seeing it. Good to go!"

"Okay, group, keep a sharp eye. Eliam watch our six! This is getting a little too easy."

"Yeah, my thoughts exactly," he said in agreement.

"Yeah, well, the hard part's yet to come," Norris said, matter-of-factly. "Once Raj gets in and finds Sarah, we know there's going to be people around, so trust me, it'll get real interesting right about then."

The team cautiously found their way to the central hall connection, and as described, it was a medium-sized room where three different corridors teed off in opposite, curving directions away from it. Standing out from one wall of the room was an island where two people could work side by side, one at a terminal, the other at a desk-like offshoot. Raj made it to the terminal and everyone else took up positions down the adjoining corridors keeping an eye out.

Raj made good time circumventing the security of the base's systems. He was acting as if he were the best-of-the-best, full of spunk and self-confidence, successfully and stealthily navigating their systems in his efforts to acquire their needed information: accessing the base's internal sensor arrays to see where all the current inhabitants of the base were located.

"How's the saying go? 'Bongo!'" he commented to the others.

"That'd be 'Bingo,' Raj, I think. And you're *from* Earth?" Norris added, laughing at the mis-comment.

The others smiled too, glad for their apparent fortune.

"Sarah's in Quadrant-B of the main complex. And as you can see…" He was feeding the intel real time via ocular screen-shots to the others. "She's in a room by herself. The adjacent room is fairly large, with…with a dozen people in it. They're all lying down, it looks like. Either they're all resting, or we've got more people in trouble than we originally thought. And looking around, it appears that there are only six other individuals in various places in the rest of the base. This's good! Two are in the base's main control room. One is in the next room down the corridor from the one Sarah's in, and three are spread out: one each in two other rooms, and one walking down a corridor as we speak, but not in our direction. All appears to be…" He paused abruptly. "Oh shit!" he said suddenly.

"What?" Tomlinson asked, immediately reacting to the comment.

"What?" Norris also added.

"The ships, there are two of them. But they're not hard docked! That means I can't get to them! But, that's not the bad news, guys."

"What do you mean that's not the bad news. That's pretty fucking bad news! That means we can't get into their systems, mask the approach of our ships when it's time to bring them in! Isn't that right?" Norris said with obvious concern.

"Yes, that is exactly what it means!"

"So what are you fucking talking about, *'that's not the bad news'*?"

"Their ships, they were just disconnected from their hard docks a few minutes ago."

There was a short silence.

"*Shit!*" Tomlinson said.

"Yes, that is what I said," Raj commented, knowing that they were now getting the point.

"What's that mean?" Eliam asked logically, processing the information just as he'd said it, already arriving at the answer before it actually came.

"What it means, is that we've probably been pegged and they figured we'd try to hack them! That's what it means!"

The team went silent again.

Everyone was thinking of the next move.

"Well, its two things: Either its coincidence, or it's a fact. We're not seeing any defensive activity. But, there's no reason they'd decouple their ships, unless they were about to leave, or because of what you just said. It's bad timing no matter how you look at it. Raj, it's both ships, right? Both ships we're undocked, just now?" he then thought to ask.

"Yes, both ships!" Raj answered.

"Maybe they are leaving?" Tomlinson offered.

"Yeah, maybe! Either way, there's no turning back. We came here to do a job, and we're going to do it. I say let's tighten up our diaper straps, and let's get on with it," Norris said.

Chapter 60

"I agree with Sergeant Norris. We have to move on. Here's what we're going to do: Raj, first make sure all our present intel is ready in a care package, standard op, you'll have a copy for back up; Norris and I will have the primaries; if we're in an overall no-win situation, he or I will launch it; *we* make the decision; if we're out of the picture, you're up. Got it?!"

"Care package?" Eliam asked.

"A quick emitter," Raj started to explain. "Information is condensed, loaded into a pulse emitter, and set for a quick launch. Basically, if I saw I was going to die, I could slap two pads in sequence—using either hand—and off it goes. Our suits are built with them, here and here." He pointed to the spots. "The system records and downloads data to the package every two seconds, as well as whatever else you want to add and/or program into it. The emitter is set to launch the packet on request so our ships can have our current intel. What they do with it depends on the situation, but at least they'll have the information. The packet is encrypted and can only be opened by the receiver, but launching it will definitely give your position away, which we don't want to do. It's a last ditch effort if there are blackout protocols in effect, which we are most definitely under."

"I see, makes sense."

"Data-share links' up, and...okay, we're synced," Raj added, nodding at Sergeant Tomlinson.

"Okay, good. Here's the rest. We're going to stay the course and get Sarah. When we get there, Eliam, you'll go to her. I'll cover the areas here and here, Sergeant Norris will cover here," he indicated the locations on their shared VF panes by a shaded area: green for his, and yellow for Norris'. "I'll check out the large room with all those people first, though I've got a feeling they won't be the threat. The single guy down the hall can sit as far as we are concerned right now. But, I'll take him out, too, if needed, with Raj's help. Raj, you'll cover that passage at this point, here.

"Sergeant, you'll cover this passage between us and their people. If they approach, you'll need to head them off at about, here. That's as far as they go. As soon as we get Sarah, we'll head your way. I'll cover the rear. We'll meet up with you, here, and head back the way we came until we get to this point. From there, this is the shortest route to the docks," he said, shading the area so everyone could follow.

"Without being able to hack their ships, ours won't have the advantage of surprise. But they're going to have to come in one way or another in order to get us out. And they're waiting on us to get them some data, but the question is do we get a package out to them before, or after we get to the docks?"

He paused for a moment.

"Comments, anyone?" he asked.

Everyone was staring down toward the floor, thinking hard. Norris then sounded off.

"At the docks, I say when we get there we find the best location to defend ourselves, launch our care package at that point, and then wait!"

"Or, we can take the offensive and attempt to disable the few people who're here, and then do the same," Raj offered.

"Not a bad idea, worth considering. There is one question we haven't asked yet, though: do we know if anyone is on either of their ships? That little fragment of intel needs to be in the package." Norris asked.

"We would've known that, had they been hard docked, but no! I could've used the base's sensors to check, but if I had it would've been like throwing up a flag. As of this moment we just don't know."

Everyone thought through the options.

"If we try to take the offensive, they might be prepared—knowing that we're here. We might get bogged down, worst case trapped if we do. No, I agree with Norris. I say we get to the docks. That's our best chance to meet up with our ships. Plus, we might be able to do something from there to help them on approach, depending on the base's defensive capabilities, I don't know. Raj, see what you can bring up along those lines from the base's schematics." Tomlinson went silent, still thinking hard.

"On it," Raj said.

"I agree, we get Sarah and get to the docks," Eliam stated firmly. "If anything, we might be able to get one of their ships to use as a last resort! Regardless, I'd say the docks are our best bet, too."

Everyone looked around at each other.

There were nods across the board.

....

Eliam stayed back a little as Sergeant Tomlinson and Raj slid down the walls opposite each other holding their NERV weapons in the ready position to drop and fire. They soon came to the point where their corridor teed off. To the left and down a short way was the large room with all the people. Sarah was to the right. On past the door to Sarah's location, and at an additional distance of another fifteen meters, was the entrance to the other room where the single figure had been located. As the men made their way, they intensely watched their VF panes. The figure was not moving, had in fact not moved at all since it was first observed.

Sergeant Tomlinson snaked around the corner and rushed to the door of the room. He put his ear to it, but all he could hear was the sound of humming machines. Again his intuition told him there was no threat. But he wasn't about to open the door to find out. He took a small wire out of his suit and slid it under the door. The camera-tipped tool fed back the images of what was inside to his VF. He saw only beds with people laying on them. Tubes were in their arms, and some type of B-CID was on their heads. He needed no other explanation;

they were human product awaiting shipment. He shook his head in disgust. A further quick scan told him that there weren't any other threats.

He left the room and joined Raj at the corridors' junction. Together they made their way to the room Sarah was supposedly in and Sergeant Tomlinson checked it the same as he'd done at the other. Inside he saw a figure on a single bed; it had to be Sarah. The room was less clinical, and otherwise empty except for the motionless body, apparently as incapacitated as the others. Tomlinson checked the door handle and to their good fortune, found it was unlocked. He then motioned for Raj to take up position down the hall toward the second room, following through by calling Eliam in next.

Sergeant Tomlinson nodded to him, opened the door and took position opposite Raj outside.

Eliam stepped into the room, made a quick scan of the layout, and then went to the figure—it was Sarah. He wanted to speak out her name, tell her he was sorry for getting her involved in this, and tell her he loved her. But he knew he should remain as stealth-minded as possible. All he wanted was to do what he'd choreographed in his mind a thousand times before arriving there: stick her with the serum, disconnect all the feeds going into her, remove the B-CID, pick her up and carry her to her freedom, and he, hopefully, to his redemption.

Eliam wasted no time. He opened a thermal pocket on his pant leg, pulled out the injector, and lifted it to her arm. He was just about to stab her with it when he saw the red flashing warning light in his VF pane. He then fell backwards onto the floor, suddenly finding himself in total and unequivocal darkness, unable to move.

Eliam then felt some of the oddest feelings he'd ever felt in his life. In fact, his senses were reeling with such odd intensities, that he could think of nothing but the strangeness and severity of them. His skin felt as if it were rippling; his nostrils seemed to twitch at the odd mixture of odoriferous scents it was encountering. His hearing seemed to sway from one ear to the other and then oscillate in circles of subtle tones and echoes; and without explanation, he seemed to taste some sort of coppery, bitter, metallic taste. One sense would dominate his attention, and then another.

It was overwhelming.

·······

Sergeant Tomlinson was startled by the onslaught of the severe change, but not as completely as Eliam. He was an educated and disciplined fighter. He immediately sensed that something was blocking his natural sensory pathways, replacing the normal feelings he was accustomed to. He had been trained, in depth, on how to center one's mind and focus when one was thrust into combat situations where sensory overload could kill a man just as predictably as a sniper's bullet.

The darkness enveloped him just as it had Eliam, but the Sergeant recognized the change quickly enough that he was able to adapt and keep his head about him. The fluctuations and surges of incoming neural signals nearly incapacitated him, but he held them at bay and fought their debilitating effects as he tried to determine his situation.

He knew from sheer sense that something was seriously wrong, and he promptly surmised that it had to do with his implanted B-CID. It was somehow malfunctioning, or faltering in its core processes. Logic then asserted its universal reason and he immediately arrived at the conclusion that it was being compromised, in some way being controlled. It had been hacked.

The notion struck him as if a blow, even as his senses oscillated and morphed unpredictably sending waves of incongruent feelings into his brain. The realization was quickly authenticated in his mind along with the conclusion that the odds were in favor of the supposition that he was not the only one being affected by the sensory altercation.

It was then that he made his decision.

Without feeling, without corresponding sensation, without sight or sound aiding him in his task, he imagined in his mind his right hand reaching down. He focused with the intensity of a Ninja Master attempting to break blocks made of solid concrete. He imagined it so fully that in reality his hand reached down and summarily tapped the two spots on his suit, as his mind screamed out *"Black Hack!"*

He didn't know it, he didn't sense it, all he could rest in was the faith that it had happened. He then fell into a heap and held on, alone in his mind with a whirlwind of disproportionate feelings pummeling his brain.

·······

Eliam didn't at all understand what was happening. He just lay there, feeling himself roll uncontrollably, as if on waves of pure motion, his mind completely challenged by the engrossing sensations. And then just as suddenly, his Visual Field became inundated with light as he heard the voice speaking to him.

"Hello, Mr. Zaris. You have no idea how pleased I am to meet you. I knew you'd find your way here, sooner or later. I must say I am glad it was sooner, though it has interrupted a portion of my work, which I brought up here to finalize as I waited. But that's of no consequence. It will be completed on time, and even be augmented a bit for my customers as a result of your visit.

"But you must forgive me. It seems I've already started rambling, and I've thoughtlessly neglected to introduce myself. We've never met, Mr. Zaris. I am Davian Adorjan. I, too, am from Hoame...originally, anyway. We have a common thread of association, Mr. Zaris. Your grandfather and I were acquaintances. Friends actually, of a sort, though that changed some time ago. But again, I am getting ahead of myself. How about we start with a little one-on-one time? I know of a little place."

Eliam suddenly found himself standing in the open, looking up at the tiered entryway of what appeared to be an ancient building. Columns of ornately carved, stacked stone blocks rose twenty meters high before him, holding an even more ornate roof of sculptured stone trusses. He could see that the structure sat atop a mountain crest and looked out across a vast plain of other mountains and hills and dry valleys.

One specific mountain appeared to have been sheared off, its summit completely gone and its new, flat plateau carved with long, straight imposing lines of immense earthworks. Along the vast expanse of terrain Eliam saw huge areas carved out in the shapes of various creatures: monkeys, birds, and snakes, among others. There were also enormous carvings on much of the slanted soil, and on the shear sides of the distant mountains in the shape of odd symbols, and geometric patterns. It was colossal in its expanse.

Eliam felt warmness on his skin, sensed the dry breeze in his hair, along with that feeling of smallness one gets while standing in the presence of enormity. He turned to see the origin of the voice speaking to him. There to his side was a man sitting on a huge, ornately carved stone throne of sorts, elevated much higher than where he stood. The man was dressed in a purple, imaginatively-embroidered robe, with accoutrements of gold inlayed into the fabric. He wore gold jewelry on his fingers and wrists and around his neck. And he had a crown of gold on his head. Even the sandals he wore on his feet looked to be stitched with gold thread.

The two made eye contact.

Davian Adorjan smiled at the recognition with an expression of superiority.

"I suppose there is something to be said of my banishment here on this planet. Even though it has been difficult, there appears to be redemption and salvation on the horizon. I was actually on the verge of deciding my existence was of no more importance. It's uncanny…no, ironic really. One minute I was resolved to experiencing some sort of self-administered state of non-existence, wholly fed up with this purposeless life, you understand. No familial support or encouragement; no reason to go on; I simply felt as an insignificant insect crawling in some nondescript direction, with no idea of where I was going, nor why I'd been.

"Then, I was offered liberation. Oh, it's understandable, now. I've come to believe one attains what one deserves, in the end. That goes for an individual, as well as for a people. Sufferings and persecutions are but stepping stones of learning on the way to fulfillment. And I see now that my turn has come."

He smiled, as if filled with euphoric joy and happiness.

Eliam tried to make sense of what was happening. His mind bristled with the rush of data arriving at his brain. He thought to speak, but he could not think of a question.

"At a loss for words, Mr. Zaris? Astounded and in utter shock at the influx of sensations pouring into your brain; I'd imagine so. Oh, don't feel deflated by it; it's not your fault in the least. For you see…it is mine!"

Davian Adorjan narrowed his eyes, displaying a sinister countenance that would shake any earthly man. Suddenly, Eliam felt electrical shocks coursing up his arms and legs. They were at first tingles, but grew into painful, ratcheting jolts to his body and bones. For an inestimable amount of time he shook from them, but then they abated.

"You can say ouch, if you so desire, Mr. Zaris. I'm sure that hurt quite a bit," Adorjan said, with an ostensibly concerned voice.

Eliam seemed to gain back a semblance of consciousness. Though mumbled, he at least got some words out.

"What…what are you doing? I…don't understand!"

"Well, of course you don't understand. I know that feeling very well. It's exactly how I felt when my friend—your grandfather—stabbed me in the back, which was totally unexpected and incomprehensible to me. In fact, it really messed me up! I still haven't gotten over it. That's why you're here. Because I need to work that particular part of my life out, you see? You know, undergo some regenerative therapy, a little self-intervention. And that's how you're going to help me, Mr. Zaris. Oh, and yes, I neglected to tell you. Your friends here are going to help as well. I wouldn't want you to be alone in your distress, as I was. No, no, no! I'm not completely merciless!"

He laughed.

Eliam then noticed his three companions. They were just sitting there on the bare, hot ground next to the building, apparently as immobilized as he was. Their faces were filled with pain. They shared a difficult, but encouraging nod.

"What is this place?" Eliam then asked, turning back to his apparent captor.

Davian Adorjan waited for a moment.

He looked out and took in the vast surroundings before speaking.

"Fair question, this is a creation of mine. A representation of the mysterious region of the Earth called Nazca, in the country of Peru on the continent of South America. Exquisite detail, don't you think? I particularly like it because of its historical significance. You may not know this, but it was actually a mining installation settled by our people multiple millennia ago.

"Do you see all those carvings and shapes? Those were made by the indigenous peoples of Nazca, who were encouraged to do so by ours, actually. Most don't know it, but it was merely due to a little friendly competition, driven by a few engineers who were also amateur artists who, over a time, tried to out-do each other in their spare time by using the Nazca people as their sculpting tools.

"The legend goes that the one who made the hummingbird won, simply because the solitary judge deemed it so—he was the overseer of the entire mining project who liked the Earth species of bird primarily because of their small stature, their iridescent colors, and the fact they could fly backwards. The winning engineer won a significant portion of gold to take back to Hoame, they say. Reward for his hard work and creativity, as well as for the pleasing of his superior. That is the way of things, and always has been. Is it not?

"However, you're actually asking why you are all here, specifically. Well, I suppose I could have started in any one of the numerous creations I've built for myself, but this one is significant because it, as I said, reminds me so much of our heritage. When we—as a people—happened upon this planet, we

were its Gods. We were appreciated and worshipped and em-
ulated simply because of our advanced technology and our superior intellect, and rightly so. In return for their veneration,
we helped them rise up out of the animal kingdom by helping
them understand their environments. We taught them basic
concepts that would help them flourish and prosper and advance, which, in turn, would help us by providing us with an
increasingly valuable commodity, which is the point of it all.

"You see, you are the extension of a family line that robbed
me of my destiny. I was to become an integral and important
part of this heritage, but due to no fault of my own, I was
shunned by my rightful caste, and left to become one of the
primitives. This unfortunate position was attributable to your
grandfather who falsely accused me of brazen divergence
from our core charge, tainting forever *my* name, within the
families of the *Ankh*.

"However, as I mentioned earlier, I now believe people
ultimately attain what they deserve. And all of you are living
proof of that fact. Those men," he pointed to the other captives, "I'm sure you know, have been hunting me for quite
some time. They wish to imprison me further, simply because
I choose to live out my heritage. We are these peoples' Gods;
we have been for millennia, and we have the right to wield
them as tools, to spend them as currency, or to destroy them
if we so desire! It is our heritage!"

Eliam couldn't believe he was hearing this. It was rhetori-
cal nonsense.

"You're *insane*!" was all he could find himself saying. He
was immediately regretful of the outburst.

"*Uhmm, right*…not what I wanted to hear!" Adorjan said,
with a deep growl, his eyes swelling with revulsion.

Eliam suddenly swayed and writhed in agony.

Chapter 61

"What happened to them? What are we going to do? They have to know the packet was sent. Surely they picked it up!" Athena asked, growing more worried. "They had to!"

Colonel Ravine sat there at the table, hands folded, studying the data along with the others. He looked up to her with understanding.

"Yes, we know. That's about all we can guess for sure. Apparently they were in a situation where they had no choice," he said, returning to his review. "No indication of what happened, just Tomlinson saying, 'Black ha...' whatever that means. The recording was cut off before he could tell us what happened. From all intents and purposes, we're in the dark. We don't know what happened to them!"

"Do you think Sarah is alright?" Oscar asked softly for the third time, seemingly forgetting he'd asked it mere seconds before. Again, he nervously rubbed his hand over his face and then through his hair.

"I don't know, Oscar. But we're going to do something. We just haven't figured out exactly what that's going to be, yet," the Colonel offered.

"We need to go in!" Lem said. "They know we're here, that someone's out here. But they don't know where, or how many, or what we're capable of. That's something! At least we have that going for us!"

Atol just sat there nodding in agreement, his eyes darting from one person to the other.

The colonel looked directly at the men, and then back down at the data he was studying.

"True," he said. "But they have two ships, and this intel informs us the big one is more than a match for ours, though fortunately the small one appears to be a transport with no weapons. And as previously mentioned, they're probably expecting us, at least by the fact that they'd recently undocked, and most definitely know about the package," the Colonel said firmly.

"True, but we have the tactical advantage in that we are combat pilots and…and…!" Lem answered sternly, with due respect in his voice, but he could think of no more advantages at the moment.

The Colonel took a deep breath and nodded in agreement.

"*Colonel, there is a low-emissions voice message resonating on all channels. Origin, the Moon base,*" *Sanguine* said, speaking through *The Adora's* internal audio system. Everyone looked at each other with apprehension.

"Audio, *Sanguine*, please," the Colonel said promptly.

"*Yes, Colonel.*"

There was a short silence and then the cabin filled with the voice of Davian Adorjan.

Hello! This message will be sent only one time. It is for those who are the co-collaborators of the four people I now have in my possession, and who are all under my full control. It is doubtful that they are here alone, and whether it is a single entity—or ship—or an entire armada awaiting some sort of communication from them to come to their aid, I assure you they will not respond, due to the fact that they were most certainly not successful in their endeavor to infiltrate this base in their attempt to subdue its inhabitants.

So, what to do? I will offer an admission. It is in the interests of the inhabitants of this base to be able to leave it in due time. If this is prohibited for whatever reason, by whatever efforts, small or large, we can assure you of the consequential demise of your friends and collaborators, post haste. Again, what to do? Well, your choice. However, I will offer this one last admonition. There will be no negotiations, no trades, no banter, and no attempts at doing so. We will leave uninhibited, or they will all immediately cease to exist. Goodbye!

Everyone seated around the table just sat there and stared dumbly at each other. Each person was in deep reflection considering the words they'd heard. A full minute passed before anyone spoke. It was Oscar that made the first comment.

"You *are* going to go get Sarah?!" he said simply, matter-of-factly, more a statement than a question. There was no fear or trepidation in his voice. The comment was delivered with the steadfast correctness of a man expecting action based solely on logic and sheer decisiveness.

Everyone looked at him, in awe of the determination and strength of character they suddenly saw. It was as if something long lost had just arisen within him.

Colonel Ravine recognized that look, for he understood it well.

"Yes, Oscar. We're going to go get Sarah!" Colonel Ravine said resolutely.

·······

"We don't have time. We'll plan on the way. We need to get going, now. I know Adorjan, and our people are not comfortable in the least. They have no time!" the Colonel spoke to Athena in response to her counsel to wait and further discuss some sort of plan.

"Engines powered up, Colonel," Lem said from the captain's chair of *The Adora*, via their shared AF.

"Copy," he replied.

"Athena, I hear what you are saying. But we have to go, now. All we know at this juncture is that we're going to deliver another Fermium-Pulse Emission and use that as a cover to get in. We'll wait until we're out of their range before sending the programming. We're going to bounce it off our deep space probe and then on to the Sol station from there so they can't track it, impacting the base in exactly…sixty minutes."

"So you think another Fermium blast will do the job? Just like that?" she asked, with trepidation.

"Well, yes! Hey, don't worry. Trust me! One element of surprise is never enough, and there are a few more left in these old bones." He smiled. "Listen, you stay with Oscar and keep safe out of range. If you don't hear back from us in a reasonable amount of time, have *Sanguine* get you home by the safest route. You can trust her. She's a good ship! *Sanguine,* you copy that?"

"Yes, Colonel, I copy!"

Athena was almost in tears imagining what they were going up against. She stopped him for a brief second, held his arms firmly and looked him in the eyes, speaking to him silently, passionately. He nodded, gave her a slight smile, and then turned and headed down the tunnel to his ship.

Within seconds *The Adora* was taking off and heading in the opposite direction from the base, taking a circuitous route in order to afford them the most favorable approach vector. They would need every edge they could get.

"Soooo…Colonel, what exactly *is* our plan?" Lem asked, as he flew the ship at fantastic speeds and as close to the Moon's surface as possible in order to avoid detection.

"Well, in about five minutes we'll be in a good position to send out the command program to launch another Pulse Emission. And afterwards, well, I was wondering, Atol, you used to be pretty good at computer graphics, if I remember?"

Lem curiously looked over at him.

"Yeah! Why?" Atol answered.

"I thought we'd make a short promotional video!"

Lem and Atol looked at each other with lowered eyebrows.

·······

"I suppose none of you will tell me what I'd like to know: where and/or how many are out there which oppose me. I assure you I could make you tell me, but I have much greater things to do than play games with you—your personal torment will be delivered upon you soon enough, regardless of your cooperation. And I assure you, I'm not worried in the least about your friends out there, seeing that I've been given a most valuable tool of control and persuasion—one of the perks of my new employment package."

He smiled with pride.

"I know that you *three* are currently affiliated with the *Curia Equitas.* Come to secure me and then turn me over to the IPCH? But let me ask you, the inimitable Colonel Ravine wouldn't happen to be among you, would he? Could it be that he is out there? I'd so love to meet him! You wouldn't want to introduce me to him, would you?"

He paused for a moment thinking he might catch a twitch of an eye, or an abrupt turn of the head.

"No answer, just looks of scorn? So predictable! Oh well, as I said it's of little consequence. I do realize that you are all full of questions though: How did I lure you up here? Why the Moon? How is it that I came about such power? What are my sinister plans? 'What might, perchance, become of me?'…which seems to be a favorite of all captives, according to studies?" He said it with an air of sardonic humor, looking back at them with arched brow as he paced from one area to another.

"I do want you to know, however, just how much I take pride in my creativity. I am relatively creative about it, and I think you will be impressed. And you know, I find myself actually looking forward to revealing some of these things to you, simply because I know how it will serve to make you that much more fearful and apprehensive knowing the pain you're all about to endure as a result. Trepidation is such a driver of the emotions, and the bowels, is it not?"

Davian Adorjan snickered malevolently.

The men had been moved to a small room next to where Sarah was located and secured in simple chairs against a wall. No restraints held the men, the control Davian Adorjan had over their B-CIDs rendered sufficient restraining power over them. Essentially they were paralyzed, unable to move voluntarily due to the fact that their nervous systems were for the most part cut off from their brains. Adorjan paced the floor on the other side of a long table from them as he manipulated the environment they all found themselves in.

"This is a creation I use to remind me of the devastation caused by the countless wars that have occurred on our planet. The detail is actually very accurate. I take pride in my creativity, as I said. These are my personal worlds, and as such—as you'll soon realize—they reflect my feelings and beliefs about things.

"I have a rather nice one that I now share with Sarah, Mr. Zaris. I thought you'd like to know that. We're getting very close her and me, *intimately* close. I'll take you to her in a little while, so you two can say goodbye. That is if she even remembers you; I'm curious to see. And by the way, I should remember to thank her. It was her in the first place that provided the 'lure' to bring you to me. Once I acquired her I found that she had been tagged with a neuronal-tracer. I assumed immediately that it had to have been you who'd done it, seeing that you felt she might be in danger from that little botched attempt in the countryside to acquire you. It's so hard to find good help these days. But, I should count it all as providence I suppose, since now I have you and the other people I was hoping to secure, and all from one stroke of genius. I amaze myself sometimes."

Davian Adorjan absorbed the look of disdain Eliam Zaris gave him. It made him smile, as he knew it would. He then looked out over the scene before them.

"That's the Arc-de-Consi over there. You remember? A few hundred years ago, when that all came about. The roots of the Reform, back before it was even given a name. That's where a force of degenerates like yourselves stormed the Arched City of Consi in the western hemisphere, brutally killing about a half-a-million people in protest of the believed disparity of classes—the lower caste's war against the higher castes.

"That particular event incited a goodly portion of the lower populace to rise up over the next hundred or so years demanding reform, and equality, and equal rights. Before that event, there had been a general, societal peace that had spanned thousands of years. But people just couldn't be satisfied with their personal birthrights. They demanded they be given equal wealth, of which they didn't inherit, nor earned, nor deserved. And since, because of that uprising, over six billion people have suffered and perished—a third of the past population of Hoame.

"I find it ironic that this movement of undeserving peasants eventually caused such catastrophic suffering and loss, when what they were supposedly fighting for was the *release* from suffering. The opposition wars against the ancient caste system, in truth, only made the system more obviously viable and imperative. There will always be those of superior intellect and stature, by birthright, as well as those not. It's in the nature of things. Even on this backward, third-world-planet it has been duly recognized. What is it they call it: natural selection…survival of the fittest? It's the way things are. It's the nature of the universe!"

He paused and froze in place looking off in the distance as if he was thinking.

"Questions? *Questions*, yes! You had questions. Why the Moon? Why…the Moon? I moved my operations up here—temporarily, mind you—so I could have an unencumbered opportunity to fulfill a few of the tasks that I've been charged with as a result of my new employment, the main one being the securing of a few representatives of the *Curia Equitas* group that have been working here on this planet, you see.

"It turns out that my employers know that you have been stowing away certain 'captured' members of their families for future delivery unto their pathetic little court system for eventual trial. And it's come under my task to render a few of you ineffectual, and then ship your pitiable asses back to them so they could garner the needed information in order to, per chance, find their family members and ultimately set them free. You see, I'm not the only one being hunted!"

He took a deep breath and then smiled broadly before continuing.

"Now then, 'how is it that I came about such power?' That's probably obvious by now, at least on the surface. My new employers are very influential and have an ingeniously clever ruse they are in the middle of perpetrating, and I just happened to be in the position to help them, seeing how you've been hunting *me* for some time. Consequently, part of our agreement, and in accordance with my other pending assignments, requires that I have sufficient influence to carry them out, you see? Hence the power. I can't share exactly what it is, but I assure you…it's powerful! That's why you can't get out of those chairs, by the way."

Again, he smiled broadly.

"Now, 'What are my sinister plans?' and 'What will become of you?' Oh, well, I guess I already shared all that! How ridiculous of me! Well, at least regarding the three of you vermin. But, Eliam Zaris, what's to become of you? What is my evil plan for you? I must say I was in an incredible position when my employers approached me. You…*you* of all people were smack in the middle of something that my employers were also in the middle of. I call it providence, merely an added incentive for me to accept their lucrative offer. In truth, if they'd just let me have you, I'd probably have been satisfied and helped them anyway after all these years.

"But, here you are, one of the Zaris family. I have some interesting experiences planned for you. Oh, don't worry, I'm not going to torture you—well, maybe just a little, but not for an extremely long time. No, I have something life-long for you, and I'm excited about moving on to it. You see, my entire future was taken from me by your grandfather. I had to live as vermin, as a primitive, undeservedly condemned to a lower-caste life, in this prison. So, I thought it fitting that I do the same to you, Mr. Pendaghast."

The others looked up at the man, bewildered. It was only Eliam that understood what he was alluding to.

"Yes, that's right, gentlemen. Did you know that this man before you isn't really Eliam Zaris? He's actually a very bad man named Arthur T. Pendaghast. He's wanted on the European continent—on Earth—for crimes against humanity: embezzlement from numerous non-profit groups that feed the hungry and bring medicine to the poor; he's funded countless terrorist efforts to undermine governments, which led to the deaths of thousands of people, including numerous bombing attacks on hospitals, and schools, and children. And to top that off…he's an acknowledged pedophile!"

Davian Adorjan smiled again at his creativity.

"Like I said, Adorjan, you're *insane*! And did you know that big, long, drawn out sentences are a sign of a small mind, trying to compensate for a small mind?" Eliam finally spoke, not really caring about the consequences this time.

The others glared at Eliam strangely.

Eliam looked back at them, suddenly noting their semi-accusatorial expressions.

"He's going to frame me! Get it? Adorjan is Pendaghast, see? He's the sick-o! That's why they probably left him on Earth!" Eliam said, sneering at Adorjan in disgust.

The others turned back to the man and just glared at him with outward disdain.

For a moment Davian Adorjan was at a loss for words. He guffawed at both accusations, yet chose not to address them.

"Whatever! But you should know my little plan for you has already been set in motion. All you need is a little cosmetic surgery, a little brain work to tweak the mannerisms, and seal up a few of those personal memories, and wouldn't you know, the decades-long manhunt will finally come to an end. Justice will be served! You'll spend the rest of your life going from one prison to another, serving out your multiple sentences; living day-to-day just trying to stay alive. And only you and I will ever know about it!"

The others looked at Adorjan as if saying that they would know.

He looked at them in return.

"Sorry, but you guys will be pretty much dead by then, actually…sorry!"

He shrugged and then smiled.

"Hey, I know! Why don't you and I go see Sarah now? That'd be nice! Wouldn't it? Here, why don't you guys go and hang out in my rendition of Hades for awhile, check out the brimstone fountain, it's pretty spectacular. But don't worry. Remember, the pain is all in your head!"

He laughed once more before he and Eliam blinked into another of his creations.

·······

The two arrived without any sense of motion.

Eliam found himself seated in a comfortable chair in the entertainment area of some bedroom. He looked around, unfazed from the abrupt transition, but then gasped as his eyes fell on Sarah. She was lying on the large bed, her eyes closed as if taking a nap.

"*Sarah*! Sarah my love!" Adorjan spoke as he approached the bed and then sat down beside her.

Sarah's eyes fluttered open. She was silent for a moment but then spoke softly.

"Davian," she said. "I guess I was napping."

Eliam noticed that she spoke slowly and simply, as if she were tired, and drowsy.

"Sarah, I missed you. Come, give me a kiss!"

Adorjan leaned in and helped her sit up. He then slowly put his arms around her and dropped his face to hers. Sarah seemed to be in a daze as she turned her face up to his. They kissed slowly, passionately.

Eliam gritted his teeth. He wanted to get out of the chair and charge the man, but he couldn't move. He couldn't even speak when he tried. He was nothing more than a piece of furniture. He felt so weak and powerless.

Suddenly, mid-kiss, Adorjan's eyes swelled to wide open, and he just sat there as if listening. Eliam then heard him speak.

"What? Coming in? I'm on the way! Perhaps this will entail some more fun or profit?"

He let Sarah fall back to the bed. Her eyes closed as she sunk into the pillow. Adorjan then turned to Eliam.

"I presume we're going to have some more visitors. Tell you what, why don't you join your friends and check out the fountain while you wait. Other matters require my attention at the moment."

Chapter 62

"Davian Adorjan! You've got my people. I'm coming in after you and I'm going to kill you! You piece of shit!" Colonel Ravine beamed the message across the gray expanse of the moon's surface as his ship barrel-rolled between two opposing sheer cliffs off in the distance from the base.

Davian quickly made it to his quarters and sat down in his special chair. He then engaged his senses so as to tie in with his equipment's, and within a moment he was feeding all the sensor data from the base and his ships' into his visual and audio fields. Within seconds he saw *The Adora* racing his way. It was flying somewhat erratically, and again he heard the voice speak.

"Adorjan, you piece of shit! Do you hear me?"

Adorjan was at first stupefied with the odd announcement. But he calmly weighed his options and decided to answer.

"My...my, whoever this is, you're exhibiting some very base emotions. Yes, we see you coming! And just who might this be?" he asked, intentionally exuding composure.

"This is Colonel William Ravine. Like I said, I'm coming in after you, Adorjan."

Davian Adorjan narrowed his eyes, made his posture rigid. He was clearly a little taken aback.

"Uhmm, I suppose you didn't hear my previous message then...the one about killing these people, if there were any attempts at rescue or negotiation?" he then said.

"They're already dead! I know that, whether they are now, or will be later. You'll see to that; I know that. And so will I be in a short time, either from you or from this cancer eating me up. So I don't give a rat's ass about capturing you and turning you over to some court that'll take half a lifetime to make up their minds as to what to do with you. I'm just going to come in there and kill you now, and save everyone the bill for the room and board your sorry ass will cost. So there, you piece of shit!"

Davian Adorjan was at a loss for words. He gauged the distance of the ship coming at the base and concluded that he had barely half a minute to adjust to his new situation.

"I suppose bringing some of the prisoners before you and making you watch their pain and torment wouldn't do any good then?" he asked as he searched his mind for ideas.

"Nope, I'll just turn off communications and come in anyway. Just so you know. I'm going to blow the shit out of your fancy ship there, and then destroy the base and every one inside."

Adorjan came back quickly.

"Uhmm, you do realize that I have about a dozen people here from Earth. Innocent people! Amongst them, several children! They're still alive and viable. And you're planning on killing them all, I take it?"

"Yep, probably have no mind left after you've had them for awhile. They'll be better off in the long run! Almost there, shit-wad!"

Davian Adorjan scanned the oncoming ship. There was only one life form on it, a single man, a single desperate man, for that matter. Suddenly Davian Adorjan became uneasy. He brought his fist to his lips and rubbed them nervously. He read the scans quickly, took in all he could for the time he apparently had.

"You do realize the power of this ship I have at my disposal, in comparison to yours? I'm sure you have scanners, correct? I assure you it is fully outfitted and operational!" he then added, even though his ordinance load was in truth only at about seventy percent.

"Yep, like I said…fancy ship! And do you realize I am a seasoned combat pilot, having done this very thing over a thirty-year period, in seven different wars, and don't give a shit? It doesn't matter if you've got ten ships! I'll kick your ship's ass and then I'm going to come in there and kick your ass, Adorjan! So pull your fat head out of your stupid little butt, and clean that crap off of your glasses, because I want you to see this coming," Colonel Ravine said sternly, making his ship do another unbelievable barrel roll, its swept-back wings nearly scooping up moon dust as they whipped over it.

Davian Adorjan didn't waste another moment. He had no time to get his pilot, which wouldn't do much good in a combat situation anyway, seeing that he was just a commercially employed asset. He then quickly pulled up all his remote VF Panes for the larger of his ships and immediately fired up its systems. As he did so, he promptly configured his VF to that of the vessel. His chair suddenly became the cockpit, and he placed his hands on the controls. He was now a drone pilot.

Though Adorjan was uncharacteristically nervous, he was not inordinately unstable. He'd had numerous outings in his newer ship and was mostly familiar with its functions as well as its potential. He'd blown numerous things up over the short time he'd had it, mainly for the thrill of it, at least he had that going for him. But what he was waiting for, and where his confidence lay, wasn't in a ship-to-ship confrontation. He was waiting for this Colonel Ravine to get into range so his 'cloud of influence,' as he'd come to call it, would envelope this maniac of an enemy, and he could make him literally fly himself into the ground without even taking a shot.

Suddenly, Adorjan saw a missile coming at him at three times the speed of the craft that launched it. He immediately engaged counter measures and trusted the onboard defense systems to time the volley. They erupted from his tail and lofted toward the oncoming threat, just as Adorjan lifted the ship off the landing pad and put it into full defensive mode.

The missile hit a piece of counter-ordinance and blew itself into oblivion. Just as it happened, another missile flew off the Colonel's wing and headed for Adorjan's ship. He saw it coming as well and again launched counter-measures. This time the missile, which must have contained a learning program, swerved and avoided most of the counter-ordinance, but it too come upon a piece of flaming decoy and it blew up as well.

Colonel Ravine's ship then let off a volley of Plasma-pulse fire as it stormed straight into close range of Adorjan's ship. The series of pulses strafed his shield-protected hull, doing little damage except to the energy levels of its shields in one particular area, dropping them by seventeen percent.

Adorjan attempted to engage his enemy now that he was well within range; he sent out the codes and was ready to react with overriding commands as soon as they did their job of unlocking the Colonel's B-CID security protocols. But nothing happened and Adorjan didn't understand. He tried sending the codes out once more, but again, nothing happened. He suddenly wished he'd focused his attention on something else, for in passing his enemy had just strafed the base's mechanical wing section attached to the docks, completely destroying its sensor arrays on the roof, and was now flying off away from him at incredible speed, arching his craft in a huge loop for a return pass.

Adorjan watched his monitors and thought desperately of what to do next. He realized he had little choice at that moment but to fight. He increased his forward shield power to maximum, lifted the ship higher and began flying it toward the oncoming enemy, veering slightly to the left to correct for angle; he then launched two of his own missiles and darted to the side.

The Colonel's ship also launched two missiles at nearly the same time and the four projectiles passed each other within mere meters on the way to their prey. Colonel Ravine saw the threat heading for him and he took evasive actions against them by quickly altering his vector and increasing his speed. The missiles turned and matched his changes and were coming in fast, positioned to strike him in the side in mere seconds. The Colonel then turned his ship thirteen degrees and headed for a large escarpment in the distance. He slowed his craft just enough to make the timing perfect and at the last second, he punched it hard and the missiles zinged past his tail and dove into the rocky cliffs, exploding into billows of disintegrated rock, and dust, and fire.

Adorjan watched as it happened, even as he attempted to do a similar thing with a small hill. He only succeeded because he set off another volley of counter-ordinance, one of which strafed the hill and confused the missiles. Both ships repositioned themselves and went at it again, aiming head on and each strafing the other with Plasma-pulses as they passed. Adorjan sent out the codes again as they neared the base, ready to follow with commands, but again nothing happened. He was at a loss for an answer.

"I think I saw an empty flight deck back there, Adorjan. Don't tell me you're not even in that thing. You're not are you? At least that's what my sensors are telling me now. You cowardly bastard, you're droning it, aren't you? Sitting on your ass in some little room on the base, just imagining being a man, instead of really being one, isn't that right? Well, I guess I've been targeting the wrong place then. I think I'll change that!"

·······

"I've never heard the Colonel speaking like this," Sanguine said, as they sat there watching and listening to the battle.

"Nor have I, Sanguine. I'm surprised he opted to relay the feeds from *The Adora* out over an open channel. If we picked it up, you'd think Adorjan would notice," Athena stated.

"Yes, possibly. However, I doubt if Davian Adorjan is even thinking about scanning the open frequencies at this juncture of time."

"Wow, I can't believe I'm actually watching and listening to a spaceship battle on the Moon!" Oscar said. "This Dementia is some powerful stuff! Have I told you that I think you're very pretty," he then added, looking at Athena.

·······

Colonel Ravine's targeting was right on as he strafed Adorjan's ship in that one area again as they passed. They both arced and banked and went at it again, but this time Adorjan made a hit on the Colonel's ship and knocked out one of his core stabilizers. He could only bank effectively and tightly now in right hand turns, but he did his best to hide that little bit of information as the two pummeled each other with pass after pass.

Adorjan was mostly in defensive mode, firing off counter measures and letting his ship take the abuse in his attempt to protect the integrity of the base. He'd not expected to have to do that, but he and his onboard defense computers were doing a good job of it, at least he thought so. But that's what the Colonel wanted him to think. The Colonel was hell bent on keeping Adorjan reacting, instead of acting, and as such he continued the barrage of missiles and strafing runs from all sorts of odd angles. In fact, it was his flying skills that proved the most powerful contributor to his effectiveness, confusing Adorjan at most every attempt at targeting.

"One more run should do it," the Colonel said to himself as he rolled and weaved past the counter-barrage Adorjan was throwing at him. On his next approach he was headed straight at Adorjan's ship when Adorjan simultaneously launched four missiles at him. The distance was too short for the missiles to acquire their targets and the Colonel knew it by experience. He sped up and used the configuration of the oncoming missiles as a timer for yet another spiraling barrel roll and his ships wings sliced right through the space between the projectiles as if he were a bird flying through the dense branches of a forest canopy.

As he neared Adorjan's ship he was completely upside down relative to his enemy's fuselage, which is exactly what he had planned, and at just the right time he shot off a volley of vertically-aimed Plasma pulses which took out Adorjan's last remaining shields in that area and destroyed his sensor packs located aft of the ship's flight deck.

"That'll do it! About out of fire power anyway," the Colonel said to himself, gratified at his success.

Adorjan screamed out a curse as he realized from his safe position in the base that his ship's capabilities had just been severely compromised. He could fly and target his weapons individually, but due to the fact that his sensors were out, he couldn't trust the computer's defense systems to locate enemy ships—or anything for that matter.

He was too angry to be afraid at that moment, and he banked in the tightest loop he could at that speed, and then headed after the Colonel. His anger swelled exponentially as he sped on and it was mere seconds before he was in range again, doing everything he could to match his enemy's erratic maneuvering. In doing so he suddenly felt intuitive of the positioning and launched a missile at the Colonel's ship, setting the targeting parameters according to where he imagined the ship might be as a result of its next maneuver. The move proved amazingly accurate and effective, because the Colonel's vessel did exactly as he'd thought, moving in that direction and into the missile's path. Suddenly the missile hit the tail of the ship.

Colonel Ravine was watching his rear screens the whole time and anticipated the strike. At the last second he sent all power to the rear shields just before impact. The move kept the entire ship from exploding, however, it was over. The ship was a 'dead stick' as it'd always been referred to in aviation, and it was going down hard. The cabin was filling with smoke and systems were sparking and going dead all around him. The Colonel smiled as it hit the Moon's surface hard and skidded toward the base. It started to shake violently, but stopped its forward motion just before its hull was breached from the severe battering. Again, the Colonel smiled.

Davian Adorjan would have risen out of his seat and done a dance, if it weren't for the fact that doing so would disconnect him from remotely piloting the ship. He cheered and relaxed his anxious breathing. He then decided to take his final revenge and blast this lowly piece of vermin into oblivion. He moved his ship into range and opened communications for one last comment. When he did, he saw the renowned Colonel William Ravine sitting in the pilot seat of his ship. It was rapidly filling with combustibles and the nearly unconscious Colonel was waking to the fact that his ship was on fire, and so was he.

Adorjan watched as the Colonel screamed in horror as the flames began to engulf him. He struggled to undo his harness, but his hands were on fire and suddenly his entire body was aflame in an uncontrollable swirl of corrosive fire and burning gases. The screams came in pitiful shrieks, and then the communication ended, the flames burning the ship, and all its contents.

Davian Adorjan took his finger off the launch button and just smiled.

"Why waste another missile!" he said, laughing arrogantly. "Burn you…how did you state it? Let's see, you…'shit-wad'?" he then laughed hardily as he steered the ship back to the landing pads.

Chapter 63

Athena sat there in tears.

Oscar had a dreadful look on his face.

They'd listened to every word of the battle, rode the waves of anxiety and fear as it unfolded, and then seen its sickening conclusion.

"What do we do now?" Athena whispered, her face turning pale.

There was a measure of deafening silence before *Sanguine* spoke.

"I take you home, as Colonel Ravine commanded," the ship said, picking up on the comment.

There was more silence, more staring, and the air was heavy with desolate certainty. The finality of *Sanguine's* words seemed to spark something in Athena. Her feelings of loss, of despondency, suddenly exploded into emotions of anger and determination. She shook her head from one side to the other. Disbelief morphed into reality, and reality into resolve.

"No! We're going to do something!" Athena said, emphatically.

Sanguine responded immediately, an odd tension in the ship's artificial voice.

"There is nothing we can do. I do not have sufficient combat facilities to infiltrate and assume control over the situation. Colonel Ravine's ship has been severely disabled, it has no remaining crew aboard, and our entire complement of resources has been subdued by Davian Adorjan's efforts.

"Our only hope at stopping him completely is for me to initiate a self-destruct sequence, obliterating myself, the base, and all its occupants. That will stop his efforts; however, it will have several unwanted consequences:

the end of our lives, as well as the resultant attention the observable ex-plosion on the Moon will garner: the turning of eyes and ears and interest of every nation on the planet Earth. I am still processing possibilities and surmising outcomes, however, I have not yet recognized any potentially successful alternatives."

"We have to figure out how they overcame our people. These were men of extraordinary training and resolve. Ador-jan said he had them under his control. If he'd killed them, he would have bragged on the fact. But he didn't. He said he had control of them. How?"

"I do not have that information," Sanguine answered, in an ap-parently deflated voice.

"You might, and you might not know it. S*anguine*, please display the last five minutes of their care package, and play back the audio of what Sergeant Tomlinson said. Put it on repeat."

Sanguine obliged.

Athena, along with Oscar at her side, looked at the data and listened as the end of the transmission was played over and over.

"Black ha…black ha…black ha…black ha…"

"'Black ha…black ha…! What does it mean?" Athena asked tersely to the air. She thought about it, and then contin-ued. "He was fine and in motion and was guarding that corri-dor. He was in a situation that demanded all his senses be alert. He wasn't caught off guard; he didn't fight anybody; we heard no sounds of gunfire, or the sizzling sound of a NERV being activated, or anything, nothing. It was total silence, total atten-tion on his part, and then something just hit him, and he was trying to say something: 'Black ha…, Black ha…!'"

Oscar's face contorted several times as if it was itchy and he was trying to relieve the feeling without scratching it with his hand. He stepped back from Athena and just stared again for a moment before speaking.

"Black…Hack!" he said softly, as if remembering some-thing.

Athena turned to look at him.

"What?" she asked.

"Black-hack," he repeated.

"What's that, Oscar?"

Before he could answer, *Sanguine* chimed in.

"Black-hack is an old term used by computer systems hackers. It is a derivative of Black-out Hack. A Black-out Hack is one wherein a hacker, once he or she has overcome a system's security codes and gained entry, delivers a program virus, or stream of nanocytes, depending on the circumstances, which serves to shut off all flow of data into its systems as a whole, or to its internal systems in a configuration. With no flow of data into its core processor, the system is essentially in the dark and cannot function."

"You mean, like sensory deprivation?" Athena asked.

"Yes, that is correct."

"What could do that in this case? With the guys? To Tomlinson?"

Sanguine processed for a moment and then answered.

"The security protocols for their B-CIDS would have to have been compromised, and then a transfer of streamed data would have to be injected into their operating systems, whereby the proposed hacker could set up the respective barriers, stopping the flow of sensory input into their brains. A Black-out Hack would then result."

Athena sat back in her chair and thought about it.

"That seems impossible!" Athena uttered. "That would mean that they are in their minds, just floating in there without any connection to the outside world at all. It'd be like…like having advanced Alzheimer's disease; the synapses blocked, no information in the form of sensory input, or memories…could…pass!"

Athena suddenly looked at Oscar. His blank look said it all. She continued.

"It'd be like being trapped inside an AVTR program, and not being able to control it or get out! Always at the whim of the hacker and whatever data stream—or Streamplace—they'd choose to input—good, or bad."

"Yes, that is essentially the case," *Sanguine* started, *"a good analogy, doctor."*

Again Athena looked at Oscar.

"Oscar, how did you know about this?"

"Know about what?" he asked.

Athena didn't follow up with another question; she just narrowed her eyes.

Another long silence permeated the ship's cabin.

"How'd this maniac get the security protocols to their B-CIDs? And how can we block it ourselves?" Athena then asked *Sanguine*.

"I do not have sufficient information to answer that question."

Athena thought about it again.

"Well, that's what we have to figure out!"

....

"No, you cannot go. One, you have an active B-CID and would be susceptible to compromise. Two, even if you did not have one, you have no training, nor the sufficient skill-set to complete a mission of this magnitude," Sanguine stated matter-of-factly.

"What about Oscar?" Athena affirmed.

"What? What about me?" Oscar said, overhearing them and feeling worried, yet not sure why.

"Oscar Whiting suffers from a debilitating disease. He is not capable of altering the outcomes of any of the potential scenarios we've discussed," Sanguine retorted.

"Yes, now…in his present condition, but what if I give him Sonilyn-7?"

There was a short silence.

"Sonilyn-7 is a drug which was developed as a preemptive aid for those who have the clinically -determined predisposition toward the diseases of dementia, as well as used as an ancillary treatment to clear the synapses of the brains of those who have been illegally brain-rused using artificial means. That is why we brought it along to use on Sarah in this case. It will help her recover from the recent attempts of altering her brain functionality.

"The probability is low that it will have any effect on Oscar Whiting. Sonilyn-7 is not intended as a cure for the naturally-occurring, long term effects seen in patients who have already exceeded the somnolent-cohesion levels that are present from unmitigated plaque build-up in a human brain over time, nor especially regarding people of his age.

"Studies have shown that below-moderate success rates have been seen during experimentation for such conditions, but were far out-weighed by the resultant detrimental side effects observed following its use; negative effects were recorded in every case study, including the brain deaths of several study participants. Therefore, it is open to doubt that it would work at all for our purposes. It cannot be allowed."

Athena became irritated at the ship. She was logical, and practical, and knowledgeable, but she wasn't exactly thinking out of the box.

"Yes, perhaps, but, what if it did. Listen, *Sanguine.* Hear me out. Let's look at the facts then. Oscar Whiting has no B-CID! He is a twenty-year veteran of Earth's U. S. Navy. He was a dedicated and trained Navy Seal, a combatant and professional soldier, although yes, it was some time ago. Be that it may, that means he has had exemplary training, and he's seen combat. He is also an educated scientist, a space and NASA trainee for their astronaut program, as well as a computer systems engineer by trade. He understands a host of things applicable to this situation. On top of that he's kept in pretty good shape for his age, and he came along voluntarily. Not to mention his daughter is in dire peril, along with numerous other people, including *us* if we just sit here on our collective asses, *Sanguine*! Do you understand that?!"

"I'm sorry, Doctor Athena. I do not have sufficient data to suggest that proceeding in that direction will render the desired results."

Athena was growing increasingly perturbed at the ship.

"If there is anyone else, or any other scenario we can present, then please speak up. But I see no other options. I propose we inform him of the situation, and ask him. If he says no, then no it is. If he says yes, then at least we have something to try. We can coach him prior to, and as he goes in. We can use simple, low emission communication and route him cautiously to where he can do the most good, wherever that may be. I don't know? But it's something! It's something we can do! We've concluded that there has to be a transportable device of some kind in there—a server, or terminal, or something—somewhere that is keeping those people—*our people*—locked up in some mental nightmare, of God knows what, and someone has to go in and shut it down, *Sanguine*! Do you hear me?!"

She stopped and waited. Sanguine fell silent for an extended time.

"Sanguine! I asked you did you hear me?!" Athena shouted.

"Yes, of course I heard you, Doctor. Your logic and reasoning now appears marginally…sound, though I'm not sure why. The facts suggest otherwise, but I have to say, something in me…agrees. I…I don't know why. I'm unsure, but I…I agree, Doctor Athena Mauropolin. We should proceed as soon as possible."

⋯⋯

"Oscar, Sarah is in danger. So are Eliam, and the team we traveled here with. I know you would want to know the truth, and I know you would want to help, so here it is. What I am going to ask you…what I'm going to ask you to do, could be dangerous. And you could die. But, Sarah might die, regardless. So could all the other people, including us if we don't do something!"

Oscar Whiting had a blank look on his face, but then recognition gained a hold and he seemed to understand.

"What can *I* do?" he asked blankly.

"Oscar. You know I'm a doctor. I can give you a drug that will help…*may* help, give you back your mind and memories for a time. Now, it may not work at all. *And*, it may eventually make your situation worse. Oscar, it may even kill you. I wish I could make you understand the full situation here, but I'm afraid I can't. All I can say is that you are Sarah's best hope for surviving. If you say yes, I will administer the drug. You may feel odd at first. It may make you worse, like I said. But, if it works, you will remember much of your past experiences and knowledge.

"Oscar, someone is holding Sarah and my team against their will. Again, they are in danger and might die soon. If you choose to help, choose to take this drug to get some of your facilities back, we are going to ask you to go on a mission to help them. Maybe even save them, Oscar. And we wouldn't even ask if there was no other…"

She couldn't finish her sentence.

Oscar spoke boldly.

"Give it to me!" he said, his eyes glistening.

"Thank you, Oscar," Athena said, reaching out and holding his hands in hers.

She quickly rose from the chair next to him and retrieved her medical kit from the space in the bulkhead. She removed the container and took out the injector. She checked it, made an adjustment, and then gave him the shot in his neck.

Oscar immediately sat back.

His eyes closed.

·······

"I am taking off now. We should have little problem avoiding detection since Colonel Ravine was successful at disabling the sensor packs on both the base and their ship. However, I am going to follow the terrain very closely in order to doubly insure our safe arrival. It is doubtful, but they could still have observers at the base watching," Sanguine said, cautiously.

"Yes, good idea *Sanguine*, I was wondering about that. William took out their sensors purposely it seems. I imagine it was because of Lem and Atol. They could be trying to get into the base as we speak," Athena surmised.

"Yes, that is my supposition as well, Doctor Athena. However, we can't know for sure. What we do know is that they both have active B-CIDs, which renders them susceptible to compromise if our theory is correct. Though they may be initiating a last incursion effort into the base, they may not be successful in their attempt. It would be prudent on our part to assume that they will fail as the others have," Sanguine said honestly, if not brusquely.

"Yes, I agree, unfortunately. I just hope they weren't on the ship with William."

Neither said another word for a few moments, as they considered the discomforting notion.

Athena looked over at Oscar who was now sitting there with his eyes wide open. She rose from her chair, grabbing her medical kit in transit to him. She sat next to him and immediately initiated a bio-scan.

"How do you feel, Oscar?" she asked, fearful yet hopeful.

"My feet are cold."

"Yes, well, your body is probably forcing most of the blood to your brain. It's trying to flush out whatever contaminates that might be there. It's a natural reaction. Do you feel any different, besides that?"

He didn't say anything at first. He just sat there with an odd look on his face. But then he smiled a large smile and peered into Athena's eyes.

"I know I kept telling you I thought you were pretty. I don't mean to retract that, that is a fact, but it was rude of me to do so, so many times, I think. I'm sorry!" he said sheepishly, humility or the extra blood in his head making him blush somewhat.

Athena smiled back at him.

Suddenly Oscar appeared to become emotional. His eyes fluttered and he turned his head down as they darted from side to side.

Athena noticed.

"Are you alright?" she asked, looking from him to her bio-unit's readouts.

He didn't answer. He just sat there and seemed oddly occupied.

"I think I'm remembering things. I've been such an odd-ball the last few years. I'm ashamed of myself."

Now he was literally in tears, and crying profusely.

Athena quickly became worried. She could tell something was happening. His emotions were heightened and he was apparently deeply attentive to the thoughts rushing through his mind. She wasn't sure if this was good or bad.

"I've been such a burden to...Sarah! *Sarah*!" he suddenly repeated, looking up to Athena. He then looked around, seemingly noticing where he was. He looked back at Athena.

"This is real!" he said, not a question, but a statement of realization.

"Yes, Oscar. This is real. You're on a ship, *Sanguine* is her name. *Sanguine*, please say something."

"Hello, Oscar," the ship said.

Oscar looked around again, seemingly realizing that no one was there but them, remembering the trip up there, the ship, the Moon.

"We're on the Moon?"

Athena saw a smile cross his face.

"Yes, Oscar, we are."

"Can I see?

"*Sanguine*, can you please open the port side windows?"

With the request three windows went from opaque to crystal clear. Oscar's eyes suddenly became as wide as saucers.

"Oh my God! It's true! I wasn't imagining it?"

"No, Oscar, you weren't. What do you remember?" she asked, again looking at his bio-readout.

"I…I remember having to go to that awful nursing home. I remember you coming and talking with me and then we left. We went to a ship, I…I thought it was a delusion. I…I…Sarah is in trouble? You said she was in trouble! Where is she? What kind of trouble?"

"She's been taken, Oscar, by a bad man. He's got our team, too. They're on a moon base. They went there to try and rescue her, but now they've been captured. We're on our way there now, Oscar!"

"Colonel Ravine, he died in that ship!"

Suddenly sadness gripped Oscar again and the tears returned.

"Oh my! It hurts to remember! I feel so odd. This isn't good; no, this is good, this *is* good! What can I do? I don't know what to do! We're on the Moon! My God, I can't believe it! We're flying across the Moon's surface! Sarah's on the Moon? How could that be? She's been taken! She's in danger! The other people, Lem, Eliam, yes, Eliam! He came and visited me, with Sarah. They're from another planet! He knows a lot about NASA. NASA, I worked at NASA. I was in the astronaut program, hoping to be one to go to Mars! But we're on the Moon! Sarah's in trouble! We have to go to her and help her, help the others."

He stopped talking and turned to Athena.

"You gave me something. You gave me a drug. I said you could. It's alright! It's supposed to help me with my memory, I remember!"

Athena listened intently as he continued to ramble.

She couldn't imagine his feelings right now.

According to the bio-readouts, Oscar was okay. His heart was beating fast, and his blood pressure was high, but not abnormally so, but the amazing thing was that his nervous system was now operating in some sort of hypersensitive-mode. He was increasingly becoming more attentive and focused. In fact, he even looked different: younger, more intelligent, sharp and professional. Yet he just kept rambling, as if his mind was bringing up things that he had not thought of in many years.

"Oscar, try and slow down. Your mind is racing."

"We are approaching the base, Doctor Athena," Sanguine announced.

Athena looked out the window and took a deep breath. She'd been so engaged with Oscar and his altered condition—from a medical standpoint—that she'd nearly forgotten what they were about to do.

"Oscar, we are…"

"Yes, I heard the ship. We're about there. My mind *is* racing; I haven't thought this much in forever. I have such feelings, too. I can't explain it. I feel like I want to laugh and sing and tell a joke, yet at the same time I want to cry; everything is so hard. I feel so sad, and so happy. I feel like I want to lecture, and strategize, and fraternize, and debate. I could really go for a cold one, too. A tall one, an ale, a lager, a pilsner, a draft; a dark one from a micro, a pub, a bar, a lounge, or club. I…wow! I'm remembering so much!"

"Oscar, remember, try to slow down. Take a deep breath. Are you ready to go over what we need you to do to help Sarah?" Athena asked to help him focus again.

Oscar abruptly stopped talking as he thought of his daughter. He put his head down, apparently embarrassed about his behavior.

"I'm sorry," he said, and he started to cry again.

"Perhaps this wasn't a good idea," Sanguine said.

Athena didn't respond, but she was thinking the same thing.

Oscar heard the ship and saw the fear on Athena's face.

"No…" he said. "No, I can do this. I need to go help Sarah and the others. I just need to calm myself and stay focused. There's no other way, you said so yourself. So, let's go over this. Help me concentrate! Tell me what I need to do! Please!" He wiped the tears from his eyes, and sat up straight. He took a deep breath and blew it out hard, and then did it again.

"Okay, Oscar. Listen, I understand. I'm a psychologist. What you need to do is keep a core picture in your mind. When you feel like your mind is wandering with thoughts, tell yourself to bring up that picture. It will help you focus. Use one of your favorite images of Sarah. It will be your center of focus, and it will help you associate your thoughts and decisions based off that. Do you understand?"

He nodded and took another deep breath.

"Yes, I've got it. Sarah, my daughter, she's in trouble. I see her. Someone has taken her and I need to help. Go on; tell me what I need to do."

Chapter 64

"We have arrived. It now appears that due to the terrain I will not be able to get close enough to dock directly with the Breach-Lock device the team installed. Oscar will have to make it there on his own. He will need to travel a distance of one hundred and eleven meters to do so," Sanguine said plainly.

"Walk on the Moon?" Oscar repeated, completely shocked by the thought.

"Yes, it appears that way, Oscar," Athena answered. "Can you do that?"

He looked out the window at the glowing gray surface; he then turned and smiled at Athena as if he were just a big kid. His face was red, and tense, but his eyebrows were high and his heart rate, which had calmed somewhat, suddenly picked up again.

"Are you serious? I'm going to do that?"

Athena smiled.

....

"Okay, Oscar let's go over it one more time. In the Breach-Lock you activate the door and the pressurization at the control panel inside—it's easy: close, pressurize, and open. It's clearly marked. When inside, you will essentially go the same way as the others according to the map you'll have. When at the airlock, it should activate the same way. Raj's data states that he isolated it from the system, so it would work independently. Hopefully it still has power and will operate. If not, you can't get in. In that event, turn around and get back to the ship. Okay?"

Oscar nodded.

"But if you do get inside, keep alert and proceed cautiously along their same route until you come to this intersection." She pointed it out on the map. "The others went this way, but we want you to go around this way. It will take you to the same location, but from their data it will keep you the safest distance from any of their people until you get close, at least according to their last positions. After that, you'll have to scout out where people might be on your own. You can use this portable surveillance cam," she put her hand on the unit which was lying on the table. "It's for seeing around corners and under doors."

Oscar nodded again.

"We can converse with you using this communicator. It is a low-emission device that shouldn't be picked up by their systems; that is what it was designed for. It uses a band of the spectrum not normally used for audio transmission—a little technique developed by Raj sometime ago for the team as a back-up device, but it'll work for us in this case. Also, they shouldn't pick you up due to your suit; Raj set that up as soon as they got in, and you'll be wearing the same type with the same built-in array. And we can't trust a standard visual feed not being detected by them either, so you'll have to tell us what you're seeing as you go along.

"And you have to remember that even though their systems won't track you by motion, or any other type of presences sensors, it doesn't make you invisible. They will still be able to see you if they're looking directly at surveillance screens. So you need to travel quickly when in the corridors, and stay hidden if you can when not on the move. Hopefully, they'll think that the danger has passed because they took out the Colonel, and maybe they've lowered their guard. All we can do is hope that's the case.

"Now, the most important thing, *Sanguine* and I agree, what you're looking for is a portable server device, as you would call it. It'll look like a small, yet highly sophisticated computer: a laptop, or a case, or a box of some sort. It will have its own energy source, but still might be plugged in to the base's systems, but not necessarily so. It is most likely Adorjan's Cloud Generator, the hub of power for all he's doing. It is the source of the control he has over Sarah and the others. It will be close to him. He wouldn't have it built into a ship, or the base. He'll have it in a compact, mobile configuration for quick transportability. It has to be shut down, or destroyed. By doing so, the others—if they're still alive—should get back control over their B-CIDs. You remember what we described to you these were, right? The B-CIDs?" she added, testing his memory.

"Yes, Brain Computer Interface Devices. Adorjan has the codes to unlock them, to hack them—a Black-hack—and he's used them to block their natural sensory input into their brains, most likely replaced the input with his own—probably torturing them right now with it."

Oscar couldn't believe he was saying what he was saying. It seemed so improbable—impossible—but then again, he was on a spaceship, on the Moon, and was in the process of going out on a life-or-death mission to stop a group of madmen from another planet who can essentially hack other people's brains.

"Good! Yes, that about sums it up, Oscar. The key is this Cloud Generator! Shut it down, or destroy it. That way the team can regroup and might have a chance of stopping Adorjan—you'll be taking a cache of extra weapons with you. We have to use every means! If we don't stop him and he gets away, we'll never be able to. He'll disappear with the team, and with Sarah, and we'll never get them back!"

Athena nearly choked on the last few words, fighting back her strong emotions.

Oscar saw the sincerity, as well as the fear in her eyes. It only served to make him more determined.

Suddenly he thought of something.

"How long will the effects of this last? The drug?" he asked.

She hesitated, turning her eyes down away from his for a moment. Athena then looked him straight in his eyes.

"We're not sure, Oscar. It could be the rest of your life, or another few minutes. We just don't know! And believe me, we wouldn't have even asked if there were another way. I wish I was the one going. It's my team in there. But…but there's…" Athena choked up again. She covered her mouth with her hand as more tears flowed down her cheeks.

"It's alright, Athena," Oscar said. "It's my daughter in there as well. Doing this, we…we may be giving them a chance, at least. If I don't screw up." He smiled at her, trying to lighten the moment. "I'm going to do everything I possibly can to make this happen, Athena. So, if you're not sure about the time, then…then, well, I guess we'd better get to doing this now!"

He reached out his hand to her.

She received it and held it as he took his other and wiped a tear from her cheek.

She smiled a sad smile and then nodded.

Chapter 65

Oscar stood there inside the ship's Air Lock.

He heard the muffled sounds of the pressure seals engaging and the whirring noises of the outer door as it channeled sideways, disappearing into the hull. Oscar was now looking out at the ethereal moonscape he'd only dreamt about. He took a deep breath and stepped out onto the ramp, bounce-walking his way to its end.

He hesitated at the bottom, noticing that the base of the ramp was sunk deep into the powdery soil. Suddenly a plethora of images streamed through his mind: the Apollo missions of nearly a century before; the more recent missions by the other countries; the newer probes and test stations established for crew training for their Mars missions that were at this moment underway.

Oscar nearly lost his breath at the realization that he was actually there.

"One small step for Man; one giant leap for Mankind!" he said, uttering the words dramatically.

He then stepped out onto the barren soil. He looked at his feet and saw the dust rise around them. He took a bouncy step and then looked back at his footprints. His heart was about to leap out of his chest.

"Wow! I think I'm going to pass out!" he muttered.

"Oscar, whatever you do, don't do that!" Athena said through his ear piece.

"Copy that, Houston!" he answered, smiling, yet trying to fight the sudden imposing dizziness.

Athena scrunched her eyes tighter, wondering what he'd meant.

Moving in apparent slow motion, Oscar looked in the direction of the base. His heart was beating faster as his head resumed its cacophony of whirling imagery.

He took another step, feeling the reduced gravity. He took another, and then another. After a few more steps, he stopped, turned around and looked back at the ship, its full fuselage now in view against the backdrop of the velvety dark universe beyond.

And then Oscar screamed.

"YEEAAAH BAAAABBBY! I'M ON THE MOON! WHOOOH… AHHHH PEOPLE! I CAN'T… FREAKING… BELIEVE THIS! I'M ON THE MOON! I'M … ON… THE MOON! MY GOD THIS IS BEAUTIFUL!"

Oscar then took off running, leaping and bounding distances greater than any long jumper on Earth could ever hope to be able to achieve. As he did he continued to utter in quick succession, a host of things he'd forgotten over the years which he was now freshly remembering: facts, figures, events, history, all the things that had given his life significance and purpose and joy over the years. But now, they were all returning in spontaneous eruptions of thought and emotion, his excitement suddenly and dangerously getting the best of him.

"You scum-sucking, shit-eating maggots, most of you aren't worth the time it takes to blow… my… nose. You're probably going to die of a heart attack on your first little run. So why don't you just quit right now and SAVE US ALL THE TIME!"

Oscar bellowed, as his face twitched and his eyes darted about. He leaped and then shouted, leaped and then shouted. Yelling out the thoughts that were coming into his mind, as fast as they were coming.

"Science is the study of *what*, religion, the study of *why*. That's where it all starts, and that's where it all ends!

"Imagination is greater than knowledge!

"To be or not to be, that *is* the friggin' question!

"Dust in the wind, all we are is dust in the wind!

"Two lost souls swimming in a fish bowl!

"Nothing to fear but fear itself!

"Space, the final frontier!

"The Force, the Source, the Dark side!

"War is hell!

"A tragic comedy!

"Vitruvian Man, The Last Supper…Divinci!

"The Sistine Chapel, The Creation…Michelangelo!

"Oh my God!

"Jesus, my Jesus!

"Where art thou!

"Lord help us!

"Give us this day, our daily bread!

"Chicken Soup!

"Food for the soul!

"Meat and potatoes!

"Coffee and ice cream and chocolate!

"*God*…am I hungry!

"Uh oh, I think I gotta pee!

"Not good…not good!"

Oscar kept yelling as if the words were just spilling out of his mouth, each time marveling at the freshly spawned memory, smiling excitedly with an overwhelmingly joyous look on his animated face.

"What is happening?" Sanguine inquired of Athena, who was sitting at the window watching Oscar grow smaller in the distance as she, too, listened intently to his rambling.

"I don't know. It seems that his memory is returning with a vengeance. It's…it's…" She stopped for a moment and thought. "It's got to be the stimulant. We added a neural stimulant to the Sonilyn-7 for Sarah. It's intended to help counteract the sedatives that are usually used when trying to do what Adorjan's doing. I'd forgotten about the stimulants. They're giving Oscar an excessive amount of energy. It's the excitement of him being on the Moon, combined with the stimulant. He's on a roller coaster that's going way too fast!"

"Is he in danger?" Sanguine asked candidly.

Athena looked to the front of the ship before answering.

"Danger? Are you serious? He's on the Moon, in a space-suit, by himself, yes he's in danger! On top of that his head is about to explode. Yes, I'd say he's in a bit of danger! But there's nothing we can do except try to calm him down."

She immediately turned to the window and started talking to him.

"Oscar! Your heart is racing again. You have to calm down! Do you hear me?"

The onslaught of internal reminiscence apparently drowned out her voice. And his attention was further diverted when he landed on a rock at the end of a leap and went down on his hands and knees. Athena gasped when she saw it.

"Oh my God!" she exclaimed.

Oscar just stayed there, entranced, now watching his gloved fingers slowly plow through the thick powdery soil. He started to remember his childhood it seemed, scooping up handfuls of the stuff as if playing in a sandbox. He then began drawing figures and shapes with his finger; started humming a kid's tune that had just come into his head. He then got an angry look on his face.

"Johnny Barnes you're a bully. I'll show you, one day! I'll kick your ass to the Moon and back! You just watch, Barnes! One day! One day! To the Moon…"

Oscar suddenly seemed to realize where he was.

He froze his motions and blinked hard.

His breathing nearly stopped altogether.

He next rose up and sat back on the heels of his boots and just looked around with a bewildered expression. Then, he seemed to intuit something and he looked up. It was at that moment he saw the Earth on the distant horizon glistening like a glass covered globe.

"Woooow! Would you look at that!" he said softly, now suddenly overcome with awe.

"Oscar! Oscar, do you hear me?"

He turned his head slightly as if he had, and then answered.

"Yes, I hear you. I fell down," he said, sounding as if he were a little kid and was embarrassed.

"*This was not a good idea!*" Sanguine started. "*He is quickly becoming disoriented and losing control of his faculties. We have put his life in danger! We must call him back!*"

"No, he's alright!" she shouted to the ship. She then turned back to the window. "Oscar, remember that core focus we discussed? Focus on Sarah, Oscar! Do you see her? Do you see Sarah, Oscar? Do you remember?"

Oscar suddenly saw his daughter in his mind's eye. He then looked around at where he was and the memories returned. Recognition molded his face.

"Yes, I see Sarah. I have to help her. I have to get to the base," he said, his burning eyes seemingly bulging out of their sockets.

"Yes, Oscar. You can do it! Get up and go to the base."

He rose carefully and began a more controlled stride toward his destination.

Athena swallowed hard and started crying again.

·······

"It's not real!" Eliam repeated for the umpteenth time. He moaned as he felt the burning creep up his legs. He darted again to the right, and then to the left as he tried to run up the mountain side. To where he had no idea, it was all on fire. But moving was all he could do, so that's what he did. He didn't know how long he could last through this, he thought. Suddenly, he heard the tormenting rhetoric again from that booming voice above.

·······

"Eliam, say, how's it going down there? Just wanted you to know I'm back. All is good. And how are you these days? By the way, I had a little run in with your friend and cohort, Colonel Ravine. He was a tenacious bastard; I'll give him that. He was coming in to kill me apparently and rescue all of you, if that were possible. But superior intelligence prevails. I think it quite the irony that I was able to watch him literally burn to death in his little spaceship. He screamed like a little girl. I guess he was your last best hope, huh? Sorry! I'm just telling you this so you can become more despondent and depressed about your own situation. Trying to be thoughtful here! Anyway, I was about to tell you a few things when we were interrupted.

"Now, I know you probably never knew any of this. But I thought it might be important for you to learn more about your family, Eliam. Do you think you could spare a minute? Good! Well, let's see. Your grandfather and I were friends—close friends—as I was saying. Anyway, we actually chose that assignment I was talking about earlier. Or did I mention it? I can't remember! Nonetheless, we'd been on several others together, on Hoame anyway. And we thought it'd be fun to go to Earth for what should have been a simple hunt-and-pick expedition.

"We understood the criteria given by our administrators: all women, young, DNA configuration certified, of course. Intelligent, attractive, from areas in alignment with our customer's specific requirements, you know? It was a mostly enjoyable assignment. The side perks were especially nice. It was like being on vacation. We'd choose our scouting locales based on the criteria and had fun intermingling with the natives, often joining in their carnal festivities, so as to fit in."

Adorjan laughed at his innuendo.

"Anyway, all was good, and we had our quota, and it was the last few hours there. I thought it'd be an experience to see the actual limits of this one particularly annoying specimen—which didn't at all meet our criteria by the way—when I induced varying degrees of sexual discomfort. She reacted as expected, but your grandfather opposed the practice adamantly. We were somewhat intoxicated, and I suppose the man's true self just came out, which I could forgive, in the short run. But, he totally changed on me and wouldn't let it go. He contacted the admin's, showed them a play-by-play that he secretly recorded, and then by their orders apparently, left me there.

"Oh, they contacted me for follow up on several occasions. Let me know that I was under disciplinary observation, and that if I cooperated, I would be allowed to return to Hoame and my former status if I continued my scouting for them. At first, I wasn't amused. Especially so after I learned that I was suddenly obliged to stay there for a ten-year duration before further consideration. Well, I was incensed, and they knew it. All of a sudden I was branded incorrigible and ten years turned into a hundred. Oh, I found it prudent to at least try and cooperate, over time, out of necessity. At least I found a few advantages in doing so. And so here I am.

"I was betrayed by your grandfather, Eliam, in more ways than one, mind you. Part of the compensation package we were offered on this particular trip was that we—if we so chose—could pick a companion to bring back to Hoame with us. Ours to keep.

"I chose this one beautiful specimen. As it turned out, Alexander Zaris took her instead. That would be your grandmother, Eliam. I bet you didn't know that. I could have been your grand-daddy! Anyway, that little fact only served to make matters worse. Surely you understand? And now it's going to be worse for you. Terrible how we inherit the good as well as the bad due to our family's discordant choices, is it not? I've waited a long time for this little turn-about play. So can you guess who my choice is this time around, Eliam Zaris?"

Eliam looked up into the virtual sky and he about sank down into the flames in a heap of despair as he saw the images of Davian Adorjan holding the scantily-dressed, Sarah Whiting in a provocative pose, as she started kissing him passionately on the lips.

....

Oscar made it to the Breach-Lock. But before he climbed inside he turned and marveled at the moonscape before him. He wanted to play out there forever; enraptured by the majesty of it; immersed in the magic of its other-worldly allure. But the thought of Sarah brought him back to reality and once more he became determined.

He climbed into the lock and initiated the sequence.

Within seconds he was inside the base.

Oscar double-timed it to the central airlock, only seriously losing focus once when something he saw sparked a flood of memories regarding his stint in the military. He jostled with the emotions he'd had at that particular time: fear, feelings of inadequacy, loss of direction. But Athena talked him back to reality and he was on his way again. Still, as he progressed he couldn't help but spill over with comments from all the waves of memories coming back to him.

"Ben Collette, NASA Crew Committee Chair. Haaaa! Dickhead! I'm on the Moon! What do you think of that!

"You canned me every time I tried!

"Always not good enough!

"You said I wasn't capable!

"You said I'd never make it!

"Well I did, you elitist asshole! I'm on the Moon, and you're still a NASA slug."

Oscar laughed at the thought as he approached the airlock.

"At the airlock, Athena," he said, as he studied the control panel.

"Good, is it powered?"

"Yes, it appears to be. Lights are on"

"Good, *Sanguine* will talk you through the operation."

Sanguine immediately began to speak.

"The central pad on the main panel is the Operational Control; push the larger button to initiate Entry mode, and then turn the lever a quarter turn to the left. That will start the depressurization. Once it is complete, a green light will appear."

Oscar followed the instructions.

"Okay, it's done. Green light is on."

"Turn the door lever to open. Enter the lock. Shut the door and push the pressurization control button on the pad inside."

Again he did as the ship instructed.

"I hear the pressurization," he said, pausing. "Okay, it's complete. I have a green light here, too. Good to go!"

"Oscar, once inside test the atmosphere before taking off your helmet, do you copy?" Athena said abruptly.

"Copy!"

He opened the door and entered the base, shutting the airlock behind him.

"Inside! How do I test the air?"

"On your suit's left arm, press keys seven and one, in that order, and then the enter key." Sanguine instructed.

"Done," he said. "Okay, I have…seven green bars, except one is kind of red at the top."

"Which one is red?" Sanguine asked.

"Third one from the left."

"How much of the bar is red?"

"Only about ten percent, maybe. Is that bad?"

"No, it is alright. It indicates a higher level of carbon dioxide, most probably from the internal systems of the base shorting out during the disruption from the Fermium-Pulse Emissions. You will be alright. It does not indicate dangerous levels."

"But keep an eye on your readout, Oscar and let us know if there are any changes. Okay?" Athena added.

"Copy that!" he replied.

Oscar grasped the levers on the sides of his helmet and released the seals. He then folded the helmet back as he'd been shown. He hesitated but then breathed in some air through his nose. It was alright he determined, but he suddenly felt dizzy again as he took a few deep breaths. It didn't matter. He had come to help Sarah.

Chapter 66

Oscar stood there in the hallway looking at the map.

He'd not encountered anyone on the way so far, but every step made him a nervous wreck. And the adrenalin coursing through his veins didn't help calm him. His emotions were starting to get the best of him again, and as a result he was crying, breathing hard, and his face was twitching. But he pressed on as he brought up that image of Sarah in his mind. It worked to help him focus, but suddenly a host of memories about her childhood—including her mother—began to flood his conscious mind

"No…*no* you can't do this," he whispered as he ran down the corridor. "Sarah needs you! I…need you, Jen! Please don't do this! Listen, there's a reason for this. You just have to believe that! I…I, what can I do? Just tell me what I can do?"

"What's he talking about?" Sanguine asked.

"I don't know. But he's getting really emotional about it. I can hear it in his voice," Athena answered. "Oscar! Can you hear me?" she asked, trying to get his attention.

He did not respond at first, but within a few seconds he answered.

"Yes, I hear you."

He was weeping.

"Oscar, where are you? Tell us where you are. And whisper; make sure you keep your voice down. This is Athena, are you okay?"

There was more silence for a moment, but then he started again.

"Yeah, I'm okay. I…I just came to a corner. No one around! I'm about to that room. I'm going to stop talking now. I'm going to see if Sarah's there."

Athena took a long deep breath. Her eyes were wet and she fidgeted in her seat with the tension. Maybe *Sanguine* was right all along. Maybe this wasn't a good idea, she thought.

·······

Oscar slipped the wire under the door and looked at the handheld readout. It was a large room. To one side was what looked like a hospital bed against a wall—someone was in it. In the middle were two large islands of cabinets topped with counter tops, and to the other side was an arched walkthrough which led to an adjoining room, it too was filled with central cabinets and tables, and along the walls were more cabinets and glass-door-covered shelves, and in the back was what looked like an office with a desk, with more cabinets surrounding it. The room looked like a lab.

Oscar turned the wire toward the bed again. It could be Sarah, but he wasn't sure. He sniffed the mucous back into his nasal passages and tried to get a grip, but his emotions were difficult to control. He wasn't sure what to do. Go in and see if it was Sarah. But, what if it wasn't? Should he go to another door? Keep searching? The intel they reviewed said this was the room the team thought Sarah was located in. Perhaps it was.

Oscar looked intently at the small screen again, trying to turn the wire to get a better image. But it was no use. It didn't make it any better. Suddenly, he heard a noise down the hall. He held his breath and listened with every auditory effort he could muster. He didn't hear anything again. He looked back the way he came, and then down the other way where the sound came from. He felt so exposed. He then knelt there in front of the door as if to hide.

What do I do? He thought.

Sweat began to bead on his forehead.

He said a short prayer, and then decided.

Oscar stood up and tried the door handle.

It turned without resistance.

He slowly swung the door open.

There on the bed lay Sarah.

Her eyes were closed.

Oscar quickly entered the room and shut the door quietly.

He stepped further into the space and then suddenly remembered he had a pack with weapons in it. He felt like a stupid fool having not gotten one out long before now. He rolled his eyes and as silently as possible took the pack off his back and opened the flap. He hurriedly reached in and pulled out one of the NERV pistols Athena had briefly reviewed with him. He threw the pack over his shoulder and clicked the safety off of the weapon.

He then moved the last remaining few meters into the room, looking carefully around the corner into the adjoining areas, afraid, but ready to shoot anybody who may be there. Fortunately, the entire space was empty. His heartbeat slowed a little with the relief.

Oscar immediately lowered his guard and ran to Sarah. Tears filled his eyes. She was breathing, and she seemed alright. She had a B-CID on her head. The sight reminded him of what Athena had described he may find when he located her.

"Sarah," he whispered as he laid the weapon on the bed.

He reached down and touched her arm softly with one hand, her brow with the other. There was no reaction. He stroked her hair back. He did it again, but still no reaction. He then remembered what Athena had said; *Give her the shot as soon as you find her!*

Oscar moved quickly and opened the flap on his suit below his left breast. He reached inside and removed the small, sealed case. He opened it and then took out the pistol-shaped injector. He didn't hesitate. He stuck her in the neck, right in the vein where Athena had told him to. He sighed with relief. Then he carefully removed the B-CID from her head.

He didn't want to, but he knew that his next move was to leave her and start looking for that case, or whatever it was, and hopefully find some of the others. If he couldn't do any of that, then he realized he didn't know what to do. It was a miracle that he made it this far, he considered. His heart sank with the reality, and fear filled his cramping stomach.

....

Oscar wiped the tears from his eyes one more time as he readied himself. But suddenly, a swooshing sound caught his attention, bringing him back from the torrent of his rushing thoughts.

"And just who might *you* be?" Davian Adorjan uttered.

Oscar jerked when he heard the voice.

He thought about the gun.

He started to reach for it.

"Now now, you'd better just leave that right there," Adorjan said dramatically.

Oscar's hand froze in midair. He slowly turned his head and saw the man standing there behind him. His heart about leapt out of his chest. The man had a chromed, Earth-made, semi-automatic pistol aimed at his back.

"That's right. Better just leave that alone! Now step away!"

Oscar moved to his left as commanded. As he did he put his hands up and slowly turned toward the man.

"As I said, just who might you be? Ahhh yes, same suit, I see! Yet another vermin comes-a calling, probably with the rest, no doubt. So you've just been hiding all this time, I take it? Timid are we? Finally decided to scamper out? No matter…"

Adorjan went silent, seemed to concentrate on Oscar as if trying to think him dead. He just stared at him with a probing, intense look on his face. He then looked past Oscar to the desk in the back of the room, and then back at him.

"Huh, curious!" Adorjan said in a near whisper.

It was then that he looked at Sarah and noticed the injector syringe on the bed, along with the B-CID.

"What did you do?" he shouted in anger. He stepped closer as he motioned with the pistol for Oscar to move farther away. "You gave her something. What?"

Adorjan then moved directly in front of Oscar and raised the pistol. It was now pointing at his head. Oscar's eyes focused intently on Adorjan's, his mind racing as was his heart. Then, something caught Oscar's attention and he looked past the man. Adorjan noticed the diverted attention. He quickly tried to react but the object caught him just below his left ear and knocked him sideways with a terrible force. He immediately became disoriented and lost grip of the gun, dropping it to the floor.

Oscar smiled largely, yet at the same time had an astonished look on his face.

"You're...*dead*," Oscar said.

Athena and *Sanguine* heard Oscar's words.

They were both momentarily stunned by them.

"Oscar, what's happening?" Athena nearly yelled, sitting up on the edge of her seat.

There was another moment of silence, and then Oscar answered.

"Colonel Ravine, he's here!"

....

Colonel Ravine moved farther into the room. He quickly kicked the shimmering firearm away from Adorjan. It banged up against the island in the center of the room stopping its slide. Adorjan had fallen to the floor, but he wasn't out cold. He was mumbling and trying to raise his head off the floor.

"You okay, Oscar?" the Colonel asked.

Oscar was dumfounded, thinking he was seeing things, but he answered anyway.

"Yeah, I suppose. As okay as can be!"

Colonel Ravine noticed Sarah lying there on the bed. He took a quick scan of the room, and then looked back at Sarah.

Adorjan could barely lift his head off the floor, though he was trying.

"Stay down, shit-wad! Now why in the world would you be bringing a real projectile weapon up to a moon base? Don't you know you could depressurize the entire place and kill everybody inside including yourself?! Are you an idiot, *and* just plain stupid?"

The Colonel went to Sarah, checked her pulse and felt her skin.

"I gave her the shot," Oscar said proudly.

"Good, that's good Oscar!"

He then turned back to Adorjan.

"And just so you know, I took out your men on the way in. Your work is finished here. So just sit tight and I might let you sleep for the ride back. I do have some questions for you, though. Which I'd advise some swift and accurate answers. It might just help you out when you go before the *Curia Equitas*. Like, who from the *Renasci* gave you the keys to this place? And how were you able to take out my guys so easily? You're not that smart or well manned from what I've seen!"

Davian Adorjan sneered at the man as he lay there, holding the side of his throbbing, bleeding head, trying to fight off the intense dizziness.

Oscar processed his questioning.

"He's got the codes to those, things. *Sanguine* and Athena said there's a server, or something, here somewhere; it was able to hack them, their…their B-CLIDs, or whatever," Oscar offered, glad that he remembered it.

"*What*? Seriously? Now I wonder how this came about, Adorjan? You must have some new friends in higher low places. But we'll have to save that for another time. Why don't we start by you telling me where my people are?"

Colonel Ravine suddenly remembered Oscar's condition, and the improbability of his actually being there on the base.

"And how is it you ended up here, Oscar? You're the last person I figured on seeing in this place. Is that Moon dust I see on your…?"

Oscar didn't hear the rest of the question; the whizzing charge flew by the Colonel and he was cut short. Fortunately for him, the Colonel had heard the footfalls in the corridor a second before the attack. He flung himself to the side just in time, sliding on the smooth floor into the adjoining room, but the pulsed-electrical-charge grazed his left arm as he did so, though not doing any damage other than causing a little numbness. As he flew through the air, he turned and fired back toward the doorway. The people outside saw it coming and ducked out of sight. The Colonel's rounds missed altogether, fizzling out against the wall beyond them.

He quickly pulled himself against some cabinets, and twisted up behind a lab stool just as two men leaned into the doorway at different elevations and started shooting at him again. The small, nerve-tweaking rounds also fizzled out, a couple hitting a cabinet, the others the corner of a counter top and the wall, missing their intended target.

Colonel Ravine returned fire immediately. He hit one of the men in the arm as he recoiled back away from the shots. As the man fell, another caught him in the shoulder taking him out.

Oscar sought cover at the other end of the island and was kicking himself for not having a weapon to help out. He kept looking around the corner, trying to assess the situation, wondering frantically what to do. He then noticed Davian Adorjan moving toward his handgun, which was lying on the floor next to the island's base.

Oscar panicked. If Adorjan made it to the gun, they might be done for. He had to do something, but what? He waited for a few more seconds but then realized he might have waited too long. He burst out from around the corner, leapt through the air and tackled Adorjan just as he'd laid his hands on the weapon. Adorjan smashed against the floor and up against the cabinet base as Oscar landed on top of him with force.

The remaining man in the doorway turned in to take another shot at the Colonel, but his eyes were temporarily diverted when he saw Adorjan being decked by some other guy. That was enough for the Colonel to get off a shot and make it count. The man took a full hit to the chest and fell back, writhing spasmodically.

Adorjan, still disoriented from the blow to his head, managed to get his hand around the pistol and attempted to swing it around at Oscar. The two struggled violently. Oscar hit

Adorjan in the face with his fist as he grabbed Adorjan's hand with the other, trying with all his might to divert the weapon away from him, but Adorjan was much stronger and he muscled the weapon toward Oscar. When in range he discharged the gun into Oscar's chest. Oscar lost all control at that point and Adorjan rolled him off onto the floor.

Adorjan then swung around as fast as his dizzy head would allow, attempting to get his bearings on Colonel Ravine, but as he did he put his face right into the Colonel's weapon. At point-blank range, the Colonel pulled the trigger and shot Adorjan in the head. The pulse wouldn't kill him, but Adorjan wouldn't wake up, or be right in his head for quite some time.

That was probably not going to be the case with Oscar Whiting.

Colonel Ravine saw in stark detail what had happened. He roughly nudged Adorjan with his weapon to make doubly sure he was out, and then anxiously made it over to Sarah's father and helped him sit up against the cabinet.

"Oscar, you old fool. Look what you went and did. You got yourself shot! Dammit! You got the stuff, Oscar...you know that! You got the stuff! You saved my ass just now! Dammit! Oh, Oscar... You're going to be okay! You're going to be okay! You hear me?" the Colonel mumbled, quickly trying to do whatever first response measures he could, yet immediately recognizing the severity of the situation.

Oscar looked down at the wound.

He was bleeding profusely.

"You have to take out the server. The others, I saw Adorjan looking over toward the desk...in there." He pointed. "I remember. I...I think it's in there," Oscar said, as he held himself, wincing from the pain.

"Right, Oscar! Right, you just wait here, okay. Here, you put your hand here and press hard! Hard! You hear me!" he said with force.

Reluctantly, the Colonel rose and hurried to the desk.

As Oscar indicated, there was a case sitting against the wall behind the desk. He knew exactly what it was. He then fired at it with his weapon, but it appeared to have little effect. The

Colonel swiftly ran back and retrieved Adorjan's weapon. He then went back and fired three shots into the case. The insides of the device sparked and smoked. If it was working before, it wasn't now.

He then turned back, saw Sarah laying on the bed, and her father sitting there in a rising pool of blood.

His eyes suddenly swelled with tears.

Chapter 67

Sarah's eyes fluttered open and she saw Eliam sitting next to her. She felt odd. Sleepy, yet her heart was racing as if she had drunk too much coffee. She smiled at Eliam. He smiled back, yet his lips were tight together and he looked ragged and worn and on the verge of crying. She squinted her eyes, silently asking him what the matter was. She then tried to speak.

"Hey there, you okay?" she asked, blinking away her drowsiness, and realizing her throat was scratchy for some reason.

A tear immediately formed and ran down one of Eliam's cheeks.

She noticed and suddenly became very concerned.

Eliam swallowed hard and began to tell her.

. . . .

Sarah was beyond shaken.

Who could make up a story like that? All it took was for Eliam to point outside a window, and she was convinced. At least she thought. She could have lost her mind. But if someone had lost their mind, how would they even know they'd lost their mind. All she could do was trust what Eliam had said.

Her father lay dying in the next room. And he didn't have much time.

Eliam helped her to her feet and together they walked to the adjoining space. On the way she saw several unfamiliar people: Lem, Atol, Sergeants Tomlinson and Norris, all in the office area of the lab sitting and talking with Colonel Ravine.

Waiting for her at the arched doorway was Athena. She had a serious, yet empathetic look on her face. As Sarah approached, Athena spoke.

"Hi, you're Sarah. I'm Dr. Athena Mauropolin. Listen, I know this is hard! But he doesn't have much time. He's holding out for you, I think, Sarah. He's in there." Athena pointed to the corner of the room.

She saw the bed sticking out from behind a curtain.

Sarah looked back to Athena for any hope at all.

Athena just took a deep breath and dropped her eyes.

Eliam helped Sarah a little way farther.

"I'll be right out here, Sarah," he said.

Sarah looked at him, her face pale white and blank.

She nodded.

Eliam backed up to stand by Athena as Sarah rounded the curtain.

Oscar Whiting was lying on the bed.

They'd bandaged him up the best they could and covered him with several blankets to keep him warm. His eyes were closed.

"Dad," Sarah said, but her voice crackled and sounded weak. She tried again. "*Dad!*"

Oscar Whiting slowly opened his eyes.

He smiled a faint smile.

"Hi Sarah."

"Hi Dad! Do you believe this? We're on the Moon. *You're* on the Moon, Dad!"

He gave out a little laugh, but it was quickly strangled by the intense pain.

"Yeah, *yeah!* Did they tell you I got to walk on the surface?"

"No, Dad, really?! They let you do that?!" she said, trying to hold back her emotions. Tears welled in her eyes, but she held them at bay.

"Yeah, it was better than I'd ever imagined. I felt so close to God, Sarah. I really did! I could have stayed out there forever. And I want that, Sarah. I asked the others to leave me up here. I just wanted you to know; that's my wish. Out there, anywhere…anywhere's fine. And thank them for me Sarah, please! It meant so much to me!"

Oscar again twitched and wrenched his body, convulsing with the pain.

Sarah started for Dr. Mauropolin, but suddenly stopped, reluctantly coming to grips with the fact that there was nothing anyone could do. She turned back to her father.

"Sure, Dad!" she said. "If…if that's what you want. I love you, Dad! I love you so much!"

Sarah held his hand and put her face to it; she rubbed it on her cheek and then kissed it.

"I love you too, Sarah. I always will!" he coughed and winced again. He caught himself and struggled to breathe as he tried to gain back some composure. "Sarah, listen. I don't have much time. I want you to believe for me Sarah. To believe in yourself, and don't be afraid. Get out there and take those chances; don't give in to fear and frustration; believe in yourself, and that you have a purpose; we all do, Sarah. I know that now!

"It's all going to work out, Sarah. It's going to be fine! Just look at me! I finally got to walk on the Moon!" he then laughed the most joyous laugh anyone could ever utter.

"And listen," he struggled to continue. "You put on one of those hats your Mom made us, once in awhile, okay? Remember, you can talk to her if you do. And me too, okay? Just remember that! I…I love you…Sarah!"

Oscar Whiting closed his eyes, and within another moment, stopped breathing.

Sarah wilted.

She rubbed her eyes and then her nose, disbelieving what had just happened.

She then slowly bent down and kissed her father on his forehead.

"I love you too, Dad!" she whispered.

Sarah wept for what seemed like an eternity.

Chapter 68

They remained on the Moon for several days.

Colonel Ravine and his people attended to those Adorjan had abducted the best they could. Most were responsive to the Sonilyn-7, but a few were too far gone. They would further be taken care of once back on Earth, and the team had help for such a task, but it would not be an easy road to travel for any of them.

Oscar Whiting was buried some distance away from the base. Far enough away that he could have his own place and no one would ever bother him. The entire group flew out to the site in *Sanguine* and they had a service fit for a king. A small cross of titanium adorned the end of his grave. Colonel Ravine had made it out of some parts from the base, placing it at the grave himself. He spoke a few words as the senior official at the ceremony. And to everyone's surprise, even *Sanguine* had said goodbye, speaking in a soft and emotional voice. The rest of that day was followed by long spans of quiet and reflection.

When Sarah was up to it, Eliam told her the rest of what had happened. She was struck with horror, and yet with honor, at what everyone had gone through to save her, especially regarding her father. He'd saved them all, Eliam, as well as the others had confessed. It broke her heart to hear of such admiration and respect for her father.

Two days later, in the evening after a meal together, everyone began to open up and talk about all they'd been through. Sarah mostly sat silent and listened. She hadn't in her lifetime ever imagined being involved with such people or events. Awe was not even close to how she felt.

Colonel Ravine finally revealed to everyone what had happened to him in his battle with Adorjan. He spoke humbly, as if he were honored to still be alive.

"After leaving *Sanguine's* position we programmed the Pulse Emission to arrive around the same time we expected I'd be engaged with Adorjan. In route, Lem and Atol climbed into a couple of Cryo-units and they took another route to the base—their idea. A great idea, except it didn't quite work out as planned. I'd say providence had a hand in it...for all of us."

He abruptly lowered his head, appearing to have an emotional moment.

Everyone noticed and understood.

He cleared his throat and then started again.

"Anyway, we all arrived at about the same time. While I was occupied with Adorjan they waited outside on the surface at a maintenance lock by the ship docks until the Pulse arrived. For added effect, I timed *The Adora's* positioning with the Pulse, and strafed Adorjan's, as well as the base's sensor packs at exactly the same time it arrived. It took them out, and in effect left an open door for the guys to get in unnoticed. At least that was the plan!"

"So what happened to you? We saw you burn!" Athena remarked, cringing from the memory.

Colonel Ravine grinned before answering.

"Well, I knew *The Adora* couldn't hold out against his ship. He just had more of what *The Adora* didn't. And I knew that going into it. So, Atol here did some creative graphics work on the way and made it look like I was sitting in the captain's chair with the flight deck on fire. Oh, I was in the chair, but the flames were added. The effect looked real enough. And I thought I did a pretty good job of acting the part!"

Everyone suddenly got it.

They all smiled at him, looking at each other and shaking their heads.

"Yeah, I'd say you did! You about gave me a heart attack, William Ravine!" Athena said, somewhat angrily.

The others looked at her strangely.

They'd never heard her call him anything except Colonel, or sir.

"Yeah, well, I'm sorry, Athena. I knew Adorjan would completely destroy my ship with me in it once I'd spent my entire arsenal. It's just his style. And I didn't really feel like dying that day, so we came up with the plan to make it seem like I was burning to death, that way Adorjan would just let me burn. He's a sick bastard! And we knew that. Fortunately, the ruse worked.

"Anyway, I got into a Cryo-unit to make it seem like my vitals had died along with me. After about fifteen minutes I got out and started to make my way into the base the same way as Lem and Atol were planning to do, except I found them just lying there outside the lock. They were breathing, but they weren't moving. Of course, at the time I didn't understand why. Now I do. When Adorjan sent out the codes to shut down my B-CID, it shut theirs down before they could even get inside."

"Interesting! And why didn't the codes shut yours down?" Eliam asked abruptly, intrigued.

The Colonel smiled.

"Upgrades!" he said simply.

"Upgrades?" Athena asked, also extremely curious now.

"The guy is old school!" Lem interjected. "He hasn't downloaded an upgrade for his B-CID for the last twenty years. He's running an old system!"

"*Ancient*, if you ask me!" Atol added with a smile.

Everyone's eyebrows raised in sudden understanding.

Athena smiled big, too.

"Hey, like Lem said, I'm old school. I don't need all that fancy, buzz-and-whirr stuff you young people think are the greatest things since breast milk. My old system runs just fine, thank you very much."

"So, the codes Adorjan had can only hack the recent iterations of the core SB operating systems?" Eliam thought to ask.

"Yeah, apparently that's the case," the Colonel started again. "Imagine, being able to block all sensory input and at the same time take away conscious control of your unit—control of your brain. Talk about the true definition of a hack. It'd be like being in a coma, and then waking up in whatever AVTR program he wanted you to be in, and there's no way to control the input. It was probably like being in a nightmare, and you couldn't wake up. I can only imagine!" He paused, thinking about it. "But, I guess by you guys having been there, now we know!" he said solemnly, shaking his head sideways, looking around to everyone, empathy and compassion molding his rugged face.

They acknowledged his sentiment with their nods of affirmation.

"What now?" Sergeant Tomlinson then asked. "Someone got Adorjan those codes, and wrote the invasive protocols. And if he had them, others have them. How do we protect against that?"

"Good question. Raj and I have discussed it and there are some possibilities. But more importantly, what we have to realize here is that something bigger than this is going on. Someone really high up is starting to pull some serious strings. How and why is yet to be determined. But, thanks to Adorjan, at least now we have some leads to go on. Raj is working on recovering data from his Cloud Server, but we don't know if anything is salvageable enough to help us, yet. We'll just have to see."

"There's something we're forgetting," Athena offered. "Sarah! She's got a life and it's been seriously disrupted. Her father disappeared from that nursing home and now he's passed away. How is she going to deal with that when she gets back?"

Sarah had only briefly thought about it. But now her mind was churning with understandable apprehension regarding the subject.

"Yes, I'm glad we got to that. Sarah, we're going to help you. Don't worry! Raj..." he began to ask, "Would you go over with Sarah what we discussed?"

"Yeah, it'd be my pleasure, Colonel. Don't worry, Sarah. What you're going to do is write a letter to the home and tell them that your father just showed up on your doorstep; you were incensed with their poor security and over the last few days you were keeping to yourself and talking to lawyers. That will put them on the edge to do just about anything to protect their reputation. Then, you'll tell them that you're not going to press charges and request they send the proper release forms for you to sign to remove him from their care. But, if you ever hear of even a small infraction regarding their incompetence, you'll offer all this to the press. They'll send the forms, probably let a few people go as a result, but keep it hush-hush as not to suffer any further consequences. This can also be the reason for your absence from the program, which is still something you need to consider, as I understand."

There was a silence as everyone thought about it.

"You know, whether you still want to be a part of it? After all this?" Eliam interjected, looking deeply into Sarah's eyes.

Sarah studied his sincerity, and then looked around at all of their matching expressions. She'd nearly forgotten about the program.

"And Sarah,' Raj continued. "I'll help with acquiring a death certificate for you sometime later, too. Okay? From the 'other state' where you transferred your father to," he smiled. "But in the interim, you can just tell everyone he wanted to go live on the east coast, or in Europe, or somewhere. Maybe he was just sick of California and wanted a different landscape to be in every day.' He smiled again. "But, that's up to you."

Sarah tilted her head back and nodded a sincere thank you as tears starting welling in her eyes. She cleared her throat and asked a question.

"What's going to happen to Bolt—Adorjan, I mean, and his people?"

Colonel Ravine offered the answer.

"They're in Cryo-units, and they'll soon be en route to a holding location where they'll be held until their time comes up for trial before the *Curia Equitas*."

Sarah opened her eyes widely in puzzlement.

The Colonel answered her silent question.

"The *Curia Equitas* is an international, intergovernmental court. They'll be tried for crimes against humanity."

"When their time comes up? And when will that be?" Sarah asked, truly curious.

"Probably quite a while, actually, what with the backlog and all the political changes underway on Hoame. But don't worry, they're secure and won't be hurting anyone ever again."

"Where is this holding place?" Eliam asked, also curious.

"Well, I can't say exactly where, by order of the court. But, it's a remote location, a long way from Earth I can assure you."

"That's why the Cryo-units have propulsion systems!" Eliam stated, nodding, the fact now dawning on him.

The Colonel smiled.

"Yes, exactly! They'll be joining others like them, wait out their time. We've been doing this for quite some time now. It's what we do!" He smiled at his team.

"That reminds me, Colonel. Adorjan said that he was actually after you guys, because his new 'employers' wanted to acquire some of your people, because they wanted to know where this holding location was. Apparently some of their people are there, and they know this," Eliam added.

"Yes, I don't doubt it. Fortunately, we deprived them of that information. In fact, none of us actually know where it is, exactly. We have encrypted coordinates that we use when making a deposit, as it we call it. We just know it's a long way away from here, and Hoame."

Eliam again nodded his head in understanding.

There was another long silence, and then Sarah spoke.

"Listen, I want to thank all of you. You saved my life!"

Sarah choked up for a moment, but then continued.

"And whether you know it or not…you saved my dad's, too. He hated having to live in that home, as much as I hated having to put him there. You gave him the chance to live the adventure of his lifetime; one he'd worked all his life for, in truth. And you probably have no idea what it meant to him! But he talked about it before he passed; it meant everything to him! He died a happy man because of you; instead of in some shallow, meaningless existence eating crappy food waiting for his turn to just come around. I can't thank you enough for that! And I know he would say it was 'providence' as well, Colonel! I think I believe that now, too! Thank you...thank you all!'"

Sarah looked intently at Colonel Ravine and the others; she then smiled a sad, grateful smile, as the tears ran down her face.

The Colonel looked back at her knowingly. He just nodded and offered a humble smile in return. But he wasn't prepared to say right then what had suddenly come into his mind. He just thought of a little project he needed Raj and Atol's help on. He smiled even larger at the thought.

Chapter 69

Davian Adorjan's eyes suddenly popped open.

He blinked a couple of times and without turning his head, looked to one side and then to the other.

His eyebrows sank in confusion.

He then turned his head and took in a greater perspective of his surroundings. He was in some kind of archaic, shabbily decorated, dingy parlor room of some sort. It contained a dozen large table-cloth covered, round tables, each having five or six mismatched chairs surrounding them. The walls had cheap rippled paneling on the bottom, with painted drywall on the top. The walls, too, were grimy-looking, in bad need of a paint job, and there were numerous holes and assorted blemishes and places where outlines could be seen where missing pictures once hung.

The sparse furniture around the perimeter of the large room consisted of a few uneven, dusty shelves with old picture frames on them, along with a few odd looking statuette figurines that looked to be old souvenirs from someone's past travels. In one dominant corner there was a large, big screen TV hanging from the wall that tilted downward. It, along with most everything in the room, was dusty. It was then that Davian Adorjan noticed the smell. It was the smell of urine and ammonia and methane mixed together. The awful disgusting odor turned Adorjan's stomach. He then instinctively raised his hand to cover his nose, only to notice that his hand was wrinkled and splotched and old looking.

As he sat there in confusion studying his physical extremities, he heard voices coming from a connecting hallway to the room. Adorjan turned his head and upon looking up saw at least a dozen and an half people walking into the room. They were all gray-haired, old, and slow moving. Some with walkers, some with canes, and some with none of either but were still navigating the tables at a careful and clipped pace, holding onto the backs of chairs as they passed them. Each made their way to a particular table: two or three here, four at that one, most with only one. They all proceeded to sit down. Some talked and whispered and made subtle gestures and quick glances Adorjan's way. Several just seemed to talk to no one in particular, mumbling as their hands nervously shook. Some just stared blankly down.

"Hello there!"

Adorjan heard the voice.

He looked up to see an old man with a pot belly standing next to him.

Adorjan just stared.

"Well, you deaf? I said hello?" the man exclaimed.

Adorjan looked around again, annoyed. He then looked up at the man once more.

"Where am I?" Adorjan asked sternly.

"Where are ya? You're in the Golden Years Retirement Home! Where do you think you are? What, were you asleep when they moved you in?" The gruff man just stared at Adorjan. He then sat down at the same table one chair over.

"Family couldn't take care of ya, huh? Didn't make enough for retirement while you was working? Is that your story? Most common one in here. You never hear tell of someone rich and well to do, with a loving family, just up and choosing one day to come to a place like this."

Davian Adorjan's mind was swirling. He felt oddly out of place, and was trying to compensate for the peculiar feelings.

"What's that smell?" he asked the man as he looked around at all the seemingly disgusting people.

"Smell…*smell*? What do ya think that smell is? It's a retirement home. You got Alzheimer's? You demented or something?" he asked as he stared at Adorjan quizzically. "I asked what's your story? You embarrassed about it? You ain't one of those ventriloquist-types who talks out their asses, are you?"

Adorjan turned his head back toward the man. He suddenly wanted to reach out and strangle him, but as he thought about it, his knuckles suddenly flared up in pain. The oddly timed association unnerved him.

"I'm Davian Adorjan. I'm a member of the *Ankh*, my family bloodline goes back thousands of years. I'm from the planet Hoame. I am a genius, and as a result a billionaire, and I have control over innumerable politicians and world leaders. I am not a…a ventriloquist, or whatever that is you said, and I assure you I do not talk out of my ass!" he said imperiously, his emotion causing him to raise his voice.

Everyone in the room glanced his way, but then turned their heads back to their conversations.

"Right! Dementia, just like I thought," the man said.

At that moment several middle-aged people began bringing serving trays in on a couple of rolling carts. They then took a metal tray off a cart and quickly placed one in front of each of the people, including Adorjan.

"Alright, dinner!" the man then said.

Adorjan looked at the disgusting three-course meal, each in its own little depression on the tray.

"What is this?" Adorjan asked, feeling like he was about to vomit from the new mix of smells under his nose.

"Fish sticks! It's Fish Stick Friday. Everyday is Fish Stick Friday here at the Golden Years Retirement Home!"

The man then smiled largely, showing his mouth of crooked, stained and missing teeth. He then licked his lips.

"Welcome to the Golden Years, Mr. Adorjan!" the man said.

Chapter 70

"I see the crowd is in near-absolute awe of Earthbridge Consumer Technology Division's over-the-top demonstration of their 'Smartbrain' computer interface technology. This year's Blue-Dot Convention will go down in history as one of the most prolific expositional conventions its consumers have ever experienced! I'm certainly impressed and thrilled to be here!" the show's announcer proclaimed, his dramatic delivery adding to the excitement.

"I must say, I didn't think it was possible, but we are made of atoms, and atoms generate electrical signals, and electrical signals do transmit all the information from the outside world into our brains via our sensory organs—eyes, ears, etc. It does make sense that sooner or later someone would discover a way to tap into that stream and learn to input like signals to and from the brain via it. Wow, talk about a game-changer!

"I have yet to try the technology, but I assure you I will be one of the next in line to do so when the opportunity arises. But, until then I suppose I'll just have to entertain myself and imagine what it'll be like until that moment occurs, along with the rest of you. However, to help us all imagine what it will actually be like, Earthbridge Consumer Technology Division now presents their one-on-one Q&A with the live version of their team of intrepid test subjects.

"Ladies, gentlemen, all people of the consumer world, without further comment, let me hand it over to our surprise Q&A commentator. He's a radio and web personality, he's the author, speaker, and famed disambiguating prognosticator we all know and love—and hate, at times." He laughed, as did the crowd. "It is my pleasure and honor to introduce to you, the all-around inexplicable interloper and puzzlingly popularizing pundit, *Jonathon Raker!*"

The crowd roared when the unsuspected name was revealed, especially as the man himself appeared from the small, spacecraft-looking capsule that had mysteriously set on the side of the stage for the presentation's entirety. The man exited the pod-like cubicle, walked to the edge of the stage and took a slight bow. He then waved his hand as the lights dimmed and the large curtain behind him seemed to dissolve into sheer nothingness, revealing the seven people adorned in plain street clothes, sitting on tall director-like chairs in front of a huge backdrop of multidimensional screens, each oscillating between excerpts of their previously shown documentary amidst images of the new device itself.

Even the team had no idea that Jonathan Raker, of *Raker's Slant* would act as official commentator during the final public Q&A session. They were all thrilled, yet at the same time apprehensive and nervous to say the least.

"Hello everyone!" he said, taking another slight bow to the crowd. "And hello to you the neo-brain sojourners of time and space and the future! Let's go forward, shall we?"

The crowd applauded again, as did the team. The lights then shifted, creating a mystical, surreal aura about the stage. It was akin to the start of a rock concert. Soft, dissonant music added to the ambiance, fading into the background as Raker began.

"Before asking specific questions of our distinguished panel, let me reiterate some of the previously presented highlights of this seemingly miraculous technology! This device is the literal integration of your smartphone, and your brain. Hence…*Smartbrain.*"

The people applauded.

"With this technology everything you can do with your smartphone, you can purportedly do with the device and more.

"First and foremost, input from the device interfaces—*streams*—directly into your brain.

"That's the game-changer here, and as a result,

"You will be able to see images, in your brain, without the need of your eyes,

"You will be able to hear sound, in your brain, without the need of your ears,

"You will be able to communicate, as if telepathically, through manifold modes and methods,

"You will be able to feel, and taste, and even smell, in your brain, all due to the direct feeds into your brain, through this device, all in augmentation to your natural senses.

"In addition,

"You will be able to operate all aspects of the device through thought,

"You will be able to stream to distant places, be in different spaces,

"You will be able to live, and interact, and exist in a host of worlds you'd never thought possible, all created by you! *Streamplaces* will become our new frontiers! Of course, that is for the public—for *YOU*—to ultimately choose!"

He finished with a bow of his head.

The crowd erupted again.

Jonathan Raker walked over to his own chair and sat down facing the team of panelists.

The crowd's applause and cheers settled down and he began.

"Alright, on to the first question, but it won't bother you all if I take an impartial stance in our little Q&A now, will it?"

The crowd erupted in earnest, knowing that Jonathan Raker could be no other than Jonathan Raker.

"Thank you…thank you! Good! Alright, we can begin. I will ask a few questions, as moderator, and then we have numerous topics of inquiry that have been gathered from the brief public surveys conducted at the start of the convention. So, I'll start. First question goes out to the entire group. Anyone can answer, just be kind and don't step on other peoples' egos, please!"

They all smiled.

"Biggest question that has come to us: Is it safe? This technology interfaces directly with the brain; some people obviously have an issue with this. I suppose the concern here is whether or not it might scatter our brains, or turn us all into zombies, or something."

The crowd laughed and applauded slightly as the group looked around at each other deciding who would answer.

Everyone's eyes settled on Dr. Robert Redding.

"Okay, Dr. Redding, your question then," Raker said.

"Well, we've been shown the results of test after test. The input into the brain is of the same frequency and substance that our normal senses has been discovered to use. That in effect was the breakthrough, as we understand it—learning just how our senses package and send information to the brain. And due to this, the technology affords downloading to the brain just as naturally. No one to our knowledge has experienced any adverse reactions from this, except the tendency for drop jaw."

"'Drop jaw?'" Raker asked.

"Yes, you know the kind that happens when you're amazed and your jaw opens up to say WOOOOOW!"

The crowd erupted into cheers and laughter.

Raker calmed them quickly with a mere wave of his hand.

"But, no. So far, it has been safe. And as a doctor, I'd say it is harmless to the body. Some people may find they might become overly addicted to it, like any video game or TV show, but in and of itself, it is innocuous, safe. It has passed all the scrutiny thrown at it to date by the leading agencies, I understand." Dr. Redding finished.

"Well, good! I suppose time will ultimately tell, as it always does. Okay, next big question: Will it be expensive? And I might add, won't a goodly portion of society be left out, as it were, if this proves to be so?"

Everyone looked toward Wena Paravin.

She immediately acquiesced.

"Well, we're not privy to the pricing structure of the units, as of this point. But I'd say at first it may only be in the hands—on the heads—of those who can afford them, as with any other technology that has come around. But, as volume increases and if competition is allowed—which it should be in my opinion—prices will drop, just as it did with computers, or smartphones, or personal conveyances. Economics is economics. Things will eventually balance themselves," she finished.

"Yes, that makes sense. Okay, next question…"

Jonathan Raker paused for a moment as if thinking. He then started again.

"Okay, let's put these lackluster questions aside for a moment. How about we jump right in and get to what the public really wants answers to, shall we. Okay, in what ways or forms will this new technology draw out the inherent *bad* that we oftentimes find dwelling in the human heart?"

The panel heard the question clearly.

Their expressions however revealed that the question would not exactly be an easy one to answer. In fact, no one even offered to comment. Raker seemed to pick up on it immediately, wasting no time reiterating the query.

"Oh, come on, Dr. Redding already alluded to the fact that people might become addicted to it. I mean, take a trip on any commuter rail and you can see that people don't interact anymore. They sit there in their own little worlds, entertaining themselves with their personal world-monitors, oblivious to the other life forms around them. In restaurants, you see couples sitting there for long periods of time not conversing, not interacting, and not even looking at each other. Instead they're engrossed with their own personal, electro-moronic fixations. How is this technology going to be any different? In fact, because of its very nature, as has been described to us, won't it in fact make this phenomenon worse?"

He paused and waited for a moment, looking at the people. No one answered.

"Declan Stewart, entertainment aficionado, what do you think? Did you find you were so absorbed with the experience that you didn't care about anybody else around you?" he asked.

The man fidgeted in his chair.

He made an effort to speak, but obviously found it difficult.

"Well, I…I have to admit I was absorbed with the experience. It is mesmerizing at times, to say the least. But that doesn't necessarily mean that I didn't—don't—care about others around me. I mean, what you're talking about is a social choice, I think. I actually found it an efficient way to interact with others. On levels that other mediums lack."

"Really," Raker said. "It broadened the experience of interaction with others, you're saying?"

"Yes, that's what I'm saying," he replied.

"Interesting," Raker offered. "It's my understanding that inherent to the technology is the ability to augment our natural selves, with made-up or exaggerated personality traits, especially when using the AVTR programs as described. People can 'self-personify' any attribute they wish to, just because they now have the capability to do so. Doesn't that afford the opportunity to be something we aren't, to the point of misrepresentation? How is that going to affect business transactions, commerce, as well as personal and corporate integrity? How are we to know who, or what entity, is actually real anymore, when we now have the tools to so easily misrepresent who we truly are?"

Again, no one was forthright with an answer.

"How about you, Ms. Goens, what do you think about that? I mean, if all business can now be completely conducted via whatever personas we wish to present, will the danger not exist to also misrepresent what is true and good and real in our business and personal dealings?"

Furley Goens seemed to exhibit a guarded position.

She thought for a moment, and then answered.

"I suppose humans have always been that way, able to personify whomever they wished in order to come across as something they're perhaps not. That's a human trait, not necessarily a result of technology, or this particular technology specifically."

"Perhaps, but back to the point of addiction, wouldn't you agree that those who are addicted to something exhibit a greater tendency to justify further addictive behavior? So how is this any different than say, your smartphone, your computer, or your TV?"

"It isn't, I suppose. But again, as you raised the question, 'in what ways or forms will this technology draw out the bad that is often found in the human heart?' What was stated earlier is the answer to your question, it is also my answer. This technology is no different than any other. It's the human element, not necessarily technology, which is the cause of the inerrant behavior of people, individually, as well as on collective scales. That's the reality of it!"

Furley smiled, looking to the others, acknowledging their silent agreement.

"Well, alright then," Raker said. "Let us look at the reality position. Let's say that due to the fact that the 'neo-reality' this technology creates—as it appeared in your documentary—is so convincing, so compelling that humanity begins to prefer that reality over true reality. Let's imagine the possibility that because you're dealing with an avatar, you might develop the tendency to become insensitive, simply because of that fact, instead of behaving as one does when in the physical flesh when dealing with someone else, also in the physical flesh. What then? Are we destined to evolve to where we only live in a false reality, numbed to the sensitivities of others, simply because it is convenient, or easier? And after living that way for such a length of time, will we ever again know what true 'human' reality is? Is there no danger in this? Condoleezza Ghee, what are your views on this?"

Condi repositioned herself in her seat now that the attention was on her.

"Reality has always been a subjective thing," she said. "Just as value is a subjective thing. When humanity got tired of getting soaking wet every time it rained, we altered our reality by going into caves, or building dwellings. When we got cold, we made clothes; when we felt limited to the distances walking afforded us, we rode horses, created trains, automobiles, and airplanes. This is no different.

"Those are technologies just the same as Smartbrain. And humanity has never let the tendency toward insensitivity stop them, just because they dealt with each other, one physical being to another physical being, as you mentioned. On the contrary, humankind has a full history of insensitivity toward each other, *especially* when in a face to face reality. So again, as Furley pointed out, it's not necessarily the technology, it's the bad and/or—I feel—the good that dwells in the heart of humans that is, and makes, the difference."

The crowd applauded, as did several of the panelists.

"Well, I see I have succeeded in making my point then. Alright, we have numerous other topics gleaned from the brief surveys of the visiting public at the start of the convention. Let's see," he said, scanning a small tablet. "What about the privacy issues. How is privacy handled? Anyone?"

Nelson Baurle, the communications engineer, raised his hand slightly.

"As we understand it…"

....

Colonel William Ravine and Eliam Zaris sat together at the edge of one of the many elevated food courts looking out over the central convention auditorium Earthbridge's presentation was being conducted at. They were some distance away from the stage, but people were crowded in all around them. It was only the third largest hall at the expansive convention center, yet there were more people in attendance there than all others combined—thousands were packed into the relatively small wing.

The ambient din of all the people should have been louder, but everyone seemed intentionally aware of that fact and strove to keep their voices down in order to hear what was being said by the group over the sound system. Eliam and the Colonel listened intermittently, and without verbalizing their speech, began their own conversation through their shared B-CID-generated audio fields.

"Did I say I hate crowds?" the Colonel asked, his lips smirking as a guy standing next to him bumped him yet again with his hip.

"Yeah, me too, this is crazy. I'm just glad we're not down there on the floor," Eliam answered.

"You got that right. You'd think that old guy Justin Timber…Bieber, or whatever, was back in the building doing a show or something."

Eliam laughed.

"I'll be glad when this is over."

"Copy that!"

"Sarah seems to be doing okay."

"Yeah, so-so. It's only been a month, but she's adapted pretty well. I know she's not exactly liking this right about now. She doesn't like crowds either."

"Yeah, well, at least she doesn't have three-hundred-pound goober-grape here slapping his big ass against her," he said silently, but then opened his mouth and blurted out a warning to the large effeminate man adorned in tight purple pants. "Hey, I understand your excitement here, but if you bump me with that ass of yours one more time I'm going to throw it over this railing!"

The man looked down at the Colonel suddenly realizing he was about to receive his wrath, so he apologized sharply and used his massive weight to push the crowd a little farther away from their table.

"Thank you for your cooperation," the Colonel said to the man. He then turned his attention back to the presentation.

"You're good to have around," Eliam offered with a smile, again only speaking through the B-CID's shared audio field.

"Thanks. Which, by the way, brings me to something I wanted to talk to you about. We'd like you to consider joining our team," he said pointedly.

Eliam turned to him with a surprised look on his face.

"Really?" he replied, his lips unmoving.

"Yes, you come highly recommended."

"I do? Highly recommended? Recommended by whom?"

"Well, that's classified, for now. But we'd like you to consider it. We need someone with your experience and expertise."

"What, you mean someone who's adept at being captured the first time out on a dangerous mission? You mean someone like that?"

The Colonel smiled largely.

"Don't underestimate yourself. You showed courage and resiliency. Besides, the whole team was taken out on that one. Not anyone's fault. It's because of that possibility recurring that we need you. We'd also like to make the same offer to Sarah."

"Sarah!? Seriously?" Eliam was stunned. "What do…" he started to ask why but was interrupted.

"Shhhhhh! I want to hear this," the Colonel said, nodding toward the stage.

·······

"…how exactly would this make a difference? Furley?" Raker asked, reservation in his voice.

Furley Goens again repositioned herself in the chair before answering.

"The environment is of the highest concern. That is my personal, as well as my public position; everyone knows that. We've become a world of insatiable consumers in order to create and sustain our supposedly irreplaceable economies. There's nothing wrong with possessions, and material things, but doing it the way we're doing it—to the levels we've done it—is exponentially threatening all of us. Everyone's sick of hearing it, so we just ignore it, and because of that it's only getting worse.

"Smartbrain technology can help turn this around by simply helping satisfy our insatiable hunger for things, and variety, and entertainment, by doing so synthetically, yet with a realism that more than gratifies our intrinsic human needs. And it can do it at only a fraction of the resource usage and negative impact on our remaining environment's fragile and failing systems.

"Now, I'm just a kid in many people's eyes. I know that. And I don't have all the answers as to how jobs can be saved, or replaced, or transitioned or how world politics should be conducted to make this a reality, or a host of other questions that need answered. There are a lot of other smart people out there that can do all that.

"But, what I do recognize is the basic fact that where it once cost a *thousand* parts of energy to make something, or to do something—never to get those parts back mind you—we can now do the same thing with only *ten* parts, and all combined we only have, say, a *million* parts in the first place, we'd be very unwise to continue wasting the remaining parts we have left.

"I don't know about you, but I understand the meanings of infinite and finite, and we wouldn't have very 'smart brains' if we don't get around soon to applying those terms to our planet, and our lives. I'm just saying! To me it's simple! It's basic math! But hey, I'm just a kid…what do I know?"

The crowd erupted in applause.

• • • • • • •

"I like simple. Way to go, kid!" Colonel Ravine said, nodding.

"Yeah, good point," Eliam added. "Too bad people can't stay focused on the simple facts. This planet's headed the same way as Hoame was and still is in many ways. You'd think *we* would've been smarter sooner."

"Yes, true. But that's why we decided to come here and help. Maybe someday seeing what happened to another planet—when the time comes—might instill enough 'simplicity' to turn this one around before it's too late. That's the idea anyway, huh?" the Colonel said, pausing for a second before thinking of something. "By the way, I've been meaning to ask. Why aren't you down there with everybody else? You're a major part of this whole thing."

Eliam answered silently without looking at him.

"Don't like the lights and attention. They all worked hard and there're plenty of people to help out down there. Don't appreciate the public thing much; I prefer to stay in the periphery for the most part."

The Colonel nodded in understanding.

"Did you tell Sarah about Sonilyn-7; what it's going to do to her?"

Eliam glanced at him, and then looked back at the stage and to Sarah.

"No. I haven't. The time will come. I'll tell her though. And that reminds me, what were you saying about Sarah joining the team?" Eliam suddenly remembered what the Colonel had said.

"We want to ask her if she'd be willing to join the team as well, at least for a special project or two."

"Special project or two, what type of projects?" Eliam's eyes thinned.

"Classified!"

"Classified?" Eliam asked through their shared audio field as he turned and looked at the man. "You know you're not saying much here."

Colonel Ravine smiled.

"Which leads me to ask, I want to invite you and Sarah to come on a little trip. Athena will be there. It'll be warm, tropical—in the periphery, if you're wondering—and it'll only be for a couple of days."

"I guess if I ask where, you'll tell me…"

"Classified!" the Colonel said with another smile, just staring forward.

"Well, I suppose that could be arranged. I'll have to ask Sa…"

"Shhhhhh!" the Colonel nodded to the stage again.

·······

"…so what is the definition of a 'smart brain,' then?" Jonathan Raker asked, going with the flow of the conversation. "How about you this time, Ms. Whiting? You've been the quiet one throughout the afternoon. What are your observations regarding the subject?"

Sarah looked intently at Furley.

Furley gestured back encouragingly with her eyes telling Sarah to go ahead; it was her opportunity to answer the question this time.

Sarah smiled back and then turned to the crowd.

"Well, I think everyone here, in one way or another, has touched on the definition of 'smart brain.' Condi said it when she mentioned that reality and value are subjective things. Furley just stated it when she said that it's as simple as just doing the math. I think having a smart brain requires us to critically review and assess our present circumstances based upon the past conditions that brought us here, and then find the courage and resourcefulness—the bigger purpose—in order to alter our thinking and behavior so we can undergo the needed change, whatever that may be.

"The hard part is human nature. We seem to have the tendency to want to remain in our 'familiar' zones at all costs, until the last minute, selfishly, oftentimes to our detriment, as well as that of others. But, if we'd just do the math, we'd see that we have to change, we have to find the faith to do so, but first, we have to believe in ourselves, that we *all* have a purpose and a contribution to make in life. And once you realize that—what *your* purpose is—that's when life truly starts for us. And that's what makes all the difference. My father had taught me that since I was a little girl; at first I didn't get it either, but he was right all along. This Smartbrain technology may not have all the potential we think it's going to have, but *we* do, and it's only going to be as 'smart'…as *we* are!"

Sarah finished.

Everyone saw the raw emotion she displayed, along with her glistening eyes.

Within seconds the hall erupted in applause again.

Chapter 71

Sarah's mind was spinning as she watched the ocean waves billowing below her.

It had only been a little under two months since their experiences on the Moon. Sarah was trying to adjust to her new lifestyle, and not having her dad. The thing with the nursing home had worked out, but keeping tight lipped and making things up for her friends like Cybil and Condi, was much more difficult than she had first thought it would be. But things were going along okay.

Colonel Ravine had asked them to join him and Athena on the short trip. They would be filled in completely upon arrival as to the purpose, he'd said. Eliam was as apprehensive as Sarah before they left, but the Colonel had insisted on the clandestine nature of the trip, though he had assured them they would be significantly enthralled when they learned what it was about.

Sanguine landed stealthily in an open area just inside the jungle line far enough in that she couldn't be seen from the beach. A rough-looking, four-wheel drive vehicle was waiting there for them and after the short jaunt down a dirt road they pulled up to an austere series of island hut-styled, yet modern buildings. They curiously and calmly walked to the entry of the largest structure, knocked on its rustic wooden door, and were then summarily greeted by the not-so-late Professor Dunes—alive and in the flesh.

Upon seeing him, both Eliam and Sarah spontaneously erupted in emotional gasps of awe-generated surprise. Eliam

lunged at him with joyful abandon, hugging him affection-
ately. Sarah did the same, even though she'd only shaken the
man's hand a few times before. She couldn't help herself, she
realized. She'd learned from Eliam the kind of man he was,
and just what he'd given his life to do.

Now he was here, back from the dead.

When excitedly asked the obvious bevy of questions, the
Professor only mentioned a few epigrammatic reasons for his
now-apparent ruse, laughing humbly at their child-like anima-
tion, stating that there was indeed a lot he needed to discuss
before they'd understand his full reasoning, but unfortunately
he'd had something very important come up that would occupy his attention for a short time longer, if they could forgive
him the absence.

The Professor offered his apologies, encouraged them to
settle into their rooms, and again stated that they would talk
at greater depth during dinner. He then introduced them to a
middle-aged man named Dr. Narita Occo, who was apparently an associate scientist and friend of the Professor's, and
who proceeded to show the three to where they would be
staying. He was a pleasant man, articulate, and obviously well
educated. Sarah and Eliam were then shown to a small two-
roomed, block-walled hut, Colonel Ravine and Athena to two
separate rooms in the main house. The accommodations were
simple, highly ascetic, yet pleasant.

In their all too brief initial conversation, the Professor
mentioned the need of stepping aside, of confidentiality, of
careful preparation. They didn't understand any of it, per se,
and could barely contain themselves during the wait, speculating about all sorts of scenarios. However, they hadn't needed
to wait too long, and in less than an hour, they were all back
together in the main house of the small compound.

·······

"Thank you for coming, and again, my apologies about the
interruption, and the secrecy," the Professor started, "but
when you hear the reasoning, perhaps you'll better understand. However, before we get too deep into it, how about we

get something to eat? I took the liberty of having some food catered in from a small tourist village I know of some distance away. It's a spread of some of the local cuisine, and I guarantee it rivals anything you can find on any shore, in any part of the world."

At his motion, he invited them through a passage off to the side, and into a large outdoor covered kitchen. On two tables were numerous heated serving trays of seafood: heaping portions of crab, shrimp, lobster, oysters on the half, clams, and fish. There were steamed vegetables, and sauces, and rice, along with numerous varieties of drinks.

"Wow!" Sarah said, looking at the arrangement. "This is enough food and drink for three times as many people."

"Yes, but it'll keep for the duration of your stay; I wanted to be sure there would be plenty," the Professor said. "Please...*please*, help yourself!" He motioned to the tables.

The six of them fixed plates and made their way to an umbrella-covered round table aesthetically positioned in an open patch of sand just off the kitchen. They sat down and began. From their new perspective they could see the ocean and a beach down the small knoll from which they sat, and off in the distance in the other direction a span of lush tropical hills rose up behind the property.

They all ate heartily with only brief conversation, mostly regarding the savory taste and freshness of the food. All but Sarah got up and went back for seconds. After everyone returned and started again, Sarah suddenly narrowed her eyes with the curious thoughts entering her head, making note of the raw enjoyment with which the others ate their food. Each seemed to have the exact same expression on their face: one of sublime joy. She then remembered those looks from various other times: dinners and lunches throughout the course of the project, or on her dates with Eliam. Her curiosity got the best of her. She nearly blurted it out.

"Listen, I can't wait any longer. I'm really sorry! I appreciate the food, thank you Professor. And I don't know about anybody else, but I'm about to die here with all this waiting. Pardon my excitement, but I'd like to know what's going on.

And by the way, what is it with you guys and seafood anyway?" Her thoughts had suddenly returned to their expressions of sublimity.

They momentarily stopped mid-chew and looked at her, pondering the question. Dr. Occo just sat back and smiled knowingly. Eliam looked around at everyone, and then turned to Sarah and offered a succinct reply.

"The seafood here is…is just so good, Sarah, compared to Hoame."

Sarah tilted her head, trying to consider a possible deeper meaning to the simple answer. Eliam noted her expression. The Professor understood her curiosity as well and decided to add his efforts to Eliam's.

"I imagine Eliam has told you a little about Hoame, our planet, Sarah?"

She nodded her head slowly.

Professor Dunes looked at Eliam and Colonel Ravine, querying them as well. He saw the looks in their eyes and decided to continue.

"Hoame is an ocean planet like Earth. However, it is made of far smaller continents, and even more island nations and provinces—the majority of its population living on the coasts."

He nodded, seeing if she understood yet.

Sarah returned his gaze with still-questioning eyes.

The Professor continued.

"Well, as a result, the vast majority of food for its population has historically come from the oceans, as opposed to inland agriculture. Unfortunately, before the people of Hoame wised up—at least to some measurable degree—Hoame's oceans were depleted and polluted, nearly made barren from our ignorance regarding population and sustainability. Our ignorance—and insolence—nearly destroyed our planet. Fortunately, though after centuries of war—long story, short—the remaining populace started getting things under control again.

"Hoame's ocean resources were reconditioned, by artificial means Sarah, on a titanic scale—it was a leading precedence set out in the Reform Movement. Anyway, intense inlet farming and ocean cultivation applications were the priority. And by doing so, things got reestablished. But again, it was by artificial means. The food produced as a result, though capable of giving nutrition and sustenance, left much to be desired regarding variety and flavor. Hence, Earth's food is much more pleasing to the palate, I guess I should say, than the food most people on Hoame can even remember, much less hope for. So, as Eliam so eloquently and honestly indicated…the seafood on Earth is really, really good! Compared to Hoame's, you see?"

Sarah nodded her head, now with a fuller understanding; at least she thought. Smiling, she shook her head and let out a soft giggle. She picked up a clam, put it in her mouth and then smiled larger.

The others smiled back as they finished the last morsels of their once-enormous helpings.

·······

"Sarah's right, Howey! It's about time for some answers," Eliam said, a level of antipathy now unmistakable in his voice.

Professor Dunes picked up on the intonation and both men's facial expressions seemed to change at the same time. Sarah noticed immediately.

"Well, I have some business to attend to," Dr. Occo said. "If that's alright, I think I'll just let the five of you catch up a little. It was very nice to meet you all. Perhaps I can show you around the island tomorrow; if you would like. Thank you for the wonderful meal, Professor."

The Professor looked up slightly and acknowledged the look of respect the man gave him.

"My thanks to you, Narita-san," he said, bowing in his chair slightly.

Dr. Occo smiled, rose and bowed slightly to everyone. He left heading toward the garage and the distant side entrance in what Eliam surmised might perhaps be their lab, if indeed there was one.

The Professor looked up at them, grinned and nodded with acknowledgement.

"Okay, yes! On with it as they say," he laughed slightly, but then got serious. "Eliam, I have something unfortunate to tell you, son. You see…I am *Ankh*!"

Eliam heard the words, but he wasn't at all assured of their meaning.

"What?" was all Eliam could find to say as he raised his eyes to his uncle and mentor.

"I am *Ankh*," he said again, but continued before Eliam could respond. "I have been part of the *Renasci* for a long time, Sarah." He began speaking mainly to her, knowing that she probably knew little of their actual backgrounds.

"I helped propagate the movement, nearly from its onset. But in truth, it was—*I* was—part of something larger. You see, when the *Renasci*—the renewed, the revived, Sarah—first established its roots, it was as an understandably rebellious offshoot of those within the *Ankh* that rallied in the political arenas for change. These were its beginnings, and the climate was ripe for transformation, what with the environmental problems, the devastation from the centuries of in-fighting between cultures and ideologies. All of it set the stage for the Reform to happen.

"And to elaborate a little further, for you especially Sarah, the Reform's demands were basically this: that the *Ankh* re-linquish its ages-old powerbase in favor of a more democratic governing organization. Some of the basic tenets written into the original charter were fundamental freedoms and human rights. Especially regarding Hoame's, shall I say dubious inter-actions with the planet Earth.

"You see, Sarah, for millennia the *Ankh* controlled the people with a despotic system of castes and classes. It was this way for so long, simply because it had just been this way for so long. And they did it with religious fervor and extremism. Because of that, the possibility of change was barely even im-agined. That is until the people of Hoame learned of recent changes here on Earth—over the last several hundred years, to be exact—in your country, the United States, which actually helped serve to inspire and launch Hoame's final reforms. However, change does not come easy, anywhere, especially for those who are old and programmed in their ways."

He took a deep, seemingly regretful breath and exhaled hard. He then humbly looked at Eliam, reading his eyes. Eliam was waiting for an explanation.

Sarah looked back and forth between the two trying to understand.

The Professor continued.

"Eliam, when the *Ankh* began to realize that the Reform—*the Renasci*—weren't just going to go away like all the other movements, they did what they have always done best: manipulate whomever they could in order to crush any opposition to their way of life. In this case, many loyal to the *Ankh* turned and seemingly became supporters and propagators of *the Renasci*. As they always have—even within their own ranks—they planted eyes and ears within the movement. Up until recently, I was one of those, Eliam."

Eliam's reaction was one of complete disbelief. He shook his head, silently mouthing the word no. Sarah kept looking back and forth between him and the Professor waiting for the next comment.

"You can't be!" Eliam started. "You…you've helped the Reform in so many ways, helped drive the efforts toward change. I don't understand! How could you do that, be *Ankh*? Howey! Please, explain that to me. How?"

He took another deep breath, humbled by the obvious rebuke in Eliam's voice.

"Well, I've often said to be careful who you trust, and for how long. When I finish explaining, I think you'll understand."

The Professor looked over to Colonel Ravine and to Athena. Their eye contact spoke volumes. The two just nodded their support.

"Let me explain…"

"I wish you would," Eliam said sternly with heightened emotion.

The Professor understood his reaction.

"Eliam, inside *the Renasci* is a group who are still *Ankh* at the core. Except, they too have evolved and changed over time, and unlike the *Ankh* as a whole, they have seen the need for change. Though, the changes they are setting out to make only include themselves. In fact, they now couldn't care less about their roots and history on Hoame. All they care about now…is Earth!"

Sarah snapped her head to attention when he'd said it. The Professor knew she'd react to the statement. He looked into her eyes and offered what seemed to be condolences. Sarah's expression invited him to continue.

"Earth? The *Ankh* has always been interested in Earth," Eliam repeated.

"Yes, but for different reasons than what I am about to tell you. They've abducted its people, enslaved them for their own purposes, used their ignorance and adolescent pettiness to play their games of war, killed its people for fun and sport and experiment; they've used its resources to augment their wealth, so on and so on. But they've never chosen to move here and take it as their own…until now."

"*What?*" Sarah exclaimed with utter astonishment.

The Professor and the Colonel glanced at each other again, sharing yet another bevy of unspoken thoughts.

The Colonel spoke next.

"That is correct," he started. "They are planning on using B-CID technology, along with other new, yet characteristically insidious methods, to circumvent the powerbases of Earth's leadership and then physically move here to start over, a new *Ankh*, a new planet which to them is by and large still full of resources and opportunity, except that now *they* will be its new governors. They plan on making it theirs."

"You're *Ankh* as well?" Eliam asked, his voice filled with disdain.

The Colonel looked at Eliam.

"No, and in truth, neither is Professor Dunes."

"What? You just said you were!" He quickly turned his attention back to the Professor.

"Well, I was. Like I've said, be careful who you trust, and for how long. I was *Renasci* from its inception. But I became what they mockingly call themselves: the '*Re-no-sci*', or the 'knowledgeable.' I did this from the beginning because I knew we needed to know what their plans were, just as they needed to know ours." He smiled.

"You mean you're a double-agent, or whatever?" Sarah asked in amazement.

The Professor smiled again, as did the Colonel.

"Yes, that is correct. I suppose your term illustrates the position as well as any other."

"That's right," the Colonel also added, "the Professor, more so than I. He's been in between the lion's and the bear's teeth for quite some time now. It was only with the recent developments that he felt it necessary—compelled—to step aside, serve the cause from behind the scenes. In doing so, he has actually helped the cause of *the Renasci* in ways that none of us can even imagine."

They all looked at the Professor with curious eyes wondering what that meant exactly. He picked up on it.

"How did I get to be a part of it? That's what you're asking, isn't it? It's a fair question. Time and chance, I'd say. I made no qualms back then about which side I chose to camp with—primarily the Reform movement and its philosophies. However, I was not an active participant in any sub-movement, though many were actually gaining strength and notoriety around then. I was working on my Professorship at the time and was heavily into the applied sciences side of Brain Interface Technologies.

"The *Ankh* had always used substances and programming techniques to coerce others into doing what they wanted—that's been well known—but when a breakthrough came that tied BCI to brain programming and conditioning in a totally unprecedented way, they approached me. Though I was neither the initiator nor the inventor of the technology, I was involved in many of its side applications that they were interested in, and as a result they approached me. Also, they wanted to test my loyalties to the Reform, I suppose, so they pushed themselves on me.

"One of the recruiters also just happened to be a relative of a research scientist that my own father collaborated with way back in the past, and because of that I suppose, I was confided in to a degree, told of the *Re-no-sci* and its long-term plans—though at the time it didn't include taking over the Earth, but was somewhat in opposition to the *old Ankh*, which I appreciated to a point.

"Basically, I was offered the opportunity to join and work with them. So I had a choice. Say no and be threatened with ruin and possible death over the course of my life, or say yes and have the opportunity to ingratiate myself into their ranks and perhaps do some long term good as a result. I chose the latter.

"I do deeply regret the negative impact that decision has had on countless, nameless people." He went silent, bowing his head for a moment, suddenly flushed with emotion. "Nevertheless, I kept telling myself that the ultimate good that would come from it should outweigh the cost! At least that's what I keep telling myself. Regardless, this is how it has all unfolded."

There was silence for a few moments as everyone rode their own wave of thought and emotion. Suddenly learning all this created a host of other possible assertions, and one of these led Eliam to ask another round of questions.

"*The Renasci—Re-no-sci—*are planning on leaving Hoame? Taking over and controlling Earth? How could they accomplish such a thing? That sounds impossible. There can't be many of them, not enough anyway, so how?"

The Professor looked upon him with a grave expression.

"As I said, B-CID technology," the Professor reiterated.

Sarah slowly shook her head side-to-side as the realization seemed to come to her.

"You said BCI and…and programming techniques. You mean they're going to use the technology to get control of our minds! That's possible?"

Sarah looked at Eliam unbelieving. He glanced back at her and then turned once more to the Professor.

"Yes, unfortunately, it is," the Professor said solemnly. "William mentioned a moment ago some new developments. First, the *Ankh* does not want B-CID technology on Earth, that's why they enlisted Davian Adorjan's help, initially, in order to stop it. The reasons are many, but basically they wanted the people of Earth to stay the way they've been for most of their history: backward, indigent, slow, and undeveloped, limited to this planet alone, in the dark as such, so they could continue to use it in the ways they have in the past. Allowing B-CID technology to proliferate would create an unprecedented paradigm change that would literally launch humanity into the realms of higher intelligence, and eventually, out into the stars. And without question, they are accurate in those assumptions.

"And it is for those very reasons that the true *Renasci* want Earth to have the technology. They also believe it is only fair after the millennia of abuse the people of our planet have reaped upon yours without you even knowing it. Also, one critical component of the plan of the *Renasci* is for Earth to be contacted soon, eventually leading to a galactic co-existence, the sharing of knowledge, and resources and commerce and the like, as well as to bring about a certain level of redemption. The *Ankh* wants none of this and are out to stop it however they can. The *Re-no-sci* on the other hand wants B-CID technology to proliferate because they will be able to use it to control people."

"How so?" Eliam asked.

Sarah nodded, seconding the question.

"The technology has been compromised," the Professor simply stated.

"*Compromised*!? You mean like with what Adorjan was doing," Eliam inquired anxiously.

"Yes, exactly. The software inside has been circumvented with a type of viral nanocytes. They can make it do things it wasn't originally intended to do. Such as halt feeds into the brain causing neural blockages, create hallucinations, alternate

realities in the mind, along with a host of other things, combined with it the use of new chemicals for long-term, sustained control, once they get a hold of certain key people
they'll be after!"

Sarah gasped. Her great fear of losing her mind gripped
her in a state of horror as she remembered what had just recently happened to her.

"You have to be kidding!" she said, her voice weak and
scratchy.

"No, I'm afraid not. Those whom they choose to set in
motion can be initiated simply by sending out an activation
code to a particular device's software, and within a few short
seconds those under the influence can find themselves in a
coma, or standing in front of an oncoming train singing a
child's nursery rhyme, or walking a bomb into a crowded
chamber of politicians thinking it's a bouquet of flowers, or
giving an order to deploy a sortie of nuclear-tipped missiles.
It is all similar to what Adorjan was trying to do to you, Sarah,
except the process was interrupted, fortunately, in your case."

His serious tone silenced everyone.

"My God!" Sarah said, looking down.

"This has to be stopped!" Eliam said. "There has to be a
way?"

"Yes, there is, but let me continue with the explanation.
There's more. I'm sure you're still wondering how I could
have done this, and *why* I chose to end my existence, as it were.
Well, the simple fact is…"

"He didn't do it!" the Colonel chimed in. "None of us
knew its extent until just a few months ago when we received
word from one of our operatives on Hoame; she informed us
of the development. We also learned from her that they were
going to assassinate the Professor because he was increasingly
showing signs of disloyalty. She died getting the information
to us."

They all understood.

The Colonel continued.

"The Professor was privy to the project, knew of its potential, even a few of the preliminary applications, but he

didn't know the extent of which they were planning on using it with Earth. And nor did I. However, it has been confirmed. Adorjan was initially trying to stop the technology by means of breeding fear and panic regarding its safety, in alignment with the *Ankh's* instructions, in order to ruin its reputation and thereby its marketability. Stop it in its tracks from being proliferated on the Earth."

"You said 'initially.' You mean that's changed?" Sarah inquired.

Professor Dunes continued where the Colonel left off.

"That's right. We've learned that the *Re-no-sci* contacted Adorjan and convinced him to join their ranks. It was a proposition he couldn't refuse. He was offered a place in their future hierarchy, which was what he essentially lost all those years ago because the *Ankh* exiled him to Earth, which he blamed on your grandfather, Eliam. Along with that, he'd be allowed to occupy the Moon base, keep his business of trafficking going from there, and the crown of his new employment package was to have the opportunity to get his revenge on the Zaris family through you, or through Sarah, I suppose was the case. But that bit of self-aggrandizement proved to be his downfall, fortunately for all of us.

"You see, the *Re-no-sci* have somehow gotten control of the designers of the newest upgrades to the technology and added their nanocytes, as well as an access to be able to activate them at will. And they obviously had at some point in time given Adorjan these access codes. That's how he was able to hack your B-CIDs on the Moon. Fortunately, some people didn't get the newest upgrades, so his control was hindered. And, thanks to your father, Sarah, his plans were stopped altogether. He saved us all, Sarah! And because of that we might have a chance."

Everyone just sat there in silence considering his words, especially regarding Sarah's father.

Sarah nodded a teary-eyed thanks to the man.

He responded with a humble nod in return.

"So, the technology is still going to be allowed to be released anyway?" Sarah then thought to ask.

"Yes. It must be, for the reasons I mentioned earlier! The *Ankh* believes that Adorjan was successful in implanting their virus. Of course they're misinformed; the break-in at the labs was only a ruse on Adorjan's part, but the *Ankh* don't know that. They believe he succeeded. They'll freeze their efforts for the most part as they wait until the technology gets released; of course it won't have the effect they expect once it is. But by then it will be too late to stop it.

"And, as expected, the proliferation of it will happen. And also as expected, the rich and famous, and especially the multitude of leaders around the world, will adopt the technology, we assume, and very quickly. And within a certain amount of time—depending on the saturation point—the *Re-no-sci* will then make their move and start the chain reaction: a series of nearly incomprehensible ruses and manipulations that will change the Earth politically and economically. And as a result, the *Re-no-sci* will be behind the doors manipulating the strings of those who will be running the planet from then on. I know it sounds impossible, but it isn't."

"It has to be stopped!" Sarah insisted.

"Yes, that goes without saying," the Colonel said.

"But how?" Eliam asked.

The Colonel and Professor Dunes looked at each other knowingly. They seemed to nod at each other. Professor Dunes then spoke candidly.

"Someone has to get the codes to unlock the software in the B-CIDs. The problem's in the core software that came from Hoame, which is downloaded to each B-CID in its manufacturing, but there's no way of locating it, much less immobilizing it without one critical thing…its originator codes, the keys to the nanocyte configurations. Having the codes will allow the nanocytes to be disabled permanently. There's no other way! It can be done remotely, once we have them, without anyone even being aware of the initial danger, but that's the only way."

"Yeah well, okay, so, how do you do that?" Sarah asked plainly.

"That's easier said than done. The *Re-no-sci's* lead scientists have them. And I was the only one who had a chance to retrieve them. However, I'm dead, you see. Someone else has to go to Hoame and infiltrate the *Re-no-sci*. We were thinking of you two!"

Everyone then looked at Eliam and Sarah.

Chapter 72

"How could you possibly expect us to accomplish this?" Eliam asked.

The Professor, Athena, and the Colonel again looked at each other knowingly. The Colonel answered the query.

"Well, you're from Hoame, you're an incredible engineer, you've been working with the technology for years, you're *Renasci*, and Sarah's from Earth and she's a very good actor! Oh, and we'll be around, too! We still know people there," he said, glancing at Athena, who nodded her head in agreement.

Sarah looked intently at the group, completely stunned. She didn't say a word.

"Because Sarah's from Earth, and she's an actor? How could that...?" Eliam started to ask the question, but a notion suddenly began forming in his mind; he quieted and thought about it. Tilting his head, he looked at Sarah.

Sarah noted the hesitation. She then chose to speak.

"How did you know I was an actor?"

They all smiled.

The Colonel answered.

"Street Shock Adventures!" he smiled larger.

Sarah invited a better explanation with her confused expression.

The Colonel smiled again and continued.

"About a year ago I just happened to be at the Casa-Del-Sol resort on the outskirts of L.A. You remember the place? I witnessed you and your fellow actors perform a ruse on a group of people. I was impressed. So, I picked up one of the cards your team left lying around. Because of my line of business, I researched your troupe—and you especially, Sarah. I found out about your background, your particular vocation, your father being at NASA—I kind of connected with all that, and the experience stuck with me. Anyway, when the pool came up for prospective candidates for the project, I gave Howey your name. I think it was providence that you were chosen for the opportunity."

"Really, you saw the gig?" she asked, all of a sudden flattered.

The Colonel nodded and smiled.

"What was it about?" Eliam asked, knowing about her troupe, but suddenly curious.

The Colonel offered his take first.

"I believe it was set up for a business group who were on a team-building exercise, by the company's president, if I'm not mistaken, or something like that. Wasn't that about it, Sarah?"

"The CEO, in fact, set it up," Sarah started, now even more flattered. "The president was one of the dupes actually. The CEO, which was also the owner, wanted the group to recognize the importance of adaptation to circumstances; to be able to react accordingly with assertiveness, yet maintain professionalism and composure when things changed abruptly and confusingly. They were a new branch, I think, of their company's investigative business, or something like that."

"Interesting! Eliam said. "What was your part?"

"I...I played a woman who was supposedly infiltrating their organization through one of their top managers—who kept denying he knew me—apparently hired by one of the guy's rising subordinates. It was kind of an internal test to see how the ranks would work together, or against each other, a loyalty thing, I guess. We knew things from the owner that I was able to throw around to make it seem that I actually did have inside information. One of our troupes played my bodyguard, and one was actually hired by the owner as a new employee and planted a week earlier before the event. It went over like clockwork. They were all confused. I don't imagine they fared really well in the eyes of the owner; they were nearly at each other's throats."

"Yes, they were. They became exceedingly verbal with each other there toward the end. I was seated close to their little party and heard everything. It was only afterwards when all of a sudden the body-guard guy stopped it by holding up his Street Shock ID, along with Sarah and everyone else, announcing their ruse that *I* actually saw it for what it was. Like I said, it was impressive," the Colonel offered again. "Yeah, I doubt they fared very well in the owner's eyes, either." He nodded in agreement to Sarah.

Eliam looked at Professor Dunes and then the Colonel.

"So that's how Sarah was selected?"

The Colonel nodded his head.

Professor Dunes then spoke.

"There were numerous reasons that went into her being chosen, as with the others. The point now is that from all this, you, Sarah, would be a great asset to the *Renasci's* efforts at stopping what seems to be, unfortunately, already set in motion. I know it may be hard to grasp, but if the *Re-no-sci* succeeds in doing what they're planning, they'll be able to get an inexorable foothold in your business and political arenas—behind the scenes—and once that happens, it will be nearly impossible to weed them out."

"The Professor's right," the Colonel joined in. "We have to stop them now, the *Renasci* plan on making official contact with Earth in the matter of just a few years. The technology is essential for this to happen, for many reasons. Hoame's cultures are centered on it, and once Earth has it as well, contact will be the next step. It will open vast doors of communication just as two cultures finally learning the same language does. If the *Re-no-sci* succeeds, that will all change."

Eliam just looked down and shook his head.

He spoke his next words as much to himself, as to the others.

"So, we go to Hoame and figure out a way to infiltrate the *Re-no-sci*, somehow acquire the originator codes, bring them back to Earth, use them to develop security protocols to over-ride them, in order to prevent the capability of them being able to hack the B-CIDs, which are already being released to the mass public...to the world-wide markets, as we speak? Wow, now that should be simple!"

Sarah heard him and just stared into nothingness, mesmerized by what everyone had just said.

There was silence all around.

....

Dinner was over and the evening had fallen upon the group. All Eliam and Sarah could say was that they would think about it. The others, impressing upon them the critical element of time, asked for an answer by the end of their stay. The two reluctantly agreed. They then decided to leave the group and together go off to explore the beach.

They strolled away and left the others at the house, walking for awhile, enjoying the twilight, and then finding a couple of lounge chairs to settle into under the clear, star-filled sky. Their conversation at first was filled with reiteration of the obvious questions and then long bouts of quiet and contemplation. As they sat in the chairs sipping on a couple of drinks, they began to talk.

"I'm sorry, Sarah, for getting you into this!"

Sarah looked over at him. Even in the waxing darkness she could see his glistening eyes.

"It is what it is, my dad always said. It's not like I was forced to get into the program or anything. I chose to. It just happened. It's not your fault."

"No, maybe not, but I still feel responsible. I could have just left you alone, and none of this would have happened."

"It still would have happened, just another way. The *Re-no-sci* would still be doing what they're doing. It's just that I would be sitting at home, eaten up for the rest of my life regretting what I'd done to my father. You'd still be in the middle of all of it."

"Yeah, I suppose you're right. But, I'm still sorry."

They looked at each other and then started to observe that their faces were increasingly becoming brighter. Both noticed simultaneously. They looked toward the water and saw the Moon rising largely up from the horizon. They watched silently as it ascended majestically. Eliam then made an unexpected comment.

"Huh, it's a full Oscar!"

Sarah looked back at him with surprise, and then back to the full Moon. They could see the spot on its rim where her father was.

"Yes, it is. Thanks for saying it like that!"

They just stared at it for a minute, thinking and remembering.

"I'll say it that way the rest of my life; I was honored to meet your dad, Sarah…honored! I want you to know that."

"Funny, he told me the same thing about you. Of course that was after he talked to you about NASA."

They shared a subdued laugh.

"What do you think he would suggest you to do? You know, about going to Hoame with me."

She looked back at him again, and then returned her gaze to her father's resting place.

"You say that like you've already decided to go."

He was silent for another moment.

"Yes, I have to go. The Professor's right. I have the background; I have the knowledge; and I have the duty. My family would want me to, if they were around. We did terrible things to the people of Earth over the centuries. It has to stop. It has to be reconciled, and that means the *Re-no-sci* have to be stopped. I guess I'm just the one who's best able to do that. Must be providence," he said, smiling a quirky smile as he looked over at her.

She was looking at him again, smiling at his smile.

"Well, I'd say it was providence we're both here."

There was more silence as they again stared at the Moon.

"I know what my dad would say. He'd say, 'Sarah, our lives have a purpose. It may take a long time for you to realize that. But one day you will. And when you do, that one day will truly be the start of your life!'" Tears slowly ran down Sarah's face as she finished. She just stared at the Moon, in that one location that forever she would look at when she gazed upon its mysterious, luminous face.

"I may be crazy, it may be the onset of early Alzheimer's, but I'll do it. I'll go. That's what my father would want me to do," she said.

He looked at her, tears in his own eyes.

"Hey, I've been meaning to tell you. You'll never get Alzheimer's, or dementia."

Sarah looked back at him, confused by the odd comment. "*What*? What do you mean?"

"The Sonilyn-7, the shot your father gave you. It's basically a cure for the disease. It's what Athena gave your father that helped him keep himself together so he could help us. It wouldn't have cured him; it only works on the synapses of those who don't already have the long-term plaque damage. But, it's essentially a cure for it. And you'll probably live twice as long now, too. Aging starts in the brain. I wouldn't doubt it if you live to be a hundred and fifty now, give or take a few years."

Sarah was dumbfounded.

"And just when were you planning on telling me this?" she asked, with a slight yet perceivable scowl.

"Uhm, I was waiting for a time like this." He smiled. "And there's something else I wanted to tell you, Sarah!"

"Yeah, and what's that?"

"I love you! I love you very much!"

Sarah lost her breath for a moment. She then got up and edged her way into his chair putting her face next to his.

"I love you too, Eliam. And I'll go with you!"

Their lips touched slightly.

Eliam suddenly withdrew, looking deeply into her eyes. His lips tightened.

"Listen, before you say that, you have to understand what it means. Remember when I talked about the *Ankh*, and how they mostly live in their own, created worlds?"

Sarah looked into his eyes, tilted her head with the memory and then nodded.

"Well, that's where we'll have to spend most of our time while we're there, in *their* worlds. And I can't begin to describe how odd and surreal some of the places we're going to have to go may seem. It's not just that it's going to be strange for you, it's going to be dangerous, Sarah! For both of us! We could fail—most probably *will* fail, and probably die!" He paused and softly caressed her cheek with his fingers. "I don't want that! You don't have to do this! I can do it myself!"

Sarah studied his sincerity.

She then looked up at the Moon again.

"Yeah, well, we all die. It's how we live that's important. My dad always said that too. It's not just about me! Something tells me I need to go, that I need to be with you!" She turned back to him. "That's what I'm going to do!"

They stared at each other for another brief moment, and then sunk down together into a long, deep kiss.

Chapter 73

Sarah's eyes opened when the warm light from the window fell upon her face. She realized it was morning and the new day was about to start. She lay there thinking for a few minutes, considering what her life was going to be from then on. She looked over at Eliam who was still sound asleep. She rose quietly from the bed, stepped into the bathroom and dressed, then quietly made her way out the door for a short morning stroll on the beach.

She walked toward the sunrise for awhile, breathing in the salty air, and taking in the beauty of the place. She thought about her life; what it was, where it was going, what it was going to end up like. She wouldn't have guessed all this would have happened to her in a million years.

She looked up into the sky. The Moon was gone, having settled back in its own slumber, but there was freshness in the air, and light, and warmth, and life. And just as her father had said, when that day comes, it would truly be the start of her life.

She was ready.

Sarah turned to walk back in the direction she had come, but was stopped in her tracks at the unexpected sight. Not too far from her was a man sitting in one of the beach chairs she and Eliam had used the prior night. He hadn't been there when she'd strolled by them only moments before. He was wearing normal street clothes, light-brown denim pants, a light blue faded shirt, and a thin jacket. He had longish hair, grayed on the edges. It was the man she'd seen those other times before.

Sarah remained cautious but started walking toward him out of curiosity. When she arrived, the man looked at her and beckoned her to sit.

Sarah hesitated but then sat down.

"You're the man I saw at the clinic and on the street that day. And, somewhere else, I can't remember. What are you doing here? Who are you?" she asked sincerely.

The man took his gaze off the horizon and turned to her.

"Hi, Sarah. I'm Myzel. You can think of me as a helper, a messenger, a teacher, whatever you wish. We do all have a purpose in life, Sarah, and a contribution to make. I'm just fulfilling mine. I came to help you."

"Help me?"

"Yes, help you. There's something you must know!"

He reached over and pinched her arm slightly.

He then smiled.

"Avatar," he said.

"What?" Sarah asked, not sure what he meant.

"Flesh! All flesh…are Avatars!"

. . . .

Sarah's eyes opened when the warm light from the window fell upon her face. She realized it was morning and the new day was about to start.

Chapter 74

"They're calling it 'Smartbrain': your field-of-vision is the monitor; images, motion, and sound feed directly into your neural pathways; activation, operation, and navigation, accomplished by your thoughts; Apps and Cloud Sources, apparently under development. Many are already speculating that this will be the technological game-changer of the century."

. . . .

"Yes, everyone, that was an excerpt from a previous program aired not too long ago with the breaking story about this new technology coming our way. Well, it's been six months now since its release, so in the closing segment of the program we at Raker's Slant thought we'd offer a little updated commentary about said technology!

"The device has been selling off the proverbial shelves since its release. It's proving to be the number one Christmas item we hear, historically exceeding all other items including Playboxes, Nerd-Oids action figures, and those long-lived colorful building blocks that snap together to make children's worlds a more constructive place!

"All of the Smartbrain-7, as they've come to be known, are doing their media parts to flaunt their fifteen minutes of fame by doing commercials and video spots and assorted other Reality TV. All except the enigmatic Ms. Whiting, who seems to have just fallen off the planet somewhere? Oh well, one out of seven's not bad, now is it?

"Anyway, the new technology is in many ways proving to be an insurmountably ubiquitous part of the human lifestyle, whether we like it or not. We can only hope it proves out over the long run. But, only time can be the true judge.

"Oh well! I think I'm going to take me and my little antiquated tablet out of here, go have a nice seafood dinner, and read a good old fashioned ebook as I eat!

"This is Jonathan Raker of Raker's Slant! Stay tuned for more breaching news and inclined commentary!"

G. F. Smith is married, has four talented and successful grown children, several awesome grandchildren, and lives in the picturesque, forested hills of Brown County, Indiana, near the renowned Pioneer Artist Colony known as Little Nashville.

Other books by G. F. Smith:

subjected: the series

The **subjected series** was written to be read in any order.

Available in Print and eBook Formats

www.gfsmithbooks.com

Dear Readers,

   Thanks for reading! I sincerely hope you enjoyed the book and will enjoy my others as well. Also, if you do find them interesting, and/or compelling, a quick online review (Amazon, B&N, Goodreads, etc.) would be most appreciated; it's really easy to do actually, and one or two sentences would be more than fine. My thanks go out to you again! Stay curious, and all the best to you and yours!

~GFS